HOSTAGE

Also by Don Brown

Treason (Navy Justice Series, Book 1)

BOOK TWO

DON BROWN

THE NAVY

JUSTICE SERIES

HOSTAGE

ZONDERVAN™

GRAND RAPIDS, MICHIGAN 49530 USA

We want to hear from you. Please send your comments about this book to us in care of zreview@zondervan.com. Thank you.

ZONDERVAN™

Hostage
Copyright © 2005 by Don Brown

Requests for information should be addressed to:
Zondervan, *Grand Rapids, Michigan 49530*

Library of Congress Cataloging-in-Publication Data

Brown, Don, 1960–
    Hostage / Don Brown.
      p. cm.—(The Navy justice series ; bk. 2)
    ISBN-13: 978-0-310-25934-3 (pbk.)
    ISBN-10: 0-310-25934-7 (pbk.)
    1. United States. Navy—Fiction. 2. Courts-martial and courts of inquiry—
Fiction. I. Title.
PS3602.R6947H67 2005
813'.6—dc22
                                        2005015807

Interior design by Michelle Espinoza

Printed in the United States of America

---

05 06 07 08 09 10 11 • 17 16 15 14 13 12 11 10 9 8 7 6 5 4 3 2 1

*This book is lovingly dedicated to my wife of twenty years,
Rhonda W. Brown.*

*May the Lord bless her and keep her, may the Lord
make his face shine upon her, and give her peace,
this day, and forevermore.*

*With much love, this Ninth Day of August,
in the Year of our Lord, two thousand and five.*

CHAPTER 1

In the hills near the Dean E. Smith Center
South Campus, University of North Carolina
Chapel Hill, North Carolina

Lying on his belly in the thick underbrush, the gunman peered through the powerful magnifying scope. It was about two hundred yards down the hill, he estimated, from his position to the main entrance of the brick arena.

Close enough for a shot. Far enough for an escape.

Students flocked like massive herds of sheep through the building's glass doors, their heads and faces grandly visible through the crosshairs of the scope.

Dozens of infidels sacrificed to Allah's glory in an instant. His heart raced at the thought. His breathing quickened. He caressed the cold trigger with his finger, waiting to squeeze it. Longing to purify the sinful American ground with spilled blood.

Whistling wind whipped through the tops of the Carolina pines. A surge of excitement, like an electrical shock, shot through his body.

My destiny is with Allah the Merciful, who controls the wind.

He pulled his trigger finger from the cold steel. His glorious destiny would depend on patience. For a bit longer.

The blood of the redhead and her companion would ensure his place in Islamic Glory. He would await their emergence. Allah would bring them from those doors at the anointed moment. And when they appeared in the crosshairs, he would execute Allah's vengeance and justice.

All praise to Allah! Blessed be the prophet — peace be upon him.

Dean E. Smith Center
South Campus, University of North Carolina
Chapel Hill, North Carolina
UNC Versus Duke: Halftime

Lieutenant Diane Colcernian tried in vain to protect her eardrums from the spontaneous, alternating chants of the boisterous crowd.

"TAAAAAR!"

"HEEEEEELS!"

"TAAAAAR!"

"HEEEEEELS!"

Diane's date, Lieutenant Zack Brewer, pumped his fists into the air, contributing to the baby-blue cacophony now reaching ear-splitting levels.

His excitement mimicked that of a kid under the Christmas tree, a beaming kid handsomely decked out in his "Carolina Blue" T-shirt with the interlocking *NC* on the front. Hers, a gift from Zack, was identical to his and to twenty thousand others in the Dean Dome.

He screamed with exhilaration when one of the Carolina players, a Rashad somebody, dunked the ball. She smiled, shaking her head in bemused disbelief.

"Let's just wear jeans and Carolina stuff," Zack had said earlier. "This is the Duke game. The fans will be so pumped up we'll never get spotted. I promise."

She believed him. After all, basketball wasn't that big of a deal when she was an undergraduate student at the University of Virginia.

Promises, promises.

They sat three rows behind the Carolina bench, so close to the court they could hear the famous Duke coach unleash a profanity-laced tirade, first at his players, then at the referees, and then, at halftime, at the crowd as he trotted off the court with his team. Zack, who had warned Diane earlier that the Duke coach was known for spewing such obscenities, not to mention appearing in tacky credit card commercials, cupped his hands and joined the thousands of UNC fans in a cascading chorus of boos aimed at the Blue Devils as they disappeared into the tunnel under the Dean Dome.

When the boos turned into a groundswell of applause, Diane sensed she was being watched. A man sitting behind them tapped her on the shoulder and pointed to the large electronic screen over center court.

There they were on the jumbo screen, displayed for everyone in the arena and anyone who happened to be watching on national television—the image of her flaming red hair and Zack's cute dimple.

"So much for anonymity, Lieutenant," she said. Then, sheepishly, she smiled and waved at the camera. Another surge of applause followed.

"You look great on the JumboTron," Zack said as he waved at the camera.

"You said we weren't going anyplace they have cameras."

"You think they won't have cameras at the White House?"

His comment brought a nervous quiver to her stomach. "Thanks for reminding me." Their image faded from the screen, replaced by half-time statistics showing individual scoring totals for the Carolina and Duke teams.

A moment later, as the Carolina dance team moved and shook to the rhythm of Chicago's "Twenty-five or Six to Four," courtesy of the UNC pep band, a skinny young man bounded up the aisle from courtside. "Lieutenant Brewer, I'm Jason Silverstein with the Tar Heel Sports Network. Rick Blixon asked if you could come down for a halftime interview."

"Who's Rick Blixon?" Diane raised an eyebrow at Zack.

He shot her an incredulous look. "He's *just* the color guy for the Tar Heel sports broadcast. That's all."

"Oh, *that* Rick Blixon. Well, why didn't you just say so?" She gave him a sarcastic smile.

"Do you mind?" His eyes still sparkled.

"It won't take long, Lieutenant Colcernian," Silverstein said. "Rick's right down there at courtside." He gestured toward a table just to the left of the now-empty Carolina bench where Rick Blixon was motioning them to come down.

"He sees us!" Zack said, grinning.

My date has ice water in his veins in front of a jury, handles press conferences like a pro on national television, but acts like some giddy kid when some sports guy I've never heard of wants to talk to him.

"Look, he wants you too." Zack pointed to Blixon, who now held up two fingers as he waved them down. "Come on. It'll be a blast."

Diane met Jason Silverstein's gaze, and when he nodded, she said, "Oh, all right."

"Thanks." Zack gave her a quick peck on the cheek, then stood, and following Silverstein's lead, escorted her down the center aisle to the court.

Rick Blixon extended his hand first to Diane, then to Zack. "Welcome back to Chapel Hill," he said, still shaking Zack's hand.

"Good to be back," Zack said.

"We're on a commercial break right now, but I'd love to do a quick interview if you're up to it." The question was directed at Zack.

That was fine with Diane. She'd gotten enough publicity to last a lifetime and hoped that after their upcoming visit with the president, she could return to being just a normal naval officer.

"Y'all just have a seat on either side of me." Blixon handed them each a headset.

Diane settled into her chair. "You're not going to interview me too, are you?"

"He's the Carolina grad," Blixon said, "but maybe just a couple of comments?" He gave her a puppy-dog smile. "After all, you're part of the package."

She leaned forward, looked around Blixon, and shot Zack another raised eyebrow.

"She doesn't like publicity," Zack said, chuckling.

"Tell you what," Blixon said as the Carolina dance team wrapped up their routine. "How about if I ask him most of the questions but just get a hello or something from you. Our listeners would appreciate it."

Before she could answer, an unidentified voice came through her headset. "Three, two, one, live."

"And welcome back to the Smith Center," Blixon said into his microphone, "where the Tar Heels, shooting a blistering 65 percent from the floor, go into the locker room leading the Duke Blue Devils by a score of 45 to 35. And we have two very special surprise halftime guests joining us today. UNC grad Zack Brewer—*Lieutenant* Zack Brewer, I should say—the most famous JAG officer in the navy, and his much better-looking partner, who isn't a UNC grad but is also a product of the Atlantic Coast Conference. Today we also have with us University of Virginia graduate Lieutenant Diane Colcernian.

"Good to have you both here, Lieutenants."

"Hi, Rick," Zack said. "Go, Heels!"

"Hi," Diane said.

"So what brings you to Chapel Hill?" This question was directed at Zack.

"Carolina versus Duke, Rickie," Zack said. "There's no greater rivalry in sports."

"I hear through the grapevine you've got an appointment in Washington."

"Yes, that's true. We've been invited to the White House."

"To see the president?"

Zack nodded. "Yes, we're scheduled to meet with President Williams day after tomorrow. Then we're headed back to California or wherever the navy wants to send us."

"I'm sure the president will congratulate the two of you on your stellar performance at the Olajuwon court-martial. So let me add my congratulations too."

"Thanks, Rick. We believe justice was done."

Blixon turned to Diane. "Tell me, Diane, what was it like facing Wells Levinson in court?"

So much for the simple hello. "A formidable challenge," she said, frowning. "Wells Levinson is the most famous lawyer in the world."

Blixon turned again to Zack. "The whole world followed this court-martial on television, in the papers, and over the Internet. Your closing argument has been called spellbinding by many legal commentators. You compared Levinson to Harry Houdini and accused him of trying a sleight-of-hand trick to fool the jury."

"Thanks, Rick. The Heels have been spellbinding in the first half."

Diane was becoming more uncomfortable by the moment. Because of the death threats they received after the trial, she and Zack had been trying to keep a low profile. She hoped Blixon would take the hint from Zack and change the subject.

He didn't.

"Now, Wells Levinson, as we all know," Blixon said, "had never lost a case—until he faced you guys in court. We all saw his public reaction on TV. But what about his private reaction? Did he shake your hand and congratulate you on a case well tried? Or do famous lawyers just not do that?"

"I'm just a naval officer trying to do my duty. I think Diane would say the same thing. I'd never met a famous lawyer before I met Mr. Levinson," Zack said. "So I don't know how famous lawyers react. But let me put it this way: Mr. Levinson wasn't a happy camper when the jury came back."

"Diane"—Blixon turned back to her—"ever go to any basketball games at UVA?"

"A few."

"Which ones?"

She sighed. *At least this was a better topic than the trial. But not by much.*

"Whenever Carolina came to town, there was always a hoopla. Our other big rival was Virginia Tech."

"What was it like, going to those games?"

Diane never fully understood this fascination with college basketball. Sure, she was a Virginia graduate, and UVA was in the basketball-crazy ACC with Carolina. But she'd never seen this kind of fanaticism at the few games she attended at University Hall. Of course, she wasn't about to tell Rick Blixon that.

"I always went with a group of girls from my sorority. At UVA, sporting events are more like social outings. We always lost to Carolina and always beat Tech. But aside from those two games, basketball wasn't that big of a deal in Charlottesville. Certainly nothing like this."

Rick turned back to Zack. "These three Muslim chaplains, all U.S. Navy officers, were convicted of murder, conspiracy to commit murder, and treason. What's next for them?"

Zack looked annoyed. "The defendants received the death penalty. They are scheduled to be executed in two weeks at Fort Leavenworth, Kansas, unless the U.S. Supreme Court blocks that execution. We're waiting for word on that, and that word could come at any time."

"Carolina grad Lieutenant Zack Brewer, and UVA grad Lieutenant Diane Colcernian, both Navy JAG officers serving our country in some very difficult times. Thank you for joining us on the Tar Heel Sports Network."

Diane heard another round of applause, although not quite as sustained as the first. She looked up and realized that a large contingency of fans in the arena were listening to the broadcast on their radios.

"Thank you, Rick." Zack took off the headphones and shook Blixon's hand. Diane did the same. They got up from the table at courtside and turned around. Two uniformed Chapel Hill police officers were waiting.

A worried-looking officer came toward them, adjusting his tie. He furrowed his brow, and when he spoke, his voice was serious. "Lieutenants, I'm Captain Rogers, Chapel Hill PD."

"Everything okay, Officer?" Zack asked.

"I think so, Lieutenant, but if you two could follow me, we'd appreciate it."

Diane met Zack's eyes and nodded. "Sure."

As they followed the officer back up the stadium steps, the pep band struck up the music to "Fame." Two other uniformed officers stepped in behind them. Now that their anonymity was compromised, fans shouted their names as they walked by. Some reached into the aisle, trying to get a handshake or pat them on the back. The police officers moved in as if they were personal bodyguards.

When the party reached the top of the steps to the main-level concourse area, the officers turned them to the right and then escorted them into an elevator. A moment later, the doors opened into a large conference room somewhere under the stadium.

A silver-haired man in a light blue sports coat stepped forward. He smiled and extended his hand. "I'm Ralph Meekins, Lieutenant. Director of operations for the Smith Center."

"Zack Brewer, Mr. Meekins." Zack extended his hand. "And this is Diane Colcernian."

"Yes, I recognize you both." Meekins shook Diane's hand. "I apologize for this, but there's been a bit of a problem."

"What kind of a problem?" Diane's heart skipped a beat.

"To be honest, just after the network cameras showed you two in the stands, we got some telephone calls."

Diane exchanged a worried glance with Zack.

"Let me guess," Zack said to Meekins. "Threats?"

"I'm afraid so."

"Death threats?"

Meekins nodded, and Zack reached for Diane's hand.

"From callers with Arabic accents?"

"Sounds like you're already familiar with the problem," Meekins said.

"It was bad the first few days after the trial ended," Zack said. "The FBI has a few leads, but that's it. Over the last few months, they've subsided—none in the last sixty days." Zack paused, frowning. "I shouldn't have agreed to that radio interview. But when Rickie asked, I'm such a big fan I couldn't resist."

"The radio interview wasn't the problem. I don't think too many terrorists tune in to Willie and Rick," he said, referring to two of the radio broadcasters for the Tar Heel basketball games. "The problem was the brief head shot when the camera panned to you before halftime. The calls came in almost instantly, *before* you went on the radio."

Meekins worked his jaw, looking worried. "On behalf of the University of North Carolina, please accept our apologies for your inconvenience.

Unfortunately, after the television contract is signed, we don't have a lot of control over where the networks point the cameras."

"It's not your fault," Zack said. "It's mine." He looked at Diane. "I should have picked some other time to bring Diane to a game. I'm sorry."

He turned to Meekins again. "What specifically did the threats say?"

Meekins hesitated. "You sure you want to hear?"

"We can take it," Diane said. "Go ahead."

Captain Rogers of the Chapel Hill PD stepped forward. "Well," he said, "one of the callers said, 'When the redhead walks outside of the stadium, we're going to blow her away.'"

Diane shivered. Zack put his arm around her shoulders.

"We had three or four other calls in a matter of a few seconds. One said, 'Allah will kill the godless infidels.' The other said, 'The pagan JAG officers will die.'" Rogers looked grim. "I'm sorry. For what it's worth, I'm ex-navy. Boiler tech on the USS *Valley Forge*," he said. "You guys did the navy proud."

Zack ignored the compliment. "Mr. Meekins, these might be crackpot calls, and I hate to miss the second half of the Duke game, but out of precaution and for the sake of the fans' safety, maybe we should leave now."

"That's up to you, Lieutenant," Rogers said.

Zack nodded to Diane. "Let's get out of here."

The gunman, still lying on his belly, brought the scope back to his eyes and squinted. The doors were open now, and through the cross-hairs, very small streams of infidels were trickling out.

From this distance, the high-powered thirty-aught-six bullet would do the job. Nailing one would be easy. Nailing both would be more problematic, but not impossible if that were the will of Allah.

May both deaths today be Allah's will.

Still, he might get only one shot. One shot—fired in a war that neither began today nor would end tomorrow.

The one shot *must* count.

Even a single kill would be a great symbol of victory. Especially if he could draw the blood of the infidel accusers before the Americans killed the three heroes of the faith they had convicted.

Now the task was Allah's.

Allah surely would bring them out these doors.

Allah surely would give him a clear line of sight.

Allah would steady his hand for the moment of glory.

He had been so patient. Would this, now, be his appointed moment of destiny?

Praise be to Allah for his beneficence, and blessed be the prophet Mohammed. Peace be upon him!

Ahmed Sadat brought the scope back to his left eye, closing his right. A young brunette woman came out the door. He put the crosshair on her temple and held it there as she walked from left to right.

Ready . . .

Aim . . .

Infidels streamed out the glass doors. His breathing quickened and deepened. His moment would come soon.

He worked the bolt action on his rifle, chambering a bullet. The distinctive, sharp clacking sound of the bolt action brought goose bumps. This was the final countdown of the mission that would forever mark his place in the history of holy jihad.

All glory to Allah for his beneficence.

More infidels filed out of the building. The thought of the loud *bang* echoing through the woods, causing the swine to scamper in a panic, electrified his soul.

A well-figured, redheaded woman, wearing a light blue T-shirt and blue jeans, walked out the door. Breathing deeply, he adjusted his high-powered scope for another look. It was her! Or was it? Surely it was. Such a beautiful woman. What a waste this would be.

And the infidel Brewer was by her side!

Allah had given him this moment.

The woman and her partner turned and walked up the hill away from him.

Now is the time to act. Praise be to Allah!

He brought the back of her red, wavy hair into the center of his crosshairs and rested his finger on the cold steel trigger.

Now!

The rifle jumped. Half a second later, there was commotion where his shot had landed. He looked through the crosshairs of the scope. Some of the infidels ran like stuck pigs. Others waved their arms frantically. The redhead had disappeared. So had her partner.

Praise be to Allah. His bullet has drawn the blood of the infidel.

The sound of the first siren confirmed that his window for escape was narrowing. He dropped the rifle in a ditch, then raced through the woods to a parking lot, where another operative was waiting.

"We must go, my brother," Ahmed ordered. "Now!"

"Did you accomplish your mission?"

He waved the driver on, and the vehicle's tires squealed as they headed from the parking lot.

"The infidel witch who called for the death of our Muslim brothers is dead."

"Praise be to Allah!" the driver shouted.

"And blessed be the prophet—peace be upon him," Ahmed said.

CHAPTER 2

Office of the Commanding Officer
Navy Trial Command
Building 73
32nd Street Naval Station
San Diego, California

Commander Bob Awe, twenty-five-year JAG Corps veteran and senior trial counsel at the JAG Trial Service Office in San Diego, stepped into the office of Captain Glen Rudy, his commanding officer. He wore working khakis with the silver oak leaf of a commander pinned to his collar.

"Any word from them, Bob?" Rudy wore the standard naval officer's working-khaki uniform with the silver eagle of a navy captain on one collar and the gold and silver mill rind of the Navy JAG Corps on the other.

As the officer directly above Lieutenants Brewer and Colcernian in the chain of command, he was as eager as Rudy to hear from them. "No, sir, Skipper," he said with regret. "I've tried both their cell phones, and all I get is voice mail. Last I heard from Zack, they were planning to attend that basketball game in Chapel Hill, then drive to Washington for their meeting at the White House. They were supposed to drive to the NLSO—Navy Legal Service Office—at the Washington Navy Yard."

"Humph," Rudy snorted, then rose from his chair. He turned his back to Awe, crossed the room, and stared out his window at a navy frigate getting underway in San Diego Bay. "I *knew* we should've arranged for a security detail to go with them. It's been too soon to assume the threats were over."

"With all due respect, Captain, President Kennedy had a security detail, but that didn't stop a long-range sniper rifle. Plus, the colonel was griping about having to detail extra marines for round-the-clock surveillance."

Rudy's gaze was still fixed on the frigate. "Nothing from Captain Buchanan at NLSO Washington?"

"I just got off the phone with him. Neither Zack nor Diane has called in."

Rudy grunted. "I feel helpless, Bob. I just wish we could get the details about what happened."

"I'm sure the press will release the names of the victims soon," Awe said. "Once they're identified and the families have been notified."

"Or their command has been notified." Rudy turned to the television in the corner of his office. Tuned to CNN, the TV showed the image of a middle-aged male reporter standing outside the front doors of a large East Coast hospital. The sound was muted, but closed-caption text scrolled across the bottom of the screen:

> Memorial Hospital still has not released the names of the victims from this afternoon's sniper shootings in what is believed was an assassination attempt on Navy Lieutenants Zack Brewer and Diane Colcernian. CNN has learned, however, through sources speaking on condition of anonymity, that two people are confirmed dead, including a woman fitting Lieutenant Colcernian's description. Hospital officials are withholding names pending positive identification of the victims.

Rudy grabbed the remote control off his desk and punched it, causing the screen to go black. "Let me know if you hear anything."

"Aye, aye, Skipper."

"That will be all, Commander."

Their escape route took them on a northerly route from the scene. The driver checked his rearview frequently for signs of pursuers. So far, so good. Or so it seemed. Mostly tractor-trailers, SUVs, and thousands of nondescript cars zipping along at sixty-five miles per hour in both directions. Not a single law-enforcement vehicle. At least not in the last hour.

As the vehicle crossed the James River Bridge, revealing the sight of the late-afternoon orange sun reflecting off the modest Richmond skyline, the driver reached down and punched the car radio. The AM scanner found station WRVA, the 50,000-watt news station and self-proclaimed "Flagship Station of the Old Dominion." A female reporter was in the middle of a newsflash.

"The Associated Press now confirms one death in that sniper shooting believed to be an assassination attempt on Navy Lieutenants Zack Brewer and Diane Colcernian."

The passenger, who was trying to doze, woke with a start, her eyes widening.

"Twenty-two-year-old Maggie Jefferies, a University of North Carolina coed, was shot this afternoon by a sniper as she left a men's varsity basketball game between North Carolina and Duke. Jefferies, who was a senior speech communications major from Wilmington, is believed to be a victim of mistaken identity. Described by her friends as a beautiful young woman who was slender with red hair and green eyes, Jefferies bore a strong physical resemblance to Navy Lieutenant Diane Colcernian, who also attended the North Carolina–Duke game this afternoon with Lieutenant Zack Brewer, a Carolina graduate."

The passenger's eyes met those of the driver's.

"Brewer and Colcernian, the Navy JAG officers stationed in San Diego who prosecuted the high-profile court-martial of *United States versus Mohammed Olajuwon* in which three Muslim navy chaplains were convicted and now face the death penalty, were in Chapel Hill as part of an East Coast tour on their way to meet President Williams in Washington later this week. Both university and law-enforcement officials are reporting that when network cameras caught the JAG officers watching the game, death threats followed. Brewer and Colcernian opted to leave the game early for security reasons, we are told, and their whereabouts are unknown."

Diane reached over and took Zack's hand.

"Officials are saying that Miss Jefferies came out of the exit Lieutenant Colcernian most likely would have used, had she stayed for the remainder of the game. Authorities are treating this as an act of terrorism, and the university president, the governor of North Carolina, and the White House have issued statements condemning the shooting.

"Meanwhile, in sports, the Virginia Cavaliers ..."

Zack punched off the radio.

"Oh, dear heaven, that poor girl," Diane said. "They were trying to kill me, and they got her." Tears streamed down her face. Trembling, she withdrew her hand from Zack's, buried her face in her hands, and wept. Zack put his right hand on her shoulder, massaging her neck while steering the car into the far-right northbound lane of I-95 with his left. "I wish it had been me." She opened her purse, fished out a tissue, and tried to stem the flow of tears. "I feel like it's my fault. Her family ..."

"I'd better call the skipper," Zack said awkwardly. "Let him know we're okay." He picked up his cell phone, powered it up, then punched the speed-dial number for Captain Glen Rudy, JAGC, USN.

"Skipper?... Yes, sir, we're fine ... Yes, sir. We just found out. We heard on the radio ... She's here ... She's pretty shaken up. We're in Richmond. Northbound Interstate 95. Just crossed the James River, coming up on I-64 split off to Williamsburg ... I understand ... That's a direct order ... Aye, aye, sir."

Zack looked at Diane's tear-stained face, and his heart filled with anguish. He breathed a prayer for strength. "Skipper says I'm to call him back in thirty minutes if we haven't heard anything from him before then."

The first flashing blue light appeared five minutes later as they passed the Parham Road exit just north of Richmond. Immediately, Zack's cell phone buzzed.

"Lieutenant Brewer."

"Lieutenant, this is Sergeant Scott, Virginia State Police. I'm right on your rear bumper, sir. You guys okay?"

"We're fine, Sergeant. But I must confess that this is the first time I've ever been happy to see a flashing blue light on my rear."

"It's a privilege to be on your rear, Lieutenant. And I promise, no tickets this time."

"Thanks."

"Lieutenant, I want you to drop your speed down to about fifty-five, then stand by for further instructions."

"Okay." Zack tapped the brake, disengaging the cruise control, and watched the speedometer needle drop from seventy to fifty-five miles per hour.

"Good," the trooper said. "You okay on gas, sir?"

"Half a tank," Zack said. Another blue-and-silver Virginia State Police vehicle with lights flashing came out of nowhere, whizzed by the rental car, then pulled in directly in front of them.

The trooper in the rear car spoke again. "That's why I wanted you to slow down, Lieutenant. We've got two other squad cars headed our way to join the party."

A third trooper, charging from the rear at probably eighty miles per hour, pulled his squad car even with Zack. He flashed a quick salute at the tip of his Smokey Bear hat.

"Whose gonna be catching the speeders in Richmond today, Sergeant?"

"Speeders have a holiday for a couple of hours. They just don't know it yet," the sergeant said. Just then, a fourth squad car zipped past the three others and pulled into the very front of the caravan.

"You guys escorting us all the way to Washington?"

"Wish we could," the trooper said. "The governor made the offer, but the navy had other ideas." Zack did not respond. "Here's what we're gonna do. Just follow the lead car with the flashing lights."

"I'm with you, Sergeant."

Five minutes later, Zack saw the squad car in front flash its right turn signal, and the trooper in the car to his left gave him a hand signal, which Zack interpreted to mean that the makeshift motorcade was about to exit Interstate 95. They took Exit 92B, the Ashland exit, and made a left at the top of the ramp. In another five minutes, they were driving into the entrance of Randolph-Macon College, about twenty miles north of Richmond. Zack stayed close on the trooper's bumper, following him to the school's small, empty football stadium.

"Follow us onto the field, Lieutenant," came one of the officer's voices over a loudspeaker.

As the sun slowly surrendered to twilight over central Virginia, the small caravan of flashing blue lights proceeded slowly through the open end of the stadium, past a sign that read "Home of the Yellow Jackets," and came to a halt in one of the end zones.

"What are we doing?" Diane asked.

"Being protected, I hope," Zack said.

The state trooper in the car behind them got out and walked to the driver's side window.

"You two okay?" The officer wore the gray uniform and black Smokey hat of the Virginia State Police.

"We're fine, Officer," Zack said. "What's the plan?"

"We're to stay with you here until the navy picks you up," the trooper said. The other three troopers who had been part of the caravan were getting out of their cars. All three carried pump shotguns. They took up positions around Zack's car like Indians circling a wagon train in a John Wayne movie.

"Any idea when that'll be?"

"Trying to get some information on that now, Lieutenant. But from what we hear"—the patrolman raised his voice against the *thwock-thwock-thwock* of the rotary blades—"it sounds like your ride is here now."

The dark silhouette of an SH-60B Seahawk, its running lights blinking, passed directly over the rental car. The helicopter slowly maneuvered into position near the fifty-yard line, and when the pilot rotated it on an aerial axis at a perpendicular angle to the end zone, a spotlight on the tail section illuminated the word *NAVY*.

"A sight for sore eyes," Zack mumbled to himself as the war bird feathered onto the field. A squad of commandos carrying M16s poured out the open bay door and sprinted across the grass.

"Lieutenant Brewer, I'm Lieutenant (JG) D. L. Cobb, Foxtrot Company, SEAL Unit 1, Virginia Beach," the squad leader said to Zack. "Our orders are to escort you and Lieutenant Colcernian to Washington, sir. My men will get your bags, but I need you and the lieutenant to accompany us in the Seahawk."

"Lieutenant, I thought you'd never ask," Zack said, then looked at Diane. Her green eyes were still bright with tears, but a small smile of relief crept across her beautiful face. "Ready?"

She nodded.

"Let's go."

Surrounded by five black-clad SEALs moving in a human circle, Zack and Diane jogged to the helicopter. As the fierce, warm air from the whirling propellers blew her red hair in a thousand directions, a master chief reached down and took Diane's hand, pulling her up into the back of the chopper. Zack stepped up behind her. The SEALs turned, pointed their guns out toward the field, as if to threaten any potential assassin who might be looking on, then backpedaled into the chopper.

The chopper lifted off in a rush, and in an instant, the whirling blue lights below were but dots disappearing into the landscape, then darkness as the chopper dipped its nose and headed north toward Washington.

CHAPTER 3

Council of Ishmael headquarters
Rub al-Khali Desert
250 miles southeast of Riyadh, Saudi Arabia

Inbound from Riyadh, the helicopter slowed, then made a low circle before feathering toward the landing pad.

Its owner and passenger, Hussein al-Akhma, raised his binoculars and looked down for a last bird's-eye view of his mighty empire. The 100,000-square-foot concrete command center, just to the left of the landing pad, was painted the color of sand. Surrounded by sixty-foot sand dunes, it appeared buried in the barren desert landscape. Powered by solar energy, and inaccessible except by helicopter, the command center housed the most modern communications and jamming equipment black gold could buy on the black market.

Al-Akhma, a Saudi national with blood ties to the royal family—second cousin once removed to King Fayel himself—was called by some a billionaire Muslim playboy, by others a devout follower and hero of the great faith. Only the latter designation mattered to him.

He adjusted the focus on the binoculars, sharpening the image of the building that housed the Council of Ishmael international headquarters. He was not sure if the Americans had seen it with their spy satellites. Most likely they could, if they wanted to. But they would never attack it. Not here in the Rub al-Khali anyway. This was not Iraq or Afghanistan. An attack here would mean an attack on the sovereign territory of the Kingdom of Saudi Arabia.

"Terrorist activities," as the leaders of the Great Satan called them, were treated with a double standard by America's criminal presidents.

Be it Carter, Reagan, Bush I, Clinton, Bush II, or now the dog Mack Williams, America would "get tough" on so-called "state-sponsored terrorism," so long as it was allegedly sponsored by hapless, bumbling, loudmouthed regimes like the Iraqis, the Afghanis, or the Libyans.

Other nations, because of their importance to American economic interests, or because of their potential possession of nuclear weapons, got free passes from the sons and grandsons of John Wayne. Foremost among the "free pass" states were China, North Korea, and Saudi Arabia.

America would more likely drop a bomb on Westminster Abbey than shoot a slingshot at Saudi Arabia.

This calculation was foremost in al-Akhma's strategic thinking when he located the Council's headquarters here. And if the Americans did the unthinkable and launched a strike on Saudi soil, the cluster cells in Europe and the Caribbean were capable, on a moment's notice, of making September 11 look like a Sunday school picnic.

He looked down once more on his camouflaged empire. Goose bumps rose on his arms and the back of his neck. From here, strategic decisions were being considered that would finally eradicate the Zionist plague called Israel on the Mediterranean coast.

Nasser, Sadaam, Arafat, and Assad had all failed, but Hussein al-Akhma would not. Allah had given him the vision to found the revolutionary Council of Ishmael—an elite group of twenty Muslim, Arabic billionaires, all Western educated, all fluent in English, all who pledged their cumulative fortunes to the elimination of Zionism and Christianity and to the spread of the Great Faith throughout the world.

Theirs would be a subtle infiltration of Western institutions and culture. The new Islamic freedom fighter would be equally fluent in English, Arabic, and French and in some cases even Hebrew. Under al-Akhma's command, Council operatives would blend unnoticed into the godless Western landscape, gather intelligence, recruit disciples, and undermine the enemy both politically and militarily.

Al-Akhma understood all too well that the nefarious twin nemeses of Islam, Israeli-Zionism and Christianity, were propped up by the Great Satan, the United States of America. Weaken America, and he would weaken Zionism and Christianity. His vision called for crippling America by infiltrating Council operatives into its military. And in the seven years that had passed since he first brought the Council of Twenty together, he had successfully inserted numerous operatives into the United States military, primarily the United States Navy.

It all started with the Navy Chaplain Corps. The Council, through an entity called the Muslim Legal Foundation, had threatened to sue the navy if it did not admit more Muslim chaplains. The chief of naval personnel, a three-star admiral on the short list for chief of naval operations, wilted like a frail petunia and capitulated in order to keep an embarrassing lawsuit out of the public eye.

This paved the way for other well-educated, multilingual Muslim operatives. The Council secretly offered scholarship money for hard-line Muslims to go into naval aviation, naval intelligence, and the elite submarine community.

The pilot's voice resonated over the intercom, breaking into his thoughts. "Leader, if you wish, safety harnesses are available for your protection, as we are about to touch down."

Hussein pressed the talk button on his headset. "Very well, Akeem." He stuffed the binoculars under the seat, then clicked the harness across his shoulder. As members of his personal security team sat down and strapped in, he returned to his musings.

All this pointed to an apocalyptic event that would shake the world for Islam. Allah had revealed this to him. And Allah had given this cataclysm a name.

Operation Islamic Glory.

This glorious culmination of events would finally drive a wedge between the Great Satan and its moderate Muslim sycophants who were more interested in the corrupt American dollar than the advancement of Islam. From Islamic Glory, finally, a consolidated Islamic superpower would rise like a phoenix from the ashes. A superpower that would hail Hussein al-Akhma as its leader.

The time for Islamic Glory would be soon. But first, other matters must be attended to.

He smiled as the helicopter made a quick circle of the area, then lightly touched down in the center of the beige concrete.

The sun blistered the midmorning sky as the pilot cut the engines, then rushed around to open the bay door for al-Akhma. A blast of hot air rushed in as the back door slid open. Two turban-clad young men, somewhat of a ceremonial honor guard, stood at attention on the tarmac holding AK-47s just outside the helicopter door. The Council of Ishmael leader put on his sunglasses and stepped into the desert heat.

From a monolithic concrete building across the tarmac, a tall, turbaned man with a closely cropped black beard walked swiftly across the landing pad, his arms spread.

"Welcome back, Leader!" He greeted al-Akhma by dropping to his knees and kissing his leader's hand.

Al-Akhma allowed his principal deputy to spend several seconds with his knees on the scorching asphalt before he spoke. "Rise, Abdur," he said.

The deputy rose, his face dripping sweat, then planted a quick kiss on each of al-Akhma's cheeks.

"Let us escape this roasting inferno, Abdur." Al-Akhma put his hand on Abdur Rahman's back and nudged him toward the building. The men shaded the sun from their eyes as they strode quickly toward the air-conditioned entrance. Two aides jumped from the helicopter with al-Akhma's luggage and briefcases and followed the two men.

"What is our situation with the two infidel JAG Corps swine?" al-Akhma asked when he felt the blast of cool air at the front doorway. "Are they dead yet?"

"Our agent tracked them to a sporting event on the East Coast. When the American television networks showed them on television, our people made calls to the stadium, warning of their fate."

As Abdur Rahman spoke, the two men walked down a long hallway, then walked into the office of the leader of the Council of Ishmael. Al-Akhma sat down behind a desk with three computer screens on its surface. He motioned Abdur to sit in a chair just opposite the desk, facing him.

"By calling," Abdur continued, "our operatives hoped to flush the infidels into the open, ahead of the crowd. Our sniper was positioned in a wooded area, watching the exit closest to their seats in the stadium. They did not emerge immediately, as we hoped, but our sniper got off a shot, we believe, at the witch Colcernian."

"What a shame, Abdur." Al-Akhma snapped his fingers. A bodyguard brought him a glass of American Coca-Cola. "Such a beautiful maiden with the decrepit soul of an apostate. Perhaps I should not admit this, Abdur, but that woman became the object of my fantasies on more than one occasion. It is a pity that I had no chance to act on those fantasies."

A sip of coke. The crunching of ice.

"Coke, Abdur?"

"No thank you, Leader."

"And so we were successful?"

"Our sniper reports contact with the target. At least some target. The Americans are claiming we shot some college girl bearing a description similar to that of Colcernian."

"Ha!" A wide grin crawled across al-Akhma's face as he removed his turban and handed it to one of his servants. "You believe the Americans?"

"I don't know, Leader." Abdur removed his turban. "Colcernian is unaccounted for. And so is Brewer. It is possible that we got one, or both, and the Americans haven't announced it."

"Hmm." Al-Akhma scratched his scruffy black goatee. "It *does* seem that the Americans would show them on the television if we had missed. On the other hand, who can figure out the American press?"

"True, Leader."

"Public reaction?"

"Shock. Terror." Abdur Rahman broke into a wide grin. "The White House is *condemning*"—Rahman made mocking quotation marks—"the actions of the *terrorists*"—he added more quotation marks—"responsible for this *despicable* act."

"Ha!" The leader of the Council of Ishmael broke into delirious laughter. "You look just like an American when you make quotation marks. Anyway," he said, chuckling, "this is, as the Americans say, a *win-win* situation. Either we killed the swine, or we missed. And if we missed, we killed another infidel and have all the infidels whining and running for cover!" More guffaws.

"And, Leader!" Abdur bent over, laughing. "Look on the bright side!"

"What may that be?"

"You may still get Colcernian to live out your fantasies before we finish her off!"

"Ingenious, Abdur!" Al-Akhma doubled over laughing. "This calls for a toast." Abdur looked at one of the three bodyguards and snapped his fingers. "Ahmed. Two bottles of vintage Moroccan wine from my wine cellar. *Boulaouane de Gris*, please. Immediately! Pour a glass for myself and my deputy."

"Right away, Leader," the Arab bodyguard said, then returned with wine as ordered and began pouring.

"What of Islamic Glory?" Al-Akma swirled the *Boulaouane de Gris*, savored its bouquet, then downed the liquid. "How are our contingency plans progressing?"

"You say that it is of Allah, Leader"—the two Arabs' eyes met—"and I believe you." A hesitation. "But ..." Abdur took another sip, allowing the thought to linger.

"A subtle difference between us Kuwaitis and our Saudi cousins," al-Akhma snapped, "is that in Kuwait we finish our thoughts before drinking."

"My apologies, Leader."

"You were saying?"

"That I support your vision of Islamic Glory, but there has been some discussion from some of the Council of Twenty."

"Discussion? What kind of discussion?" al-Akhma roared. He smashed the wine glass against the far wall, leaving a trail of red wine across his desk and along the trajectory. "Are there those in the Council who do not support *me*?" He snapped his fingers, demanding more wine.

"Only those with a few questions, Leader. It is a hard sacrifice for a Muslim to fathom. The destruction of one of the holiest sites in Islam."

"Not destruction!" Al-Akhma stood, slamming his fist on the table. "Sacrifice!" His gaze swept the room. "Sacrifice for the greater good! What do these fools not understand, Abdur?" A swipe of the hand. Papers flying. "Names! I want names of the subversive ones."

"Leader," Abdur said, lowering his voice in contrast to al-Akhma's fevered pitch. "I assure you that there are no subversive ones. But *you*, Leader, are Allah's one true prophet on earth today. It makes sense, does it not, therefore, that you would be sensitive to hearing his voice before they would? That is why *you* are our leader. *You* and only you are Allah's visionary, Hussein."

Abdur Rahman's velvety-smooth voice, far more than that of any other member of the Council, had a soothing effect on al-Akhma's temper. Unofficially, he had become the visionary's deputy, rumored by some within the inner circle as the heir-apparent to power should anything ever happen to Hussein himself. Al-Akhma depended on his Saudi billionaire friend. And sure enough, Abdur's points were resonating. How could the other members expect to understand as clearly as he? After all, as Abdur said, he was Allah's prophet.

"Brother Abdur, once again, you are the voice of reason. I must be patient with my flock. After all, they are good Muslims." Al-Akhma spoke in a lower voice, then sat down and took several deep breaths. "Call the Council together for eight o'clock tonight. I shall again explain the need for this."

"Yes, Leader."

CHAPTER 4

Navy JAG Appellate Government Command
Washington Navy Yard
Washington, D.C.

When Lieutenant Commander Gwendolyn Hanover Poole, JAGC, USN, announced to her *Law Review* colleagues at Northwestern University, during her third and final year of law school, that she had accepted a commission in the U.S. Navy JAG Corps, she received considerable ridicule from her classmates.

"The *JAG* Corps? What are you? A warmonger or something?"

"Wendy, you're editor-in-chief of the *Law Review*, for goodness' sake."

"Are you crazy, Wendy? You were a clerk for the Fourth Circuit Court of Appeals. You can write your ticket."

"You're giving up a six-figure salary out of law school to go into the *navy*?"

Such were the protests from her well-intentioned classmates. And on several points, they were right. For ten years, the editor-in-chief of the *Northwestern Law Review*, the prestigious position that Gwendolyn Hanover Poole had held in her final year of law school, had enjoyed a direct employment pipeline to the corporate Chicago firm Cantor and Goldstein.

Though the few first-year associates lucky enough to get jobs with the large firm occupying floors eighty through eighty-five of the Sears Tower were required to sign a nondisclosure form keeping their salary confidential, rumors spread like wildfire around Northwestern: starting salary in the $200,000 range. Wendy Poole, from firsthand experience, knew this to be a fact.

Though she was not at liberty to discuss the specifics with her class-mates, the job offer she received from the firm called for a base salary of $180,000 per year, *plus* a $20,000 signing bonus if she maintained her number-one law school class rank at graduation. *Plus*, for all associates staying with the firm a minimum of three years and billing an average of 2,200 "billable hours" per year over that time, the firm would pay off, in one swoop, all law school debt. And although Wendy was on a full academic scholarship her last two years, she had accumulated $60,000 in debt from her first year before she was awarded a grant based on her first-year grades.

The startup salary—in the upper one-half percent of all first-year associates' salaries in the country—was significant, she had to admit.

The lump-sum tuition payment after three years was enticing. The prospect of doing drudgery work for senior partners who were billing seven hundred dollars an hour, the idea of carrying their briefcases into court, and the notion of working seventy-hour weeks—weekends, Sundays, and holidays just to meet the minimum billable require-ments—were not.

Despite her reservations, Wendy Poole nearly took the money and ran. Several times, in fact. Still, something inside told her money would not satisfy. The idea of becoming some high-billing senior partner's good-looking wallflower associate, even a well-paid, good-looking wall-flower associate, was more than her stomach could bear.

The call of the JAG Corps was too alluring. So what if her silk-stockinged classmates didn't understand? It was *her* life.

From her office overlooking the Anacosta River in the Washington Navy Yard, Wendy did a last-minute check of her U.S. Navy service dress blue uniform. She straightened her blouse. Good. All four sets of gold buttons were in place, shining against the dark navy blouse, accentuat-ing her trim figure.

Two and a half gold stripes of a navy lieutenant commander were sewn perfectly around the cuffs of her jacket, and the gold mill rind insignia of the JAG Corps, roughly the size of a quarter, was sewn onto each sleeve. Her skirt was cropped just slightly above her knees.

Good. Hemline within regs.

No runs in her nude-colored stockings, at least not yet. Excellent. Her shoes, medium-heeled officer's pumps with a definite feminine touch, were polished spotless.

She examined her salad row of awards to the left of her lapel. Two green and orange Navy Achievement Medals, two green and white Navy Commendation Medals, and a pink and white Meritorious Service Medal were perfectly in place. And on the opposite side, a blue and white name tag with the name Poole and the round insignia of JAG Appellate Government Command.

Good.

A touch of blush and lipstick, just about right. Subtle, not overpowering. Perfume, subtle.

Good.

Her hair was tidily pinned up in a bun, where it would fit perfectly under her white officer's cover in transit to her destination.

It had cost her maybe three quarters of a million dollars in lost salary over the last five years by turning down Cantor and Goldstein.

But none of her law school classmates had ever done what she was about to do.

In one hour, Lieutenant Commander Gwendolyn H. Poole, JAGC, USN would argue the position of the government before the Supreme Court of the United States of America.

Even after all this preparation, after all her work to prepare the brief, after all the publicity surrounding the case, the mere thought of it was surreal.

The Supreme Court of the United States.

She couldn't believe it was about to happen.

The knock on the door broke her concentration. "Ready, Wendy?"

She turned and saw her commanding officer, Captain Will MacDonald, standing at her office door.

"Yes, sir. I think so."

MacDonald, dressed in the service dress blue uniform of a navy captain, flashed a sly grin. "Nervous?"

"Not too much, sir." *I'm lying to my commanding officer. Don't lie to your commanding officer, Wendy.*

"Good. The master chief has a staff car waiting for us. Here's our procedure. We have to clear security at the main entrance to the building and then again just before going into the courtroom. As you know, cameras are not allowed in the courtroom, but our PR people tell us the press is already camped out in front of the main portico."

"Great. I'd rather drink cod-liver oil than deal with those guys."

MacDonald chuckled. "Maybe you won't have to do either."

"Remember, Lieutenant Brewer was involved in a three-day members' trial. They learned his habits, his parking place, his lunch spot. They ambushed him at every corner. And he enjoyed it."

"And he was good at it," Wendy said.

"True," MacDonald said. "But that was a drawn-out affair. This is a one-shot deal. One thirty-minute argument, in and out, and you're done. They haven't seen you yet. They may or may not even recognize us as we enter the court, unless they read the name tags. Of course they'll recognize you when you come out of the court. Just keep the comments to a minimum. Remember, this is an appeal, not a trial. Stick to the issues. Keep it short and simple."

"Aye, aye, sir."

"I'll be at counsel table with you, but this is *your* moment, Commander. The navy is depending on you, and so is your country."

"Aye, aye, sir."

"Let's go."

CHAPTER 5

800 feet above USS Harry S. Truman
32 degrees 22 minutes west longitude
35 degrees 18 minutes north latitude
327 nautical miles WSW Lajes Field, Azores, Portugal
North Atlantic Ocean

The sun, now a glowing orange ball, slipped under the western Atlantic horizon as the pilot looked back over his shoulder for his final pass on the port side of the carrier. The ocean was turning into a dark, colorless abyss, except for the narrow orange carpet on the western horizon near the setting sun. And the floating gray yardstick with flashing lights, churning a white trail of water, was now barely visible.

Passing by the stern of the USS *Harry S. Truman* at an altitude of eight hundred feet, the pilot gently banked the multimillion dollar jet fighter away from the sun and pressed his microphone.

"Flight control, Viper Leader on final approach, requesting permission to land."

"Viper Leader, flight control." This was the carrier air traffic controller. "We've got you on visual now. Be advised request for landing is granted. Proceed at your discretion."

"Roger that, flight control. Proceed at discretion."

Completing the wide, aerial loop behind the stern of the nuclear carrier, he pointed the F-14 Tomcat at the stern of the floating postage stamp.

This would be like any other landing at any other airport in the world, except the runway of this floating airport rolled in six-foot swells sliced by the carrier's hull. And the landing area on the rolling, bouncing runway was only about five hundred feet, less than a quarter of the length of a normal runway. And if the tail hook trailing underneath his fuselage missed one of the four steel cords in the aft of the deck, Lieutenant Commander Mohammed "Mo" Quasay and his navigator, Lieutenant Mark "Mouse" Price, could wind up with a cockpit full of cold, dark, North Atlantic saltwater and a free trip to the bottom of the drink.

Quasay switched his radio to the LSO—Landing Safety Officer—frequency, then dropped the plane's flaps.

Landing gear down.

Tail hook down.

"Viper 1. LSO. Call the ball!" squawked the LSO, referring to the amber light on the stern of the carrier used for visual guidance for landing.

"Roger ball!" Quasay called back, indicating visual contact with the flashing light on the back of the carrier.

Ten seconds to touchdown. No more radio contact. All landing signals would now be governed by a system of lights on the stern of the carrier run by the LSO.

Green light on.

Good.

Three hundred feet.

Two hundred feet.

The Tomcat rushed at the carrier's stern. The ship was no longer a postage stamp, but a floating steel wall growing exponentially larger by the second, rushing head-on at the cockpit.

Up! Up! Up!

Five seconds.

Three seconds.

Cut throttle.

A violent, jolting *thump* as forty tons of aircraft slammed against the steel deck. The pilot and navigator lunged forward under furious g-forces, their shoulder harnesses digging into their chests.

Full throttle!

The aircraft shook violently, its twin afterburners momentarily fighting the resistance of the powerful steel cable stretched across the floating runway, "trapped" by the plane's tail hook. Shaking under the thrust of full power, the plane came to a restrained stop halfway down the carrier's deck.

Cut power!

Quasay pulled back on the forward throttles and switched off the engines.

"Nice job, Commander." Mouse Price patted the plane's commander on the shoulder as the pilot blew a deep exhale. "That's the tenth Okay Three in a row, sir." Price was referring to the fact that Quasay had caught the third of four powerful cables stretched across the back of the runway, considered the optimum target for the highly dangerous carrier landings.

Praise be to Allah for his beneficence.

"Thanks, Mouse," Quasay flipped a switch that raised the Plexiglas canopies, allowing a rush of warm sea air into the cockpit. "We were coming in a bit low for a second. Guess I've been lucky."

"Lucky. We're still on mark for the Top Hook Award"—he referred to the award given at the end of the cruise to the pilot with the safest landing record as evidenced by the highest number of Okay Three landings—"and there's not even a close second. That's not luck, sir."

"Thanks, Mouse. I've got a good navigator."

Mouse made a comment in response to that, but Lieutenant Commander Quasay ignored it. He wasn't really interested in small talk. Two days to Gibraltar. By then he would know.

He waited as an air crewman brought a portable stepladder to the cockpit, then climbed over the side, took salutes, and pulled off his flight helmet. Quasay checked his watch. His was the last flight for the late afternoon cycle, and the next flight operations were still a half hour away.

Quasay walked alone to the rear of the flight deck, leaving the flight crew to attend to his plane. Another twelve hours until he was due back in the cockpit.

He whipped a cigarette and a Zippo out of his olive-drab flight jacket and, cupping his hand around the end of the cigarette, carefully lit it. The first draw of nicotine into his lungs preserved some of the adrenaline from the carrier landing.

Like most naval aviators, Quasay needed adrenaline. To be constantly on the razor-thin line between life and death was exhilarating. Another long draw on the cigarette. A flick of smoldering ash into the ocean breeze. He watched as the ashes blew toward the dark waters below, mingling with the churning wake behind the carrier's stern.

Back beyond the sunset's afterglow, somewhere in the growing span of ocean as the *Truman's* nuclear-powered engines pushed the carrier toward Gibraltar, the eastern seaboard of America loomed. And somewhere beyond that was his adopted hometown of Grand Rapids, Michigan.

Quasay flipped the last vestige of the burning cigarette butt into the wind, then cupped his hand and fired up another.

America had been good to him. America granted his family citizenship, afforded better economic opportunity for his parents, grandparents, brothers, and sisters. America gave him a commission as a naval aviator in its military.

Because of this, his mission for Allah would be a struggle. Everything they'd pumped into his head at NROTC and at flight school at NAS Pensacola was hard to wipe out.

Duty.

Honor.

Country.

Defending the Constitution of the United States against all enemies, foreign and domestic.

Obeying the lawful orders of my superiors and of the president of the United States.

The words from the officer's oath rang in his ears. These past seven years as an American naval aviator had been a heady experience.

In a way, he hoped that Allah would spare him the task. But if it did come, he hoped to have the strength to do Allah's will.

If he followed through with this, he would become a traitor to many and a hero to others, depending on whether this al-Akhma really was Allah's prophet.

Quasay believed him to be, but he wasn't certain.

He took another long draw on the freshly lit Camel as the sun's afterglow faded and a canopy of stars appeared in the clear sky.

In the end, his heart was not with the setting sun to the west. It was with the rising crescent moon to the east. His struggle now was determining whether the crescent moon really was calling him to unload deadly ordinance on the target in question.

Perhaps he *had* been called to this mission for a purpose beyond human understanding. He'd always wanted to fly fighter jets, even as a boy. Then out of the blue, Allah's providence had provided him the best flight training in the world.

Fate was with him. Every dime of his education at the University of Michigan had been paid for by the Muslim Academic Foundation, a New York–based entity that provided scholarships for young members of the Great Faith who attended college to pursue careers in the United States military.

The stated purpose of the foundation was to give more Muslim-Americans the opportunity to serve their country in the armed forces. Extra money was available for students who committed to enrolling in the Naval Reserve Officers Training Corps—NROTC—during college. Even more money was thrown to NROTC students following the aviation track.

The foundation not only paid every dime of tuition, books, boarding, and meals for his education at Michigan, but also paid him a living allowance of $1,500 a month.

Someone, somewhere, wanted more Muslim pilots in the United States Navy.

Later, he learned that the foundation, though based locally in New York, received most of its funding from Muslim and Arab brothers overseas, with the greatest percentage coming from an organization known as the Council of Ishmael.

He also learned that he had been scrutinized by the foundation before the scholarship was offered and was selected because he and his family were determined to be true guardians of the Great Faith by meeting the following criteria: First, his parents were less than one generation removed from immigrating to America, his grandparents having grown up in Iran.

Second, Quasay and his two sisters were educated in a private, conservative Muslim academy, The School of the Holy Prophet, located on the outskirts of Dearborn, Michigan. There, strict adherence to the Great Faith was taught. Quasay was personally recommended by the Islamic headmaster and the school's three staff imams as a young man who would adhere to the Faith above all else.

Finally, Quasay was fluent in Arabic, as were all other scholarship recipients, he later learned.

Yes, fate was surely with him.

"Excellent landing, Commander."

He recognized the voice of Lieutenant Hosni Alhad, the only other Arab-American fighter pilot on the aircraft carrier. He turned and saw the red glow of a cigarette lighting the silhouette of a man.

"Hosni, come." Quasay motioned to the pilot, then patted him on the shoulder as he stepped forward. Like Quasay, Alhad also was still in his olive-drab aviator's flight suit. "How was your landing, my brother?"

"Not quite as smooth, sir." Hosni Alhad took a long draw, then flicked the ashes into the sea breeze. "My tail hook caught the second wire." Alhad uttered an obscenity and took another draw.

"Second wire?" Quasay paused. "Not too bad. At least you did not have to make another pass." He coughed. "And at least you're not in the drink. Besides, the winds and seas picked up considerably between the time of our launch and our landing."

A brief pause. Then Alhad spoke. "With all respect, sir, the increased winds and seas did not prevent you from nailing your landing. Your skills are amazing, Mohammed."

Quasay let that pass for a few seconds. "I was lucky, Hosni. I've been lucky all these years."

"Your modesty, sir, deprives Allah of the glory due him from having bestowed such superb abilities on you." Alhad switched to Arabic, lowering his voice. "Surely our presence here, together, in the same squadron, is divinely ordained, a sign that we are to carry out Allah's mission."

Quasay looked around to make sure nobody was in earshot. He didn't like speaking in Arabic with Hosni in front of other navy personnel. On the other hand, better to use Arabic than to divulge information that would get them both court-martialed.

Under the carrier's deck lights, he could make out the presence of a couple of ATs—aviation technicians—working on a jet about thirty yards away. The increasing sea breeze would serve as an effective sound barrier.

"No email messages, I take it, Hosni?"

"Not yet, sir. And we aren't yet within radio contact of Gibraltar."

"You are excited about this, my younger brother? You realize we may both die."

"Martyrdom would be my privilege, sir."

His pupils adjusting to the nighttime conditions on the flight deck, Quasay looked into Alhad's jet-black eyes. "Are you sure this is what you want? You know, it isn't too late to back out. If the call comes, what we are being asked to do will never be understood even by many Muslims. No one will say anything if you back out."

"Commander," Alhad said, still whispering in Arabic, "they paid for my education as they did yours. There is no coincidence that Allah has placed me in this squadron, at this time, at this place, for a reason. I am convinced al-Akhma is Allah's prophet. I am ready to give my life for a greater cause. I am with you in life, and in death, sir."

Quasay smiled. "I'm glad you are sure, brother." *Even if I am not.* Then he switched to English and patted Hosni on the back again. "Get some rest. You'll need it."

CHAPTER 6

Main plaza entrance
United States Supreme Court Building
Maryland Avenue
Washington, D.C.

The car carrying Lieutenant Commander Wendy Poole and Captain Will MacDonald pulled to a halt along Maryland Avenue between the U.S. Capitol and the Supreme Court Building. Wendy grabbed her briefcase and stepped out onto the sun-bathed plaza.

The white marble Greek-revival building loomed above the plaza, its massive columns towering upward like powerful pillars of wisdom reaching to the heavens. Resting atop the columns, chiseled in massive granite for all to see, were the words *Equal Justice Under Law*.

Her gaze was fixed on the proclamation of justice, broken only by the flight of pigeons alighting from their berth under the great sign and fluttering to the plaza just a few feet in front of her. As the pigeons pecked at some peanuts being tossed by two little girls and their mother, Wendy realized her heart was in a sudden flurry. Until now, the idea of arguing before the Supreme Court of the United States was an esoteric concept to be dealt with in the future.

But being here, stepping onto the plaza, witnessing the majestic building and the hundreds of spectators and media gathered on the plaza and the marble-columned portico steps—reality hit her like a cold, wet washrag in the face.

Please, Lord, give me strength.

"Captain MacDonald? Commander Poole?" Two middle-aged police officers in navy blue uniforms were standing by the car. "We'll be escorting you into the building and into the courtroom. If you'll follow me, please?"

"Lead the way, Sergeant," Captain MacDonald said.

The policemen led the two JAG officers straight down the middle of an open, roped-off passageway toward the steps leading into the building. Several hundred people crowded along the ropes, standing behind a dozen armed, uniformed police officers who guarded the inside of the cordoned-off passageway. Wendy noticed several signs and placards carried by some in the crowd.

Navy Justice: An Oxymoron

Free the Chaplains!

Capital Punishment = State-Sanctioned Murder!

Kill the Chaplains!

The Real Problem? Judeo-Christian-Yankee-Zionism!

"Who *are* these people?" Wendy mumbled under her breath.

"Professional court watchers," one of the officers volunteered. The foursome strode down the plaza toward the most famous courthouse in the world. "There are always a few newbies for each new case," the officer added as they neared the base of the steps. "Other than that, it's the same nuts holding different signs. I think they're on retainer by interest groups trying to influence the court."

When they reached the bottom step, the sergeant halted, then mumbled something into his handheld radio.

Wendy looked up at the blue sky, again taking in the towering columns that reached to the heavens. The sergeant was still on his walkie-talkie, talking about the security check.

"Are you here on the Olajuwon case?" a woman shouted, standing behind the rope just to the right of the steps in an area designated for the press. "Priscilla McNally, *Washington Post*," the woman shouted again. Wendy recognized the name. "Are you Commander Poole?"

Wendy glanced at Captain MacDonald. "It's okay to identify yourself," he whispered. "They'll see you in the courtroom anyway. But no comments about the case."

"Aren't you Commander Poole?"

"Yes, I am," Wendy said. *Hurry up, Sergeant.*

"Commander, it's almost unheard of for the Supreme Court to hear argument on a motion for a stay of execution. Do you think this is a sign that the court may in fact block the execution of the chaplains?"

"Ready, ma'am? Sir?" The sergeant motioned the JAG officers to follow him up the steps.

Wendy turned and smiled at Priscilla McNally. "Sorry, I can't comment on that right now."

"But, Commander ... Isn't it unusual ..."

The reporter's voice faded as a female police officer snapped, "Place your briefcase on the belt, ma'am. Wendy stepped through a metal detector just inside the large doorway.

"Your arms out, ma'am," the woman said. Wendy assumed a spread-eagle position, doing her best to maintain a sense of dignity. "Sorry, ma'am. We're required to do this even for the attorneys."

Wendy did not catch that. Her eyes were roaming around the "Great Hall," the palatial, pure marble hallway with Roman columns leading to the door of the courtroom itself. She looked up and saw eight cylindrical gold chandeliers hanging by gold chains from a red-and-gold-checkered ceiling as the female police officer waved an electromagnetic wand under her arms, behind her rear, and down the front of her chest. Then a delayed reaction made her realize that the officer had spoken to her.

"That's okay, Officer."

"Good luck, ma'am," the female officer said.

"This way." The sergeant motioned them across the marble floor. The echo of their clicking steps bounced off the columns and ceiling as the foursome walked toward the courtroom. The sergeant pushed open one of the huge double doors, then stepped back for Wendy to enter.

Already, a packed gallery sat in hushed reverence on both sides of the aisle. Wendy stopped just inside the chamber, her eyes wide as her gaze swept the regal scene before her.

Across the room, beyond the packed gallery, nine raised black chairs, still empty, loomed like thrones reserved for exalted princes. And in the very center, the chief justice's chair stood out like the throne of the king.

Behind the thrones rose four Roman marble columns draped with red velvet curtains. In the center of the gallery over the chief justice's chair, a round white clock hung suspended from the ceiling.

Down in the center of the well, about four feet below the justices' platform, was the podium from which she would argue. As if to add more pressure, a small spotlight illuminated the counsel's podium.

"Follow me." The sergeant motioned, breaking Wendy's trance. She fell in line behind the sergeant and Captain MacDonald and strode down the center aisle between the spectators. The sergeant pushed open a mahogany gate separating the gallery from the counsel area and directed Wendy and Captain MacDonald to be seated at the large counsel table just to the right of the spotlighted podium.

A few seconds later, another Supreme Court policeman escorted two U.S. Marine JAG officers through the same gate and directed them to be seated at the counsel table to the left. Fit, trim, dressed in green tunics with their hair closely cropped, Major Andy Goldstein and Lieutenant Colonel Patrick Rafferty were from the Navy JAG Appellant Defense Division in Washington. Both were familiar to Wendy. She had argued against them many times before the Armed Forces Court of Criminal Review.

Goldstein looked over at Wendy and nodded, but he did not smile or show any other emotion. Rafferty looked straight ahead and did not make eye contact.

"All rise!" a deep voice bellowed as nine black-robed justices emerged through the curtains draped behind their thrones. "The Honorable Chief Justice and the Associate Justices of the Supreme Court of the United States. Oyez! Oyez! Oyez! All persons having business before the Honorable Supreme Court of the United States are admonished to draw near and give their attention, for the Court is now sitting. God save the United States and this Honorable Court!"

Wendy's gaze settled on an older man in a pinstriped suit standing to the far left of the nine chairs. *The clerk of the Supreme Court.*

"This Supreme Court for the United States of America is now in session." The clerk's deep voice resonated throughout the palatial courtroom. "Please be seated."

Wendy's knees weakened as her hand found the chair's armrest. She tentatively pushed the chair back from the counsel table and, with all the dignity she could muster, lowered herself and focused her eyes on the chief justice.

Thank God they don't let TV cameras in here. The whole country would see me hyperventilating.

"The clerk will call the first case." The black-haired, double-chinned chief justice drew out the words in the Alabama drawl for which he was known.

Lord, calm my nerves.

"Call *United States versus Mohammed Olajuwon et al.*," the clerk bellowed. He sat down and seemed to disappear in the shadows behind the spotlights illuminating the nine lords of American jurisprudence.

"We'll hear from counsel for the appellant." Chief Justice Rayford Moore twitched his dark, bushy eyebrows. "If I'm not mistaken, that would be Major Goldstein?" He nodded toward the marines.

Andy Goldstein stood and flattened his green marine jacket against his already very flat waist. With a row of colorful service ribbons on his chest and a single legal pad in his hand, he stepped to the spotlighted podium between counsel tables.

"Mr. Chief Justice, associate justices, may it please the court." Goldstein's hands clutched both sides of the podium. His voice sounded firm, commanding, but his knuckles looked white. "I am Major Andrew Goldstein, United States Marine Corps, with Navy JAG Appellate Defense, and along with Lieutenant Colonel Patrick Rafferty, I represent the petitioner-appellants in this case."

Goldstein's gaze dropped to his legal pad. "Briefly, the facts of this case are as follows—"

"We know the facts, Major!" the chief justice snapped. "Tell us why we should stop the execution of these three chaplain officers, all of whom have been convicted by a court-martial of their peers."

The interruption seemed to jar Goldstein's concentration. Wendy saw his eyes rise from the legal pad, saw him lock stares with the chief justice. A stunning moment of silence followed as Goldstein appeared to gather his thoughts.

The chief justice intimidates even the marines.

"Because, Mr. Chief Justice ... because of governmental misconduct." Goldstein lifted his right hand from the podium. "The government's whole case started with a navy investigator who broke into a witness's car—without probable cause—and began gathering evidence on which the government got its conviction. We submit that this was tainted evidence"—he chopped the air with his right hand—"and this court should block the execution based on that reason alone—"

"But, Major!" Associate Justice Edna Rouse Winstead, the court's newest member and a former congresswoman from Wilson, North Carolina, removed her reading glasses. "This navy investigator you're referring to is Special Agent Kilnap, correct?"

"Yes, ma'am, Justice Winstead," the marine said.

"Isn't it true," the attractive fifty-year-old said, "that even if *some* of Kilnap's activities were improper, this evidence against the Muslim chaplains would have been discovered anyway?" Winstead raised her eyebrows, flashed an owlish look at Goldstein, then put her glasses back on.

Goldstein took a sip of water. "That's the government's argument, Madam Justice. Obviously we disagree with that argument." Goldstein glanced at Wendy, who looked at her watch.

Twenty minutes until I argue. Lord, make my knees stop shaking.

CHAPTER 7

River entrance
The Pentagon
Arlington, Virginia

Diane stepped out the massive front doors of the Pentagon's river entrance, the side of the great limestone building overlooking the Potomac River. She gazed across the river, soaking in the view of the Lincoln Memorial, the Washington Monument, and in the distance, the dome of the U.S. Capitol. Even in late winter, with spring threatening to burst forth in the form of cherry blossoms, Washington was one of the world's most breathtaking cities.

"We're gonna be late." Zack glanced at his watch as he followed her out the door a moment later.

"Attention on deck!"

Diane snapped to attention, ignoring Zack's comment, then rendered a sharp salute. Zack also snapped to attention and saluted as the judge advocate general of the navy, Rear Admiral Joseph Stumbaugh, accompanied by his personal aide, Lieutenant Commander Kirk Foster, exited through the river entrance doors.

Stumbaugh returned the salutes. "At ease, Lieutenants."

Two government staff cars, the first a white Crown Victoria, the second a white Taurus, had been dispatched by the navy to carry the JAG contingent on the short drive from the Pentagon to the White House. They were flanked by two squad cars, one from the Arlington Police Department and a second from the Virginia State Police.

Admiral Stumbaugh and Commander Foster rode in the backseat of the Crown Victoria. Directly behind the Crown Vic, Zack and Diane sat in the backseat of the Taurus.

They were told that Virginia State Troopers and City of Arlington Police would provide an escort from "the Building"—the name military insiders called the Pentagon—across Memorial Bridge to the base of the Lincoln Memorial, where D.C. police would take over.

As they crossed the famed old bridge, the vista of Washington unfurled before them, the Lincoln Memorial to their right, Foggy Bottom and the quaint shops of Georgetown along the riverbank in the distance. Diane turned to look over her shoulder at the soil of her native Virginia.

Her home.

She gazed at the green rolling hills behind her with thousands of white crosses planted almost like stars in a green Milky Way. Arlington Cemetery. Beneath a solitary cross, somewhere among the others, lay the body of Vice Admiral Bobby Colcernian, United States Navy.

If he could see me now, his only daughter, about to meet the president of the United States.

"Diane?" Zack caught her staring over her shoulder.

She flicked a tear from her eye.

Zack pulled a white handkerchief from his pocket and handed it to her. "You gonna be okay?" He smiled and gently took her hand as the Crown Vic and the Taurus crossed over the bridge into the District of Columbia. The cars pulled to the curb at the base of Constitution Avenue, just in front of the Lincoln Memorial, where three Metropolitan Police Department squad cars waited.

She smiled at Zack as the makeshift motorcade began rolling up Constitution Avenue toward the Washington Monument. "I've just been thinking about Daddy. How I wish he could have been here for this." She handed him back the handkerchief. "And I've also been thinking about that poor girl in North Carolina." She looked out the window to her right. A few dozen people milled about in front of the Vietnam Memorial. Some touching it, others dropping flowers at its base.

She studied Zack for a moment, glad for the strength of his hand around hers, for the understanding in his eyes. The cars stopped in traffic, then slowly started rolling again. "Here we are, about to meet the president of the United States. Probably hailed as heroes, while in North Carolina, there's a grieving family whose daughter was murdered by a bullet that was meant for me."

Zack stopped and pulled her around to face him. "Hey. Don't do this to yourself." She met his gaze, unable to look away from the compassion she saw there. "That bullet wasn't just meant for you. I was a target too. You had no control over this, Diane. Don't feel guilty. Okay?"

She didn't answer.

"Okay?" Zack raised his eyebrows expectantly, then gave her his handkerchief again.

"Okay." She attempted a smile. Something about his reassuring tone made her feel better.

"Besides, if anybody's at fault, it's me. I'm the one who insisted that we go to the game."

"Zack, you didn't know—"

He cut her off. "Look, we're getting ready to meet the president. This is a once-in-a-lifetime opportunity. Cameras will be there. Terrorists around the world will see the images. We need to show our strength. Our resolve." Though his eyes were warm, his expression was dead serious. "I know we're both feeling a lot of things right now, but we've got to put on our best game face. The navy expects it. The nation expects it." He paused and gave her arm a squeeze. "Understand?"

In that instant, he reminded her of her father. The greater the pressure, the greater his strength. She drew in a deep breath. Her father would expect no less of her. Neither did Zack. "I understand."

When the car reached the Washington Monument, the driver, an enlisted legalman from the JAG's staff, turned left onto 17th Street NW, skirting the outside perimeter of the South Lawn of the White House.

"Two blocks to the White House," Zack said.

"Can you believe this is happening, Zack? We're actually going to the Oval Office."

"After what we've been through with this court-martial"—he released her hand—"I can believe anything. Besides, once you spread your charm and that million-dollar smile around the Oval Office, it will never be the same."

"Right thing to say, Lieutenant Silver Tongue." She smiled at him, then glanced out the right rear window at the green lawn of the Ellipse behind a wrought-iron black fence. The car turned right and halted for the small contingent of marines and uniformed Secret Service personnel carrying M16s.

A marine first lieutenant, wearing a crisply starched dress blue uniform, white gloves, and white cap, rendered a sharp salute at the car bearing the judge advocate general of the navy; then he approached the Taurus, shooting another salute as the driver lowered the windows.

"Good morning, sir and ma'am," the marine said. "I'm Lieutenant MacGregor, White House Security Detail."

"Morning, Lieutenant," Zack said.

"If the two of you could please step out of the car for a moment for some standard security clearances, we'll have you on your way for your appointment with the president."

"By all means, Lieutenant," Zack said.

Diane exited the car behind him, then realized she was standing on the South Lawn of the White House. *Am I really here?*

"May I examine your identification cards, please?" The naval officers complied; then the marine lieutenant said, "And now, gentlemen, if you could follow me."

The marine led the JAG, his aide, Zack, and Diane to a small, high-tech security station on the perimeter of the South Lawn, where they stepped into an X-ray booth. Two uniformed Secret Service agents nodded their heads at the marine lieutenant, who motioned for the four naval officers to step out of the security shack and back onto the lawn.

"Admiral, if you and your party would follow me, please." The marine officer, resplendent in dress blues, was trim and well built. His voice was almost robotic.

"By all means, Lieutenant." The judge advocate general motioned for his aide, Zack, and Diane to follow him. With the marine leading, the JAG officers walked toward a small door near the hedgerows on the west side of the White House, where they were met by a navy captain, heavy gold cording hanging over his shoulder.

The marine lieutenant saluted, then said, "Sir, presenting Rear Admiral Stumbaugh and his party."

"Thank you, Lieutenant." The navy captain returned the junior officer's salute. "I've had the pleasure of meeting the admiral and the commander on a previous visit to the White House. I'll take it from here, Lieutenant. You are dismissed."

"Aye, sir." The marine captain clicked his heels, pivoted 180 degrees, and marched away as the navy captain flashed a smart salute to the judge advocate general.

"Captain Hancock, we meet again," the JAG said to the captain.

"A pleasure as always, sir." The captain then turned to Diane and Zack. "Good morning, Lieutenants. I'm Captain Jay Hancock, naval attaché to the president."

Diane's eyes caught Zack's.

"A pleasure to meet you, sir," Zack said, shaking the captain's hand.

"A pleasure, sir." Diane extended her hand.

"What's our itinerary, Captain?" Admiral Stumbaugh asked.

"If you'll follow me, I'll explain as we walk to the Oval Office," Hancock said.

The Oval Office.

"Lead the way, Captain," the admiral said.

Diane and Zack followed the attaché through an interior corridor, then along a covered walkway adjacent to the West Wing.

"As usual," the attaché said as they walked, "the president is running a tight schedule. This morning he will meet with Lieutenants Brewer and Colcernian privately in the Oval Office, and then we will all move out to the Rose Garden for a brief ceremony."

"Did you say he wants to meet with the lieutenants *privately*, Captain?" Admiral Stumbaugh's voice projected a tinge of disappointment.

"My apologies for a poor choice of words, sir. Both you and Lieutenant Commander Foster are also invited into the Oval Office. By privately, I meant no press will be in the Oval Office meeting. Of course, the president wants all four of you at his side both in the Oval Office and in the Rose Garden."

The attaché checked his watch as the group approached a reception area. "We're right on time." A gray-haired woman sat behind a desk. Four muscular men with shifting eyes and icy looks flanked an ornate door behind her. The men wore dark business suits, closely cropped haircuts, and small earpieces with wires reaching to their suits. Two stood guard to the left of the door; the other two, hands clasped, stood to the right.

"Hello, Captain Hancock." The woman's eyes twinkled. "I'm Gale Staff, the president's appointments secretary. And you must be Lieutenants Colcernian and Brewer. I recognize you from television."

"And this is Admiral Stumbaugh and his aide, Lieutenant Commander Foster," Hancock added quickly, as if to ensure that the navy's senior JAG officer wasn't totally overshadowed by two lowly, albeit widely recognized lieutenants. Hancock turned to Stumbaugh. "Admiral, you remember Mrs. Staff?"

"Ma'am." Stumbaugh gave a gentlemanly nod.

"Yes, I remember the admiral too. Good to see you again, sir," Gale Staff said with a smile. "You are right on time, and if you'll wait for a moment, I'll see if he's ready."

The secretary picked up her telephone. "Sir, Admiral Stumbaugh, Lieutenant Brewer, Lieutenant Foster, and Lieutenant Colcernian are here." A brief pause. "Yes, sir." She looked at the attaché. "Captain, the president is ready."

Diane's heart jumped. *I'm not really here.*

"Admiral, Lieutenants, follow me, please." Hancock stepped to the large ornate door, opened it, and announced, "Mr. President, Admiral Stumbaugh, Lieutenant Brewer, Lieutenant Foster, and Lieutenant Colcernian."

Diane followed the Admiral and Zack into the spacious Oval Office. The tanned, silver-haired man she had seen on television a thousand times rose from behind his huge mahogany desk. Two other men stood with him.

"Admiral, Lieutenants, please come in," President Mack Williams said in his native Kansas twang. Then, smiling, he crossed the room to meet the officers just inside the doorway. He wore a dark pinstriped suit and red tie, looking every bit as powerful and charismatic as he did on TV.

As the president shook the admiral's hand, Diane noticed two more burly men in dark suits, arms crossed in front, flanking the inside door.

"And you must be Lieutenant Colcernian," the president said, turning to Diane.

"Yes, Mr. President." His handshake was firm. Yet undeniable warmth radiated from the man.

"Thank you for coming," he said, as if she'd had a choice when summoned to the White House by the president himself.

"It's an honor, Mr. President."

"Admiral, Lieutenants, I'd like you to meet Secretary of Defense Erwin Lopez." The president gestured to a middle-aged Hispanic man standing a few feet to his left. The secretary of defense shook hands with all the officers.

"And this," the president announced, "is our White House chief of staff, Mr. Wally Walsh."

A balding man who, like the president and the secretary of defense, was also a fixture on national television, stepped forward and offered his hand.

So this is Wally Walsh? The mastermind behind the president's political fortunes. Diane flashed her trademark modeling smile at the almost sloppy-looking man with the reputation for being a political genius.

"Everyone, please have a seat." The president gestured toward a group of chairs facing his desk. When they were seated, he lowered himself to his seat, then continued. "I invited you here to personally thank you for your service to our country. I know this was a challenging court-martial, but your performance and the verdict were a victory for America in the war on terrorism."

"Thank you, Mr. President," Zack and Diane said, almost in unison.

"You know"—the president's eyes met Diane's—"there was initially a heated debate in this very office over who should prosecute this case." Looking amused, the president scanned all the officers' faces. "My attorney general felt the justice department should prosecute. He meant well, but he thought our JAG officers were too inexperienced." The president exchanged raised eyebrows with the secretary of defense. "But Secretary Lopez here felt that the military should prosecute. And Admiral Stumbaugh assured me that he could find the right officers to do the job." He grinned. "And he did."

"Thank you, sir." Diane said. "But in all honesty, Lieutenant Brewer deserves the credit. His performance was outstanding. I'm just honored to have been on the team."

The president leaned back in his chair, smiled, crossed his arms, and raised an eyebrow at Zack.

"Mr. President," Zack said, "Lieutenant Colcernian is naturally modest, which is one of the many qualities I admire about her. In all honesty, I doubt we could have won without her. And I have to credit Admiral Stumbaugh for detailing her to the prosecution team."

The president burst out laughing. "Okay, okay," he said, holding up his palms. "I can see the navy is still the same kiss-up society it was when I was a Navy JAG officer."

That brought obligatory chuckles from everyone in the room, except for the two Secret Service agents, whose hard faces did not flinch.

"I'd like for you to know, Lieutenant Colcernian," the president continued, "I agree with Lieutenant Brewer. I watched you on television. Your opening statement was magnificent."

Diane felt herself blushing. "Thank you, sir."

"And you, Lieutenant Brewer"—the president's gaze shifted to Zack—"your reputation as a crackerjack trial lawyer preceded you."

"Thank you, Mr. President," Zack said.

The president took a sip of coffee, exposing a cuff link bearing the presidential seal. "I understand that you're the only JAG officer in history to get a defense verdict at the Newcomb murder trial at the Naval Justice School."

Diane grinned as Zack's gaze dropped to the floor. *Here it comes.*

"I got lucky," he said, looking back at the president.

"Son, there's nothing lucky about that. That's the toughest moot court assignment I've ever been exposed to." The president took another sip of coffee, then leaned forward. "My apologies. Anybody care for coffee or anything to drink?" He lifted his mug emblazoned with a "Fighting Jayhawk" logo.

A few responded, and two white-jacketed navy stewards poured steaming black coffee from porcelain pitchers. Diane and Zack declined.

"Anyway," the president continued, "I remember that case vividly from my days there. I got stuck with the role of defense counsel and, like everyone else, got my rear end skewered." He chuckled. "I'll bet the prosecutor in your case must've felt pretty bad to be the only prosecutor to have lost." Another chuckle.

Zack's gaze dropped again.

Should I tell him that I was the prosecutor, the only prosecutor in the navy ever to lose that case, and that I hated Zack's guts for three years because I wanted to win that award for my dying father?

"Thank you, sir." Zack blushed.

I've got to bail him out.

"Mr. President," Diane said, "I happened to have witnessed Lieutenant Brewer's performance in that case."

The president caught her eyes and smiled.

"It was truly magnificent," she said.

"Well, I think you are both magnificent," the president said as Zack gave Diane a thank-you wink. "And if there's anything I can ever do for either of you, all you have to do is call my appointments secretary. I'll see to it that you get her private number."

"Thank you, sir," Zack and Diane said, almost in unison.

"I hate to interrupt, Mr. President," Wally Walsh said, "but we're all due in the Rose Garden in three minutes."

"My trusty chief of staff makes sure I'm in front of the media at the appointed time." The president stood and motioned for his seated guests to rise. "If you all will follow me."

★

"Ladies and Gentlemen, the President of the United States." A voice boomed over the White House loudspeaker as two plain-clothed Secret Service agents pushed open the door leading outside into the Rose Garden.

Applause and the clicking of several dozen cameras were heard as Diane and Zack followed the president to the Rose Garden. The late afternoon sunlight of early March bathed the floral panoply of daffodils, tulips, and a variety of red and yellow rosebuds in the world's most famous garden.

The president stepped to the mahogany podium with the presidential seal on the front. Diane, Zack, and the others formed a straight line behind the president. The battery of television cameras and microphone-toting reporters reminded Diane of the sharklike media circus that she and Zack had endured during the Olajuwon court-martial. A fleeting queasy feeling twisted her stomach.

"Please be seated," the president said to the press.

"Today, we mark the recognition of another significant victory in the war against terrorism." Diane squinted under the barrage of flashbulbs as the president continued. "The convictions rendered in the court-martial against navy chaplains Olajuwon, Reska, and Abdul-Sehen send the message that our country will root out and aggressively prosecute terrorists, no matter who they are and no matter where they are.

"At this time, I'd like to ask Navy JAG officers Lieutenant Zack Brewer, Lieutenant Foster, and Lieutenant Diane Colcernian to step forward." The president turned and motioned for Zack and Diane, who walked forward and stood by the president, one on either side. Cameras clicked and flashed.

"For their professionalism in waging this important legal battle on behalf of the government," the president said, "I am pleased to announce that these officers are today being awarded the Meritorious Service Medal."

A round of polite applause followed from the press.

"Normally this award is given by the secretary of the navy through the service member's commanding officer. But today I've gotten special permission from Secretary of the Navy Arthur Hardison and Captain Glen Rudy—these officers' commanding officer—to personally decorate Lieutenants Brewer and Colcernian for their professionalism in service to our country."

A chuckle rose from the gathering—as if the president had to get the secretary of the navy's permission to do anything.

"At this time, I'd like to ask the secretary of defense to step forward."

Erwin Lopez moved forward to stand beside Diane. He held an open black velvet box. Inside, two pink and white medals lay on the velvet. He handed the president a citation, which he began reading aloud:

"Lieutenants Zack Brewer and Diane Colcernian, Judge Advocate General's Corps, United States Navy, for your outstanding professionalism in the performance of your duties to the naval service, in serving as trial counsel in the case of *United States versus Lieutenant Commander Mohammed Olajuwon et al.*, a case of extreme importance not only to the naval service, but also to the United States in this country's continued battle against international terrorism" — he paused — "on behalf of the United States Navy, it is my honor to decorate each of you with the Meritorious Service Medal. On behalf of a grateful nation, please accept my congratulations."

The president applauded. The media and military guests followed suit. Then the president stepped in front of Secretary Lopez and lifted one of the pink and white medals from the black velvet box.

"Ladies first." The president smiled as he pinned the MSM on Diane's dress blue uniform. "Congratulations, Lieutenant." When the president shook her hand, goose bumps rose on the back of her neck.

The president pinned the medal on Zack, whispering, out of earshot of the press, but not out of Diane's, "They say your nickname is Silver Tongue." She saw Zack grin as the president shook his hand. "Congratulations, Lieutenant."

The president turned back to the podium. "Let's again show our appreciation for these fine naval officers." Another round of applause followed.

"Our time is short," the president said after a moment, "but I'll take a couple of questions."

"Mr. President, as you know, arguments are taking place at this very moment in the U.S. Supreme Court about whether the death penalty will be imposed against the defendants whom these officers prosecuted." Diane recognized the strident tone of the questioner's voice. It was ABC's Jack Williamson, seated in the front row, sporting his notorious black toupee. "How would you answer charges, Sir, that this ceremony was strategically timed to coincide with today's arguments to somehow influence the court's decision?"

"This ceremony was planned *before* the Supreme Court scheduled arguments on the execution, Jack." The president grasped the podium.

"It's purely coincidental." He chopped the air with his right hand. "And unless the justices are watching us on television, instead of listening to arguments, I doubt they'll even know about this ceremony." The president checked his watch. "I see that our time is up. Thank you all for coming."

"Mr. President ..."

"Mr. President ..."

The president smiled, waved, and ignoring the shouted questions, turned and motioned his guests to follow him back into the White House.

CHAPTER 8

A s she awaited her turn to stand before the world's most powerful court, the last thirty minutes seemed like an eternity to LCDR Wendy Poole, JAGC, USN. The courtroom was a hornet's nest, with the justices grilling Major Goldstein with a relentless barrage of questions about the government's conduct in the court-martial of *United States v. Mohammed Olajuwon et al.*

The court's collective thinking was hard to read based on the justices' questions. Some of the questions, at least those asked by the four liberals on the court, seemed sympathetic to the defendants.

The four conservative justices, those appointed by Republican presidents, were often antagonistic in their questioning of Major Goldstein. So much so that Wendy, though she didn't particularly care for Goldstein, almost felt sorry for him. Chief Justice Moore, a southern Democrat but with old-school conservative ideas on some issues, was the most difficult to read. He would probably cast the deciding vote that would seal the chaplains' fate.

The yellow light flickered on the counsel podium. Goldstein had three minutes. Wendy tuned out the spirited exchange between the justices and the marines and concentrated on her opening statement. The red light flashed, followed by "Thank you, Major," from Chief Justice Moore.

Goldstein took his folder, turned, and sat.

"The court will now hear from the government." Chief Justice Moore's voice rumbled through the courtroom like the growl of an angry grizzly bear. "Commander Poole?"

Wendy's knees trembled as she pushed back her chair, picked up her legal pad, and rose in front of the crowded gallery.

"Thank you, Your Honor." She smiled as she stepped to the podium, feigning an air of cool confidence. She placed her legal pad and brief on the lectern, then looked up. The eighteen eyes of the black-robed lords of American jurisprudence bored into her. She felt the weight of their silent stares.

"May it please the court." The first five words of her introduction came out just as rehearsed. "I am Lieutenant Commander Gwendolyn Poole, JAG Corps, United States Navy, and I represent the government in this case."

Chief Justice Moore leaned forward, scowling. "It sounds like the government built its case around a dirty agent, Commander!"

"Mr. Chief Justice, the whole purpose of inevitable discovery, a doctrine developed by this very court, is to balance the needs of justice, even if a mistake is made by a police officer. If an officer makes a mistake in the collection of some evidence, but if other evidence would have been discovered despite that mistake, justice requires that the rest of the evidence be admitted.

"A mistake?" Associate Justice Edna Winstead whipped off her glasses, managing to contort her face so she looked appalled. "Commander Poole, your Special Agent Kilnap of the Naval Criminal Investigative Service *broke* into a car parked on a navy base, *without a warrant* and *after* a federal magistrate specifically *denied* his request for a warrant. Isn't that so?"

"Justice Winstead, we don't condone Mr. Kilnap's actions. But the prosecution did not try to offer into evidence anything that was found in the car. The tape recordings in which the chaplains acknowledged their involvement in this plan to commit murder were made after and independent of the incident you are referring to."

Associate Justice Mona Shepard of Massachusetts, a staunch death penalty opponent, was the next to speak. "Kilnap was a dirty agent, wasn't he?"

Wendy eyed the frail little gray-haired woman. "Justice Shepard, I'm not qualified to evaluate Special Agent Kilnap's professionalism. He made one mistake in the case, and that was it. And as I say, we haven't offered into evidence anything found in the warrantless search of the car. Agent Kilnap did not make a mistake when he tape-recorded the chaplains' admissions of their involvement with the murder of the Israeli ambassador and several members of the naval service and the murder of innocent civilians during a San Diego church service."

"But a conviction is one thing." The court's most liberal justice whipped off her granny glasses. "An *execution* is quite another." Justice Shepard wiped the lenses of her glasses with a tissue, then pushed them back on her nose. "Don't you see a problem with an execution associated with dirty police work? Why shouldn't we just order this to be commuted to a life sentence? Would that not be a reasonable compromise?"

"With respect, Your Honor, no, this court should *not* order commutation to a life sentence for these terrorists masquerading as naval officers. Not if this court is satisfied that the subsequent evidence, that is, the tape recordings especially, would have been discovered *in spite of* the agent's illegal actions. It was *this Supreme Court*"—Wendy chopped the air with her hand—"that formulated the inevitable discovery exception in the 1984 case of *Nix versus Williams*. And in this case, the military judge found the illegal break did not assist Special Agent Kilnap in obtaining the taped confessions of the chaplains.

"Kilnap was planning to follow Aziz's car from the naval air station anyway. He did not need a warrant to tail the car. He followed Aziz into the Shoney's restaurant where Aziz met with one of the defendants. Kilnap did not need a warrant for that. And he taped the confession of Chaplain Reska in the restaurant, a public place, where there is no reasonable expectation of privacy. At that point, probable cause was generated and court orders were properly issued for all subsequent tape recordings of the chaplains' telephone lines. So the subsequent evidence was *not* tainted by Kilnap's illegal action, and therefore, the chaplains were convicted based upon legally acquired evidence."

"You really believe that?" Justice Shepard glowered down from on high, her elbows resting on the table, her hands steepled under her chin. "Do you really think that the illegal break-in did not give Kilnap an inherent advantage in leading him to gathering confessions? As I understand the record, Commander, Kilnap not only broke into Petty Officer Aziz's car, but also *bugged* it—and in the course of bugging it, he overheard a mobile phone conversation between Aziz and the chaplain about meeting at Shoney's. Isn't that right?" Justice Shepard raised her left eyebrow.

She's boring in on my case's weakness.

"Yes, Justice Shepard, your memory is correct on that portion of the record. But—"

"But"—Shepard wagged her crooked index finger before Wendy could change the subject—"isn't it true that Kilnap knew to go to Shoney's because he overheard the mobile phone conversation from the illegal bug he planted in the car? And without the tip about going to Shoney's, no other evidence would have been gathered, and we wouldn't be here. Sounds to me like the whole investigation was tainted from the illegal break-in of Aziz's car. In other words, your conviction was from the fruit of the poisonous tree, wasn't' it?" Another wag of the crooked finger.

Wendy took a deep breath. Shepard was the court's most feminist, fire-breathing liberal. Her response here could be pivotal to the government.

"That argument, the fruit of the poisonous tree argument, is the very argument that the defense counsel, Mr. Levinson, made during the court-martial, Justice Shepard." Wendy took a sip of ice water from a paper cup to slow the pace of Shepard's interrogation. "Captain Reeves, the military judge, carefully considered that, but he found based on other evidence that Kilnap planned to follow the car anyway. In other words, he believed the tape recordings would have been *inevitably discovered*"—she made air quotation marks—"following *this* court's decision in *Nix versus Williams*, and he rejected the defense argument. Judge Reeves had the right to make that finding, and absent an abuse of discretion, his decision must stand. Abuse of discretion would be impossible for the defense to argue because there was other evidence in the record for this case on which the judge based his decision."

"What other evidence?" Justice Shepard snapped.

"Special Agent Kilnap testified," Wendy quickly responded, "that he planned to follow Aziz's car out of the naval station parking lot with or without the recording and that he never let the car out of his sight as he tailed it. In other words, Kilnap didn't need the illegal conversation to follow Aziz to Shoney's. He was *already* tailing the suspect's car when the transmission device he planted picked up Aziz's voice and the conversation about Shoney's.

"Kilnap began his pursuit *before* hearing the information about the rendezvous point at Shoney's. The point is, Justice Shepard, Kilnap would have followed Petty Officer Aziz to Shoney's with *or without* the illegal bugging of Aziz's car. He would have gotten his evidence anyway.

That's why the *inevitable discovery* doctrine trumps the defense's fruit of the poisonous tree argument."

"But, Commander"—another wave of the crooked finger—"isn't believing Kilnap sort of like believing the fox who testified he wasn't planning to enter the henhouse?" A few snickers rose from the gallery.

"Your Honor, it's up to the trial judge to assess credibility, to accept or reject testimony. And while Kilnap's initial actions are not admirable, Judge Reeves found his testimony to be truthful. The defense had an opportunity to cross-examine on this point and was unable to contradict Kilnap's testimony."

"Commander"—Wendy looked to her left and recognized the court's most conservative justice, Associate Justice Jack Miller of California—"you've talked a lot about this court's decision in *Williams versus Nix*." Miller paused to toy with his handlebar moustache. "But what about *Brady versus Maryland*? And specifically our requirement in *Brady* that the prosecution reveal exculpatory evidence *prior* to trial. Did that happen in this court-martial?"

He's throwing me a softball. Thank you, Justice Miller.

"I'm glad you asked that, Justice Miller," Wendy said as the yellow three-minute warning light flashed on. *Thank God. Stretch out this answer to keep Shepard off your back.* "The navy prosecutor in this case, Lieutenant Zack Brewer, first discovered Mr. Kilnap's error. Lieutenant Brewer discovered the warrantless search *after* the trial began. But to his credit, Brewer immediately informed the court." She paused for a sip of water. "Judge Reeves stopped the trial and allowed the defendants to make motions to dismiss and for a mistrial. Judge Reeves heard the evidence and denied the motions. The defendants lost, and now they want to have their cake and eat it too."

Red light.

"Commander Poole, your time is up," Chief Justice Moore growled, "but because we ran over with Major Goldstein, in fairness to you, the court will give you one minute to wrap up your thoughts."

"Thank you, Mr. Chief Justice." Wendy took a deep breath. Her entanglement with Justice Shepard was over. "Mr. Chief Justice, distinguished associate justices, *this* court formulated the inevitable discovery doctrine back in 1984 to prevent miscarriages of justice. That doctrine was formulated in part to keep murderers seeking to hide behind technicalities in the law from walking the streets again."

Wendy's gaze swept from left to right. Her day before the United States Supreme Court was about to come to an end, and every justice, appointed over time by five different presidents, was focused solely on her.

"And this case, Your Honors, *is* about murder. Not just a single murder, but *multiple* murders within the armed services. Not just random acts of street violence, but calculated killing by radical Islamic terrorists, disguised as members of the naval service, encouraged by the calculated plotting of the defendants, who spread their distinguished brand of hatred under the offices of the United States Navy Chaplain Corps.

"Captain Reeves did not err in ruling that inevitable discovery applies in this case. Justice screams out that his ruling was correct. These defendants should be executed for their actions, and we urge this honorable court not to block those executions.

"Thank you."

"Thank you, Commander," the chief justice said in a milder voice. "We are in recess."

"All rise," cried the clerk of the Supreme Court.

CHAPTER 9

Council of Ishmael headquarters
Rub al-Khali Desert

Hussein al-Akhma sat alone in his office, a remote control in his hand, his crossed feet propped on his desk. He pressed the record button, then watched the live broadcast from Washington. A very attractive blond American woman in a U.S. Navy dress blue uniform walked down the steps of the United States Supreme Court Building. She wore a white naval officer's cap with a gold eagle and anchors, and as she stepped behind the microphones, the camera caught her sparkling smile and deep blue eyes. They reminded him of the pristine waters of Lake Zurich.

Why are the most beautiful women always on the enemy side?

He pointed the remote control at the television and pressed the volume button. The sound of her velvet-smooth voice came from the broadcast half a world away:

"We are pleased with our briefs and with our argument. Other than that, I'm not going to comment further. The decision is now in the hands of the Supreme Court. Thank you."

A woman of few words. A smile crawled across Hussein's face as the woman in the navy dress blues turned and walked away. When the image shifted to some talking head in the American studio, he rewound the tape to the image of Commander Poole, froze it — and smiled. *Like delectable, poisonous fruit.*

The sound of three knocks came from outside his office door.

"Enter." Hussein turned off the television as a black-bereted member of his elite palace security force stepped in. The olive-skinned guard wore a thick black mustache and the standard Council of Ishmael security force uniform consisting of a sidearm, a drab-green uniform, and combat boots.

"Leader, Mr. Rahman is here," the guard said.

"Send him."

Hussein stood as Abdur Rahman stepped into the office.

"Leader," Abdur said affectionately, then stepped forward and planted kisses on each of Hussein's cheeks.

"The execution party is ready, Leader." Hussein sensed a lack of enthusiasm in Abdur's voice.

"You do not approve of what I am about to do, Abdur?"

"Leader, I approve of all that you do. But I believe Khalid meant no disrespect by his comments in the Council meeting."

"Khalid was a member of the Council of Ishmael!" Hussein slammed his fist on his desk. "To fulfill our vision of reclaiming the world of Allah, we must be of one accord. Even if he meant no disrespect, he allowed his tongue to run recklessly by calling into question the divinely inspired vision Allah has given me. Intentional or not, there must be unity."

Hussein ran his hand through his hair. "Do you not understand this, Abdur? Khalid must die." He snapped his fingers, and one of the black berets appeared with his white blouse and turban.

"Yes, Leader, I understand. But weaker members of the faith may at first have trouble accepting what you plan to destroy for the greater good."

"Precisely." Hussein slipped his arms into the white gown. "Khalid is weak. We cannot have weak brothers on this elite council. It is too dangerous for the common good." He slipped a white turban on his head. "Besides, I have not even yet given the final orders for the execution of Islamic Glory."

"It is as you say, Leader." Abdur bowed as Hussein walked from behind his desk.

"Let us witness the atonement. Only the spilling of blood can satisfy Allah's fury."

Hussein and Abdur left the building and stepped out into the blazing sun. Hussein halted, put a cigarette to his mouth, and snapped for a lighter. A security guard stepped forward.

He took three draws on the cigarette, then stamped it into the sand. Donning a pair of sunglasses, he motioned for Abdur and the guards to step with him out into the desert.

It was just as he had ordered. About thirty yards away stood a small podium. To its left, six members of the white-turbaned security force stood at attention, armed with fully loaded, Russian-manufactured AK-47s. To the right of the podium, a temporary spectator's gallery had been set up, consisting of sixty folding chairs, each occupied by Council of Ishmael members and other high staff officials who would learn an important lesson this day.

The accused, twenty yards in front of the firing squad, was bound to a wooden post with heavy ropes. A black blindfold covered his eyes, a stark contrast to his white robe. Already he dripped sweat, and his chest heaved for oxygen.

Council members rose as Hussein stepped to the podium and spoke into the microphone. His voice, amplified by powerful speakers, boomed across the desert floor.

"What Allah has ordained, let no man put asunder. You may read the charges." He nodded to Abdur, who stepped to the podium and pulled from his pocket the formal indictment. The paper flapped in the wind as Abdur pressed it against the podium.

"Having publicly called into question the leadership of the servant of Allah, Hussein al-Akhma, ordained leader of Allah on earth, Khalid Mohammed el-Shiek, a member of the Council of Ishmael, hath called into question the judgment of Allah himself, and therefore hath committed the crime of blasphemy, for which there is but one punishment satisfactory to Allah." A pause as the hot wind blew across the desert sand. "Death."

Another pause as the white robes and turbans of the witnesses fluttered in the hot desert wind.

"No," the accused wailed. "Please, Leader." He twisted against the thick ropes that bound him to the post. "Mercy, I beg of you, Leader."

Hussein stepped back to the podium. "Do you repent of your sins against me, Khalid Mohammed?"

"I repent, Leader." The man's voice cracked. "*You alone* are Allah's messenger on earth."

"And you will never again publicly question my judgment?"

"Never, Leader." More sobbing. "In the name of Allah. You have my word."

"This man has asked for mercy." Hussein looked to the members of the Council. "What shall I do?"

They stared back at him but did not answer.

"Shall I offer clemency at this late hour?" Still no response. "Will no one answer?"

The wind whipped; the traitor wailed. There was no other sound.

"Remove his blindfold," Hussein ordered.

The execution squad leader stepped forward and pulled off the blindfold. Hussein studied Khalid Mohammed's face. Sweat trailed down his forehead. His bloodshot eyes pleaded for leniency.

"Because you have asked for mercy, I shall grant it."

"Thank you, Leader!" Khalid sobbed. "Praise be to Allah!" Khalid's voice cracked.

"Praise be to Allah, indeed." Hussein motioned for the firing squad captain to approach. "Bring me a knife so that I may personally cut the ropes."

"I shall always serve you, Leader," the man cried.

The squad captain handed Hussein a glistening bayonet that had been affixed to his AK-47. Then Hussein slowly walked the short distance from the podium to the accused.

"Because you have asked for mercy, I shall grant it," Hussein whispered.

"Thank you, my leader." Uncontrollable sobbing from the formerly condemned man, now reprieved. "I shall follow you always."

"Shhh." Hussein brought his left index finger over his lips, as if lulling a baby to sleep. With his right hand, he held the bayonet high over his head, and as the chrome blade reflected the brilliant midday sun, he plunged it into Khalid's esophagus, but not deep enough to kill. Blood spurted as Khalid gasped for air and writhed.

"Die, traitorous swine!" Hussein twisted the knife, then forced it deeper until the tip of the blade jutted through the back of Khalid's neck. The man's head dropped, and blood flowed from his mouth.

The hot wind swept a wave of sand over his feet in the direction of the seated council members. He turned to them. "Will anyone else publicly question me?"

More sand whipped across the desert floor as he studied their terror-filled faces. "Is there no one else who wishes to question Operation Islamic Glory?"

They sat silently, looking straight head, as if afraid to make eye contact.

"Very well. You have seen the penalty for questioning the vision and divine will of Allah. Islamic Glory, the vision directly from Allah, which this dead swine questioned"—he waved his hand back toward the limp, bleeding body of Khalid Mohammed el-Shiek—"shall drive an irreparable wedge between the Great Satan, the United States, and her lackey Zionist puppet, the Israeli occupation force masquerading as a Jewish government in Palestine. America shall lose her influence forever in the Arab world, leading to the birth of the first legitimate Arab superpower, of which you shall form the ruling council, and of which I shall be the leader.

"Yes, it will require giving up something dear to Islam, but in the end, this will mean sweeping growth for Islam throughout the world."

He eyed them once more. Were there any other traitors among them? Had he perhaps made more than one mistake in his selection of these, the chosen ones?

"We are with you, Leader!" one of them shouted.

"We shall never forsake you. You are Allah's chosen one," shouted another.

"Cast your eyes upon the bleeding body of the traitor," Hussein said. "From this day forward, let it be known that the vengeful blood of Allah shall be upon those who oppose him and question his prophet."

He turned and walked to the corpse. Blood still oozed from the throat and mouth. Hussein grabbed the bayonet and pulled the steel blade, dripping with dark red blood, from el-Shiek's throat. Then he walked behind the post and cut the ropes from the traitor's hands and body. El-Shiek dropped to the sand, his body a lifeless heap.

A sense of exhilaration filled Hussein at this power over life and death. A smile crossed his face.

"Death to America!" he shouted.

"And to her Zionist puppet, Israel," his followers responded.

"Come, my brethren, there is work to be done for Allah's kingdom."

He kicked sand in the bleeding face of el-Shiek's body, then motioned Abdur Rahman to follow him back into headquarters. It was time to make a decision on Operation Islamic Glory.

CHAPTER 10

The main dining room inside the Officer's Club at the historic Washington Navy Yard was like most Zack had visited around the world: bright, open windows, simple gold chandeliers hanging from a pristine ceiling, white-clad navy stewards moving about with a uniform dignity.

Live music was always a part of the O-Club scene. And in this case, a gray-haired black man, whose smile reflected unrestrained joy, provided exquisite light jazz on a baby grand Steinway in the far corner of the room.

From time to time, a saxophone player joined in. The first notes of "Misty" flowed with velvet sweetness from the sax just as the host announced that Captain MacDonald's table for his party of six was now ready.

"We're still waiting on two more," MacDonald said. "The judge advocate general, Admiral Stumbaugh, and possibly the secretary of the navy."

That announcement brought a pop-eyed stare from the host. "Captain, I can assure you that my staff will be on the lookout for the admiral and the secretary, and we will promptly escort them to your table upon their arrival."

MacDonald wore the regulation uniform of the day in the D.C. area for late winter–early spring: navy dress blues with gold buttons down the jacket and the four gold stripes of a navy captain on his lower sleeves. He glanced at his watch with obvious irritation.

"Very well," he said, "but please make sure these gentlemen aren't left waiting."

The host motioned for the present members of the MacDonald party, including Zack, Lieutenant Diane Colcernian, Lieutenant Commander Wendy Poole, and Captain MacDonald, to follow him to their table.

After having been honored by President Williams in the Rose Garden, Zack felt burned out by the limelight and longed to return to being an anonymous JAG officer, away from the camera's blinding glare. Besides, he was looking forward to just being alone with Diane.

But they had been invited to the O-Club for dinner by the commanding officer of the JAG Appellate Government Division, who, in Zack's opinion, was undoubtedly hoping that the judge advocate general or maybe even the secretary of the navy might join them.

After all, it was an extraordinary day for the JAG Corps: national television exposure at the White House, then at the Supreme Court. MacDonald could still be tapped for JAG, and it was all about timing, as Zack well knew.

Lieutenant Commander Wendy Poole, who sat just to his left at the elegant round dining room table, was under MacDonald's command. A good commander could rightfully take credit for the success of his subordinates, and MacDonald had done just that because Wendy Poole worked directly for him. And so when MacDonald glanced repeatedly at his watch when salads were being ordered, he was, Zack surmised, still contemplating the whereabouts of the guest of honor, the judge advocate general of the navy.

"Do you have anything light?" Zack asked in response to the steward's question about his salad dressing preference.

"Light ranch, light Italian, and we also have a raspberry vinaigrette, which seems to be a favorite here, sir," the steward said, standing over Zack's shoulder with a pen and pad.

Zack glanced at Lieutenant Commander Poole, who looked quite buoyant from her Supreme Court appearance. "Any suggestions, ma'am?" He caught her eye. "This is your O-Club."

Captain MacDonald's cell phone chirped, and before Wendy could respond, the captain stood, bringing Zack and the two female officers to their feet. He excused himself and stepped away from the table. Zack, Wendy, and Diane resumed their seats.

"First of all, Zack, you can drop the 'ma'am.'" Wendy smiled. "'Wendy' will be fine. At least in private. I'm not all that senior to you." She glanced at Diane. "That goes for you too, Lieutenant Colcernian. Please, in private call me Wendy."

"Thank you," Diane said.

"I understand, sir," Zack overheard Captain MacDonald saying on his cell phone. "Midnight tomorrow."

"Did you decide on a dressing, sir?" the naval steward persisted.

Zack glanced at Lieutenant Commander Poole. "You were about to make a recommendation, ma'—Wendy?"

"I agree with the steward," she said. "You've got to try the vinaigrette."

"Raspberry vinaigrette it is," Zack said.

Captain MacDonald stepped back to the table, and the three stood. "Ladies and gentleman, I've got good news and bad news." MacDonald grinned, motioning them back into their seats. "Which do you prefer first?"

"Bad news first, please, sir," Wendy said as the senior officer.

"Admiral Stumbaugh called. The bad news is that neither the JAG nor the secretary of the navy will be joining us for dinner."

What a shame.

"The good news is"—the captain grinned broadly—"the Supreme Court has ruled." He crossed his arms, smiled, and leaned back in his chair.

"Already?" Wendy Poole gave him a puzzled look.

"Split decision. Five to four," MacDonald announced in a flat voice. "The petition for a stay of the execution has been *denied*."

"Denied?" Wendy sounded incredulous.

"Executions at midnight tomorrow." A proud smirk crossed his face.

As three stewards arrived with trays loaded with salads and beverages, Zack turned away from the table to look out over the Anacosta River. His gaze followed it out to where it met the Potomac. He felt sick. The men he'd prosecuted were going to die. They were traitorous murderers; yet they were still human. And by midnight tomorrow, all hope for their salvation would be gone.

Forever.

"And here's the other good news," MacDonald said. "SECDEF wants you two in Leavenworth tomorrow to witness the executions."

Zack turned back to the table, feeling as though a cinder block had dropped onto his stomach. He and Diane stared at each other for a moment. Without turning away, he said, "Sir, will Lieutenant Colcernian be accompanying us?"

"That's a negative," MacDonald said. "Security reasons, I think. Sorry, Diane."

She seemed reluctant to tear her gaze away from Zack's, but finally she looked at MacDonald. "That's okay, sir. This is one I'll gladly pass up."

"Anyway," MacDonald continued, "I'll be accompanying you two. We catch a C-9 out of Andrews at 2200 hours tonight."

Tonight?

"Diane," MacDonald continued, "the Admiral says to remind you that you've still got another week of leave before you're to report back to San Diego. We've had you under pretty tight security here in Washington. We'd like to think that the incident with the sniper is past, but those guys are still out there on the loose.

"The admiral isn't ordering you to accept marine protection, but he thinks it would be a good idea. And for the record, so do I."

Diane sipped her water, then met Zack's eyes again. By now, he could read her expressions. And the brief glance she just shot him with those enticing green eyes was one that he had seen many times on her pretty face: a feisty look of subtle defiance. She could be so hardheaded. Which, ironically, was one of the many attributes he found attractive about her.

"I'll be fine, Captain. They wouldn't have found us last week if some numbskull hadn't shown us on national television. No more Carolina games for me." She raised a brow at Zack. "Besides, I need to relax for a few days. If the admiral's technically not ordering that I accept marine protection ..."

"Diane," Zack snapped. "Don't be foolish." He shot her a stern glare, as if that would do any good. "You can't travel back to San Diego in anonymity. Your face is too well known around the country." He took her hand. "I *insist* that you accept marine protection."

"Insist?" she said with a laugh. Then she touched his arm, serious again. "Really, Zack. Don't worry about me." An all-confident smile lit her face. "I'll be fine."

"Well, then." Captain MacDonald checked his watch. "We'd better be going. Anyway"—he handed Diane a business card—"we have to get rolling. I'll arrange for our command master chief, Master Chief Gimler, to pick you up in just a few minutes. He'll take you anywhere in the city you'd like. The master chief will be instructed to stay with you while you're in Washington and provide support for you here. You need to rent a car, he'll take care of it. Or if you want a ride to the airport, or the mall, or whatever you need, Master Chief Gimler will be your shadow in the nation's capital." He glanced at the card in her hand. "You've got my number and also the number of the JAG's aide, Lieutenant Commander Foster. Call either of us if you change your mind about an escort back to the West Coast."

"Aye, aye, sir."

Captain MacDonald inclined his head toward Zack and Wendy. "Commander, Lieutenant, we need to get going. There are a couple of things I need to brief you on." He glanced at Diane. "Take care of yourself, Lieutenant."

The idea of leaving Diane here, by herself, made Zack sick. After all this time . . . after fighting like mortal enemies, then coming together to prosecute the most publicized court-martial in history, after all that had happened between them in the aftermath. He turned down a congressional seat in part because of her. They'd traveled the country together, escaped an assassination attempt, been honored by the president of the United States. Together.

And now to be separated suddenly? By the chirp of the captain's cellular phone? This wasn't how it was supposed to end. Was it? But as Captain MacDonald said, duty called. Duty always called. And Zack was first and foremost a naval officer.

"Lieutenant Brewer. Are you coming?" MacDonald and Wendy had already taken a few steps away from the table.

"Captain?"

MacDonald turned. "Yes, Zack?"

"With the captain's permission, may I have a word with Lieutenant Colcernian for just a few minutes?"

"Sure, Lieutenant." He glanced at his watch again. "Five minutes, okay?"

"Thank you, sir."

"Meet us outside." Captain MacDonald turned and escorted Wendy through the door.

"So. This is it?" She managed a smile. He opened his arms, and she stepped into his embrace. "You know, the navy has rules against public display of affection."

"Who cares?" He hugged her tightly. "Wait here."

"Where are you going?"

"I'll be right back." He stepped to the piano, pulled a ten-dollar bill from his wallet, and then whispered into the ear of the saxophonist. Two long-stemmed roses were in a vase on the baby grand. Zack took one and walked back over to Diane. "For you."

"Zack." She smelled the rose and grinned up at him, her green eyes bright.

"You know, once in a while we get a special request." The saxophonist's deep voice boomed over his microphone. "To lay down the saxophone and to sing." He flashed a broad, gleaming smile in their direction. "And I am pleased to report I have just received such a request." A dramatic pause. "From Lieutenant Brewer to Lieutenant Colcernian."

A stunned gaze crossed her face.

"And Lieutenant Colcernian, Lieutenant Brewer asks you for the honor of this dance."

His voice, like the sound of his saxophone, was smooth velvet. He was Satchmo, back from the grave, bellowing golden tones from the great love song from *West Side Story*.

"There's a place for us.

"Somewhere a place for us."

Zack took Diane's hand and led her to the parquet dance floor.

She fell into his arms. They danced, slowly. A few others joined them on the floor.

"There's a time for us. Someday a time for us. Time together with time to spare. Time to look. Time to spare. Someday ... Somewhere ..."

The applause from the onlookers told him that the song was over. It was time to go. He couldn't speak; there were no words to express all he felt for this woman, this feisty, stubborn, beautiful, compassionate woman.

He kissed her on the lips, prayed silently for her safety, then turned and headed toward the exit.

CHAPTER 11

Council of Ishmael headquarters
Rub al-Khali Desert

The interruption of regular programming, feeding live images of the United States Supreme Court Building into the television sets in the intelligence room of the Council of Ishmael headquarters, sent Abdur Rahman scrambling out the door. He turned left down the dark hallway, then right, then headed straight to the office of the titular leader of the Council.

"I must see the leader. Now!" he barked in Arabic at the two black-bereted guards posted on either side of the door. "Tell him it's urgent!"

Abdur Rahman was the one member of the powerful Council of Twenty with enough clout to get Hussein al-Akhma's personal body-guards to interrupt the most powerful man in the Arab world outside the Saudi royal family. Two seconds later, the guard reappeared and motioned Abdur into Hussein's inner sanctum.

"What is this emergency, Abdur?" Hussein al-Akhma, in his favorite white robe, stood as Abdur entered.

"Leader," Abdur responded, panting, "American television is about to announce their Supreme Court's ruling on the death penalty for our operatives."

Hussein reached for the black remote control on his desk and pointed it at the television in the corner of his room, preset to CNN.

"Sit." Hussein motioned Abdur to sit down as an image of a disturbed-looking black man appeared on the screen. Holding a microphone, he stood in front of a marble building, fidgeting with an earpiece in his right ear. It was the famous American reporter Bernie Woodson.

"I understand that we have breaking news from the White House on a presidential order concerning the executions," he said. "And we're going to take you now to the White House, where CNN's Tom Miller has more information on that order."

Woodson's image faded, and in its place appeared the familiar visage of a middle-aged white man, wearing a dark blue business suit and wire-rim glasses. He held a microphone identical to Bernie Woodson's with the CNN logo. Electronically superimposed across the bottom of the screen, in both English and Arabic, were the words *Tom Miller, CNN White House Correspondent*.

"That's right, Bernie," Miller said, holding his microphone in his left hand and touching his earpiece with his right, "CNN has in fact just learned that the White House, reacting to the late-breaking news from the Supreme Court lifting the stay for the executions of the three chaplains, has released a presidential directive concerning the specifics of the executions. And I've just been handed a copy of that directive, released by the White House press office, which reads as follows."

Miller held a document in front of him and began to read as the same text scrolled on the screen:

I, Malcolm P. Williams III, pursuant to the authority vested in me by the Constitution of the United States as Commander in Chief of the armed forces of the United States, and also pursuant to my authority under the Uniform Code of Military Justice and various other directives and regulations pertaining to the United States military, do hereby issue this directive to the Secretaries of the Army and Navy, through the Secretary of Defense.

Whereas a general court-martial of the United States Navy, having convened and considered certain charges and evidence brought against officers of the United States Navy, namely Commander Abdul-Sehen, Commander Mohammed Olajuwon, and Lieutenant Commander Mohammed Reska, all members of the Navy Chaplain Corps; and whereas said general court-martial, after having considered the evidence against these officers, returned with a verdict of guilty on all charges and specifications and sentenced said officers to death by execution; and whereas military procedures and regulations require that all death penalty sentences may be carried out only with the approval of and by order of the president: Now, therefore, I order that the Secretaries of the Army and the Navy, and all military personnel under their jurisdiction, shall carry out the following instruction with regard to the final fate of these defendants.

The defendants shall be moved immediately by military transport from the United States Navy Brig in Norfolk, Virginia, to the United States Disciplinary Barracks at Fort Leavenworth, Kansas, an institution under the jurisdiction of the United States Army.

A United States Navy execution team shall accompany the condemned defendants to the USDB, and the Navy execution team shall carry out execution of these defendants at midnight tomorrow, in accordance with procedural instructions handed down by the Secretary of the Navy.

United States Army personnel are directed to provide full logistical support to their Navy counterparts, including use of USDB facilities and any and all other support as may be necessary to carry out this sentence.

Upon completion of the executions, the bodies of the defendants shall remain in United States Navy control for proper disposition.

It is so ordered.

Malcolm P. Williams III
President of the United States

Miller finished reading the statement, paused, then looked up into the camera.

"So there you have it, the first presidential order authorizing execution of naval personnel in over 150 years. And in case you're wondering why the defendants are being transferred to Fort Leavenworth, an army installation, the White House press office issued a statement explaining that technically, both navy and army regulations suggest that executions of all military personnel are to be carried out by the army. In this case, the president, himself a former Navy JAG officer, moved the site to Fort Leavenworth as a symbolic gesture that the armed forces are united in combating terrorist infiltration."

Abdur expected a legendary outburst of temper from Hussein al-Akhma at such bad news. Slinging papers from his desk to the floor, shattering the first pane of glass in sight. Even worse, brandishing his pistol and killing in a fit of rage. He'd done it before.

Instead, the leader of the Council of Ishmael, like an angel from Allah, stood behind his desk in white linens, his arm outstretched, pointing toward the television set, holding the remote control in his hand. His eyes were transfixed on the now-blank screen, and his face had an eerie, blank expression.

"Praise be to Allah," he said. "And blessed be the prophet Mohammed—peace be upon him."

Hussein turned his eyes toward Abdur. These were eyes that Abdur Rhaman had never seen before on the face of Hussein al-Akhma. Instead of black and piercing, they were dark and soft. Almost glowing. Hussein seemed possessed by something strangely serene.

"The time draweth nigh, Abdur," Hussein said softly, almost in a whisper.

"Of what do you speak, Leader?"

"Don't you see, my brother? This moment is a gift from Allah. This is the beginning of the end for his adversaries." Hussein's eyes seemed to gaze into space, at something unseen, just over the top of Abdur's head.

"It is as you say, Leader," Abdur blurted, uncertain of what to say to the human apparition standing before him.

"Only a moment longer." Hussein smiled, his eyes now sparkling. "In the holy name of Allah the merciful"—he extended his arms to his sides, raised his palms to the ceiling as if in worship—"hasten your coming glory."

CHAPTER 12

Execution chamber
United States Disciplinary Barracks
U.S. Army Base
Fort Leavenworth, Kansas

2330 hours

Zack waited in the corridor just outside the execution chamber with a handful of other navy dignitaries, including Captain Will MacDonald, Lieutenant Commander Wendy Poole, the judge advocate general of the navy, and the chief of naval operations. A handful of reporters also stood outside, silent.

An army protocol officer, an African-American major wearing U.S. Army green, his boots clicking and echoing as he marched down the shiny passageway, approached the group with a clipboard.

He stopped in front of the chief of naval operations, clicked his heels, and shot a smart salute. The CNO nodded, said, "Major," but did not salute back, reflecting the long-standing tradition of those in the army saluting indoors while those in the navy do not.

The protocol officer, in a stern voice and with a grim face, said, "We'll file you in according to rank, first the CNO, followed by the judge advocate general." The major studied the sheet provided to him by navy public affairs. "As the junior-most officer present, Lieutenant Brewer will enter last. Then we will escort members of the press in, who will be seated in the back rows." He looked at the CNO. "Admiral, is there any other way that I may be of service to you and your party?"

"No, Major," the navy's highest-ranking admiral said. "You may proceed."

"Very well, sir." The major again smartly saluted, then opened the large wooden door to the viewing gallery of the execution chamber.

Zack waited for the admiral, the JAG, and other senior officers to file in, then followed Wendy into the white antiseptic-smelling viewing gallery. One wall was made of glass paneling. Behind it were three empty gurneys with bags presumably containing lethal agents. The senior officers sat in wooden folding chairs in the front row; Zack and Wendy sat in the last two chairs of the second row.

Zack glanced at the round clock on the wall: *2330 hours. Thirty minutes to midnight.*

Eerie silence permeated the room. Not a sound from the dozen or so press members occupying the two rows behind him. Only the sound of pencils furiously sketching the scene, from the two media artists behind them. No cameras had been allowed.

Zack didn't want to be here. He'd never seen anyone die and had never fathomed watching someone he'd prosecuted die. His heart ached. He missed Diane more than he could have imagined, though he was glad she had been spared this sickening scene.

The army protocol officer interrupted his thoughts. "Excuse me, Lieutenant Brewer?"

"Yes, sir?" Zack stood.

"Could I see you for a moment?" The major waved Zack into the hallway outside the viewing chamber, then closed the door. He briefly wondered if somehow, miraculously, he might be excused from having to witness the event.

"This is a bit unusual, Lieutenant," the major said, looking hard into Zack's eyes, "but there's been a rather strange request I've been asked to pass along."

"Yes, sir?"

"One of the chaplains has asked to see you."

Dear God. If a chaplain is asking to see me at a time like this, something is terribly wrong. They've gotten Diane.

"Major, is everything all right?" Zack's heart pounded like a jackhammer.

The major gave Zack a puzzled look. "Lieutenant, do you understand what I just said?"

"Sorry, sir. It's been my experience that when a chaplain comes calling out of the blue, it's to bring bad news. I was worried about a family member or possibly Lieutenant Colcernian."

"Lieutenant," the major persisted, "you *don't* understand. I'm not talking about a Christian chaplain like you or I might see in a time of personal crisis. I'm talking about one of the *Muslim* chaplains you prosecuted."

Zack stood for a moment, his mouth agape, his body temporarily paralyzed. "Wants to see me?"

"Time's running out, Lieutenant. These executions take place by order of the president at midnight whether you see him or not. It's your decision."

"Which one?"

"Lieutenant Commander Reska."

Zack's heart dropped through his stomach as his palms beaded into a cold sweat. He hadn't wanted to come, let alone talk to one of these guys.

"That sort of thing's allowable?"

"The navy's running this execution, but your guys have pretty much been relying on our guys all night. We told them we would try to grant a condemned man's last wishes. Anyway, you've got about twenty minutes if you want to do it. Personally"—the major's eyes bored into Zack—"I'm not sure that I would. These guys are traitors to this country. But it's up to you." He glanced at his watch. "Either way, I need a decision, Lieutenant."

"Where are they?"

"They're in three separate holding rooms. They've eaten their last meals, and now they're strapped on gurneys. Navy corpsmen will wheel them into the execution chamber, simultaneously, about five minutes till midnight."

Zack's stomach knotted. He checked his watch: 11:35. "Okay, Major, I'll do it," he said, then wondered why he'd agreed, or for that matter, why he was even here.

"Follow me, please." The major motioned to Zack. He walked down the hallway, stopping at a door flanked by two armed marines in combat fatigues. "He's in here, Lieutenant. You can go in, if you'd like."

Why are you putting yourself through this, Zack? You don't have to do this.

"I don't mean to rush you, Lieutenant, but we're on a tight time schedule."

Because you'd wonder the rest of your life, that's why.

Zack grasped the cold, round steel doorknob. He gripped it, nodded at the major, then turned it a quarter of a rotation clockwise. He heard a corresponding clicking sound, then pushed open the door.

The room, its walls, floor, and ceiling, was all white, lit by five oblong fluorescent bulbs hanging from the ceiling. Two navy corpsmen, standing guard at opposite corners of the room in their enlisted "crackerjack" blue uniforms, shifted from parade rest to attention as Zack stepped in.

The accused was strapped on a gurney in the middle of the room, robed in white, his feet facing opposite the door. A heart monitor, registering each beat with a beep, hung on a stainless steel stand beside the gurney.

Zack motioned the corpsmen to return to parade rest. They complied, and as he stepped around Reska, he met the condemned man's piercing black eyes.

"At last, my chance to speak face-to-face with the great Lieutenant Brewer."

"There's nothing great about me, sir."

"You prosecute me, convict me, have me sentenced to death, yet you still call me 'sir.'"

Zack studied Reska's face. "At this moment, you remain my superior officer. I respect your rank, your office. That does not change, even though I have no respect for the crime you committed."

A slight smile crossed Reska's face. "You amaze me, Lieutenant. My backers spend millions to hire the greatest lawyer in the world. But look at us now. Levinson is nowhere to be found. Yet you are here with me. And I am about to die."

Zack let his words resonate for a moment. "Was there something you wanted to talk about, Commander?"

"I wish we had more time to talk, but my time is short."

"Yes, sir."

"But you were right."

"Sir?"

"In your closing argument you said that I shot Petty Officer Aziz and dumped his body in the Atlantic. That's exactly what I did. I invited him on a fishing trip, then took him out in the cruiser supplied by the organization. I helped him bait his hook, and when he cast his line over the side of the boat, I blew his brains out. He never knew what hit him."

Zack cringed. "Yes, sir. I was confident that I was right about that."

"He trusted me, Lieutenant. I was his chaplain. But those who funded me, and the other two who will die with me tonight"—Reska hesitated—"they worried that Aziz would talk." Reska's eyes rolled off into space. "You see, Aziz did plant that bomb in the F-18, just like you said. So they pressured me to take care of the problem."

Zack thought he saw a film of water in the chaplain's eyes. "Why are you telling me all this now?"

Reska looked at Zack. "Because I never felt good about killing Petty Officer Aziz. Something seemed wrong about it. But they claimed it was Allah's will. I accepted that and carried out my orders."

"And you no longer feel this crime was the will of your Allah?"

"You're the lawyer, Lieutenant. You tell me. If this were the will of Allah, then would I be here now, strapped on this gurney, about to die?"

"Your question presupposes that 'Allah's will,' as you call it, really matters. I don't believe Allah's will matters. I believe Allah is a powerless relic."

Reska squinted. "You do not believe in God?" He sounded disappointed.

"I didn't say that. I said I believe Allah is a powerless relic. My study of history tells me that Allah was an Arabic moon god, one of many gods, whom Mohammed allegedly had a vision of. That's why the symbol of Islam is a crescent moon. With respect, sir, I believe the god of Islam is nothing but a polytheistic entity that became an evil figment of Mohammed's imagination and is powerless to affect the final outcome of world affairs."

"And do you believe there is a god powerful enough to, as you say, 'affect the final outcome of world affairs'?"

Zack looked into the man's face. In the final minutes of his life, he was searching for something.

Why me? Why is this grave responsibility on my shoulders?

"Yes, Commander, I do believe there is such a God."

"My time is short, Lieutenant. Who is that God?"

"He is the one true God. The living God of Abraham, Isaac, and Jacob."

"Hmm." Reska smiled. "And what would this God say to me, a man about to die, a man who has murdered and sinned against him?"

Help me, Lord. Give me the right words.

"He would say repent of your sin. That the hour of salvation is now, Commander. That his Son spilled his precious blood for you, and that if you will confess the Lord Jesus with your mouth, and believe in your heart that God raised him from the dead, you will be saved."

A peaceful smile crossed Reska's face. "You will be in the gallery when they take my life?"

"I'll be there."

"My eyes will be on you, Lieutenant, and I will consider the words of your God in the moments I have left."

"Good-bye, Commander," Zack said, touching the man's hand and looking into his eyes. "I'll pray for your soul."

"Good-bye, Lieutenant," Reska said, still smiling peacefully. "Thank you."

Zack stepped into the hallway and checked his watch. Ten minutes until midnight. The major led him back to the viewing gallery, where all eyes followed him as he took his seat beside Wendy.

She whispered, "Is everything okay?"

"I think so." He still wasn't sure what had just transpired.

Through the dividing wall of glass, Zack saw the doors open in the back of the execution chamber. The same navy corpsmen pushed the gurney carrying Lieutenant Commander Reska into the execution chamber. Two more corpsmen followed, rolling in Commander Mohammed Olajuwon, the senior Muslim chaplain in the navy, at least for the next few minutes. Another pair of corpsmen appeared with the third condemned chaplain, Lieutenant Commander Charles Abdul-Sehen, and all three gurneys were then raised to an upright position, facing the gallery. Microphones were positioned beside each gurney.

Zack noted the clock on the wall behind them. *Eight minutes to midnight.*

A navy captain, wearing the breastplate of a Navy SEAL, walked into the execution chamber, followed by three medical officers who would pronounce the chaplains' deaths.

The captain nodded, and the corpsmen swabbed both arms of the accused with rubbing alcohol. IVs were inserted into both arms of each prisoner. One contained a harmless saline solution. The other carried the lethal dosage of potassium chloride. In this way, neither corpsman could be sure he actually administered the killing agent.

When all six IVs had been inserted, the navy captain stepped forward, his back to the audience, his face to the condemned men, and spoke into a microphone, his voice reverberating into the gallery.

"Commander Mohammed Olajuwon, Chaplain Corps, United States Navy; Lieutenant Commander Charles Abdul-Sehen, Chaplain Corps, United States Navy; and Lieutenant Commander Mohammed Reska, Chaplain Corps, United States Navy, having been convicted by a general court-martial for the offenses of murder, conspiracy to commit murder, and treason, and having been condemned to die for these offenses, and such execution order having been signed by the president of the United States, effective midnight tonight, you will now each be given a maximum of one minute to make a final statement, should you so choose.

"In keeping with tradition, and in accordance with the regulations of the naval service, the senior officer, Commander Olajuwon, shall have the opportunity to speak first.

"Commander Olajuwon, do you wish to make a statement?"

From the center gurney, Olajuwon leaned over toward the microphone positioned beside him. "I do, sir," he snapped in a defiant voice.

"Very well," the captain replied. "What say you, sir?"

Olajuwon's eyes shifted back and forth like a windshield wiper in slow motion. "I say, glory to Allah, and to the prophet Mohammed—peace be upon him. I say . . . death to America!" His black eyes shot blazing sparks of rage as he held his neck back, his face to the ceiling, and in an almost worshipful moan, said, "Glory forever to Islam. May Allah forever bring jihad against all who oppose the Great Faith. Death to Christian and Jewish infidels!" His eyes closed, and he fell silent.

"Lieutenant Commander Abdul-Sehen. Is there anything you wish to say?"

"Death to America! Death to her Zionist puppet, Israel!" Abdul-Sehen looked up at Zack and Wendy, then appeared to be looking at the other officers, dignitaries, and press representatives. "Death to the United States Navy!" Following Olajuwon's lead, Abdul-Sehen then dropped his head back and closed his eyes.

"Lieutenant Commander Reska. Would you care to make a final statement?"

Reska opened his eyes. "Yes, Captain."

"Very well. You may speak."

Reska looked straight out into the center of the galley. "To the families of Petty Officer Aziz and Commander Latcher, I say, I am truly sorry. And to Lieutenant Brewer . . ." He paused, his eyes searching the gallery for Zack; when their eyes locked, he said simply, "Thank you." A pause. "That is all."

Zack lifted his gaze to the clock on the wall behind the condemned men. The minute and hour hands were already aligned on twelve, waiting for the second hand to catch up. *Fifteen seconds. Ten seconds. Five Seconds.*

"Administer toxicants," the captain said, prompting all six corpsmen to turn small plastic screws on the bags hanging on each side of each chaplain. Liquid flowed through the plastic tubes into the men's arms. Olajuwon and Abdul-Sehen flinched as the high dosages hit their veins. Reska simply closed his eyes and smiled.

It was as if all three simply fell asleep. Ten minutes later, the medical officers declared them dead. Zack closed his eyes, grateful that Diane hadn't been subjected to this.

For Zack Brewer, the case of *United States v. Mohammed Olajuwon et al.*, at long last, was over.

Council of Ishmael headquarters
Rub al-Khali Desert

It is over. They are gone," Abdur Rhaman said to Hussein al-Akhma. "In the name of Allah the merciful, order execution of Islamic Glory."

"It is as you say, Leader."

CHAPTER 13

Point Cires, Morocco
Southern shore of the Strait of Gibraltar

1700 hours

The sun had inched slowly to the west all afternoon, ducking in and out of an intermittent cloud cover. Its frequent disappearances brought an unwelcome chill from the strong sea breeze. And each time the glowing orb reemerged from its annoying game of hide-and-seek, it reappeared with less warmth.

The dark blue waters of the eastern horizon flirted with the ebbing sunlight, turning it into a kaleidoscope of reds and purples. Waily Rahmin turned away from the direction of his occupied homeland to face the narrow eight-mile strait in front of him.

His heart jumped as the slanting sun clipped the top masts of the gray warship entering the strait. He pointed the high-powered telescope at the sleek man-of-war, then brought his right eye in contact with the lens.

The view revealed a stream of churning water in the ship's wake. A slight adjustment overshot the strait altogether, the early evening lights from Point Marroquí on the Spanish side, eight miles away, now in view.

Waily blurted a curse word in Arabic and then lowered the telescope slightly. This time the image of the sharp, sleek bow with the hull number 50 painted on the side, ploughed through the water from the left of the oval view. Next, the blocklike superstructure came into view, rising above the waterline, followed by a steel cross mast. And then a second, higher steel cross mast. Flying just behind the second steel cross, the red, white, and blue rag known as the Stars and Stripes.

"*American warship! American warship!*" Waily Rahmin shouted in high-pitched Arabic.

That proclamation brought two other members of the watch team rushing to his side.

"Where?" Tariq Tamman demanded.

"There." Waily pointed out at the Strait of Gibraltar.

"Valley Forge class cruiser," Tariq observed.

"Here comes another!" Waily swung his telescope to the left as an identical warship came into view.

"You are witnessing the lead ships of the battle group," Tariq said. "I have seen this many times before. The Great Satan headed to our homeland to terrorize our people with its ships and planes and missiles." The watch leader paused, the wind whipping through his black hair, as a third ship trailed in the wake of the other two. "The carrier should appear over the western horizon within the next hour or so."

Tariq, the eldest of the team, brought his binoculars to his eyes and scanned to the left, toward the Atlantic. "Very good work, Waily."

"Thank you."

"How old are you?"

"Twenty-two," Waily said.

Tariq put his hand on Waily's shoulder. "Keep watch for the carrier. When it appears, you shall have the honor of announcing its sighting to the Council, my son."

Waily pondered the idea of Hussein al-Akhma learning his name. The name of a loyal sentry on watch, waiting on the front lines in the battle against the great enemy of Islam. At the thought, chills shot down his spine.

The wind grew stronger and colder as the large orange ball kissed the western waters of the Atlantic. But the adrenaline that pumped from Waily Rahmin's chest warmed his body. Just last year, he volunteered to die for Allah by strapping dynamite to his chest for a mission in a bus on a crowded street in the West Bank. How disappointed he felt when another martyr was chosen instead.

Now, for the first time, he understood why Allah had deprived him of that opportunity for glorious martyrdom. He was born for this very moment! This he now knew with all his heart. What a blessed man he was.

"*Aircraft carrier!*" Someone shouted in Arabic. Waily turned and saw the third watch-team member, Misbah Mudar, pointing excitedly to the left.

"I see it!" Tariq said.

Misbah's excited shout jolted like lightning through Waily's body. He snapped his right hand against his forehead, almost like the British saluted when they occupied Palestine, then squinted in the direction Misbah pointed, at the orange reflection of the dying sun on the water ... at the distinctive, dark gray silhouette of a flattop pushing through the water, its superstructure growing larger by the moment.

Waily swung the telescope around to the left. His hands were shaking as he tried to bring the ship into focus.

"Can you make out the number?" Tariq scanned the horizon with his binoculars.

A deafening roar distracted Waily before he could answer. He moved his gaze to the strait. Two U.S. Navy jet fighters, both with twin turbofan engines shooting fire, streaked like missiles toward the Mediterranean. His eyes followed the jets until they disappeared an instant later.

Waily looked back toward the carrier, this time finding it clearly in his telescope. He fidgeted with the focus mechanism once more, bringing into clear view the large white number painted on the superstructure: 75.

"Seventy-five, sir," Waily said. "I can see it now."

"Ah, the *Harry S. Truman*, just as expected," Tariq said. "Are you prepared to make the call, Waily?"

"It would be a great honor, sir," Waily said.

A moment later, Tariq handed Waily a cell phone. "Minorca is on the line."

Waily took the phone and, just as he had rehearsed a hundred times in his mind, spoke into it in Arabic. "Minorca, Morocco. The whale is in the bottle. Seventy-five. Repeat, the whale is in the bottle."

Static nearly obscured the voice on the other end. Finally, Waily heard, "Acknowledge, Morocco. The whale is in the bottle. Seventy-five."

"The whale is in the bottle," Waily repeated, then hung up as the chopping sounds of two U.S. Navy helicopters, each with blinking running lights and a trailing stream of smoke, grew louder and closed in.

"Break down the telescopes," Tariq ordered. "We must get out of here."

CHAPTER 14

Port Mahon, Minorca
Balearic Islands
Western Mediterranean

2100 hours

The obnoxious ring made the gray of her eyes fade to nothingness. Carlos blinked once, twice, then realized his summer holiday on the French Riviera had ended last week. The telephone had ruined his dream.

Another hideous ring. He cursed under his breath as his eyes slowly adjusted to the dark: the faint image of the modest bureau at the foot of his bed, the four bedposts pointing toward the rotating ceiling fan.

Perhaps it is her, he thought when the buzzing did not stop. The thought energized him to roll onto his side, reach over to the small wooden table beside his bed, and fumble for the telephone.

Thinking of the woman, he used an inviting tone. *"Sí?"*

"The whale is in the bottle," a male voice said in Spanish. "Repeat, the whale is in the bottle."

"The minnow is in the pond," Carlos grunted, his mood deflated.

"The whale is in the bottle. Repeat, the whale is in the bottle."

"I will be down in five minutes," Carlos said in Spanish. He slammed down the phone, flipped on a lamp, stepped into a pair of tight-fitting blue jeans, and pulled a black turtleneck sweater over his head.

Carlos was not sure what was meant by the phrase, "The whale is in the bottle." His contacts never told him. The only thing he knew for sure was this: Within a matter of five to ten minutes, he would be collecting a briefcase full of sixty-five thousand United States dollars, small bill denominations. His only requirement for earning the money was cranking his forty-foot cruiser, *Bella Maria*, and giving two passengers a ride in it, full power, south-southeast to a designated point in the middle of the Mediterranean.

They were the same passengers every time. Arab chaps by the names of Falik and Ghazi. They had called on his services six times now in the last two years, and for sixty-five grand per trip, no questions needed to be asked.

By now, Carlos knew their routine. Eight hours into the trip, when the cruiser reached 38 degrees north latitude, 3 degrees east longitude—almost dead center in the Mediterranean—he would cut the engine, setting the vessel adrift. Then one man would wail something Arabic-sounding into a handheld radio.

At first, the practice was puzzling. But by the third trip, he began to suspect that the phrase, "The whale is in the bottle," was being used whenever an American aircraft carrier passed through the Strait of Gibraltar from the Atlantic, headed for the Eastern Mediterranean.

He had no proof. But it was hard to keep the passage of a United States battle group a secret. The Strait of Gibraltar, a narrow bottleneck six hundred statute miles southeast of Mahon, was so narrow a nuclear aircraft carrier could hardly hide from public view. And when, the following day, the European press announced the entry of an American flattop into the Med, Carlos began making his own deductions.

Even still, Carlos Ortega saw no harm in what he was doing. His small craft posed no threat to any vessel owned by the U.S. Navy. Ghazi and Falik weren't armed. Even if they were, they couldn't harm one of the mightiest warships ever constructed.

Carlos stepped onto the pier and saw the whites of the two Arabs' eyes. One of them, Falik, smiled, shook Carlos's hand, and handed him a briefcase. The other man carried a gym bag, which he did not give up.

"For you, my brother," Falik said in Spanish dosed with a heavy Arab accent. "It is all there, but you can count it if you like."

Carlos laid the briefcase on the dock. He looked around, and when he saw no one in the vicinity, he popped open the latches and shined his flashlight on the stacks of twenty-dollar bills. The briefcase bulged with cash, as always. And these men had never cheated him before.

"That will not be necessary, my friends," he said. "Step inside. I know you are anxious to get under way."

Four hours later, Carlos cut the boat's engines, setting it adrift on the rolling seas under the bright, starlit canopy. He checked the GPS. *38°03'02"N; 3°01'08"E*. Almost dead on mark.

The two Arabs lit up cigarettes, as they typically did, and lumbered out of the cabin and into the aft section of the boat. Following the glow from their cigarettes and against the dim radiance from the quarter moon and the Milky Way, Carlos saw them fidgeting in the gym bag.

Carlos reached into the inboard ice chest, grabbed an ice-cold beer, and took a swig as he watched the mysterious duo. They pulled the usual walkie-talkie devices from the bags, and Carlos knew what would follow: Arabic wailing, then the return trip to shore.

Falik put the walkie-talkie to his mouth. "Oscar India Golf," he said in English.

Carlos raised his eyebrow as the wind picked up, blowing in from the stern, the Spanish pennant flapping in response. He took another swig. This was the first time he had heard either man speak English.

"Repeat, Oscar India Golf."

Strange. They speak to me in Spanish. They talk to each other in Arabic. And now this.

"Oscar India Golf. Repeat, Oscar India Golf."

He lifted his beer. *For sixty-five thousand dineros, they can speak whatever language they want.*

Radio Communications Center
USS Harry S. Truman
Western Mediterranean

Radioman First Class Bob Whitlow, in dark blue dungarees and a light blue short-sleeved enlisted uniform shirt, sat at his station in front of his keyboard, surrounded by various high-tech electronic gadgets.

Something wasn't quite right. He made a note on his legal pad, then whipped off his earphones.

"Lieutenant," he said, still sitting at his duty station. He motioned to the watch officer. "Something is strange about this."

Lieutenant Doug Vandergrift strode toward him, wearing faded officer's wash khakis and a blue "USS *Harry S. Truman*" ball cap. "Watcha got, Petty Officer?"

"We've copied this message on frequency 487 MH. It's been repeated four times over the last hour, sir." Whitlow handed Vandergrift the written transcript of the strange message.

"Hmm." Vandergrift took a swig from a white coffee mug with the ship's popular, unofficial motto, "Give 'Em Hell, Harry," imprinted on the side. "Play that back."

"Aye, sir." Whitlow punched the rewind button, then the play button.

A voice on the tape said, "Oscar India Golf. Repeat, Oscar India Golf."

"Any planes doing radio checks this morning?"

"That many times?" Whitlow met Vandergrift's eyes. "At established intervals?"

The lieutenant took another swig of coffee, still looking puzzled. "Message all squadron leaders. From radio room. Please report any radio checks this AM using the sephamore call sign 'Oscar India Golf.'"

"Aye, sir."

"Meanwhile, I'm calling in intel on this one."

"Probably a good idea, sir."

CHAPTER 15

Officer's Country
(Officer's berthing area)
USS Harry S. Truman
Western Mediterranean

Are you sure?" Lieutenant Commander Mohammed "Mo" Quasay said, looking at the younger officer, a fellow naval aviator, who had just burst excitedly into his stateroom.

"I heard it myself," Lieutenant Hosni Alhad said. "I was monitoring portable radio earlier this morning. Not only that, but look at this." He handed Quasay the message from the radio room.

From: Radio Room, USS Harry S. Truman (CVN 75)
Via: Commanding Officer, USS *Harry S. Truman* (CVN 75)
        Air Wing Commander, USS *Harry S. Truman* (CVN 75)
To: All squadrons
Re: Interception of Radio Msg.

1.   Please report any use of sephamore call sign "Oscar India Golf" by any U.S. Navy aircraft stationed aboard USS Harry S. Truman.
2.   Radio room reports interception of such message from unidentified sources at regular intervals this morning.

          Very respectfully,
          D. G. Vandergrift, LT, USN
          Watch Officer

FIRST ENDORSEMENT

From: Air Wing Commander, USS *Harry S. Truman* (CVN 75)

Via: Commanding Officer, USS *Harry S. Truman* (CVN 75)

To: All squadrons

Re: Radio Room Msg. to All Squadrons, Interception of Radio Msg.

1.   All squadrons are instructed to comply with subject message, to provide written response to radio room, within one hour.

> Respectfully,
> J. E. Wesson, CAPT, USN
> Commanding

Quasay dropped the paper to the floor. "Then it is true." His eyes met Alhad's. "After all this time. After all this planning." He felt, then saw, goose bumps on his arms. The message had been reviewed and *endorsed* by the commanding officer of the *Harry S. Truman*, officially ordering all squadrons on the ship to be on the lookout for the call sign only he and Alhad knew was from the Council of Ishmael. Oh, to be alive, to have been called to this very moment in history! Allah had called him for this. He took a deep breath, hoping to prevent Alhad from seeing his tears.

"Our duty is clear," he snapped at Alhad, his voice stern in an attempt to jolt his emotions back into check. "We are but a few days away now. We will say nothing more of this until we arrive off the Israeli coast. Is that understood?"

"Yes, sir," Alhad said.

"You are dismissed."

Radio Communications Center
USS Harry S. Truman
Western Mediterranean

Lieutenant Doug Vandergrift surveyed the impromptu gathering of the *Truman*'s most powerful officers.

The *Truman*'s commanding officer, Captain William Constangy, informally convened the meeting. "What's our situation?" He looked to the *Truman*'s air wing commander. "Air Boss?"

"Cap'n," the commander said, "we've surveyed all our squadrons. No such radio check from any pilot on board."

"Intel?" Constangy eyed his senior intelligence officer, Commander Trent Fox. "What do you make of this? Anything we should be alarmed about?"

"Odd, sir," Fox said. "On the one hand, we have a benign combination of the sephamore alphabet. Oscar, India, and Golf. Seems like a harmless combination at first blush. Spoken in English, as opposed to, say ... some language like Arabic, Russian, Chinese, Korean, or the language of any other potential enemy. So assuming this was something more than a routine radio check, it doesn't seem like they were trying to hide anything from us."

"Could this have been an aircraft?"

"No, Skipper," the carrier's radar officer responded. "No aircraft in the vicinity of the triangulation. Has to be a surface vessel."

The captain frowned. "Or maybe a submarine?"

"That would mean the Russians," Fox said. "We'd know if any allied subs were in the area."

"What's your hunch, Intel?" the captain asked. "You think this might have been a radio check?"

"No, sir, Skipper, I don't."

"Shoot." The commanding officer took a sip of coffee.

"Three problems with that theory, sir. First, a radio check would not ordinarily occur at such regular intervals over time like this. Second, a radio check would ordinarily be specifically identified as such. Finally, there's no response from any other radio. So it's not like we have two vessels out there, maybe separated five miles apart, and one calls for a radio check, and the other responds, 'loud and clear,' or anything like that."

"Agreed," the skipper said, sipping more coffee. "I think the radio check theory is bogus." Another swig. "It's almost like they wanted us, or somebody on board, to hear them."

"Us or perhaps one of the other ships in the battle group," Fox added.

"But why?"

"That I can't say, sir."

"Recommendations?"

"Sir," Fox said, "we've got an approximate triangulation on the source of the broadcast, at least as of thirty minutes ago. I think we should launch an aircraft to investigate."

"Where?" the skipper pressed.

"About seventy-five miles east southeast," Fox responded.

The captain turned to his senior JAG officer, Lieutenant Commander Dewey Rouse. "If I send a chopper out with a SEAL team on board, and if we can pinpoint the source of this broadcast, what are our rights under international law? Can we board the vessel?"

"Under the law of the high seas, Skipper, we can board if we can make the argument that the broadcast threatens either this ship, one of the ships in our battle group, or the United States. Otherwise, we could have an international incident on our hands."

"Come up with an argument, Commander," the captain said.

"Aye, sir." The JAG officer grimaced.

"Let's get a chopper up."

U.S. Navy helicopter
Special Mission 448
52 nautical miles ESE of USS Harry S. Truman
Altitude 500 feet
Western Mediterranean

The bright morning sunlight was already bathing the eastern horizon when the copilot of the U.S. Navy SH-60B Seahawk helicopter saw a trail of freshly churned water marking a short streak in the vast expanse of the dark blue Mediterranean.

"Small craft in the water at nine o'clock, Skipper," the first officer, a lieutenant junior grade, announced.

The chopper's commander, a navy lieutenant wearing an olive-drab flight suit and a white flight helmet, turned his head to the left. "I see him," he said. "Let's go in for a closer look." The chopper banked left and completed one full orbit of the small craft's position; then the pilot pushed his call button.

Radio communications center
USS Harry S. Truman
Western Mediterranean

ruman, Seahawk 434." The pilot's voice was being broadcast into both the ship's air traffic control center and its radio communications center. In the room were Lieutenant Doug Vandergrift and his staff along with the ship's skipper, its air boss, its executive officer, and its senior intelligence officer.

"Go ahead, Seahawk," Vandergrift said. Every eye in the radio control room was glued on the silver and black speaker.

"*Truman*, we've spotted a small craft, maybe a forty- or fifty-footer, flying the Spanish ensign. Speed, approximately eighteen knots. At present course, she appears to be making for the Balearic Islands. Awaiting your instructions. Over."

There was an exchange of glances.

"Any other craft in the area?" Vandergrift asked.

"Negative, *Truman*. We've swept the entire area. Nobody else here."

"I think we've found our source," Fox said.

"Yes, but what are we gonna do about it?" the captain asked, as if talking to himself, then turned to his JAG officer. "Lieutenant, have you come up with a theory that will allow us to board?"

"This might be a stretch, Skipper"—Rouse toyed with his chin—"but if the radio contact that we received could be interpreted as a distress signal, or a call for help by someone on board ... this would give you grounds for boarding."

Captain Constangy's eyes twinkled as he scanned the room. "Dewey, you just might be on to something."

"With due respect, Skipper, this vessel appears to be Spanish. As you know, sir, Spain is a member of NATO. If the vessel is legitimately Spanish, and if there is nothing sinister about her intentions, we could be risking an international incident, possibly even a formal protest by the Spanish government, which we would certainly hear about, to say the least, sir."

U.S. Navy helicopter
Special Mission 448
54 nautical miles ESE of USS Harry S. Truman
Altitude 300 feet
Western Mediterranean

The navy pilot, LT Bill Cameron, USN, lowered the Seahawk to three hundred feet from the water's surface, orbiting the slow-moving small craft on the rippling sea below.

His first officer, LT (JG) William Jonson, USN, kept watch with a pair of binoculars, while the aircrew chief opened the chopper's main cargo door. The six-member SEAL team, wearing combat fatigues, their faces painted black, checked their M16s as they awaited the call from the *Truman* to board.

The small craft, flying the flag of Spain, had already failed to respond to the chopper's attempts to make radio contact. This fact was radioed back to the *Truman*.

"How's our fuel, Bill?" the pilot asked the first officer.

"Forty-five minutes, Skipper," Jonson said. "Gonna be tight."

Cameron checked his watch. Avgas was okay for now, but within the next fifteen minutes, things would get tight. Cameron had flown back to "the boat" on fumes before, but nothing taxed his nerves more. Navy choppers don't float well.

"Seahawk, *Truman*. Do you copy?"

"Roger that," Cameron said. "Copy you loud and clear."

"Seahawk, Cap'n Constangy here."

Cameron's eyes met Jonson's.

"Yes, sir, Captain," Cameron said.

"Is the Spanish vessel still unresponsive to radio contact?"

"Roger that, Captain," Cameron said. "Three attempts, all negative."

"Copy that, Seahawk. Stand by for instructions."

Make up your mind, guys. It's a long ways to swim.

The sun was now 10 degrees or so above the horizon, shining almost horizontally along the water below the chopper, illuminating the choppy ripples. Cameron made five more slow loops, and then static came over his radio again.

"Seahawk, *Truman*," said LT Vandergrift, the radio room officer.

"*Truman*, Seahawk. We copy."

"By order of the captain, you are to intercept Spanish vessel, ordering it to halt. If vessel does not comply, SEAL team is to prepare for possible boarding to halt the vessel by force if necessary, investigate, and report. Do you copy?"

That brought a collective vocal burst from the adrenaline-charged SEAL team, all of whom were monitoring air traffic control on their headsets.

"Copy that we are to attempt aerial intercept, and if unsuccessful, SEAL team to board."

"Seahawk, *Truman*. Negative. SEAL team to prepare for boarding. Repeat, *prepare* for boarding. Do not board unless ordered by the commanding officer, USS *Harry Truman*. Repeat, do not board unless ordered by the commanding officer, USS *Harry Truman*. Do you copy?"

"We copy, *Truman*. Attempt aerial intercept, and if unsuccessful, SEAL team to prepare to board. No boarding until authorized by CO of USS *Truman*.

"Your copy is correct. Execute orders immediately."

"Roger that. Executing." Cameron dropped the chopper to one hundred feet and brought the bird to within twenty yards off the vessel's bow.

CHAPTER 16

United Flight 392
Altitude 31,000 feet
Somewhere over northeastern Arizona

Ladies and Gentlemen, the President of the United States ... Thank you, Lieutenant Brewer ... Death to America!... This court-martial finds you, of all charges and specifications, guilty ... In the court-martial of the century today, the death penalty ... Today I will be with you in Paradise ... I hope to see you again, Zack ... Death to the U.S. Navy!... Help me, Zack!

"Diane!"

Amid the whining hum of jet engines, a few passengers, obviously light sleepers, punched on their overhead reading lights.

The slight hint of perfume wafted around him, and a gentle hand touched his shoulder. "You okay, Lieutenant?" a soft, feminine voice whispered in his ear.

"My apologies," Zack said to the flight attendant. "I was dreaming."

She drew her hand back. "Could I get you anything? Maybe a blanket?"

"A blanket and maybe another pillow would be nice."

"Here you are." She placed a pillow under his neck and spread the blanket over him. "Anything else I can do for you?"

"You're kind." He smiled, still whispering. "I'll be fine."

Zack closed his eyes again, praying that the revolving images—of President Williams shaking his hand in the Rose Garden, of the chaplains' eyes before they died, of Diane crying—would stop. But the image, the dream, that was the most poignant, the most emotional, was that of Diane Colcernian, in her white uniform, reaching to him, her auburn hair flaming against a mysterious dark abyss. In the dream, she screamed, crying to him for help. She was so real that cold sweat beaded on his forehead.

Why did he let her leave on her own? Surely he could have done something. He should have called Captain Rudy or Commander Awe and pleaded with him to order a marine escort to take her back to San Diego. Why wasn't he more insistent? It all happened so fast.

Because of his stunning victory over Wells Levinson, the *New York Times* called him "one of the brightest young lawyers in America." The *San Diego Union* claimed he was "the navy's best JAG officer." How he wished none of it had ever happened. The publicity had made him a marked target. His association with Diane made her a target too. A bull's-eye was on her back.

His dreams over the last two nights brought with them the full realization of what she meant to him. Zack did not feel like the navy's best lawyer as he closed his eyes and leaned his head back. Diane's abrupt absence had brought him face-to-face with his emotions. In the last two days, his feelings for her had either grown or perhaps been exposed in a way he never before fully realized.

But against that growing passion within him, he felt a wrenching foreboding he could not explain.

CHAPTER 17

Radio communications center
USS Harry S. Truman
Western Mediterranean

T*ruman*, Seahawk 434."

"Seahawk, *Truman*," Lieutenant Vandergrift said into the microphone. The ship's cadre of senior officers closed into a tight semicircle behind his station. "Report your situation."

"*Truman*, be advised small craft has refused—repeat, refused—to halt."

Captain Constangy, standing behind Lieutenant Vandergrift, grunted an obscenity, which brought all eyes in the room squarely on him. A slight burst of static followed by another message from the helo's commander.

"Small vessel appears to be a sixty-foot civilian cruiser operating on twin inboards. Cruising speed approximately twenty knots, still maintaining a course directly for the Balearic Islands. Three persons spotted aboard. Unknown if others are below deck. Awaiting your instructions, *Truman*.

Another grunt from Captain Constangy. "What kind of small craft won't stop for a U.S. Navy helicopter? Lieutenant Vandergrift, may I borrow your microphone?"

Vandergrift handed his microphone to the skipper.

"This is the captain speaking. Do you copy?"

"Yes, sir, Captain, you're loud and clear."

"Can the SEAL team hear me?"

"They all have their earphones on and are giving me the thumbs-up, Skipper."

"Good. Listen up. Drop as low as you can, insert SEAL team, detain crew, and take control of vessel. You are to search vessel and report. Use force only if necessary to defend yourselves. Do you copy?"

"This is Lieutenant Kemp, SEAL Team 3." The chopper's engines and the sound of wind competed with Kemp's voice, making him barely audible. "Acknowledge: Board, take control, and search. Force only if necessary for self-defense."

"Roger that, SEAL team. Execute boarding orders now."

"Bringing the bird in close for insertion," Cameron said. "Stand by."

Room 442
Hilton Wilmington Riverside
301 North Water Street
Wilmington, North Carolina

She drove to the hotel under the cover of darkness, parked her rental car on the street, checked into her room, and slipped under the soft cotton sheets, hoping desperately for some precious rest before the sun rose.

But her thoughts, churning like the fast cycle of a washing machine, made her quest for sleep next to impossible.

Maybe it wasn't such a good idea to come here. She wasn't sure she could preserve her anonymity. And her presence could pose a distraction for the family, which worried her.

Still, she felt compelled to be here. It was as if some invisible force, perhaps the hand of God, had drawn her here. Maybe it was just her guilt.

She flipped on the bedside lamp and reached for the remote control. News of the execution, which she had deliberately avoided, would still be fresh. She would avoid the news, if possible. Maybe she would find an old movie. Something romantic to get her mind off things.

The Sony responded instantly to the remote control, and the muted image on CNN nearly made her heart stop.

Under a flood of television lights, Zack, looking breathtakingly handsome in his service dress blue uniform and wearing his white officer's cover, was stepping out of a building into the night. At his side, Lieutenant Commander Wendy Poole, Captain MacDonald, and the judge advocate general of the navy.

A message superimposed across the bottom of the screen read, "Navy chaplains executed at Fort Leavenworth."

The officers disappeared in favor of Sally Wu, the Asian-American CNN evening anchor. Closed-captioning scrolled across the bottom of the screen, and behind Sally's image, official U.S. Navy photos of the three executed chaplains.

So much for avoiding the news. She punched the off button. With the lamp still on, she rolled over in the opposite direction and closed her eyes, thinking only of Zack, missing him, and wishing it had been her—not Wendy Poole—at his side.

U.S. Navy helicopter
Special Mission 448
58 nautical miles ESE of USS Harry S. Truman
Altitude 50 feet
Western Mediterranean

Lieutenant Bill Cameron brought the Seahawk down to just fifty feet from the surface, as close as he could come without entangling his rotors with the boat's high-rising radio antennas.

He reduced his airspeed to twenty knots, matching the boat's surface speed. With the bow of the Spanish vessel directly below the cockpit, the aircraft's rotors were blowing wind downward, making an artificial circle in the water, almost like a moving spotlight blinding a running rat.

Cameron glanced into the cargo bay to check on his SEAL team's readiness. One member manned the chopper's fifty-millimeter machine gun. Three others cocked their M16s. All gun barrels were pointed directly down, ready to pour fire onto the craft should any threat arise. Lieutenant Gregory Kemp had strapped himself into a harness and was about to be lowered to the boat by the chopper's mechanical winch.

When Kemp gave Cameron a thumbs-up, Cameron flipped a switch, activating the chopper's loudspeaker system. "Attention, Spanish vessel. This is the United States Navy. Be advised we intend to board your vessel. Do not resist, or you will be fired upon."

The helo's powerful speakers amplified Cameron's voice above the deafening roar of the engines, causing a thunderlike echo from the surface. Cameron repeated the message, a bit more deliberately, and then gave Kemp a thumbs-up.

Kemp stepped out into open space, dangling from the chopper like a spider on a single thread.

Radio communications center
USS Harry S. Truman
Western Mediterranean

What's taking them so long?" Captain Constangy mumbled, checking his watch again.

"*Truman*, Seahawk."

Constangy lunged at the radio. "Whaddya got, Seahawk?"

"Captain," Cameron said, "SEAL team has boarded with no resistance. Vessel is now halted in the water."

"Yes!" The *Truman*'s skipper punched his fist in the air. "Report, Mr. Cameron. I wanna know what's going on down there."

"Stand by, Skipper. Lieutenant Kemp is radioing a report right now."

"They must be running low on fuel," the intelligence officer said.

"He can switch to his emergency tank, but it's getting close," the air boss said.

"Launch another chopper, now," the captain ordered.

"Aye, sir."

"*Truman*, Seahawk."

"Go, Seahawk."

"Captain, Lieutenant Kemp reports three men aboard Spanish vessel. The captain has a Spanish passport. Two crew members have Saudi passports."

Captain Constangy locked eyes with his intelligence officer. "Repeat passport information."

Static. "Roger that. One Spanish. Two Saudi."

"Two Saudis," Constangy mumbled away from the microphone. "I don't like the smell of it." He picked up the microphone again. "Any weapons on board?"

"Stand by, sir. SEALS report two nine-millimeter handguns. No other weapons. Also sixty-five thousand U.S. dollars found in a leather attaché case."

"I don't like it." Constangy looked at his JAG officer. "What can we do about this, Dewey?"

Rouse chewed on his lower lip. "Captain, I agree with your instincts, sir. But I'm not sure that we have the right, under international law, to detain the vessel."

The captain bristled. "I need a recommendation, Commander. My chopper's running low on gas out there."

Rouse raised an eyebrow. "Have the SEALS ask them about the money."

"Seahawk, *Truman*. Ask them why so much cash is on board."

"Roger that, *Truman*. Stand by."

"Come on. Come on." The captain glanced at his watch.

A burst of static. "*Truman*, Seahawk. The Spanish captain says the two Saudis are purchasing the craft, and the cash is a down payment. Also, the SEALs asked them about the broadcast. The captain says they were doing a radio check."

"Bull." Captain Constangy looked at his JAG officer. "Commander, I need a reason to commandeer that boat. How about the fact that we've got a bunch of foreigners in possession of United States currency?"

"Skipper, I'm not aware of any law that prohibits foreigners from owning U.S. dollars. In fact, it happens all the time. That's part of the reason our currency fluctuates. We've got no probable cause to believe that money was illegally obtained. While the circumstances are suspicious, the vessel has every right to navigation on the high seas, a principle this country has defended for over two hundred years. There's no evidence that the vessel took hostile action against any U.S. warships."

"So what are you saying, Commander?"

"What I'm saying, sir, is that in my judgment, the vessel has not violated international law, or the law of the sea, or U.S. law. Because it has taken no overt hostile act against our forces, we do not have the right, under international law, to take any defensive measures. You're the captain, but I would very respectfully invite you to consider the fact that the Spanish are NATO members and that the Saudis are also, officially at least, our allies."

"Like a horse's rear the Saudis are our allies!" The captain slammed his fist on the table. "They kiss up to us in front of TV cameras, then fund murders in Israel and then send their kids to indoctrination camps, filling them with hate for this country." He shook his head. "As far as I'm concerned, they're all a bunch of animals."

"I agree, Captain. But all that aside, I don't think you've got enough here to provoke an international incident." Constangy met Rouse's gaze as the JAG officer continued. "Sir, as your senior JAG officer, it's my duty to give you the best advice I can. What would happen here if either the Spanish or the Saudis filed a protest over our actions in commandeering this vessel? You would most likely lose your command."

Constangy worked his jaw in anger.

"If we had solid evidence, it would be different. But we don't. Not even close. Even boarding the vessel was questionable, Captain."

Constangy grunted. "Your recommendation, Commander?"

"Have the SEALS photograph every inch of that boat, the cash, the crew. Then let's get the heck out of Dodge."

As much as the recommendation went against every fiber of Bill Constangy's being, he knew his JAG officer was right. "Seahawk, *Truman*. Relay message to SEAL commander. Photograph crew, money, and all quarters of Spanish vessel. Then retreat, at which point vessel is free to proceed."

"*Truman*, Seahawk. Roger that."

CHAPTER 18

Outside Hilton Wilmington Riverside
301 North Water Street
Wilmington, North Carolina

It was barely dawn when Ahmed Sadat parked his Aerostar minivan in front of the hotel. He smiled as he lifted his binoculars and studied the entrance.

He followed her last night all the way from Washington.

Did she really think she could just rent a car, drive from the nation's capital down to some obscure southern port city in North Carolina, and rent a hotel in the middle of the night without him following her?

Did she take him for a fool? Because his shot killed the wrong infidel the first time? The irresistibly gorgeous Lieutenant Colcernian, now without Lieutenant Knight-in-Shining-Armor Brewer at her side, sorely underestimated him.

Maybe she and Brewer had had a lover's quarrel. That thought made him smile more widely. Maybe deep down, she liked Arab men. That thought gave him a nicotine craving.

Ahmed chucked the binoculars into the backseat. At this short distance from the entrance, he really did not need them anyway. No point in raising unwarranted suspicion. Ahmed reached into his front pocket, fidgeting for a cigarette. Igniting his Zippo, he sucked in through the filter, bringing a bright glow to the nicotine-saturated tobacco. Ah, the smell of fresh smoke filling his car was invigorating.

It was Allah's divine will that he missed. This he now understood, fully. Allah, the all-knowing, foreknew that Islamic Glory was imminent. Her assassination was not yet in Allah's timing.

But what of the dead girl?

A deep, satisfying draw from the cigarette.

So what if the bullet had struck her by accident? She was but an infidel anyway. The prophet himself—*Peace be upon him*—taught that death was the proper punishment for those who either rejected or refused to submit to Islam. She got what she deserved. Allah himself willed that his bullet crush her skull. Allah had dumbfounded the American law enforcement authorities searching for him. How could they be so shallow in their understanding? Did they really believe they could apprehend a man carrying out Allah's will on earth? Fools!

Praise be to Allah! Blessed be the prophet Mohammed—peace be upon him!

Feeling triumphant, he flicked a clump of ashes out the window.

The stunning image of Diane Colcernian was impressed upon his mind, and he smiled with pleasure. It was an image of this alluring maiden in her white uniform, her shapely, tanned legs visible below the hemline of her white skirt.

He had spent months studying photographs of her. His dossier was complete with photos, going all the way back to her days as a model in Virginia.

Such an oxymoronic blend of feminine militarism. Authoritative. Intelligent. Beautiful. Perhaps Allah delayed her death as a personal reward to him. His marching orders, at least as far as Colcernian was concerned, had changed as a result of Islamic Glory. He would be rewarded by the Council, by al-Akhma himself, no matter how he dealt with her, as long as he dealt with her. The next few days would prove most interesting, a turning point in world history.

He flicked the still-lit cigarette stub out onto Water Street and fired up another.

Surely Allah's promise of maidens was not for the afterlife only.

Another puff. Another smile.

He would kill her, chain her alluring legs to cinderblocks, and dump her body into the Cape Fear River. By the time she was found, he would be across the Mexican border.

Room 442
Hilton Wilmington Riverside
301 North Water Street
Wilmington, North Carolina

The warm Jacuzzi water, swirling around her back and over her arms, was the most luxuriating tonic she had experienced in days. Maybe she would just lie here, enjoy the steam, and skip the task ahead.

No. She had come this far. She would go through with it. With a sigh, she pulled herself up out of the water, toweled off, and slipped into a terrycloth bathrobe.

It would be a morning service, according to the obituary in the *Wilmington Star News*. Eleven o'clock, to be precise, followed by a twelve-thirty burial. Driving by the location last night, which was within walking distance of the hotel, she discovered that it was a large, old-looking sanctuary. To avoid being seen, she planned to slip in the back at the last minute, wearing a black suit and dark shades, with her hair hidden under a black hat.

As she reached for the blow dryer, her purse and cell phone fell off the vanity and onto the marble floor.

With a frown, she reached over to pick up the items. A black line ran through the green screen on her cell phone, like Moses parting the Red Sea. She tried powering it off and then back on again. Same result.

She checked her watch. The service started in one hour. Time to get ready.

CHAPTER 19

251 Andropov Ulitza
Krugloye
Mogilev region
Republic of Belarus

Just before six o'clock, under the single lightbulb hanging from the ceiling of the two-room apartment, a family of six gathered around the table for an evening meal of borsch, radishes, and water. A rapid knock at the flimsy front door cut short Alexander's prayer.

He met his wife's eyes and scratched his long black beard.

Who could be at the door at this hour? Who would wish to visit a poor Belarusian Jewish family? Possibly the KGB? No one ever knocked on his door at the dinner hour. All good Jews would be at home with their families, thanking God for his benevolence and serving whatever food they could scrounge from their garden or the market.

The fall of the Soviet Union and the rise of the Belarusian Republic had ushered in a period of greater religious "tolerance." But in this poor country sandwiched between Poland and Mother Russia, the most horrific atrocities against Jews in the history of humankind had occurred. Alexander was only too aware that the respite from oppression could end at any time.

Surely nothing good could come from this. He had heard that if Jewish emigration papers fell into the wrong bureaucrat's hands, the consequences could be staggering. Rumors abounded of false criminal charges, of eviction notices from government-issued houses.

On the other hand, he had heard that a few Christians were now working in the emigration offices and that Jewish immigration papers falling into their hands were being processed very quietly, without trouble. How ironic, Alexander thought, Jews relying on Christians, of all people, to help them return to the Promised Land. Alexander had taken a gamble and submitted his paperwork. Now, with another round of furious rapping at his door, he wished he had not.

"Even though I walk through the valley of the shadow of death," he said to himself in Russian, quoting the psalmist, "I will fear no evil."

He stood from the table, exchanging worried looks with his wife and four children, two girls and two boys whose ages ranged from three to nine. "For thou art with me." He turned and stepped toward the door. "Thy rod and thy staff, they comfort me."

He opened the door to the sight of two stone-faced young officials, maybe in their late twenties, official looking in black suits, dark glasses, and crew cuts.

"*Etta Alexander Kweskin doma?*" the one on the left demanded.

"*Dah.*" Alexander nodded, trying to mask the trembling in his voice.

"*Vwee Alexander Kweskin?*" the one on the right said.

"*Dah.*" *Please, God. Protect Yael and the children.*

"*Etta dla vas, Guspadyeen Kweskin.*" The one on the right thrust a sealed envelope, probably an arrest warrant, at him.

"*Ahtcreetay.*" *Open.*

Alexander opened the envelope, then dropped to his knees.

Outside St. Mary's Catholic Church
412 Ann Street
Wilmington, North Carolina

Diane stepped through the revolving door of the hotel and onto the sidewalk. The bright colors and sweet aroma of azaleas that greeted her solidified her decision. Parking, she figured, would be a problem this morning, and she doubted she could get any closer if she tried. So she headed by foot to the large stone church, located in Wilmington's historic district.

She slipped on a pair of dark glasses, closed her eyes, and inhaled deeply, enjoying a prolonged sense of the blended fragrance of azaleas, dogwoods, and roses before turning left along North Water Street. In the hotel she had read a promotional brochure promoting Wilmington as the "port city" of North Carolina and, moreover, as the "Azalea capital of the world."

She tried dwelling on this pleasant thought as a means to combat the awful lump in her throat and the ache in her heart as she tried to suppress her tears. This way, she could say her earthly good-byes to a young woman she never knew. With the sweet fragrance of blooming azaleas along the way, and with her eyes focused on the black hearse that came into view just in front of the church, she barely noticed a black Aerostar minivan parked near the walkway.

She hoped Maggie Jefferies was a Christian. And if she was a believer, Diane knew that the sight now before Maggie Jefferies' eyes was far more wonderful than even the beautiful mounds of pink and white azaleas, drenched in the morning Carolina sunshine and blooming in clusters along the dogwood-lined streets of Wilmington's historic district.

Diane's vision blurred. Tears became impossible to contain as she stepped across Ann Street and walked toward the front door of St. Mary's.

Ahmed smiled, popped another cigarette in his mouth, lit it, then opened the driver's side door of the Aerostar and stepped out. He fell in about thirty yards behind the woman.

He could take a shot from here and definitely pick her off. But too many others were around, all headed inside the infidel church to observe the body of the infidel named Maggie Jefferies.

Maybe he would wait outside, hide behind one of the many large magnolia trees across from the church, and shoot her through the leaves with a high-powered rifle. Better yet, he thought, he could crack the top of the tinted glass window from his van, squeeze the barrel through it, and just pick her off from the side of the street.

Of course, all that would take the fun out of the chase. And he *did* have more discretion now in how he decided to deal with her. He smiled, put on his sunglasses, and followed her with his eyes as she stepped up the stairs and disappeared through the front door.

251 Andropov Ulitza
Krugloye
Mogilev Region
Republic of Belarus

Forgive me," Alexander said, still on his knees and now weeping profusely, his head bowed almost at the feet of the two black-suited young men, who had now stepped inside the door.

"Alexander. Alexander! *Sto etta?*" He heard the worried voice of Yael, his wife of seventeen years, a slightly heavy woman but still lovely in his eyes. And when he felt her soft hand on his shoulder, he looked up, then took her hand in his.

"Oh, my dear one"—he covered his eyes with his left hand—"there is news of our fate."

"What is it, my love?" She looked at him, concern in her sparkling black eyes.

"Dear one, these two bring us news of our future."

"I do not understand." She threw up her arms in exasperation. "How have these gentlemen upset you so?"

He stood and wrapped his arms around her, then saw the children, like frozen mannequins, staring at them from the small wooden table. "My dear, we are leaving."

"Leaving?"

"May I read this to my wife?" He glanced at the bureaucrat on the right.

"By all means, Guspadyeen."

"*Harasho, moi droog.*" He stepped back from Yael and unfolded the paper.

"This, my family, is a letter from the International Fellowship of Christians and Jews. It was written last Wednesday." Alexander handled it reverently, then slowly began reading in a voice trembling with emotion.

Dear Guspadyeen Kweskin,

On behalf of the International Fellowship of Christians and Jews, I am very pleased to announce your emigration request to Israel has been approved by the government of the Republic of Belarus. I am enclosing a copy of the approval letter from the Belarusian Emigration Office, which was forwarded to us, as your agent in handling this request.

As you can see, the government is approving the emigration request for you and your entire immediate family, which includes your wife and your four children.

Alexander stopped, wiping more tears.

"Is this true?" Yael stared at the mysterious duo, her mouth agape. "These are not arrest papers? We are really going to Israel?"

"Yes, Guspazhal Kweskin, it is true." The man on the right finally flashed a semblance of a smile. "I am Dimitry Popkov with the

International Fellowship. You may call me Dima. This is my brother Sasha, also with the Fellowship."

Sasha nodded his head.

"You are Jewish?" Yael asked.

"We are Christian," Sasha spoke up, now smiling himself, "but our Savior is Jewish, and our heart is with you."

Alexander's eyes met Yael's. Tears were streaking down her face. "Praise be to the God of Abraham," she said softly as Alexander put his hands on her cheeks.

"And to his Son, the resurrected Messiah," Dima added, also softly.

"Yes," Yael said. "Who could argue with such a proposition at this hour?"

"Perhaps you should finish reading the letter, Guspadyeen Kweskin," Dima said. "There is much work remaining to be done and little time in which to do it."

Alexander smiled and nodded, his hands still trembling with excitement. For a moment he caught a glimpse, he thought, of the glory Moses must have felt when he read the Ten Commandments. *A writing that could have come only from God.* And with that fleeting thought, he went back to his solemn reading.

Our offices will serve as liaison between the Belarusian and Israeli governments to arrange for the execution of all paperwork necessary for your emigration. Once all the paperwork is finalized in Israel, you must be prepared to leave immediately. Because of severe space limitations in Israel, your family will be limited to only one suitcase per person.

By the generosity of an anonymous donor in America, you will be provided a cash allotment of two thousand ($2,000.00) U.S. dollars to help you start your new life in Israel. Please make arrangements to get your affairs in order and be prepared to travel on short notice, most likely within the next two weeks.

Your liaison officers from the International Fellowship are Dima and Sasha Popkov. They will stand ready to assist you, round-the-clock if necessary, to facilitate your move to your new homeland. They will guide you through all remaining paperwork requirements, then facilitate your transportation to the airport in Minsk once the specific time for your departure is finalized.

Please accept my congratulations on your selection, which was made in a very competitive environment from a large pool of applicants. May God's blessings be upon you as you begin your new life.

You are the living fulfillment of HIS promise written by the prophet Ezekiel, who said, "For I will take you out of the nations; I will gather you from all the countries and bring you back into your own land" (Ezek. 36:24).

Shalom to you,
Rabbi Dan Eckstein
Director

CHAPTER 20

Charles E. Lindberg Field
San Diego International Airport
San Diego, California

Despite his worries over Diane, Zack found a pittance of relief when he discovered that his "baby," that is, his silver Mercedes 320, the only material possession on earth for which he admittedly had a weakness, appeared unscratched when he found her sitting in section AA, row 3, in the long-term parking lot.

He popped open the trunk, tossed in his bags, then pulled off his service dress blue jacket and laid it in the backseat.

His Guess WaterPro wristwatch showed that it was now 8:45 PST.

How would he spend the rest of the day? Technically, he was still on leave. But frankly, he really didn't feel like being on leave. Not with Diane's presence unaccounted for.

Maybe he would just jump on the first flight back east to search for her. He could take a nonstop to Washington, land at Reagan National Airport, rent a car, and start driving down I-95, hoping to bump into her at a McDonald's or something.

Use your head, Lieutenant. You can't help her with stupid thoughts.

He cranked the engine, pressed a button to open the sunroof, and basked for a moment in the warm San Diego sunshine. He opened his eyes and, adjusting them to the light, looked in his rearview at himself.

You are one grungy sight, Lieutenant, a pitiful-looking excuse for a naval officer.

Oakdale Cemetery
520 North 15th Street
Wilmington, North Carolina

It was a large, peaceful, and old cemetery, nestled in a grove of Spanish moss and magnolia trees, containing the remains of some of Wilmington's most prominent citizens, dating from the antebellum era to the twenty-first century.

She read about this place last night in the hotel room. David Brinkley, the famous broadcaster, was buried here. But the words in the brochure did not adequately describe its beauty.

Diane took her place, standing under one of the big, shady Spanish mosses, maybe twenty yards or so from the tent erected by the funeral home for the family.

As the priest made a few comments, Diane's eyes locked momentarily with those of Maggie's sister, a beautiful, green-eyed brunette, and a Carolina grad—just like Zack—who had earlier given a tear-filled eulogy about Maggie's relationship with her family and with the Lord.

The priest, in black clerical robes, finished praying and made the sign of the cross over the casket.

Shadows of clouds rolled over the green grass and gray tombstones. Wind and a sudden drop in temperature signaled that an early season thunderstorm was on the way.

The distant booms of thunder, followed by lightning, made the crowd scatter quickly. Only the family members remained with the priest beneath the tent when the first big drops of cool rain started falling.

Still, Diane could not bring herself to leave as the rain increased from a few drops to a downpour.

Violent lightning bolts ripped across the sky, followed by booming thunderclaps. The deluge from the heavens turned the image of the family under the tent into a ghostly blur. One of the family members, a man with a black umbrella, jogged toward her, splashing water from the grass as he cut across the graves.

"Won't you come under the tent with us?" He held the large black umbrella over her head. Now that he was closer, she could see he was Maggie Jefferies's father.

"I came to pay my respects, but I wouldn't want to intrude on the family's privacy." Diane took solace in knowing that her tears were being masked by the rainwater streaming down her face.

"You look familiar." The man flashed a puzzled look just as another lightning bolt split the heavens.

"I'm Diane Colcernian." Diane looked away from him, worried that Mr. Jefferies would blame her for his daughter's death. "I feel responsible," she said, her voice breaking into a sob. "I'm so sorry."

"She admired you, Lieutenant." Mr. Jefferies put his arm around her shoulders. "We all do. We don't blame you. Don't ever think that. It was her time; God called her home when he wanted her home."

The raindrops fell more heavily now. The thunderclaps grew louder, increasing in frequency.

"It's okay, Lieutenant. Please, come under the tent."

She looked into his eyes, then through the rain at the other family members, their faces turned toward Diane and Mr. Jefferies.

"I appreciate your kind words, Mr. Jefferies. Right now, you need to go back to your family. I'll be praying for you." She gave him a hug. "I've got to go."

She stepped out from under the umbrella into the drenching rain, walking through the cemetery, away from Maggie Jefferies's freshly dug grave.

Navy Trial Service Office
Building 73
32nd Street Naval Station
San Diego, California

Zack arrived just outside his office at the Navy Trial Command on 32nd Street. His office was on the far end of the L-shaped, one-story stucco building, and often he could sneak in without being noticed.

He inserted his security card into the door on the end of the building, and when he heard the electronic release of the lock, he pulled open the door.

"Lieutenant Brewer." Zack heard the all-too-familiar voice and looked up to see his boss, Senior Trial Counsel Commander Bob Awe. He was totally gray, with intelligent eyes, a pleasant personality, an eccentric penchant for collecting art, and a bit more of a potbelly than would ordinarily be allowable for a naval officer. Awe stood in the passageway, smiling and holding his trademark coffee mug.

So much for Zack's plans for an anonymous return.

"I see our celebrity has returned." Awe beamed as if Zack were his personal protégé. "We thought we might see you today, Zack." Awe extended a warm and welcoming handshake.

"Well, sir," Zack said, "after witnessing that execution, I decided getting back to work would be the best possible therapy for me right now." *Actually, the best therapy would be news that Diane is okay.*

"The captain instructed me"—Awe released Zack's hand—"if I saw you around here today, to send you directly to his office."

"Is everything okay, sir?"

"Yes." A big gulp of coffee. "I think the captain has some rather good news he would like to deliver."

"May I ask what it is, sir?" *Please say you've heard from her and she's all right.*

"Yes, of course you may ask. But I'm under orders not to say. The skipper wants to deliver this personally."

"Does he want to see me now?"

"As soon as I see you. Those are his orders." Another swig of coffee. "Why don't you drop your briefcase on your desk while I get a refill. Meet me in the skipper's office."

Five minutes later, when Zack arrived at Captain Glen Rudy's office, Commander Bob Awe was already sitting in the captain's presence, armed with another fresh cup, this one filled to the brim, probably his fourth of the morning.

"Welcome home, Commander," Captain Rudy said in a cheerful voice, then motioned Zack to sit in the big leather chair beside Commander Awe.

"Coffee, Commander?" Rudy smiled at Zack.

"Sir?" *Why is he looking at me while he's speaking to Commander Awe?*

"Would you like coffee?"

"No thank you, sir," Zack said.

"Zack"—Rudy leaned back in his swivel chair and crossed his arms—"you've done the navy proud, and you've made the JAG Corps look great."

"Thank you, sir." Zack smiled. He knew the skipper meant well, but he was tired of being praised for merely doing his job. He just wanted to get back to work, get out of the limelight, and return to life as a normal naval officer.

And he wanted Diane back. And if he ever got her back, if he ever looked again into those dazzling, incomparable green eyes, he would finally come out of the *shell* she always accused him of being in.

"I'm sorry, Skipper." Zack looked up. Captain Rudy was speaking to him.

Rudy looked at him with a curious expression. "You okay, Zack?"

"My apologies, sir. I'm fine."

"Anyway, what I was saying," Captain Rudy continued, "is that we've just received the promotion board's list for lieutenant commander. You've been deep-selected, Zack."

Zack felt his eyes widen.

"Congratulations."

Zack fumbled for something to say.

"Is my prosecutor experiencing a rare paralysis of that silver tongue of his?" Rudy chuckled.

"But, sir, I didn't think I was in zone for selection for another year."

"That's one of the beautiful things about deep selection, Commander. On the very rare occasion when the commander in chief of the United States armed forces personally weighs in and says he wants an officer promoted to the next highest rank, the selection board does not argue."

Zack sat there for a second. He had prosecuted the most highly publicized court-martial in modern history, then been decorated personally by the president with a Meritorious Service Medal. So perhaps the deep selection shouldn't have come as a surprise. But for some reason, it did.

"What about Lieutenant Colcernian, sir? Was she also deep selected?"

Rudy shook his head, then sipped his coffee. "Lieutenant Colcernian will be in the zone next year, and I *guarantee* she'll get picked up, Zack." A hesitation. "Even if I have to go to Washington myself and hold up the board, which, given her record, will be wholly unnecessary."

"I see," Zack said, then realized his tone may have conveyed his regret that Diane would not be promoted with him.

Rudy continued, ignoring Zack's disappointed tone. "The secretary of the navy has given me the authority to frock you now. If you would stand and come to attention, please."

Zack complied as Rudy rose, walked around his big desk, and stood face-to-face with him, then proceeded to unpin the silver "railroad tracks" rank of a navy lieutenant from Zack's right collar. Rudy handed the railroad tracks to Commander Awe, who was standing beside him, and said, "Commander Awe, I believe you have the oak leaf?"

"I do, sir." Awe handed a dime-sized gold oak leaf to Rudy, who pinned it on Zack's right collar, then extended his right hand. "Congratulations, Lieutenant Commander Brewer."

Oakdale Cemetery
520 North 15th Street
Wilmington, North Carolina

Surely the driving rain was a direct answer from Allah, Ahmed Sadat thought. He sat in the cabin of his Aerostar, parked along a cart path in the middle of the suddenly deserted cemetery. From his vantage point in the driver's seat, he pointed his binoculars at the blurry image of Diane Colcernian traipsing alone through the graveyard. Oddly, she wasn't even running in the inclement weather.

He thought he would have to wait until nightfall to make his move. But Allah—*praise be to him*—had provided this divine opportunity in the middle of the day!

Now was the time. He must move with haste so as not to squander this, his God-given appointment with destiny. He felt for the nine-millimeter, pulled it out, quickly worked the action, then turned off the safety and stuck the gun back in his belt. He grabbed the empty wine bottle, threw open the front door, and ran out into the thunderstorm.

More lightning bolts split open the sky, and thunderclaps rumbled as he fell in, now jogging, behind his very wet, unsuspecting target. The driving rain served not only as a veil of visibility but also as a sound buffer. As he closed in, it was obvious that she did not suspect his presence. Looking quickly over his shoulder, he determined that they were totally out of eyesight of the funeral party. Nothing now but driving streaks of rain, coming down even harder, giving him miraculous seclusion for what he was about to do.

He hesitated for a moment, unnerved by the notion that he was about to attack a creature who was the object of his carnal desires. Her black skirt was soggy as she trampled across the sodden cemetery. Her red hair—she had removed the black hat—was deliciously drenched and stringy.

Now was the time to move. Breaking into a sprint, his feet splashing water as he dodged three or four headstones, he closed in. Thunder again masked the sound of his charging feet. She turned, looking stunned that he was charging her like a raging bull. He raised the bottle and smashed it on her skull.

CHAPTER 21

Squadron briefing room
Viper Squadron
USS Harry S. Truman
Central Mediterranean

Still in his olive-drab flight suit, and feeling depleted after having just landed on the carrier from two hours of routine combat air patrol, Lieutenant Commander Mohammed "Mo" Quasay stepped into the squadron briefing room. He wasn't sure why the impromptu meeting had been scheduled by the carrier's air wing commander, but he did not have a good feeling about it. He worried that it might be related to the interception of the code word transmission.

Already, word had gotten around the *Truman* about the interception of the Spanish boat. To make matters worse, according to the ship's scuttlebutt, two of the passengers were Arabic.

This information sent the crew into a feeding frenzy, chewing on all kinds of imaginative rumors like a giant school of piranhas feasting on a piece of steak floating in the river.

Perhaps the command was falling victim to this witch-hunt paranoia. Perhaps they would question him because of his Islamic background. Or maybe they wanted to put him in the same room with Lieutenant Hosni Alhad. Or perhaps they had already interviewed Hosni. But if they had, surely he would not have given them anything, would he?

Hosni was younger and more idealistic, and therefore, more rabid, more hard-core, and more committed to Islamic Glory than even he was. Surely Hosni would let them shoot him before he said anything.

Mo walked into the empty classroom and took a seat at a desk. He placed a legal pad on the fold-down writing surface and waited. He breathed out an inaudible sigh of relief when several other squadron members walked in and sat down. Surely, if they were going to interrogate him, they would not do so in front of the whole squadron, would they?

"They should have snatched the rag heads off the boat," one of his lieutenants whispered to another.

"Snatch 'em off?" The command master chief grimaced. "With all due respect, sir, the skipper should have just blown that boat out of the water. You know they're up to no good."

"Yeah, Master Chief, but how do you prove it?" a lieutenant junior grade asked.

"This isn't a court of law," a full lieutenant said. "We're at war with these terrorists; 9/11 proved we've got to act first and ask questions later."

Mo kept quiet, letting his men rattle on as they waited for the air wing commander. He caught Lieutenant Alhad's eyes as Alhad walked through the hatch and into the briefing room. Alhad looked worried too.

"Attention on deck!"

The squadron rose, snapping to attention as the ship's commanding officer, the air wing commander, and the senior intelligence officer strode into the room.

Navy Exchange
32nd Street Naval Station
San Diego, California

Most recently promoted naval officers were happy to make their first trip to the base uniform shop to purchase the insignia of a new rank.

For Zack, his promotion meant having the Navy Exchange seamstress sew another gold stripe, in this case half of a gold stripe, onto the cuffs of his service dress blue jacket.

He would purchase new shoulder boards for his summer whites, with two *and a half* gold stripes—rather than the two of a full lieutenant. And he also would buy several sets of gold oak leaves, to be pinned to his working khakis. Then, after dropping a hundred bucks to bring his uniforms up to speed, he would make a trip to Base PSD—Personnel Support Detachment—to update his armed forces identification card.

This isn't right, thought newly frocked Lieutenant Commander Zack Brewer, stepping out of the Mercedes. He immediately received the salutes of two full lieutenants in front of the 32nd Street Navy Exchange, reminding him that he was now wearing the oak leaf of a lieutenant commander on his collar. But the salutes did not rev his ego. The promotion felt like further evidence that he was leaving Diane behind. Her absence had created an aching void within him that no promotion could alleviate.

"Lieutenants," Zack said, returning the salutes. As the lieutenants passed behind him, he again silently prayed for her safety and her return. He mumbled "Amen" and hit the speed dial on his cell phone for the third time in the last fifteen minutes.

"Come on, answer," he barked. After the tenth ring, he slapped the phone shut.

**Oakdale Cemetery
520 North 15th Street
Wilmington, North Carolina**

She staggered, then fell limp, her head barely missing a tombstone as she dropped like a rag doll onto the wet grass. The driving rain quickly washed the blood from the back of her head.

He would have to move more quickly now, before the weather cleared and this miracle of an opportunity passed.

He bent over and gently touched her jugular area with his thumb and index finger. Was that a pulse? It was hard to tell. He picked her up, slung her over his shoulder, and started jogging back toward the Aerostar.

She felt heavier than he expected as he ploughed through the driving rain, squinting to make out the image of his van, maybe fifty yards away. Maybe the extra weight was her black skirt and blouse soaking up the rainwater like a sponge. Then he realized, as his hands dug more deeply into her hamstrings, that the weight was sheer muscle tone. This beautiful infidel was a solid, lean physical specimen. Obviously the product of many hours in the gymnasium.

The driving rain pelted his face like stinging needles as he approached the van. Ahmed laid the infidel down on the asphalt cart path beside the van, then opened the sliding door right behind the driver's seat.

He lifted her from the ground, this time cradling her unconscious body in his arms, and slid her onto the backseat. He wasn't sure if she was alive or not, but Ahmed Sadat wasn't taking any chances. He pulled her hands behind her back and snapped on the handcuffs lying on the back floorboard. Then he chained her ankles together with a chain and steel padlock he had purchased from Wal-Mart.

Slamming the sliding panel door closed, he jumped into the driver's seat, cranked the engine, and started driving through the rain, his windshield wipers battling a torrential downpour. The van reached the edge of the cemetery, then turned right on Market Street as the rain lightened. *Praise be to Allah!*

Squadron briefing room
Viper Squadron
USS Harry S. Truman
Central Mediterranean

The customary "At ease, gentlemen," had not come, and they remained standing at attention for what seemed an eternity as the CO and the air wing commander stood up front, at the briefing podium, shuffling papers. Was this some sort of psychological ploy?

With his peripheral vision, Mohammed glanced at Lieutenant Hosni Alhad.

"At ease, gentlemen," Captain Constangy said. "Take your seats."
Finally.

"The information you are about to be given is classified as top secret. The purpose of this briefing is to advise you of a very dangerous situation involving terrorism."

Mohammed's eyes cut to the very worried look on Lieutenant Alhad's face.

"As you know," Captain Constangy continued, "the situation in the Middle East, and particularly the political situation between Israel and Syria, has become a powder keg waiting to explode.

"The Israeli Air Force boasts some of the world's best and most experienced pilots. However, that fact, and the fact that Israel has miraculously been able to defend herself against overwhelming odds since 1948, does very little to reassure the fragile Israeli psyche. That psyche is especially frail right now, especially in view of the fact that more than one dozen Scud missile attacks have landed erratically in northern Israel in the last week alone. The Scuds have been launched from multiple locations in southern Syria and Lebanon, and the intensity of the attacks has been increasing.

"From the first Persian Gulf War, we learned that rooting out these Scud cells is problematic. That's because these missiles are mobile, packed in the back of trucks, or Scud launchers. Commander?"

Constangy turned and motioned to the ship's senior intelligence officer, Commander W. Trent Fox III, who had inconspicuously erected an aluminum tripod easel beside the podium as the captain was speaking.

"Thank you, Captain." Fox was a skinny, bespectacled officer, with black hair and a professorial demeanor. "Gentlemen." Fox looked out at the pilots, his gaze lingering in the direction of Mohammed Quasay. "The skipper is right on the mark when he speaks of the difficulty in rooting out these Scud launchers." Fox again glanced at Quasay.

"And here's why." Fox removed a canvas to reveal several large black-and-white photographs that had been pre-positioned on the easel. "Here" — he tapped twice with a pointer in the upper right corner — "is a satellite photograph of a mobile Scud launcher. As you can see, the concept is devastatingly simple, and yet equally effective. Basically, the missiles are hauled around on trailers, something akin to a conventional big rig eighteen-wheeler that we've all seen ten thousand times on a typical interstate highway in America.

"Part of the problem here, and this has become a much bigger problem than we had in the First Persian Gulf War, is that these *tractor-trailers*" — Fox made quotation marks with his fingers — "are much faster and more difficult to find than before. These launching platforms, our intelligence estimates tell us, can run down the highway at upwards of ninety miles per hour and can barrel across the desert floor at faster than sixty miles per hour. And while the accuracy of these Scuds has not improved immensely since the First Persian Gulf War, because of the greater mobility of these tractor-trailers, our ability to hunt them down and destroy them has been imminently compromised.

"Put another way, they launch and then *haul boogie*." Fox stopped for a sip of water. "They just seem to disappear off the roads and out of the sand." He cleared his throat. "Of course, we know they aren't just magically disappearing. We believe they launch and then race off to warehouses, shelters, camouflaged bunkers, any type of shelter that makes them invisible from the air.

"On a couple of occasions, we know they have been rushed off to school grounds and hospitals."

Praise be to Allah for these brave freedom fighters against Zionism.

"These faster tractor-trailer delivery platforms pose a direct challenge to American airpower, which in this region means primarily carrier-launched American *naval* airpower. To be more effective in taking them out, we're going to have to fly lower, get closer, and be ready to pounce more quickly when there is a launch."

My plane could never fire on these freedom fighters.

"Of course, that strategy poses significant inherent risks. And here's why." Fox mounted a large black-and-white photograph of a bearded freedom fighter, holding what looked like a small cannon over his shoulder. "This is the Stinger missile. Officially known as the FIM-92A, and manufactured in the good ole U.S. of A. I know most of you have heard of it, but as a practical matter, you may not have paid too much attention since most of you are used to flying at altitudes way out of its range. However, at lower ranges, say of one thousand feet and below, it is the lethal enemy of the fighter pilot." He readjusted his glasses. "An Islamic terrorist, such as the one you see pictured here ..."

Freedom fighter.

"... can simply pop out the front door of his house or step out of a bus or automobile, fire the missile, and duck back into his hiding place.

"These nasty little weapons weigh roughly thirty-five pounds, and unfortunately, though American-made, they have fallen into the wrong hands.

"In the late seventies, the CIA supplied over a thousand Stinger missiles to the Mujahideen in Afghanistan to fight the Soviets. We all know what happened there. Afghanistan became the Red Army's Vietnam.

"To make matters worse, China stole the plans to this deadly little gadget, manufactures thousands of them each year, and turns around and sells them to rogue governments. These rogue governments — such as Syria, North Korea, and even China — slip these missiles into the hands of terrorist groups.

"This deadly weapon can splash an aircraft flying as high as 11,500 feet. That's two miles, gentlemen. It has a speed of fifteen hundred miles per hour. In other words, it can haul boogie up your fantails and run faster than any plane in the fleet. It has an effective range of five miles." Fox rested both hands on the podium and surveyed the audience with his eyes. "What all that means is that these missiles are extremely accurate. If the aircraft is less than two miles high, then it is likely that the Stinger can hit it. I'm convinced, for example, that a Stinger destroyed TWA Flight 800 out of JFK. The same is probably true of American Flight 587.

"It is a little-known fact that flight control radar around JFK picked up small missilelike objects in association with Flight 800. This has happened with several other aircraft, on which there were no hits. The missilelike blips on radar were most likely Stingers launched by terrorists, probably from small vessels in Long Island Sound. Because the Stinger is a heat-seeking missile, the only defensive mechanism is chafing. But at such low altitudes, you are extremely vulnerable to being blown out of the sky if you get too close to one of these things." With that, Fox looked at the air wing commander, Captain J. Scott Hampton. "That's about it on the Stinger's technical capabilities. I'll now turn this briefing over to the air boss."

Hampton, tall and imposing for an aviator at about six feet one, took the podium and threw a hard glance at Mohammed.

Maybe they keep staring at me because I'm the squadron leader. Maybe it is just my imagination.

"Gentlemen, we essentially have three problems that affect the military and political dynamics of this hornet's nest we're about to fly into. First, there's the problem of the Stingers that Commander Fox just told you about, and along with that, there's a proliferation of old Soviet-made SA-7s, which are shoulder-fired surface-to-air missiles similar to but not quite as effective as the Stinger.

"Secondly, there's the problem of finding the Scuds with their faster launch platforms. But there's another challenge posed by the Scuds that Commander Fox didn't mention. So far, those Scud warheads have been armed only with conventional ballistics. However, our intelligence reports that a number of the tractor-trailers have biological and chemical agents on board. Needless to say, it would be simple to switch those warheads out at any time." Hampton ran his hand through his hair.

"Which leads us to our third problem." He paused for a sip of water. "The Israelis." His eyes scanned the room.

"Now as you might imagine, the prospect of even an erratic Scud armed with chemical or biological agents makes the Israelis nervous, to say the least. And who can blame them?

"As we all know, the Israeli Air Force boasts some of the best pilots in the world. Capable of outflying any of their Arab neighbors ..."

Right. Only because of conservative Christian Republicans in Congress who seem to have taken up the cause of the Jews for some inexplicable reason.

"... but given the fragile Israeli psyche, that doesn't do a whole lot to calm the population right now. In a word, the Israelis, for psychological reasons, want more visible signs of an American presence." A pause as the air boss swept his eyes across the members of the squadron. "The Israeli government is requesting low overflights not only for military reasons, but to boost morale. So low, in fact"—he paused for another sip of water, then resumed in a slower and more somber tone—"that an Israeli who can read English can read the word *Navy* painted in black on your fuselage." Hampton's gaze swept the faces of the pilots in the room.

"That's why we've called you here this afternoon, gentlemen. We're looking for volunteers. This is dangerous duty. There are enemy Stingers in Israel, brought in by Arab terrorists intent on destroying the Jewish State. While our past record of relative safety in these types of sorties is relatively high, we can no longer say this. You could get shot down. But you will be flying for the cause of peace and doing a personal favor for your commander in chief, the president of the United States." A pause, another sip of water. "Obviously, you don't have to volunteer. No one expects you to. But if we have no volunteers, we will have no choice but to order some of you to fly these missions."

The opportunity for low overflights over Israel would make this job even easier. Surely this is of Allah. "Count me in, Captain," Mo Quasay said, standing.

"Thank you, Commander." Hampton looked around. "Anyone else?"

"I will go too," Lieutenant Hosni Alhad said.

"Very well," Hampton said sternly. "It's a small country. Two planes should be sufficient for now. Those who don't see you directly will see you on Israeli television." Hampton cleared his throat. "The rest of you will be responsible for searching out and destroying Scud launchers in Lebanon, and if necessary, even Syria, which will also be dangerous, as you know. You are not to cross into Syrian airspace, however, without specific authorization. If we need more volunteers, we will ask.

"That is all."

"Attention on deck!"

Two dozen naval aviators snapped to their feet as the captain of the *Truman*, and his entourage, exited the briefing room.

CHAPTER 22

Westbound Interstate 20
Lauderdale County, Mississippi
Mile marker 10

Racing under the stars in a westerly direction along Interstate 20, he set the cruise control at seventy miles per hour to avoid even the remote possibility of being pulled over by a trooper for speeding. The Aerostar had just crossed over the Mississippi state line when Sadat heard a faint moan coming from the heretofore lifeless woman lying handcuffed on the backseat.

His eyes fell on the digital clock on the instrument panel.

10:14 p.m.

Sadat punched on the overhead dome light, then adjusted his rear-view mirror. He saw Lieutenant Diane Colcernian move. Her clothing smelled of mildew.

"Ooooh."

He readjusted his rearview. No headlights, no cars, were anywhere in sight.

As they passed the Kewanee-Toomsuba exit, he tapped the brakes, disengaging the cruise control, then gently steered the van onto the roadside along the long, flat stretch of interstate. He killed his running lights, then reached into the glove compartment for the assortment of drugs and the packet of syringes he'd managed to purchase.

"My hands. Where am I?"

He looked over his shoulder. His prisoner was squinting her eyes at the dome light. Perhaps she would survive, and perhaps he would get her out of the country after all.

"Zack?"

She's delirious.

Sadat unfastened his shoulder harness, then electronically reclined the driver's bucket seat so he would have access to her.

A set of headlights appeared in the distance, maybe a mile down the interstate. The vehicle probably wouldn't stop. No matter if it did; he had a little present for anyone who got too close. He reached down and gripped the Uzi.

Another moan as the vehicle whizzed by, the hum of its wheels against the concrete dipping in pitch as it shot off toward Meridian.

"Oh, my head." She spoke in a painful moan, slurring her words as if drunk.

"Shhhh." He blew across his index finger, shushing her.

"Zack, is that you?"

Carnal thoughts crossed his mind. He could have his way, finish her off, dump her in the woods at the next off ramp, and escape the country.

No, that's not what Allah would have him do. Not now.

She would be more valuable to Allah alive for a while longer.

He fidgeted for a syringe, then jabbed the needle into the back of her thigh. She flinched, moaned again, and then fell back asleep.

Sadat brought the seat back up, buckled himself in, and pressed the accelerator, heading for Meridian, and points beyond.

CHAPTER 23

Navy Trial Service Office
Building 73
32nd Street Naval Station
San Diego, California

Lieutenant Commander Zack Brewer, wearing working khakis and feeling cinderblocks in his stomach, stepped into Captain Rudy's office and came to attention. His eyes saw, but his mind barely registered, the sight of the Aegis cruiser in dry dock at the National Steel and Shipbuilding Company, visible through the window behind the captain's desk, maybe a hundred yards from the NTSO.

"Stand at ease, Zack." Captain Rudy sat behind his large mahogany desk. "You wanted to see me?"

"Yes, sir." Zack looked Rudy in the eyes. "It's about Diane, sir. I haven't heard from her in three days. It's not like her."

"Have a seat, Zack." Rudy gestured toward one of the comfortable chairs ordinarily reserved for more-senior officers.

Zack sat, the thought crossing his mind for a fleeting millisecond that rank has its privileges, that a lieutenant commander enjoys a few more such perks than a lieutenant. That thought was just as instantly overwhelmed by the thought that had driven him to seek this meeting with the captain to begin with.

"Coffee, Commander?" The skipper seemed to relish using the word *commander*, Zack noticed, when addressing him. As if Zack's new rank was Captain Rudy's baby.

"No thank you, sir. I'm fine."

"Well then," Rudy said. "I'm concerned about Lieutenant Colcernian too, Zack. But she *is* on leave."

"Sir, she hasn't returned any of my calls, and her voice mail has been full for two days. It's just not like her, Captain."

Rudy scratched his chin. "Well, she's not under any orders to call in. Now, granted, I'm not comfortable with her being unaccounted for under these circumstances either. But it isn't the first time an officer has decided to slip away for some privacy. After all she's been through, she needs it."

"Yes, I know. I've considered that, Skipper. But I've called her dozens of times, and still no answer. Sir, we've got to do something. We need to get NCIS on this. Maybe the FBI." Zack felt his voice cracking, then took a deep breath. "Sir, with all due respect, in my opinion this is an urgent situation involving the safety and welfare of a fellow naval officer."

Rudy leaned back in his chair, touching his fingers together like a tepee across his chest. "You know, Zack, I have no influence over the FBI." Rudy's gaze focused outside his office window, toward San Diego Bay. "And darn little influence over NCIS, for that matter."

"I understand, Captain. But I could never forgive myself if I didn't ask you to try."

"Hmm." Rudy sat quietly for a few moments, then pressed a button on his telephone.

"Yes, Skipper?"

"Master Chief, I want you to check Lieutenant Colcernian's leave address, let me know what she left, then put in a call and see if anyone's seen her."

"Aye, sir."

A moment later, the speakerphone on Captain Rudy's desk buzzed again. "Captain Rudy."

"Skipper, I've got that info you requested," the master chief said as Zack felt his heart skip a beat.

"What did you find out?" Rudy leaned back in his chair and interlocked his hands over his stomach.

"Sir, Lieutenant Colcernian left an address in Charlottesville, Virginia, the home of a law school classmate, a Jane Morgan Swain. We checked with Miss Swain, and she says she hasn't heard from the lieutenant."

Captain Rudy's gaze met Zack's. "Look, Zack, I know you're concerned. But remember, she maybe just needed some time to herself. Give her one week. If she doesn't show up, that's when we should start getting worried."

"Skipper," Zack said, "I feel like I need to go back east to look for her."

Rudy folded his arms. "Talk about looking for a needle in a haystack ..."

"I understand, sir. But I did cut my leave short. I don't have any contested cases coming up, and ... I guess you're right, sir." Zack let his gaze drift to the sparkling blue waters of San Diego Bay outside Captain Rudy's office window. "I wouldn't know where to start looking."

Rudy stood, which prompted Zack to do the same. He walked around his desk and put his hand on Zack's shoulder. "Zack, she's courageous, bright, and savvy. If anyone can take care of herself in any circumstance, it's Diane Colcernian."

There was the sound of humming tires against asphalt. And then the excruciating sensation of something that felt like a dagger wedged through her brain. The throbbing forced Diane's eyes open. Stars twinkled against a black night canopy, and in an instant, she realized these were not stars associated with pain.

She was being transported somewhere in an ambulance at night. Perhaps she had been in a serious car wreck. Was Zack all right?

"Zack?"

No answer.

"Nurse?"

"Shut up!"

"What?"

"Shut up!" Dome lights came on in the ambulance. Diane squinted, adjusting her eyes. This was no ambulance. A hand lifted a gun from the front seat. "You are now Allah's prisoner." The light went off. The stars reappeared. "We have your lover in captivity. Try anything and he dies."

Council of Ishmael headquarters
Rub al-Khali Desert

How are things progressing, Abdur?" The leader of the Council of Ishmael stood as Abdur Rahman walked into his office for the latest intelligence update.

"Very well, Leader. The *Truman* will be in striking distance within a few hours."

"Excellent." The leader gleefully scratched his semblance of a black goatee. "Listen, Abdur. I want you to pass the word to all our operatives: From noon tomorrow until further notice, no Stinger attacks on Israeli or American aircraft."

"Understand?"

"Yes, Leader," Abdur Rahman said. "It is as you say."

301 North Water Street
Hilton Wilmington Riverside
Wilmington, North Carolina

Sergeant Larry Lineburger had been with the Wilmington Police Department for the better part of thirty years. And for the last ten, he had patrolled the same beat, the historic downtown district along the Cape Fear River and the surrounding area. Wilmington had become a chic tourist destination in the last few years, driven primarily by the bourgeoning motion picture studios that had relocated in the port city from Hollywood because of lower wages, lower taxes, and natural beauty. The downtown area around Water Street had also become quite posh. All of these factors tended to drive down the crime rate, which was fine with Larry.

He'd put in his dues and been shot at more times than he cared to remember. Leave the blood and guts to the younger guys, he decided long ago. Besides, Larry had always had a nose for the investigative side of law enforcement.

So when Sergeant Lineburger drove past the gold LeBaron Avis rental car with District of Columbia license plates for the twentieth time, his investigative nose told him something wasn't right.

Same car?

With D.C. plates?

Not been moved for three days?

Probably drug-related, Lineburger decided. *There's a bunch of drug dealers in D.C. Probably brought some of that stuff down here to sell to the Hollywood types and them young hooligans out at UNCW.*

Lineburger pulled his squad car ahead of the rental car, stopped, and got out. Cupping his hand over his eyebrows to block out the reflection of the afternoon sun, Lineburger peered through the driver's window. Nothing but a legal pad with "Room 442" written on the front. *Looks like a woman's writing.*

He gently pulled up on the door latch. *Open. Do I need a warrant? Hmm. Looks like abandoned property to me. Just trying to determine ownership.*

He sat in the front seat, behind the wheel, and reached for the glove compartment. There was a receipt from Avis.

Received of: LT Diane Colcernian,
$320.00 for Rental of Chrysler LeBaron.
To Be Returned in Five Days.

Larry double-checked the name. How many LT Diane Colcernians could there be in the country? He checked the calendar on his watch. The car was due back yesterday. Larry scratched his chin. Maybe there was a reason, after all, that he had not taken that SBI job.

CHAPTER 24

Aeroflot Flight 305
Descending from 5,000 feet
50 nautical miles east of Tel Aviv

In the back of the plane, Alexander squeezed Yael's hand as the pilot announced in Russian that they had descended to five thousand feet and would be on the ground in fifteen minutes. She smiled at him with the same dazzling sparkle that had danced in her eyes on their wedding day. For other than their wedding day, and aside from the births of their four children, no day had been as exciting as this one.

Three of their children, Anna, Rachel, and Adam, sat in front of them, almost piling on top of each other for a glimpse of the sparkling Mediterranean below. Three-year-old Sol, their youngest, snoozed in the aisle seat beside his mother. Yael leaned over her husband's shoulder, peering down at the great sea, then planted a kiss on his cheek.

"Alexander, I still cannot believe this is happening."

"Believe it, my love," he said. "We are going to Israel." They embraced for a few seconds until Anna and Rachel saw them and giggled.

Alexander blew nine-year-old Anna a kiss, causing his curly-haired doll to giggle even more; then he leaned back and closed his eyes. The pitching whine of the jet increased. His ears popped a few times during descent. A few minutes later, the bump of the wheels on the runway brought his eyes wide open.

"Da bropazhalowitz versus Israel," the Aeroflot flight attendant said. *Welcome to Israel.* Alexander's eyes widened as David Ben Gurion Airport rushed by his window.

"Praise God from whom all blessings flow! Praise him all creatures here below!"

The plane rolled to a stop, and because they were sitting in the back, the Kweskin family had to wait until the other passengers deplaned. Finally, the Kweskins stood and retrieved their bags from the overhead. Alexander led the way, the children sandwiched between their parents. He stepped through the door of the plane into the bright, sunny morning.

He paused at the top of the stairway leading down to the tarmac. He closed his eyes, deeply inhaling the pure oxygen of the Promised Land, which already seemed therapeutic to his soul, far more pristine than the smog of Mogilev.

"Come on, Papa, let's go!" The sweet voice of his daughter Anna caused him to open his eyes again to the sight of the Promised Land, the most beautiful landscape he had ever seen.

"Okay, my sweetie," he said. Anna took his hand and walked down the steps, closer and closer to the concrete. He felt the Promised Land under the soles of his shoes. He fell on his knees, kissed the ground, prayed, and wept.

Office of the Chief
Wilmington Police Department
115 Red Cross Street
Wilmington, North Carolina

I'm telling you, Agent MacGregor, something ain't right about this." Police Sergeant Larry Lineburger spoke through the telephone handset to the young whippersnapper duty agent of the FBI's local office in Raleigh. "All right."

Lineburger looked over at his boss, Police Chief Perry Laymon, and rolled his eyes. "The kid's put me on hold."

Laymon shook his head. "Feds."

"Say again?" Lineburger took a draw from his cigarette. He flicked ashes in the tray. "You want me to repeat again what I already told you twice already?"

Chief Laymon smirked.

"Oh, I see," Lineburger continued, "you've got your supervisor on the other end and he wants to hear this too?" He looked at the chief, who again shook his head and chuckled under his breath.

"Okay, here goes. I was on routine patrol of my regular beat in the riverfront area here in Wilmington, when I noticed what appeared to be an abandoned car. I proceeded to investigate, and I opened the glove compartment for clues ... What? Did I have probable cause?... Look, sir, I already explained that this ain't no drug case, so it really don't matter. Anyway, I found two things. I found a receipt from Avis Rental Car that the car was rented to Lieutenant Diane Colcernian, United States Navy ... That's enough probable cause, ain't it? I mean, how many people do you know with that name?

"How do I know it was really her?" Another drag on the half-burnt cigarette. "'Cause I found a motel receipt for the Hilton Riverside.

"So I got 'em to let me in her room, and I found her official United States Navy uniform hanging in the closet, that's how ... What?... No I didn't find no military ID card." He let out an irritated sigh. "No offense taken, Mack. What I did next was I tried to figure out why she might be in Wilmington. And I figured it might have something to do with the funeral for that Jefferies girl, being that some folks think that bullet was intended for Colcernian. So I called the dead girl's daddy. And get this ..." He took a final drag on the half-lit stub of a cigarette. "Colcernian showed up at the grave. Stood out there in a driving rainstorm, then walked off all by herself. Said she was upset, blaming herself for his daughter's death ... What's that?... No I didn't take no affidavit from him ... Because the man's still mourning his daughter's death, that's why. And his story ain't gonna change. I figured it could wait ... Uh-huh.... Uh-huh ... I appreciate that, Mack." Lineburger hung up the phone.

"What'd they say, Larry?"

"They said they believed us, Chief. They said they was gonna send a task force down here from Raleigh in a helicopter to check it out."

"When are they coming?"

"Now," Lineburger said. "They're gonna comb that cemetery for clues. Said we should rope it off till they get here."

"Good work, Sergeant."

CHAPTER 25

Westbound US 90
78 miles west of San Antonio, Texas

Midmorning

One hand on the steering wheel, Ahmed Sadat glanced over his shoulder. His prized hostage was still sleeping, thanks to the drugs supplied to him by an Islamic pharmacist in Richmond, Virginia.

Cruising along westbound US 90 for the last leg of the trip, at a conservative fifty-five miles per hour, with the Aerostar's air conditioner on full blast to combat the South Texas heat, Ahmed spotted the first mileage sign since bypassing the town of Hondo.

Uvalde — 5
Del Rio — 75

By the grace of Allah, he should be at the border in a couple of hours. After that, he would feel safer.

So far, his only concern had been stopping for gas. He paid cash to avoid an electronic paper trail. That meant leaving her in the car, alone. But the interior shades he had rigged across the back windows had kept her well hidden.

When they had arrived at San Antonio, he briefly considered taking Interstate 35 South directly to Laredo. The interstate posed less of a risk of being stopped. But he headed instead to Del Rio, where he had heard the border crossing was easier.

Two more hours to safety.

Feeling a bit bored now, he turned on the van's radio.

"We interrupt our regular programming to bring you this special report from Washington."

Ahmed reached down to turn up the volume.

"This is Tom Miller in Washington. Navy Lieutenant Diane Colcernian, one of the two Navy JAG officers responsible for the prosecution of three Islamic navy chaplains convicted by a navy court-martial and sentenced to death, is missing.

"According to the F.B.I., Lieutenant Colcernian's car was found, apparently abandoned, earlier today in Wilmington, North Carolina, where she is reported to have attended the funeral of the late Maggie Jefferies. Miss Jefferies, a University of North Carolina coed, was shot last week emerging from the Dean Dome following North Carolina's win over Duke. Law enforcement experts believe that the gunman, who remains at large, may have mistaken Miss Jefferies for Lieutenant Colcernian.

"Lieutenant Colcernian was last seen in Wilmington's Oakdale Cemetery, ironically, by Miss Jefferies' father. According to Mr. Jefferies, Lieutenant Colcernian had apparently been at the graveside service for his daughter and was spotted lingering near the grave when a driving rainstorm began. Mr. Jefferies indicated that Lieutenant Colcernian was visibly upset about his daughter's death and seemed to be blaming herself.

"This disappearance comes just three days after the execution of the three Islamic chaplains whom Lieutenant Colcernian, along with lead prosecutor Lieutenant Zack Brewer, prosecuted last year.

"At this point in the investigation, officials are not ready to declare foul play was involved in the lieutenant's disappearance, and there is no known link, at least as of yet, to terrorism.

"The FBI's local office in Raleigh, North Carolina, has been mum on the details of the investigation. That, of course, is expected to change as the investigation unfolds.

"An all-points bulletin has been issued, and law enforcement officials across the nation are instructed to be on the lookout."

Ahmed turned off the radio.

A sheriff's car zoomed by in the opposite direction on US 90. Ahmed instinctively laid his hand on the Uzi lying on the passenger's seat and looked in the rearview, half-expecting to see the squad car tap its brake lights and commence a U-turn. Instead, the car became a speck, disappearing into the distance.

Praise be to Allah!

Now it was becoming clear to him. All of this was unfolding according to Allah's plan. The bullet had been destined not for Diane Colcernian, but rather for Maggie Jefferies, so that at the appointed moment in time, during the heavy thunderstorm that Allah had sent at Maggie Jefferies's funeral, he would be able to personally capture, alive, the most celebrated American prisoner ever to fall into the hands of an Islamic organization!

Goose bumps crawled all over his arms and up his spine as several cars zipped by in the opposite direction.

In less than two hours, he would disappear across the border, away from the American manhunt, into oblivion.

He pressed the accelerator, thinking about al-Akhma's reaction upon learning that he, Ahmed Sadat, had personally brought this prisoner into the fold.

Perhaps he would become a member of the coveted Council of Twenty.

Perhaps he would become a hero of Islam.

Office of Lieutenant Commander Zack Brewer, JAGC, USN
Navy Trial Service Office
Building 73
32nd Street Naval Station
San Diego, California

Sitting alone in his office, Zack watched the CNN broadcast, live from Wilmington.

A reporter stood in front of Diane's abandoned car, babbling on about Officer Lineburger's brilliant police work. The screen cut to a picture of the lush green cemetery. A female reporter was carrying on about Diane's disappearance. A shot of Maggie Jefferies's tombstone filled the screen. The text superimposed across the bottom declared, "JAG Officer Diane Colcernian last spotted at Oakdale Cemetery, Wilmington, N.C."

Zack flipped off the television and covered his face with his hands, fearing that his worst nightmares were now unfolding.

Why?

Why had he left her at the Officers' Club alone?

He knew it was a horrible idea, and he had tried to tell her.

The image of her face, of her smile as she waved good-bye to him for the last time in the O-Club in Washington, had haunted him for days. As he closed his eyes, that image returned, as vivid as if she were sitting right there with him. He felt sick.

"Dear God, please be with her. Please, may your divine protection be upon her right now, wherever she is. Right now. In Jesus' holy name ..."

The phone rang.

Zack wiped his eyes, took a gulp of cold Dasani bottled water, then picked up the receiver. When he spoke, it was with his military bearing in a voice full of confidence. "Lieutenant Commander Brewer speaking."

"Zack?" The woman's voice on the other end was faint, making his heart leap.

"Diane?"

"No, Zack. It's Wendy. I just heard the news, and I had to call. I know the two of you must have been ... must be close."

Zack did not respond.

"Anyway," she continued, "do you know anything more than what they've said on the news?"

"No. I just heard the radio report myself. I haven't even talked to Captain Rudy yet."

"That's horrible, Zack. Hearing something like this on the radio ... Someone should have called you."

It wouldn't have mattered. Nothing could have lessened the blow to his emotions, his heart, his desperate fears for Diane. Zack rolled his chair away from his desk and thumped his fingers on the armrest. "I shouldn't have left her there alone—"

Wendy cut him off. "This isn't your fault. I was there. Remember? You tried as hard as you could to get her to accept some protection."

"She's so hardheaded," he said, staring blankly out the window.

"And that's who she is, and that's part of what makes her such a good lawyer."

"I've got a few days' leave left. I can be at Reagan National in three hours. Do you need me to come out to San Diego?"

"That's sweet, Wendy, but save your leave for something more worthwhile."

"Are you sure?"

"I'm sure."

"Look, don't give me that invincible, macho stuff, okay? I know how you guys are. You're hurting right now. I'm coming."

"No. Thanks anyway. To be honest, I'm still in shock. I need to be alone a few days to sort things out."

She hesitated. "Okay. But I want you to promise to call me anytime, day or night, if you need somebody to talk to."

"Okay."

Diane estimated thirty minutes had passed since the radio broadcast. Since then, only the sound of whining asphalt. At least her headache was not so splitting anymore. She could think more clearly now. She lay there, pretending to be asleep. Thinking. Something about the broadcast wasn't right. At least they were looking for her. That was a relief. But what was missing?

Zack.

If Zack really had been kidnapped, why nothing about him on the broadcast? Maybe Zack had been abducted and the press wasn't yet aware of it. But that didn't make sense. If they knew she had been kidnapped, surely they would have checked on Zack immediately. Wouldn't they?

Or maybe this goon was lying about Zack to discourage her from making an escape attempt. If he was going to kill her, why hadn't he already? He easily could have killed her and dumped her body somewhere by now.

She opened her eyes. It looked like the goon had tried using duct tape to tape cardboard across the back windows. But from the light coming in through the windshield, and from the cracks in the cardboard, she could tell that wherever they were, it was daylight.

Time to engage this guy.

"I need a bathroom!"

"Shut up!"

"Cram it, goon! I'm not afraid of you or your kind!" *I must have a death wish. I can't believe I said that.*

Silence.

More silence. *Let him make the next statement.*

Maybe five minutes passed.

"I see a barn." He spoke with a Middle Eastern accent. The inflection in his voice was slightly sarcastic. "I'm going to stop there. I will be watching you. Make one move, and you're dead."

A moment later, the back door slid open. Warm, humid air blew in. And then, for the first time, she saw him in full view. He had black hair and dark skin and looked to be slightly short, wearing jeans and a denim shirt. And around his waist hung a holster and a gun ... a nine-millimeter Glock.

He drew his gun and pointed it at her. "Get up."

"My hands and legs are cuffed."

He tossed a key at her. The key bounced off her stomach and fell onto the floorboard just below the seat. "This is for the handcuffs. The leg chains stay on."

"A little help would be nice."

"Facedown into the seat." She felt him tinkering with the cuffs, and then they fell off. "Out of the van. Try anything, and you are a dead woman."

She slipped, feet first, out of the van. Her feet touched the ground. The chains around her ankles were much like the leg chains on prisoners being brought into the courtroom from the brig. Enough slack to walk. Nothing more. Running would be impossible. But her hands were free ...

If she could just get at the gun.

The van was parked behind the barn, nearly hidden by high weeds. Behind the barn was a stand of trees. No civilization was in sight, but in the distance, she heard a few cars zooming by on the main road.

"Over there!"

He kept his distance but kept the gun aimed at her. She contemplated her options. With the chains around her ankles, dashing into the trees would be futile. Perhaps there would be an opportunity when she returned to the van. If she could just wrestle the gun away ...

"Hurry up!"

She waded back through the weeds. Toward the van.

"Faster!"

"If you want faster, then take these chains off my ankles."

No answer. She was near the van now. Maybe ten feet. Another car zoomed by. Unseen. Somewhere in the distance. He stood by the van's sliding door, weapon drawn.

"Get in. Lay facedown on the seat."

She would lunge at his feet. Knock him off balance, grab the gun. She hesitated.

"Move! Inside!"

Now!

Chink-chink.

He worked the bolt action on the pistol. That froze her in her tracks.

Cooperate. For the moment anyway. Try to build trust. This isn't the right time.

Just enough leeway in the chain allowed her to step into the van. She lay facedown on the seat. When he grabbed her wrist to reattach the cuffs, she thought she sensed a gentleness in his touch. Was it her imagination, or was there a smidgen of oxymoronic compassion within this monster? She had read that captors sometimes form an odd bond with the kidnapped. Was this happening now?

Compassion or not, next time they stopped, she would kill him.

CHAPTER 26

Flight Deck
USS Harry S. Truman
Eastern Mediterranean
204 miles SSE of Limassol, Cyprus

Sitting in the cockpit of his powerful F-14 Tomcat, as the flight crew hooked his jet to the giant catapult that would sling his powerful war bird out over the ocean, Lieutenant Commander Mohammed "Mo" Quasay realized his day had finally arrived.

Islamic Glory.

Until now, the top-secret plan was known only to a few persons around the world. Pulling on his helmet, then going through his final instrument check, Mo Quasay wondered how he, a simple man, was here at this time, in the Eastern Mediterranean, on the deck of an American nuclear aircraft carrier, about to launch a strike that would change the history of the world.

Looking down from the cockpit, he watched his enlisted flight crew scramble about on the flight deck, the wind whipping across the deck and fluttering their uniforms. Indeed, he had developed a modicum of affection for these, his men. No, they were not of the Great Faith, and they wouldn't understand what he and Lieutenant Alhad, in the jet behind him, were about to do.

Sure, he had had second thoughts, he reflected, punching the button on the Tomcat's instrument panel that caused the twin-turbine jet engines to slowly start their whining roar. Even still, Allah was in all of this, wasn't he?

Even now, the plan seemed to be unfolding with divine guidance. The attack message had been transmitted to the carrier with clarity. Too much clarity. And though his Muslim brothers had been detained temporarily by Captain Constangy's SEAL team, they had been released. *Praise be to Allah.*

And then Israel had requested low overflights, a mission for which he and Lieutenant Alhad were given the opportunity to volunteer. If they could avoid some overenthusiastic brother with a Stinger who may not have received al-Akhma's command to hold fire, the low overflights would make his job that much easier.

"Navigations system and weapons system check completed, Skipper. All systems go."

This was the voice of his navigator and weapons officer, Lieutenant Mark "Mouse" Price, sitting in the cockpit right behind him. Price was the main reason Mo had felt any reluctance to go through with this plan. He and Price had been in the cockpit together for a long time, had watched one another's backs, and had developed a genuine friendship. Despite the fact that he was an infidel Christian, Price was a family man, with a young wife and two small children back home in Virginia.

The thought of Lieutenant Price's fate made Mo cringe. Still, Price had had all his life to convert to the one true faith. He had not. And according to the teaching of the one true faith, even if we develop affection for our goats, sometimes we must slaughter our livestock for the greater good.

And the Koran and the Hadiths clearly teach that infidel Jews and Christians, whether we like them personally or not, are at the end of the day no greater than livestock.

"Very well, Lieutenant," Mo said into his microphone. "I'll request clearance for takeoff."

"I'm with you, Skipper," Price said cheerfully.

"*Truman*, Viper Leader. All systems clear. Ready for takeoff on your call."

"Roger that, Viper Leader," the *Truman*'s air traffic controller said. "You are clear for takeoff when signaled by the LSO. Godspeed, Commander."

Mo revved up the twin turbofans, then looked down at the LSO, who gave him a thumbs-up. Chalk blocks were removed, and Mo reciprocated the thumbs-up. A huge burst of steam shot up behind the plane, and like a giant rubber band, the giant catapult pushed and then slung the Tomcat down five hundred feet of runway and into the wind.

The jet cleared the carrier, then dropped for a second as Mo gave it full throttle. And then powerful g-forces, like a giant, invisible hand, pushed him back into his seat as the Tomcat rocketed to two thousand feet and began to orbit the carrier until Lieutenant Alhad's plane could be launched. Mo turned and banked. The *Truman* was now a small spec of metal on the surface, pushing a white trail through the aqua-blue waters of the Eastern Mediterranean.

"Viper Leader, Viper 2. We've cleared the boat. Be right with you," Lieutenant Hosni Alhad announced.

"Roger that, Viper 2," Mohammed responded. "We're on the lookout for you."

A moment later, the long, sleek twin-turbo F-14, with the word *NAVY* painted on the fuselage, appeared just to the left of Mohammed's cockpit.

"I see you, Viper 2. Let's rock and roll."

"Roger that, Leader."

Jaffa Gate
Western entrance
Old City of Jerusalem

The taxi driver, who had previously identified himself as a Russian immigrant to Israel, pulled over in front of the gate through the walls of the Old City. "Okay, this is the Jaffa Gate, my friend. Walk straight through this gate; follow the crowd for about seven blocks. You will be at the Wall in ten to fifteen minutes, depending on how fast your children can walk."

"Shalom to you, my brother." Alexander shoved a few of his remaining shekels into the driver's hand.

"Come, Yael, children, let us enter the Old City!" Alexander said excitedly.

Yael sat a little too long for his comfort in the backseat of the taxi, wiping crumbs from little Sol's mouth with a rag.

"The Temple Mount has been there thousands of years," Yael said. "It isn't going anywhere in the next fifteen minutes."

Adam, Rachel, and Anna piled out of the cab and up onto the curb.

"Come on, Mama," nine-year-old Anna called.

"Yeah, I want to see the temple!" This from five-year-old Adam.

"The temple isn't there, dummy," seven-year-old Rachel said. "It is the temple mountain we are going to see."

"No, not the *mountain*," Anna said to her younger sister. "It is the *mount*."

"*Eezveeneetzia*," Rachel retorted. *Excuse me.* Then she looked at her mother and said, "Come on, Mama, we want to see the mount."

"*Harasho, harasho*," Yael said. *Okay, okay.* She finished her dabbing and stepped out of the car. "Let us go to the temple!"

They took hands, all of them, and together stepped through the gate to the Old City, turning up the sunbaked streets, taking in the vibrant sites of Zion as they walked.

International Bridge spanning the Rio Grande
Del Rio, Texas – Ciudad Acuña, Mexico
United States – Mexico border

The Aerostar came to a dead stop on the International Bridge over the Rio Grande. On one side was the United States of America; on the other, Mexico.

It was not supposed to happen this way. Delays crossing the bridge were common on the other side. Not on this side.

Could the Americans already have gotten to the Mexicans? Were they searching vehicles crossing the border?

Through the hazy fumes spewing from the old station wagon creeping forward just in front of him, Ahmed gazed across the river at the rolling limestone bluffs dotted with cactus high on the Mexican side.

He had moved his drugged passenger from the backseat to the very back section of the van, where curtains made her visual detection impossible. He had slipped his Uzi under the driver's seat.

The Mexicans weren't heavily armed, he was told, and he was fully prepared to shoot his way through the border if he needed to. But if he did, an unacceptable level of commotion would jeopardize his escape. He hoped it would not come to that.

The station wagon's brake lights went off, and it inched forward. Ahmed followed suit, inching the Aerostar forward. More brake lights.

Then a brown-skinned Mexican guard stepped out of the guard booth and stopped the wagon.

Perhaps I should just ignore him if he stops me.

The guard waved the station wagon through, then held up his palm to stop the Aerostar.

Ahmed reached down and felt the cold steel grip of the Uzi. He flipped off the safety switch and slid it a little farther under the seat.

By instinct, his foot came down on the brake pedal.

"Hola, amigo," the Mexican border guard said, peering curiously through the window.

CHAPTER 27

Altitude 500 feet
15 nautical miles east of the Israeli coastline
Eastern Mediterranean

With the sparkling waves of the Mediterranean racing below him in a blur, and with Lieutenant Hosni Alhad's Tomcat still flying off his left wingtip, Mohammed saw, for the first time, the coastline of Palestine. Though he felt reluctant about his mission, the glorious sight of this Israeli-occupied Islamic holy land provided an unexpected jolt of courage.

Blessed be the prophet Mohammed—peace be upon him.

Dropping his airspeed to a modest two hundred fifty miles per hour, he reached into his holster and pulled out his sidearm, a nine-millimeter Ruger.

"Traffic at three o'clock, Skipper," Lieutenant Mouse Price said through his intercom headset from the back of the bubbled cockpit. "Looks like a civilian Beechcraft."

"I see him, Mouse," Mohammed lied. He activated the automatic pilot and then worked the action on the nine-millimeter. "Viper 2, be advised civilian traffic at three o'clock."

No response.

He looked out to the left at Hosni's jet. Hosni's flight officer, Lieutenant Ricky "Pip" Davis, an African-American father of three from Charlotte, North Carolina, was slumped over inside the cockpit.

"Skipper, does Pip look all right to you?" Mouse sounded worried.

Mohammed deactivated his pistol's safety. "Sun's in my eyes. I can't really see him." Another lie. "I don't want to break radio silence again. Why don't you get out your binoculars and see what's going on?"

"Aye, sir."

Mohammed took another look at the Palestinian coastline, now growing more visible by the second.

May the will of Allah be done!

He reached around the jump seat and pointed the gun at the chest of a wide-eyed Mouse Price, who sat directly behind him.

"Commander!"

Mohammed squeezed the trigger. Even with his helmet on, he could hear the *bang* reverberate through the cockpit over the roar of the jets.

Another squeeze. Then another. One of the snub-nosed bullets ripped right through Price's embroidered name tag. He slumped over, his eyes still wide open, blood now soaking through the front of his olive-drab flight suit.

He looked at Hosni and made a slicing motion across his neck. Hosni did the same. He too had carried out Allah's will.

Mohammed gave Hosni a thumbs-down, indicating lower altitude. They dropped to two hundred fifty feet from the water, and then Mohammed armed his sidewinder missiles.

And then set a course directly to Jerusalem.

International Bridge spanning the Rio Grande
Del Rio, Texas – Ciudad Acuña, Mexico
United States – Mexico border

ola." Ahmed returned the greeting, faking a smile.

"You Norte Americano?"

"Si, señor."

"You do not look Norte Americano." The guard fixed his black eyes on the empty back seat.

"Si, yo Norte Americano." Ahmed resisted the temptation to go for the Uzi.

"Why do you visit Mexico, señor?"

Because I'm an Arab terrorist, you fool. And I'm getting ready to blow your head off if you don't let me pass. "Just a tourist. Never been."

"A tourist?" The Mexican raised a suspicious eyebrow. "I don't see no bags."

"Not planning to stay long." Ahmed inched his hand toward the Uzi.

"You have identification?"

"By all means."

Ahmed reached into his back pocket for his wallet and pulled out a fake Virginia State driver's license identifying him as Samuel Shalome of 2822 Indian River Road in Chesapeake. He handed the guard the license, which was wrapped in a green photograph of Benjamin Franklin, courtesy of the United States Mint.

"Ahh." The guard's black eyes twinkled. "Mucho gracias, señor." The Mexican stuffed the hundred-dollar bill into his pocket and returned the license. "Welcome to Mexico." He stepped back and motioned the Aerostar to pass.

Wailing Wall
Old City of Jerusalem

The Temple Mount, with its despicable golden Islamic Dome, was visible for the last few blocks of their walk. But it wasn't until they reached the end of the street that they got a clear view of the Western Wall — the last remaining vestige of Solomon's holy temple, still standing proudly after three thousand years.

Oh, how beautiful it was! The sight of priests bowing and praying. Of boys from America having their bar mitzvahs in the late afternoon sunlight. Pigeons clucked across the courtyard as a flock of white doves flew by.

Surely in this place, Jehovah God still dwelt.

"Stay here with the children." He looked into his wife's eyes. "I need to go there alone for a moment."

Yael nodded her head with that beautiful, angelic smile of hers. And then, on an uncontrollable impulse, he rushed like a child to the wall, barely noticing a host of other black-robed, black-yarmulked Jewish men standing and kneeling, wailing to the Lord God.

He put his hands on it. He caressed it as if it were the most precious stone God had ever created. And he wept.

"Oh my Lord and my God," he cried. "The Father of Abraham, Isaac, and Jacob. You have brought me and my family to this holiest of sites on the earth. All praises to your holy name for your unending mercy and your everlasting goodness.

"Never take us again from this place, oh Father. Never allow us, your chosen people, to ever again be dispersed from Israel."

Alexander dropped to his knees, his tears still flowing. "Oh Father, hasten the day when your temple shall be restored. If it be your will, oh Father, let that day be in my lifetime."

A cool breeze whipped through the courtyard, refreshing Alexander's face.

"Hasten the day, oh Father, when Messiah will come."

"But Messiah already has come, my friend." Alexander turned around and, through tear-blurred eyes, saw a Jewish-looking man in a white suit. "And he shall come again."

Alexander looked down, reached into his pocket for the prayer he had written back in Mogilev. He found it, pulled it out, and looked back over his shoulder. The man in white was gone.

No matter. He had a task to perform now. It was a task he had promised God, to deliver his written prayer into the crevices of the holy wall. Gently, tenderly, he kissed the folded paper, sliding it into a crack near the ground.

A whistling sound caught his attention. Almost like a kettle blowing steam, it got louder, louder. The whistling turned into a loud scream. The ground trembled.

Alexander covered his ears.

Boom! Boom! Boom!

Screams filled the air. People scattered and dove. Debris rained as if from heaven. The ground shook. Alexander looked to the sky as two fighter jets, with the word *NAVY* painted in black, roared overhead.

"Alexander! Alexander!"

His wife's screams broke through the cacophony, piercing his heart even before he turned to see her cradling Anna's bleeding body in her arms.

Mohammed banked the F-14 to get a visual damage assessment. Black smoke billowed from the top of the Temple Mount into the deep blue late-afternoon Jerusalem sky. It appeared their mission was accomplished. He banked back to the right, looked up, and saw Hosni again on his wingtip, giving him a thumbs-up. Mohammed reciprocated, pointed the jet toward Syria, and hit the afterburners.

The Tomcat shot like a rocket, screaming over the tops of Jerusalem houses and buildings, clearing the city, streaking over rocky, mountainous regions, and finally clearing Israeli airspace.

Within twenty minutes of crossing into Syrian airspace, Mohammed was over the designated drop zone. He set the automatic pilot on a course toward Baghdad, where the plane would most likely be easily shot down, at this low altitude, by Iraqi air defenses.

Mohammed punched the eject button. The emergency ejection rockets in the cockpit shot the seat into the air; then the chute deployed. He looked around. Another white parachute, maybe a half mile away, floated down toward the sandy, rocky surface.

In a few moments, he would be rescued by COI forces operating inside Syria. He would become a hero of the New Islamic Republic.

CHAPTER 28

The Oval Office
The White House
Washington, D.C.

The president of the United States sat near the Oval Office fireplace, having tea with the British ambassador, when his chief of staff came barging in.

"Excuse me, Mr. President." Wally Walsh strode purposefully across the royal-blue rug with the presidential seal embroidered on it. "Pardon the interruption, Mr. Ambassador"—he gave the Brit a quick glance, then looked back to the president—"but this is an absolute emergency."

"My apologies, Mr. Ambassador." The commander in chief rose and followed Wally Walsh's very rapid footsteps out of the Oval Office.

"Wally, what's up?" The president's stomach knotted when he saw the ashen look on his chief of staff's face.

"Mr. President, there's been an attack on Israel."

Lord, please don't let this be nuclear, chemical, or biological. "Out with it, Wally. What kind of attack?"

"An attack on the Temple Mount in Jerusalem, sir."

"What the ..." Mack Williams stared at the ornate ceiling. The news numbed his brain. A wave of fire flashed through his chest. He would take decisive action. Immediately. He punched the wall. "We've gotta retaliate. We must show our support for Israel. Who did this, Wally?"

"Apparently we did, sir."

"Come again?"

"Israeli intelligence reports that two U.S. Navy F-14 Tomcats swooped in at treetop level and launched a missile attack."

A foreboding knot twisted the president's stomach. "How can this be?"

"I don't know, Mr. President."

"Are they right?"

"Details are still sketchy, sir. But eyewitnesses are apparently corroborating this information."

Mack hesitated. "Convene the National Security Council, Wally. We may have just started World War III."

"Yes, Mr. President."

Syrian Desert
Approximately 200 miles east of Damascus
Near the Iraqi border

Over here!" Mohammed yelled to Hosni. Both had just floated to the earth like feathers, three hundred yards apart. Hosni waved back, extricated himself from his parachute, then started jogging toward Mohammed.

"Where are they?" he panted.

"They will be here, my brother. This is why they instructed us to bail out here. It will make it easier for them to find us. Here." Mohammed handed him his canteen.

Hosni took four gulps, then handed it back. "I hope you are right."

"Surely Allah would not have allowed us to come this far, to have all this success, to open the doors as he has, only to leave us stranded."

Hosni wiped the sweat off his forehead. "I hope you are right, Skipper." He swiped his hand across his brow again. "I surely do not wish to spend the night out here."

Mohammed shaded his eyes and glanced at the sun, which was descending but still bright enough to give them full daylight.

"Maybe a couple of hours of daylight left," he said. "We've done everything on our checklist, Hosni. We've left our chutes out for increased visibility from the sky. The Council knew where we would be bailing out. They will search for us in private planes, then send a chopper to evacuate us. We were selected by al-Akhma for this mission. They will not let us fall into enemy hands. The information we possess is too valuable."

Mohammed's lecture failed to mitigate Hosni's fearful expression. "Yes. You're right. Focus on the game plan."

How ironic, thought Mohammed; Hosni's enthusiasm about this mission had known no bounds; now he was close to panic.

"Here. Drink some more water before you start getting delirious on me." Mohammed again thrust the canteen at his fellow Arab-American pilot.

"Do you hear something?" Hosni said after the first gulp.

A low roar came from the direction of the distant horizon. The roar crescendoed. "Sounds like jets."

They turned toward the sound, and then, like lightning bolts from out of nowhere, two delta-shaped fighter jets shot directly overhead from the west, maybe five hundred feet off the deck, streaking over the desert toward Iraq.

"Were those what I thought they were?" Hosni asked.

I hope not. "What did you think they were?"

"Sure looked like F-15s to me."

Bingo. "No way they could be F-15s. The Syrians don't have any. They're still using MiG-21s."

"That's probably what they are," Hosni said, as if trying to convince himself. "MiG-21s. Very similar in design to the Eagle anyway. Look, Commander. They're turning around."

Sure enough, the twin-turbofan jets were making a huge loop out over the desert.

"Maybe they saw our parachutes," Hosni said as the jets finished their loop.

"Maybe."

The jets came roaring in, this time dropping their altitude to maybe two hundred feet off the desert floor. The stranded pilots covered their ears as the jets roared directly overhead, so close this time that there was no mistaking them for anything other than F-15s.

A light blue Star of David was painted on their fuselages.

CHAPTER 29

Council of Ishmael headquarters
Rub al-Khali Desert

Leader, Leader!" Abdur Rahman barreled into Hussein al-Akhma's office so abruptly that the leader's two black-bereted bodyguards, each flanking the large desk, instinctively drew their weapons.

"Put your weapons away," al-Akhma ordered. "What is it, Abdur?"

"It is Islamic Glory, my leader! And it is a smashing success. You must turn on your television."

Hussein al-Akhma was not used to taking orders from anybody, not even his trusted number two. But under these circumstances, he overlooked his subordinate's well-intentioned insolence and complied by punching the remote control on his desk.

The image of CNN's Tom Miller materialized on the screen.

"This is Tom Miller at the White House. Shocking news is coming out of Israel at this very moment with profound national security implications. United States Navy warplanes have launched a missile attack against the third holiest site in all of Islam, the Dome of the Rock.

"According to witnesses and Israeli radar, two navy F-14 Tomcat jets, based on the aircraft carrier USS *Harry S. Truman*, while flying routine reconnaissance over Israel at the request of the Israeli government, swooped down low over Jerusalem and launched at least three precision-guided Sparrow missiles at the Dome.

"The death count is uncertain. But dozens of Muslim pilgrims were in the Dome worshiping, and many are believed to be dead.

"There is no explanation for why this happened. But the White House has issued a terse statement calling the attack a 'grave mistake and one that was not in any way planned or condoned by the United States. We are still gathering the facts underlying this tragedy,' White House Chief of Staff Wally Walsh said in a written statement, 'and we will announce the results of our investigation and take strong action in the very near future.'

"That explanation, however, is not sitting well in Islamic capitals. In Cairo, Damascus, Riyadh, Tripoli, Amman, and Teheran, not only are official condemnations flowing from each of those governments, but pandemonium is erupting in the streets, with thousands expressing unrestrained anger at the United States ..."

He hesitated, adjusting his earpiece. "What's that?

"I understand that we now have live footage, courtesy of an Israeli traffic helicopter, of the billowing, smoldering site atop the Temple Mount."

The screen switched to an aerial view of the Temple Mount, with black smoke rising into the Jerusalem sky. Miller spoke over the rotary sound of the chopper's blades.

"Okay, we have this live picture of the Temple Mount in Old Jerusalem. The smoke and flames you see rising from the site that up until about thirty minutes ago was the third holiest site in all of Islam, the golden dome, also known as the Dome of the Rock.

"According to Islamic legend, it's from here that Mohammed ascended to Allah, sometime around AD 600, which explains why it was held out as such a holy site by Muslims worldwide."

Miller paused, leaving only the sound of the chopper's rotor blades and the incredible scene of smoke and fire.

"Unbelievable."

The screen switched back, partially, to Miller, with the left side of the screen remaining on the Israeli helicopter's live feed.

"I understand our staff has found three distinguished guests to join us for some initial impressions of what we are seeing. From Capitol Hill, Senator Jarrett Lettow, Republican of California, is a member of the Senate Foreign Relations Committee; from Georgetown University, Professor Fadl Allah Bandar, Professor of Islamic Studies and a native of Syria; and from SARD headquarters in Chicago, we are joined by the civil rights activist Reverend JamesOn Barbour."

Live pictures of Miller, Lettow, Bandar, and Barbour were stacked on top of one another, like a totem pole, on the right side of the screen as the smoldering Dome dominated the left.

"We'll start with you, Senator Lettow. What's your reaction to what you're seeing right now?"

Lettow hesitated.

"Tom, you best described this a moment ago. Shocking beyond belief. Having said that, however, I would like to remind the American people that we don't have all the facts here. In fact, we really don't know why this happened. While this was considered to be a holy site by Muslims, it is premature and irresponsible, in my judgment, for anyone, including the foreign governments that you mentioned, to condemn the United States. I can say with confidence that whatever happened here was not sanctioned by the U.S. government. That's not the way we do business, Tom."

"Professor Bandar," Miller asked, "as a native Middle Easterner, and as a person of Islamic faith, what does this tragic sight mean to you and to persons of your faith?"

"Tom," Bandar started slowly, deliberately, "I'm numb right now. When the shock subsides, there will be grieving and then anger."

Miller continued. "Professor, is there any way that you can help someone who is not Islamic to see and understand what we are seeing right now?"

"Tom, this is the most shocking thing I have seen since your Twin Towers were attacked on 9/11. And in many ways," he said somberly, "it is even more shocking. How do I help Americans to understand this? To Americans, this would be like watching the national capitol, or perhaps the White House, burn to the ground. That's how important the Dome of the Rock is to Islam."

"A most sobering analogy, Professor."

"Sobering, but accurate."

"Reverend JamesOn Barbour," Miller said, "you've been an outspoken critic of this administration's war on terror. Do you agree with Senator Lettow that we should withhold judgment?"

Barbour was dressed in his trademark khaki short-sleeve shirt, like a game hunter on an African safari. "Well, you know, Tom," he replied, "I've always said it is not might which maketh right. It is right which gives us the right to use might." Barbour was animated, appearing to come close to spitting as he talked.

"Jesus saith, 'Peace be upon you.' And Mohammed saith, 'Let there be peace.' And so at times like this, *all* God's children from *all* religions should come together and strive for peace. May peace be upon our

Muslim brothers who may have lost their lives in that Dome of the Rock today."

"But, Reverend," Miller persisted, "my question was, do you agree with Senator Lettow that we should withhold judgment?" On half of the split screen, Israeli helicopter cameras showed the Jerusalem fire department spraying water onto the Temple Mount.

"You know, Tom," Barbour spat, "Jesus saith, 'Judge not, that ye be not judged.' So it is not for me to judge this administration. God will judge this administration, Tom. God knows their motives. It does seem, however, that ever since 9/11, Republican presidents have sought excuses to retaliate against Islam. Has this happened today? I want to know."

"That's irresponsible, Reverend—" Senator Lettow fumed.

"Hold on, Senator," Miller interrupted. "This question is for Reverend Barbour. Are you suggesting this attack was not accidental, that it was a deliberate, calculated, American response against Islam in retaliation for 9/11?"

"Tom. Tom!" Lettow broke in.

"Hold on, Senator," Miller said. "Let's let Reverend Barbour clarify."

"You know, Tom," Barbour spat again, "another great African American, Mr. Johnny Cochrane, once said, 'If the glove don't fit, you must acquit.' And right now, it looks to me like the glove fits."

"Tom," Lettow cut in, "I'd like to respond to that."

"Senator, I'll give you a chance to respond, but first we've got a live feed from our CNN cameras in Cairo with our Cairo correspondent, Anna Katrova. Are you there, Anna?"

The television switched to the image of a massive boulevard, teaming with thousands of angry Egyptians shouting in the streets, shaking their fists in the sky, burning effigies of President Williams, and burning the American flag.

"Yes, Tom. I'm here. Although I don't know how much longer this angry crowd will let us broadcast. They're well aware that CNN is an American news organization.

"This crowd began pouring in the streets only minutes after news broke of the attack. This is mayhem to say the least. Already thousands are on the streets, some weeping at the loss of the holy Islamic mosque. But mostly the cry is 'Death to America,' over and over again. And it appears for the moment that any goodwill the United States has built up over the years with Egypt, at least if this crowd is any indication, is gone.

"Anna Katrova, CNN, Cairo."

"And this seems to be the case from other Middle Eastern capitals as well," Tom Miller said, his face now filling the screen. "We have a live report from CNN's Adrienne Lippenour in Damascus."

CNN's attractive, Lebanese-born Middle-Eastern correspondent appeared on the screen.

"Tom, the situation here in Damascus is utter chaos. Massive outbursts of wailing can be heard through the streets as Muslims express their grief. Guns are being fired indiscriminately into the air in rage, another practice unique to the Islamic world. Reports are trickling in of pedestrians injured, a few killed, by bullets falling back to the earth and striking people on the head.

"The government, after condemning the attack—the *American* attack as it was called—is calling for women and children to stay indoors, as widespread ransacking is now beginning. The situation is dangerous on the streets, but the government's call for restraint has been ignored. Thousands of Syrians poured into the streets anyway.

"An angry mob is now gathered around the United States embassy here in Damascus, throwing bricks into the courtyard and demanding that the ambassador come out and meet with them. So far, no word from Ambassador Ari Malone, but the situation at the embassy looks dangerous, and frankly, it does not appear that the Syrian government is willing or even able to protect it, should that mob try storming the gates.

"Adrienne Lippenour, CNN, Damascus. Back to you, Tom."

"Praise be to Allah!" Hussein al-Akhma blurted, clicking off the television. "His plan is working."

"You are a genius, Leader," Abdur said reverently. "All the Arab governments are furious with the Americans, Muslim brothers are pouring into the streets, and even the Americans are fighting amongst themselves."

"The victory is Allah's," Hussein shot back. "But now, the split between America and those moderate traitors who call themselves Islamic will be irreparable. There will be, finally, a glorious political opportunity to consolidate the Arab States into a united Islamic superpower."

"With you as its leader," Abdur said.

"Yes," al-Akhma said. "If it be Allah's will." He stared at Abdur and in a suddenly snappish tone demanded, "What of the pilots who did this? Have they been detained?"

"Leader, they bailed out over eastern Syria as instructed. Our small planes are searching for them now. It should be only a few hours."

"Assad has agreed not to interfere?"

"Yes, Leader. Through our back channels, we have secured promises that the Assad administration will not interfere with, nor ask any questions about, any Council of Ishmael operations in their Eastern frontier with Iraq."

Hussein walked around his desk and slapped Abdur on the back. "We should have a drink to celebrate the end of American involvement in the Middle East. Don't you agree?"

"I am honored, Leader, to drink with you to celebrate this momentous historic occasion."

Syrian Desert
Approximately 200 miles east of Damascus
Near the Iraqi border

Lieutenant Commander Mohammed "Mo" Quasay cupped his hand against his forehead and gazed across the barren desert toward the west.

The sun was low, an orange ball setting over the direction from which they had flown. Three small single-engine planes had passed overhead, one coming in low and wagging its wings, the prearranged signal indicating that they had been spotted.

Other than that, nothing.

"To our knees, Hosni. Let us beseech Allah for his protection." He hoped the call to prayer would soothe Hosni Alhad's nerves. The junior officer had been shaking and talking of dying. He thought about ordering the lieutenant to surrender his firearm.

"Yes, Commander. Prayer is in order," Hosni said.

They fell to their knees on the desert floor, in the sand, facing Mecca. They had lifted groans of supplication to Allah for about fifteen minutes when they heard the first sound of freedom.

"Do you hear that, Hosni?"

The *thwock-thwock-thwock* was more pronounced now.

"Allah always provides our needs," Hosni said, smiling.

"Get ready for glory, my brother."

"Look!" Hosni pointed. "There it is."

The large helicopter, painted black with no markings or insignia, came skimming across the desert, hovered at a position about fifty yards from the two pilots, then gently feathered down to the surface.

"Looks like a Huey," Hosni said. "I thought the Council owned Russian-made choppers."

"The Council has enough money to buy anything they want on the black market, my brother. And hundreds of Hueys are available on the black market." Mohammed stood, and Hosni followed as the chopper's engines shut down. "Come on. Let's catch a ride to our new home."

The fighter pilots started toward the chopper as the side door slid open. In the long shadows of dusk, it was too dark to see inside. But there was no visibility problem when four soldiers, wearing camouflaged uniforms and carrying submachineguns, piled out and pointed their weapons at the pilots. Four more piled out after the first wave.

"Israeli Special Forces!" a voice shouted. "Move and you are dead."

CHAPTER 30

Situation Room
The White House
Washington, D.C.

The National Security Council was created by Congress in 1947 as part of the Executive Office of the President, consisting of the vice president, the secretaries of state and defense, the director of the central intelligence agency, the chairman of the Joint Chiefs of Staff, and of course, the president's national security director.

Mack Williams had not called an emergency meeting of the Council since he had been president, not even to discuss last year's infiltration of the U.S. Navy Chaplain Corps by radical Islamic imams. He'd hoped to finish his two terms without having to convene the Council in emergency session.

But now, with the UN Security Council about to be called into emergency session, with governments around the globe condemning the United States for what was seemingly an overt attack on Islam, and with the Middle East literally about to explode, the president had no choice but to summon the group on short notice.

"Be seated," President Mack Williams said as he entered the room. He tossed his jacket over the back of the big black-leather chair at the end of the table. Seated on the other three sides of the massive table were members of his National Security Council along with guests, experts, who might shed light on the current crisis. "All right. I want to know what happened, and I want to know now."

Cynthia Hewitt, his national security advisor, spoke first. "If I may begin, Mr. President."

"Sure, go ahead, Cyndi."

"Sir, here's what we know. At approximately 1600 hours, Jerusalem time, this afternoon, two F-14 combats, U.S. planes, based off the USS *Harry S. Truman*, did in fact fire two sidewinder missiles and one harpoon missile into the Dome of the Rock. These attacks effectively leveled the Dome.

"These planes were in fact cleared to fly over Israel at low altitudes—the Israeli government had requested such overflights by American warplanes as a means of calming continued Israeli fears about hostile Syrian intentions. So the planes were supposed to be where they were.

"After they fired the missiles," she continued, "both planes headed on a northwesterly course, crossing over the tip of Lebanon and then into Syria before disappearing from radar."

"Did they land?"

"We don't know, Mr. President." This was Admiral John F. Ayers, the chairman of the Joint Chiefs of Staff. "We do know that the Israelis scrambled two F-15s to follow their course, but you know how the Israelis are. You don't get much information, even if you are their biggest benefactor."

"But why?" The president pounded his fist on the table. "Were these pilots Jewish? Did they have an ax to grind with the Muslims?"

"I may be able to shed some light on that, Mr. President," Secretary of Defense Erwin Lopez said.

"What do you have, Erwin?"

"Sir, actually, we've checked with the navy, and not only were the two pilots not Jewish, but they were *Muslim*."

"This is getting stranger," the president said. "No Muslim in his right mind would attack that place. What about the NFOs on each of those Tomcats?"

"Both Christian, Mr. President. Lieutenant Mark Price and Lieutenant Pip Davis. Sort of average naval aviators, Mr. President. No apparent ax to grind."

"With due respect, Mr. President"—the national security advisor leaned forward intently—"it is *Muslims* who in recent times have a history of blowing up buildings. Not Christians."

"I understand that, Cyndi, but this was their building."

"Mr. President," Lopez continued, "we are going to scrutinize the psychological profiles of the pilots and NFOs. We are also interviewing squadron members and other personnel on the *Truman* to determine if anything unusual was going on with these officers before their flights."

An aide to Secretary of State Robert Mauney stepped into the room and spoke to the secretary. A moment later, Mauney nodded apologetically to the secretary of defense, then to the president. "Excuse me, Mr. Secretary, Mr. President ...?"

"You have something for us, Mr. Secretary?"

"Yes, Mr. President. We've just received a communiqué from our embassy in Tel Aviv. It appears that a commando team of Israeli Special Forces has flown into Syria and captured the two pilots of those F-14s."

This announcement brought a stir of whispers around the table.

"The Israelis," the secretary of state continued, "have announced their intentions to prosecute these guys for their illegal attack on Israel."

"You sure about this, Secretary Mauney?" the president asked.

"Yes, sir."

"Mr. President." Secretary of Defense Lopez leaned forward.

"Recognize the secretary of defense."

"Sir, no matter what they've done, or no matter why they've done it, these guys are United States Navy pilots. The navy has jurisdiction over them, and if they're going to be prosecuted, the navy should prosecute." Lopez cut his eyes to Cyndi Hewitt, who met his gaze and nodded. "The Israelis don't have a right to hold them unless they're prisoners of war, and we aren't at war with Israel.

"Besides," Lopez continued, "if we are going to find out the reasons for this travesty, we need full access to our pilots."

"Agreed, Mr. President," the secretary of state said.

"I too agree," the head of the National Security Council said.

"Do we have a consensus then?" The president's gaze swept the table. "We are going to demand—strike that—we are going to *formally request* that the Israelis turn these pilots over to the United States for charges and possible prosecution.

CHAPTER 31

Bikur Holim Hospital
Jerusalem

Get somebody up here who speaks Russian!" the attending physician, Dr. Lawrence Berman, called out. "I think there's an orderly on the second floor who just emigrated a couple of years ago." Two minutes later, a nurse entered the emergency room with the Russian-speaking orderly.

"I need you to translate for me," the doctor said in Hebrew. "Are you up to it?"

"Yes, Doctor. Anything you need."

"Good. Follow me."

They stepped through the swinging double doors, turned left down a main corridor, then passed through another door, over which was written in Hebrew and English, "Family Waiting Area."

A man in his late forties stood when he saw the doctor. His worried brown eyes seemed enormous in his sunken face. He wore an unkempt black beard and ragged clothes. A plain woman in a worn dress, her eyes red rimmed, pushed herself up heavily to stand beside him. Their three children remained seated, their eyes wide and fearful.

The man blurted something in Russian that the doctor didn't understand.

"He say, 'How is my daughter?'" the orderly said.

"Tell him that his daughter suffered severe head wounds from shrapnel and that there was great loss of blood."

The orderly translated, and Alexander Kweskin, his brows contorted, tears filling his eyes, again blurted something at the doctor that he didn't understand.

"He say," the orderly said, "'Is my daughter okay? She is my first-born, Doctor. We just came to Israel. She have to live. Will she live?'"

Doctor Goldstein hesitated, looking deeply into the man's eyes. This cup he wished he could pass to another. But he could not.

"Tell him ... tell him I am very sorry, but her injuries were too severe. We did everything we could, but I am afraid she is gone."

A look of dread crossed the orderly's face, but he nodded to the doctor. Then slowly, in a sympathetic voice, he began to translate.

Alexander Kweskin's face turned deathly pale. *"Etta nee Pravda!"* he whispered, then dropped to his knees, sobbing. *It is not true!*

"Nyet. Pazhalsta! Ne maya kraseeva Anna!" Yael Kweskin joined her husband on the floor, clinging to him, heaving, sobbing. *No, please, not my beautiful Anna!*

Goldstein nodded his thanks to the orderly. "I'll stay with them. Please, go find a rabbi."

"Yes, Doctor."

Israeli cabinet meeting
Emergency session
Government building
Jerusalem

I cannot believe the audacity of the imperial Americans!" Prime Minister Daniel Rothstein stormed. The prime minister read the communiqué again and then slammed his fist on the table. Still fuming, he picked it up, peering out at the eighteen other members. "This message has just been delivered to me from the president of the United States.

Dear Mr. Prime Minister,

At this hour of crisis and peril, the United States government and the American people join with the good people of Israel in mourning for the perilous and inexplicable attacks which occurred earlier today in Jerusalem.

While the facts and circumstances concerning the cause and motive for this senseless destruction are unclear, one thing is clear, which I wish to assure you of in no uncertain terms:

Even though it appears that American military warplanes and missiles were used in this attack, be assured that this despicable attack was not ordered, suggested, or sanctioned by the United States government.

Please take me at my word, Mr. Prime Minister. I had no advance warning or notice of this atrocity, and my government joins all the other governments in the world who have already issued condemnations against this act of violence.

Terrorism, Mr. Prime Minister, as your country knows best from having felt its indiscriminate brunt so often over the years, often manifests itself in inexplicably rotten forms. When American airliners became human-filled missiles, exploding into our Pentagon and Twin Towers, at first, rampant confusion reigned. But our government fully investigated, got to the bottom of that atrocity, and punished those involved.

Likewise, we shall punish the perpetrators of this crime.

With the Government of Israel, our long-standing democratic ally in the Middle East, we share the mutual goal of eradicating terrorism forever.

Therefore, I write not only to express my sympathies, but also to propose a plan to most effectively pursue our mutual goal of bringing the criminals responsible for this crime to justice.

To that extent, we have been informed by the United States ambassador to your country that Israeli military forces have successfully captured two American pilots whose planes were apparently involved in these attacks.

Under our Uniform Code of Military Justice, and under American jurisprudence, a citizen of the United States is innocent until proven guilty. Therefore, I cannot speculate at this time on the guilt or innocence of these pilots.

I can say this, however, that if these pilots are in the least manner implicated, they will be dealt with in a manner similar to the three Islamic chaplains who last year infiltrated our military and attempted to sow terrorist seeds within our navy.

To make this determination, however, we will need to take custody of these pilots and return them to the United States, where the appropriate investigation and action will be taken in accordance with U.S. military law.

Therefore, the United States government requests of the Israeli government that at the earliest time possible, arrangements be made for transfer of the captured pilots from Israeli authorities to American authorities for transportation to the custody of the United States Navy.

Thank you, Mr. Prime Minister, for your understanding of this request, and for your anticipated cooperation.

Very truly yours,
Mack Williams
President of the United States

With a grunt of disgust, the prime minister tossed the letter onto the table.

"Let me get this straight," Defense Minister Aeriel Levine said. "United States jets attack Israel—not the most popular site to Jews but nevertheless a site under Israeli control. Dozens of Arabs die, reports surface of Jews dying as well, *my* special forces go out and capture the pilots at great personal risk, across Syrian lines, effectively doing the Americans' dirty work for them. And now they want the pilots back. Just like that?" Levine flailed his hand in the air.

"I, for one, thought the president's letter a stroke of statesmanship," said Foreign Minister Alya Baruch. At forty-six, she was the youngest member of the cabinet and one of two women in the male-dominated group. "I was not offended. But I worry about the male ego of my friend Minister Levine. He's like a kid saying, 'I caught the prisoners, they're mine, and you can't play with them.'"

"You call an old man a kid?" Levine roared, stood, and eyeballed the attractive brunette whom the Western media was betting would become the next prime minister. "My family babysat for you while your family gallivanted around the globe. You once called me 'Uncle Ari.' Now you accuse me of acting like a child? Are we angling for *New York Times* endorsement when we run for prime minister? *Hmm?*"

"Actually, *Uncle Ari*"—that brought a few chuckles—"I prefer the endorsement of the *Jerusalem Post*."

"Okay," the prime minister interrupted. "Enough sniping. Let us focus on the task at hand. Okay, Alya, I agree that Williams's letter is diplomatically written. But Israel is a sovereign nation. And with that comes responsibility to *act* like a sovereign nation. It wasn't America that brought us back to this land. It was God." He paused, frowning. "Yet America has supported us with billions of dollars in economic and military aid."

The foreign minister leaned forward. "And they were the first nation to recognize our existence in 1948. Harry Truman came to our defense when no one else would.

"Alya, let me finish." Rothstein shook a lecturing finger at his beautiful rival. "The Arabs accuse us of conspiring with the United States to attack the Dome. If we capture these pilots and send them back to America, how will that look to the international community?" Rothstein flailed his arms through the air. "It smacks of a Jewish-American conspiracy. Every Arab head of state will say so. And the risk of war is escalated to unacceptable heights.

"And what of our own people? We undermine the confidence of the Israeli people in this government if we release these pilots to the Americans.

"These pilots must be brought to trial." He swiped sweat from his forehead. "And they must be prosecuted in Israel under Israeli law!"

Silence.

"But Williams will never go along with that," the minister of agriculture said.

"What will he do?" the prime minister asked. "Send a SEAL commando team to extricate them from Jerusalem?"

"His position is clear, Mr. Prime Minister," the agriculture minister responded. "Nothing Mack Williams would do would surprise me, including the possibility of using force to retrieve his pilots."

"His war criminals." This from the minister of defense.

"Look," Foreign Minister Baruch said. "You make very good points, sir. But if we can't trust the Americans, who can we trust?"

"No one!" the defense minister thundered. "Where were the Americans when our ancestors were gassed in Nazi concentration camps? Israel can trust only herself."

"The Americans *liberated* those camps!" the foreign minister shot back.

"Five years and six million lives later," the defense minister retorted.

"Alya! Ari!" the prime minister snapped. "Look, Alya. You raise a legitimate question. Who can we trust?" He looked around at a rare sight, the momentarily blank faces of his cabinet members. "There's really one American I would trust with this case."

Puzzled looks were exchanged.

"Lieutenant Brewer. His performance against that Jewish traitor Wells Levinson was formidable. I believe his heart is with Israel."

"Unfortunately, Prime Minister," the defense minister spoke in a much lower voice, "the lieutenant is in the United States Navy. Not the Israeli Navy."

More silence.

"Prime Minister," Alya Baruch said, "there may be a diplomatic solution to this problem that will allow us all to save face."

CHAPTER 32

Mount Helix
La Mesa, California
East San Diego County

Zack sat on the stone wall, staring out at the panoramic vista overlooking San Diego. With the magnificent thirty-six-foot white cross rising above Mount Helix at his back, and with the cool Pacific breeze in his face, he remembered the last time he visited this place, the most tranquil location in San Diego County.

He had come here in the late afternoon that spring day, having just won the most publicized court-martial in the history of the United States military. Diane was at his side as his assistant, and Senator Roberson Fowler, a powerful Louisiana Democrat, had offered him an opportunity to quit the navy and run for Congress. And win.

He had come here that day to get away from the press, and to find solace, and to pray. Beneath the large white cross, its beams turning an orangey hue as the sun made its way into the Pacific, he had prayed that day for guidance and wisdom in what to do: stay in the navy, or switch political parties and take a congressional seat as a Democrat.

Sure, he had mentioned to Diane that he was coming here and that she was welcome to join him. But he hadn't expected her to come. She was engaged at the time to a wealthy Frenchman, a benefactor from her days as a top fashion model. He figured, with the court-martial over, she would fall into the arms of Pierre Rochembeau, resign from the navy, and live happily ever after as Mrs. Rochembeau.

Besides, even though they had formed a sizzling prosecution team and were featured together in magazines and newspapers and on television, their relationship was professional. He was never really sure how she felt about him.

That afternoon when she appeared in the empty amphitheater, just under the cross, wearing a blue denim skirt, a green blouse, and large, almost camouflaging sunglasses, his heart nearly leapt out of his chest.

In that instant, he decided to turn down the congressional seat and remain in the navy.

Coming here today, watching the sun make its glorious trek toward the magnificent waters of the Pacific, feeling the breeze caress his face, absorbing the sight of the magnificent cross transformed from pristine white to a splendid orange, Zack hoped that somehow, by a miracle from God, Diane would once again walk around the corner.

But when the tip of the sun touched the Pacific, then sunk halfway down, he resigned himself to the fact that, for today at least, God had other plans.

As the private park at the top of Mount Helix closed at dark, Zack wiped a tear from his cheek and walked to his car, parked in the gravel parking lot. It would take about five minutes to traverse the narrow, crooked road down the side of the mountain.

He flipped his radio to KSDO, expecting to hear more news of the dangerous situation in Jerusalem, a crisis he had almost tuned out because of his preoccupation with Diane. Maybe, just maybe, the newscast would include a report saying that they had found her and that she was safe.

"More news coming out of Israel today concerning yesterday's mysterious attack by U.S. Navy warplanes on the Dome of the Rock. In the midst of continued protests and an emergency meeting of the UN Security Council by Russia, it appears that the United States and Israel are now in a diplomatic standoff over the fate of the two American pilots involved in the attacks.

"The pilots, whose names have yet to be released, were captured by Israeli Special Forces after they apparently bailed out of their planes over eastern Syria, near the Iraqi border.

"CNN has learned that the U.S. and Israel are at odds over who, where, and how the pilots will be prosecuted. The United States wants the pilots returned to the U.S. for a military court-martial, while Israel contends they are war criminals, whose actions led to the deaths of Israeli citizens. Israel wants the aviators prosecuted in Tel Aviv or Jerusalem by an Israeli tribunal.

"Word out of our Jerusalem bureau is that a very contentious cabinet meeting of the Israeli cabinet concluded this afternoon, in which cabinet officers engaged in heated exchanges over the Williams administration's request that the pilots be returned.

"To further complicate matters, Syrian president Ouday Assad has demanded the pilots be turned over to an Arab tribunal on the grounds that this was, quote, 'a despicable crime against the heart of Islam.'

"The Williams administration has remained mum on the standoff with the Israelis, prompting criticism from congressional Democrats and the Reverend JamesOn Barbour. Meanwhile, there has been no word on the whereabouts of Lieutenant Diane Colcernian, whose car was discovered three days ago in Wilmington, North Carolina."

Zack pulled the car to the side of the narrow road leading down the mountain.

"Lord, please be with her. Please protect her. Please, Lord, bring her home."

City Morgue No. 3
East Jerusalem

Alexander Kweskin entered the City Morgue in East Jerusalem, not far from the Dung Gate of the Old City.

A woman who had been sitting to the right of the entry door stood and gave him a quizzical look. "Mr. Kweskin?"

"Yes?"

"I am Kathryn Shadle from the International Fellowship of Christians and Jews," she said in Russian, though she looked American.

"You're the organization that brought us here. Now I wish that I had stayed in Belarus. At least my daughter would still be alive."

The woman waited a moment, then said, "We are deeply sorry for your loss."

"If you will excuse me, I must now claim her body."

Kathryn Shadle gently touched his arm. "Mr. Kweskin, we are here to help. Word has spread quickly about the death of your daughter."

"Anna was only nine years old," he said, his voice cracking.

"I've brought with me a burial dress." She held up a dainty blue dress. "It was donated from a local clothier who is a benefactor of our organization. Please accept it for your daughter, if you wish."

Alexander looked at the dress. It was so beautiful. Much more beautiful than anything he'd ever been able to provide for Anna in life. He wished Yael were here. She would be best at making a decision like this, but she had remained in the shelter with the other three children.

He did not have the money for a decent burial dress. His daughter's funeral, including the mortuary services, was being financed by the government of Israel. She would be buried in a state-run cemetery in the war-torn West Bank.

A rabbi would be provided for the simple ceremony—an act of compassion offered by the Israeli government that would not be offered by the Belarusian government.

But other than that, nothing special for his precious Anna. She would be buried in the same blood-stained dress in which she died. The same dress she wore when they stepped on the plane in Minsk, and when she held his hand as they stepped onto the soil of the Promised Land yesterday.

They had been in Israel only a day. It seemed like years. Time had stalled, uncompassionate and sinister, as it dragged out every painful moment and burned a fresh hole in his soul with every heartbeat.

He remembered the snowy morning he and Yael had brought Anna home from the state-run hospital in Mogilev. They had wrapped her little six-pound body in the warmest, thickest blanket they could find. And as they stepped out the front door of the hospital into the cold to hail a taxi, he cradled Anna in his arms.

They say that newborn babies have no sight. But on this morning, as the taxi pulled to the curb, he knew his red-cheeked, curly-haired angel could see.

Her sparkling eyes peered up at him, and she smiled, an angelic smile that could have come only from God.

The precious, holy memory accentuated his grief this day. Was his pain punishment for his sins? How could God give him such a beloved gift as this child, only to rip her from his arms, from the arms of her family?

"Mr. Kweskin?" He felt the warm hand of the IFCJ representative on his back. She pulled a handkerchief from her purse and offered it to him.

He accepted the handkerchief and dabbed his eyes.

"Yes, Miss Shadle. Your offer is kind. On behalf of my wife ... and my daughter ... we will gratefully accept the dress."

Kathryn Shadle's expression was filled with compassion. "Perhaps I could come with you to help dress her and help prepare her for burial?"

"Forgive me for not having been more gracious at first. I thank you for your kindness. Yes, I would appreciate your help this morning. This is so hard."

A middle-aged Jewish man entered the room from another door. "Mr. Kweskin?"

Alexander glanced at Kathryn Shadle, then nodded to the man.

"I am the director of the morgue, and on behalf of all the people of Israel, I am very sorry for your loss." He spoke in Hebrew, which Kathryn Shadle quickly translated to Russian.

Alexander nodded again after Kathryn had finished the translation.

"If you and your friend could follow me, please."

Kathryn and Alexander followed the man down the hallway about fifty paces, then stopped. "She is in here." The man gestured toward a closed door on the right. "I will give you some privacy."

Alexander opened the door, and he and Kathryn stepped into the sterile, tile-floored room. In the middle, under dangling fluorescent lights, a white sheet was draped over a small body.

"I don't know if I can do this," Alexander said.

"Yes, you can," Kathryn said. "I am a Christian, Guspadyeen Kweskin. The New Testament tells us that we can do all things through Christ who strengthens us. I will be right here with you, praying for you every moment."

CHAPTER 33

Ladies and gentlemen"—President Mack Williams looked around the table at the members of his National Security Council—"we've received a response from the Israelis." The president paused, sipping coffee from his favorite Kansas Jayhawks mug. "It seems that our friend, Prime Minister Rothstein, and his cabinet are, shall we say, none too keen about the prospect of handing us our pilots back."

The responses were quick, sharp, and negative, from all sides of the table.

"Now hang on." The president raised his hand, palm out. "We *do* have a response. It's not exactly what I was looking for, but I wanted to discuss this with you before I make a decision. I've asked the vice president to read the communiqué to you." The president glanced at Vice President Surber, seated immediately to his right, nodded his head, and said, "Doug?"

"Thank you, Mr. President."

The vice president pulled an envelope from his blue pinstripe suit, carefully unfolded it, adjusted his wire-rim glasses, and started reading.

Dear Mr. President,

While we, like you, do not understand the reasons or the motives for this tragic incident, we do understand and appreciate the great level of assistance and support that your great country has rendered toward our tiny nation since our rebirth in 1948.

Israel, as you know, has stood with the United States in the war on terror, as evidenced by our cooperation and willingness to share intelligence against radical Islamic insurgents operating within our borders and elsewhere.

I hope you will agree, Mr. President, that our history of cooperating with America is well established. I hope also that you will agree that from time to time, strategic allies do not always agree on the best course of action in certain situations. And in those rare occurrences when such disagreements may occur, this is by no means a sign of disrespect for the other's position or a symbol of deteriorating relations. Rather, such rare disagreements among allies are more akin to the occasional family disagreement, nothing more, and nothing less.

To this extent, I would like to take this opportunity to address the proposal set forth in your letter, wherein you have requested that Israel hand over the two American pilots our forces picked up, pilots who by all accounts, for some unknown reason, appear to have been directly involved in the attacks on our country.

Before I lay out the Israeli position in response to your request, I would ask you to remember the events immediately following the barbaric and savage attacks on your country on September 11. At that time, the United States took all actions it deemed necessary, and rightly so, to protect itself.

In many cases, the United States rounded up foreign terrorists, brought them to United States Naval facilities such as Guantanamo Bay, Cuba, detained them, and in some cases, court-martialed them under U.S. military law.

In contrast to other nations, such as France and Russia, Israel supported your country in each and every endeavor following those attacks, and will continue to do so in the future.

Now, in a manner not so dissimilar to yours, Israel has been attacked. A great landmark, known around the world, much in the way your Twin Towers were known, has been destroyed. But unlike the geopolitical situation following 9/11, where there was no national military power about to attack your country, Israel is surrounded by a host of nations hostile to her existence, nations whose militaries are at this very moment mobilizing.

Arab Scud missiles are at this hour aimed at us, bearing not just conventional ballistics, but nuclear, biological, and chemical warheads.

The Arab world claims that this attack is the product of an American-Israeli conspiracy to destroy the Dome as a prelude to the rebuilding of Solomon's Temple. While we know better, the average Arab does not.

Our government is concerned, therefore, that transporting these pilots back to America would fuel this perception, further endangering an already precarious situation. We feel that these pilots should be placed on trial here in Israel, prosecuted under Israeli law.

Having said that, however, the government of Israel proposes the following solution:

A United States court-martial would convene on Israeli soil, in Jerusalem, for the prosecution of these pilots under American military law. Israel would be pleased to have the case prosecuted by Navy JAG officer Lieutenant Zack Brewer, who, because of his remarkable performance in last year's prosecution of three Islamic chaplains, is greatly trusted here.

This solution solves our mutual national security interests by (a) assuring that the trial takes place in the country where the crime was committed, (b) allowing your military to prosecute under American military law, and (c) introducing a prosecutor who is trusted by millions in both of our countries.

Thank you for your consideration of our proposal, Mr. President. We look forward to your response.

Very respectfully,
Daniel Rothstein
Prime Minister

Vice President Surber folded the letter and handed it back to the president.

The president looked at the chairman of the Joint Chiefs of Staff, then at Cynthia Hewitt. "Other than the fact that the Israelis don't know that Brewer has been promoted to Lieutenant Commander, are there any comments?"

The secretaries of state and defense glanced at one another, as if jockeying for the chance to speak up first.

"Mr. President, you know how much I think of Lieutenant Commander Brewer," Defense Secretary Erwin Lopez said. "You also know that I argued last year to have the navy, rather than the justice department, prosecute their own members." Lopez paused for a sip of water. "I think it was appropriate then, and I think it appropriate now that the navy prosecutes its own."

The president noticed Lopez exchange looks with Cynthia Hewitt. The two were rumored to be an item around Washington. Mack had never asked.

"And while there's no doubt in my mind that Commander Brewer is our best litigator," Lopez continued, "something doesn't sit well about Israel, or any other country, telling us where we can convene a court-martial or who our trial counsel is going to be."

Joint Chiefs Chairman Admiral John Ayers nodded. "Agreed."

The president turned to Vice President Surber. "Mr. Vice President?"

Douglas Surber removed his wire-rim glasses. "I don't have a problem with holding a court-martial in Israel, and I'm also a big fan of Lieutenant Commander Brewer. But the memo doesn't address two issues we need to evaluate in advance before agreeing to such a thing."

"Please elaborate," the president said.

"First, the Israelis want Brewer because they think he can get a conviction. And that's fine. My guess is that he'd be the man the navy would select anyway." The secretary of defense and chairman of the Joint Chiefs nodded in agreement. "But who picks the defense counsel? The Israelis? If so, then we can't accept this. The Israelis must agree that the accused officers are treated like any other officers under the UCMJ, and even have the right to hire civilian counsel, which, if I had my guess, they will probably want to do."

"Good point, Doug."

"But there's one other point, Mr. President."

"Go on."

"What happens if we do get a conviction? Do the Israelis expect the officers to stay in Israel? Or what if there is an acquittal? Will they commit to release the officers?" The vice president slid his wire rims back on his nose. "I just think we need clarification in these areas before we make any decisions."

"Right on target, Doug." The president looked at his national security advisor. "Cyndi?"

"Mr. President," Hewitt said, "I agree with the vice president's concerns and likewise believe that we should seek clarification on these points. If we get the right answers, I say accept the proposal."

"That makes sense to me too," the president said. "We'll send a communiqué back requesting clarification on these points, and assuming a satisfactory response, we'll send Brewer to Israel."

"Mr. President," Admiral Ayers said, "what if we don't get a satisfactory response?"

"We will, Admiral. We'll keep requesting clarification until we get the answers we want. Look, this is a face-saving proposal for the Israelis. This will work." He paused. "That answer your question?"

"Yes, sir." Ayers nodded his head.

"Now, moving on." The president motioned to a navy steward to refill the coffee carafe, then turned to his secretary of state. "Secretary Mauney, what's this I hear about an emergency meeting of the UN Security Council?"

"Rumor has it, Mr. President, that Sudan and Libya, who, as you know, have just rotated on the Security Council, are working on resolutions to condemn the attacks. The meeting could take place as early as tomorrow. Probably no later than next week."

"Anything from the Russians and the French?"

"Condemnations against '*whoever* is responsible' for the attacks."

"Okay, Bobby," the president said, "if and when such a meeting takes place, I want you to personally go up to New York and represent our interests."

"Yes, Mr. President."

"Admiral Ayers, what's our position vis-à-vis the disposition of Arab military forces around Israel right now?"

"Every Islamic military power in the region is on full alert. In Egypt, more than two hundred tanks are being repositioned into the Sinai. In Syria, dozens of tanks and missile batteries are being brought to the border regions near Israel."

"Okay, listen." The president looked at the secretary of state. "I want back-channel communications opened with all these governments, discreetly, diplomatically warning them that hostile overtures against Israel will not be tolerated. Understood?"

"Yes, Mr. President."

"Director Early, what's the situation on the streets in these Arab capitals?"

"Mr. President," the CIA director said, "it's a powder keg. Especially Damascus. Intelligence tells us that militants could storm our embassy at any time."

"Secretary Mauney, these are your people. Do we need to evacuate?"

"I hate to say it, Sir, but I recommend evacuation of our Syrian embassy. I would hate to have a repeat of Tehran in 1979."

"Secretary Lopez, is the *Truman* the only carrier in the Med right now?"

"Yes, sir, Mr. President. The *Truman* relieved the *Nimitz*, which is on her way back to Norfolk."

"Where's *Nimitz* now?"

"Eastern Atlantic, Sir. Near the Canary Islands."

"Mr. Secretary, turn *Nimitz* around. Send her back to the Eastern Med. Move USS *Harry Truman* off the Syrian coast and evacuate our embassy immediately. Any questions?"

"No, Sir."

"Where's our next nearest carrier?"

"*Ronald Reagan* is in the Indian Ocean."

"Okay, bring the *Gipper* up the Red Sea and through the Suez. I want enough naval firepower concentrated around Israel to make the Arabs think twice before they try anything foolish."

"I will send out the orders, Mr. President," Lopez said.

"Admiral Ayers, pass the word down through the chain to Commander Brewer that I want him to prosecute these pilots. He is to begin his preparation immediately and be prepared to fly to Israel on a moment's notice."

"Aye, aye, Mr. President."

CHAPTER 34

The rattling and shaking brought her eyes wide open, and from her position on her back, she saw the ceiling and unlit dome light of the minivan. Daylight flooded in through the windows.

Potholes.

Every part of her body ached when they hit one, which was all too often. And every two minutes or so, this vehicle drove through what felt like a lunar crater, shooting knifelike pains through the back of her head. Wherever they were, wherever they were going, not much attention was paid to road upkeep.

Her stomach muscles, strong from hundreds of weekly sit-ups and abdominal crunches, helped her bring her head up, just a little, to catch a glimpse of the man behind the wheel.

The next lunar crater brought her abruptly back into a supine position.

Should she talk or not? She had read somewhere that victims who develop at least some sort of emotional bond with their captors have the best chance of survival.

If she was going to die anyway, what difference would it make? She wasn't going to get out of here unless she tried something. If he turned around and shot her, at least that would put her out of her misery.

God, please give me wisdom.

"What's your name?"

No answer. Three more bumps.

"I said, what's your name?"

Still no answer, but she saw his black eyes glance up at her in the mirror.

"What's the matter? Your mother didn't care enough about you to name you?"

"Shut up!"

"Oh. So we do speak English, do we?"

"I said, shut up!"

Count to twenty. Then try again ... seventeen, eighteen, nineteen, twenty.

"Look, I'm sorry if I made you mad. I just asked your name. What's the harm in that?"

He glared at her.

"I am a murderous Arab terrorist. That is all you need to know."

Let that sit for a moment.

"So where are we going?"

"None of your business."

Okay. Next question after the eighth bump in the road ... six, seven, eight. Ouch.

"Excuse me."

No answer.

"Hello. Mr. Terrorist."

"What!"

"I've got to go to the bathroom again."

That brought another glance in the rearview.

"You know, Mr. Terrorist, women *do* have to do this sort of thing." A few seconds passed. Using her abdominal muscles, she again pulled herself up and looked out at a sunbaked desert. In the distance she saw cacti and mountains. A single sign passed by the van.

Villa de Cos — 8
Acapulco — 255

Mexico.

We must be a couple of hundred miles south of the border. Jesus, please help me. If I can just get out of this car ...

"If you're going to kidnap a girl, you really need to be prepared for potty breaks," she said in a sweet voice.

"Okay. Okay. Can you wait just a few more minutes?"

Was that a snippet of compassion? Maybe a chink in the armor?

"Sure, I can try, Mr. Terrorist. But I'm in a lot of pain."

"Okay."

She felt the van slow down, then the slight centrifugal force indicating a right-hand turn. The road grew rougher, and a minute or so later, the van stopped.

Either he's going to kill me, or I'm going to kill him.

"Okay. You have to go to the bathroom? Here we are."

She pulled herself up and looked around again. They were in some sort of desolate area strewn with large boulders, some nearly as big as the van.

"Where?"

"Over there." He motioned to the right with his gun. "Behind that cactus."

He moved the barrel so it pointed at her heart. "I will unlock your handcuffs. But if you try anything, I will deal with you like I dealt with your friend Maggie Jefferies."

He holstered the gun, then took her wrists in his and worked the key into the handcuffs. They dropped to the ground just behind her feet.

"Now take ten steps forward, and don't look around until I tell you." She stepped forward. "Okay, turn around." She did. "Go behind the cactus."

A few minutes later, she walked across the desert floor back toward the van. The man was standing by the hood. The gun was still in the holster. He lit a cigarette, his eyes still trained on her. Maybe he was testing her. Maybe this routine had made him overconfident. Maybe he thought that because of her ankle chains, he could draw the gun and shoot her before she could reach him. Maybe he just thought she wouldn't try anything.

Whatever his deranged thought process might be, she had to try.

"Into the van, lady. We have places to go."

"I'm moving as fast as I can."

Be nonchalant. Pretend you haven't noticed the gun. Slowly she walked to the van. Gently she put her right foot up on the floorboard.

Lord, help me.

Now!

She sprang to her left, diving at his feet like a linebacker blitzing a quarterback in the Super Bowl. He fell with a thud, screaming in Arabic. She pushed herself on top of him, scratching his face with her fingernails. He pushed her face back with the heel of his hand. She reached for the holster. His hand gripped her right forearm. They rolled over and over in the dust. She screamed.

She freed her left hand. Scratched at his eyeballs with her left hand. A scratch under his eye socket drew blood. He loosened his grip and yelped. Her right hand touched the gun. She wrapped her fingers around the handle. She wrestled it from the holster.

His hand grabbed hers again. Struggling, wrestling, her finger felt for the trigger.

More screaming. More shrill Arabic.

She squeezed the trigger. A loud *bang*!

A cloud of dust rose from the floor.

Another squeeze. Another *bang*.

They wrestled and rolled on top of one another. Now he was on top of her. He pinned her hand with the gun against the dirt. Still she clung to the pistol and yanked his hair with her free hand. He cursed, this time in English. Salty sweat dripped from his forehead into her mouth.

He leaned over, forcing all his weight on her arm. Her hand was going numb. He pushed his knee into her stomach. Her strength was ebbing. She could no longer feel the gun in her hand.

He grabbed the gun and smashed her across the head with the butt.

She looked up at him. His face was in a whirlpool. Swirling, swirling, swirling ...

Just before darkness closed in, the image of Zack Brewer, handsome, trim, and tanned in his summer whites, drifted into her mind.

Then all went black.

CHAPTER 35

Office of the Commanding Officer
Navy Trial Service Office
Building 73
32nd Street Naval Station
San Diego, California

Sit down, Zack." Captain Glen Rudy motioned Lieutenant Commander Zack Brewer to one of the two big leather chairs in front of the commanding officer's desk. The other chair was already occupied by Senior Trial Counsel Commander Bob Awe, who seemed uncharacteristically serious.

"Coffee?" Captain Rudy raised his eyebrows at Zack.

"No thank you, sir."

Rudy sipped his coffee. "So how are you doing, Zack?"

"I'm fine, sir." *Don't lie to your commanding officer.*

"Zack, I think you sometimes forget Commander Awe and I used to be litigators before the navy kicked us upstairs and turned us into bureaucrats. Now, we might not have been hotshot, nationally famous JAG officers like you've become"—Rudy shot an affectionate wink in Awe's direction—"but we've both been around long enough to recognize a lying witness when we see one." He leaned back and folded his arms over his stomach. "Now, let me see if I can rephrase the question." He leaned back. "So how are you doing, Zack?"

"I think if I'm going to answer that truthfully, I'd better reconsider your offer of coffee."

"It's the fuel that makes the navy run." Rudy poured the steaming black brew from a thermos sitting on his desk into a mug, then gently pushed the mug across his desk.

Zack took a sip, closed his eyes, and felt a psychological jolt if nothing else. The much-needed actual jolt of caffeine wouldn't be far behind. "I'm not doing too well, Captain," he said, opening his eyes.

"It's Diane, isn't it, son?"

"Yes, sir." Another sip. "It is."

"You haven't looked yourself, Zack. You've seemed depressed. Now, I know your courtroom performance hasn't dipped, but Commander Awe and I are worried about you."

"I feel responsible for this, Captain. I should have insisted that she take an escort. I should have called you. I should have done something."

"Zack, Diane was on leave. Don't take this on yourself. You know, that's the very thing that may have gotten Diane in trouble. She was taking the blame for Maggie Jefferies' death—something that was by no means her fault—and it affected her thinking and her decision making. And Diane's disappearance is not your fault."

"You know, Zack," Commander Awe added, "I can give you the names of a couple of excellent navy doctors over at Balboa. There's no shame in using medication to battle depression. No one would think any less of you if you decided to do that."

Zack considered his offer for a moment. "Thanks, Commander. I don't think it's necessary yet, but I'll keep it in mind."

"We're all worried sick about Diane, Zack," Rudy said. "And we know how close the two of you have become." Zack looked out the CO's office window, across the waters of San Diego Bay toward the low-lying buildings on Coronado Island. "But I want you to put a very important concept in the forefront of your mind." That brought Zack's eyes back to Rudy's. "Son, we're at war. Not with a traditional enemy, but with an invisible enemy. It's an enemy that rears its head and kills people and then disappears.

"This enemy can strike anywhere at any time without notice. It's like a vapor that knows no boundaries. And you and Diane, by the fine job you did last year, have been at the forefront of that war just as much as a Navy SEAL out on the front lines dodging bullets.

"Zack, sometimes in war we lose our buddies. Sometimes they become missing in action. And I know that you and Diane are more than buddies. But we are at war, Zack. And just like in places like Normandy, San Juan Hill, Gettysburg, Midway, Coral Sea, and all other battles in history, we lose our comrades in battle, and we cry, and we pick up the pieces, and we keep fighting."

Zack wanted to slam his fist on the captain's desk, but instead he said, "I understand."

"Do you?"

"Sir, I've got some leave accumulated. Maybe if I took some time off, maybe I could help find her." He exhaled. "Sir, it's worth a try."

"Sorry, Commander. Not possible. The navy has a new job for you."

"A new job?" A hole opened in Zack's stomach.

"A direct request from the prime minister of Israel and a direct order from the president of the United States."

"I don't understand, Captain."

"Heard about those pilots that blew up the Dome of the Rock?"

"Yes, sir, of course."

"Israel wants to prosecute them over there; the U.S. wants to prosecute them over here. So it looks like the president and the prime minister have reached a compromise." Rudy paused. "You are that compromise."

"What do you mean?" Zack's eyes widened. "They want me to prosecute these guys?"

"Yes, Zack. In Israel."

"Israel?"

"They're still hammering out the details, but an Article 32 investigating officer is already on the way."

"Unbelievable." *How can I do this when Diane may be in danger?*

"Zack, the stakes here are even higher than last year's prosecution of the chaplains. This is an explosive international situation. War could break out, depending on how this is handled. You're the only diplomatic solution to prevent an international standoff. I know you've got the ability for this, but I need to make sure your head's in the game. Shoot it straight, Zack. Are you up to this, even, for example"—his eyes met Zack's—"if bad news comes in about Diane?"

"I need to make sure your head's in the game ..."

"You're the only diplomatic solution to prevent an international standoff ..."

"War could break out, depending on how this is handled ..."

"I need to make sure your head's in the game ..."

"Zack? You okay?"

"Yes, sir, Captain. I'm okay. And yes, sir. My head's in the game."

But if that's true, then why do I want to jump on a jet and search every corner of the world until I find her? Why do I want to kill somebody?

"You can pass the word up to the president and the prime minister that if the charges are referred, I'll get them their conviction."

CHAPTER 36

Council of Ishmael headquarters
Rub al-Khali Desert

From the day he first met Hussein al-Akhma at an outdoor café near the Limmat River in Zurich, Abdur Rahman had never wavered in his belief that Hussein was the greatest Muslim Allah had placed on the earth since the prophet Mohammed himself—*Peace be upon him.*

Al-Akhma gave birth to the vision of placing Islamic operatives within the United States military. It was al-Akhma who advocated blending into the woodwork of the American power structure, where Council of Ishmael operatives, deeply committed to Islamic domination of the world, would be Western educated, multilingual, and impossible to pick out on the streets of American cities and within the American military.

By blending in with Westerners, at least in appearance, operatives could deliver devastating strikes against the West not only from the outside, but also from within, and with the constant pounding of Western targets, including infidel women and children, Islam could, over time, wear down the Western will to resist. This would, according to the leader's vision, eventually cause America, and her Zionist puppet, Israel, to collapse. With America and Israel severely debilitated, the world would become ripe for a true Islamic revolution.

From this vision was born Operation Islamic Glory, a bold and radical plan whereby operatives—American fighter pilots within the U.S. Navy—would attack and destroy one of the holiest sites of Islam, the Dome of the Rock in Israeli-occupied Palestine.

In the flesh, it seemed like a huge gamble, but al-Akhma said that the vision was from Allah, that it would drive an irreparable wedge between the Arab States and America, and that the sacrifice of the Dome would be a painful but necessary sacrifice to forever advance the great spread of Islam around the globe.

Even Abdur himself was secretly, albeit not openly, apprehensive of Islamic Glory. Sacrificing the Dome seemed an unfathomable gamble. What if it did not work?

But the furor against America pouring out in the streets of Arab capitals was overwhelming beyond anything Abdur Rahman had ever seen.

Hussein al-Akhma had been bold beyond measure, and he had been right.

But al-Akhma, like all great leaders in history, including the prophet himself—*Peace be upon him*—despite having almost superhuman visionary abilities, could at the same time reflect an almost superhuman anger.

Like the prophet—*Peace be upon him*—had been, al-Akhma himself was ruthless, many times, in dealing with those who opposed his vision. Khalid Mohammed el-Shiek, a member of the Council of Twenty, had received a literal dagger in his throat for questioning Islamic Glory, which was tantamount to questioning al-Akhma. And there were others.

Abdur Rahman, second only to al-Akhma in the Council of Ishmael and rumored to be al-Akhma's successor, was also the one on whose shoulders fell the responsibility of delivering bad news to al-Akhma.

And so, when news reached the Council that the Israelis had beaten the rescue team in capturing the two Islamic pilots who had carried out Islamic Glory, someone had to break the news to al-Akhma.

As usual, Abdur Rahman got the dreaded job.

He pulled the report off the computer and headed to Hussein al-Akhma's office. A knock on the door brought an uncharacteristically buoyant "Enter" from the leader of the Council of Ishmael. "Ah, Abdur," al-Akhma said, rising to his feet, smiling and then kissing Abdur once on each cheek. "What is our update on Islamic Glory?"

"Leader, overall, the results continue to be greater than we could have expected. The government of Sudan, it is our understanding, is about to introduce a resolution on the floor of the Security Council condemning America for the attack. Although we expect America to veto, it is our understanding that France and Russia may support it."

That brought a broad smile from al-Akhma, who sat back in his chair and folded his arms. "Yes, the French have been moving our way ever since the second American invasion of Iraq when they refused to support the Americans and Bush the Second. What is it they say? *Vive la France?*"

"And there is even better news, Leader ..."

"And does this 'better news' call for the eating of grapes and the sipping of champagne?" Hussein kicked his feet up on his desk.

"I think eventually it very well could."

"Out with it, Abdur. I cannot stand the anticipation." Hussein snapped his fingers, and one of the black berets brought him a silver tray full of fruit, including several clusters of purple grapes. Hussein tilted his head back, opened his mouth wide, and dropped in two grapes, seeming to savor each in triumphant succulence before he swallowed.

Abdur waited until his leader had swallowed the second. "This is still preliminary, but our COI operatives in America are convinced that we have Lieutenant Colcernian and that she is somewhere in Mexico in our custody."

Hussein's eyes widened like the full moon. "Alive?"

"Yes, Leader, we believe so."

"Ah, the beautiful Lieutenant Colcernian. The infidel maiden who has found herself no longer in control." Hussein's black eyes sparkled. "Soon to be in my hands." Another half-moon smile. More grapes popped into his mouth. "As soon as we have verified her whereabouts, I want her brought here. No, no, no." He wagged his finger as he reconsidered. "Take her to a secure location. I can go to her if I need a conjugal visit." A long stream of sinister laughter. "Ah, the world condemning the Americans, the French moving to our side, and now we may have Colcernian? How much better can it get for this week?"

Now is the time to break it. "Leader, I regret to say that all has not gone as smoothly as we would have liked this week."

"Oh? You are not about to burst my festive mood, are you, Abdur?"

"Leader, it is about the two pilots who carried out the attack."

"What about them?" Hussein's feet came off his desk. His sparkling eyes turned piercing.

"I regret to say that before our operatives were able to pick them up in Syria, an Israeli Special Forces unit captured them."

"*What* did you say?"

"Factors came into play that we did not anticipate. We did not believe, for example, that Israel would penetrate deep into Syrian airspace. But we underestimated them ..."

"I underestimate no one!" Hussein slapped the silver tray off his desk. Grapes flew across the room as the tray clanged to the floor.

"You are correct, Leader. You underestimated no one. Islamic Glory is *your* vision. The day-to-day operations fall on the shoulders of others. The loss of the pilots to the Israelis was the responsibility of others."

"Yes, and I will *deal* with those responsible." Al-Akhma lifted a crystal stem glass, downed the water, then threw it almost in the direction of Abdur's head, causing Abdur to jerk back as the glass hit the far wall and shattered into hundreds of pieces.

"Of course, Leader."

"But first we must deal with the problem of the pilots. They possess information that could be fatal to our network in America." Hussein stood, folded his arms, and stared into space. "Maybe the Israelis will kill them before the Americans can interrogate them."

"Actually, the Americans and the Israelis are arguing over who will prosecute them."

"Hmm." That statement seemed to alleviate at least part of the contortion in al-Akhma's face. And then a sudden look of calm and peace came over him. It was the same radical mood swing that Abdur had witnessed in his brilliant but mercurial leader over the years. Unrestrained fury one moment followed by angelic peace an instant later. Perhaps Abdur had dodged the bullet—literally—once more. *Praise be to Allah.*

"You understand our strategic doctrine better than anyone else in the world other than me. Tell me, Abdur, what is it that our doctrine would call for at this moment?"

"Our doctrine, the strategic doctrine you have brought to us from Allah himself"—a smile of satisfaction crossed al-Akhma's egomaniacal face—"calls for us not only to use direct military action, but to attack on all fronts, military, economic, psychological warfare, terrorizing infidel population bases and even co-opting international agencies and legal means to fight the enemy."

"Precisely." He snapped his fingers, summoning a black beret to bring him a glass of wine. "And given that strategic doctrine you have so aptly laid out"—he took a sip of wine—"what specific recommendations would you make to me, your leader, with regard to how we should handle all this?" Al-Akhma downed the glass and snapped for more.

"Leader, no decision has apparently yet been made as to where the pilots will be prosecuted. That is the first issue of interest to our organization. And it seems to me that it would be better if these pilots are not returned to America."

"Your reasoning?"

"Obviously, we exert greater control over events in the Middle East. Our operatives are working in Israel. We can slip agents in and out at will from Jordan, Syria, and Egypt. If we needed, for example, to kill the pilots, an assassination would be far simpler in Israel."

Al-Akhma scratched his chin. "I see your point. But how do you suggest we accomplish that?"

"Through the United Nations, Leader."

"Oh. And am I just supposed to appear before the General Assembly, bang my shoe like Mr. Khrushchev did, and demand that the pilots not be returned to America?" Al-Akhma chuckled at himself. Good.

"As you know, and as I have said, the Sudanese government is currently preparing a condemnation resolution even as we speak. Why not expand the resolution to include a demand that these 'war criminals' be brought to trial in an Islamic country? Perhaps under some international legal theory that they have essentially committed a crime against Islam?"

Al-Akhma smiled. "Yes, yes. I like this, Abdur."

"And better yet," Abdur continued, "why not try to enlist the assistance of our French allies? They may even make the resolution for us. If they don't have the stomach, as they often don't, we can always rely on the Sudanese."

Al-Akhma was beaming now. "Very well, Abdur. Go to the French. Spend whatever you must. And do it quickly."

"Yes, Leader."

CHAPTER 37

LCDR Zack Brewer's residence
4935 Mills Street
La Mesa, California

Zack's small stucco house on Mills Street in La Mesa, about twelve miles east of the naval station, was perfect for a bachelor. It was only nine hundred square feet, assuming you counted the unheated sunroom that connected the kitchen to the single-car garage. Without that, the small house on the postage stamp–sized lot had about seven hundred fifty feet of living area. Just about enough room for Zack to cook, shower, sleep, watch a little television, and of course, work.

Oftentimes, when he finished court for the day, but in the middle of a big case, Zack would leave the naval station early, head east up California Highway 94, jump off at the Spring Street exit in La Mesa, and go home. He could get more work done at home without the phone ringing constantly and without the penny-ante interruptions from his well-meaning subordinates and colleagues.

About the only time Zack spent any significant time preparing for a major case in his office was last year, when he and Diane Colcernian had prepared for the famous court-martial of *United States v. Mohammed Olajuwon et al.*, now known in many circles as the "court-martial of the century." They had barricaded themselves at the naval station through the late hours of the night. It was during those long hours of working together that his feelings for her had begun to grow.

Before, she was physically attractive to him, and probably to every other red-blooded American male who had gotten half a look at her. Before, he had actually enjoyed baiting her in court. He enjoyed sparring with her, which proved a challenge—and heightened his attraction to her. She gave him a strange kind of high—a high only a litigator would understand—with her adept maneuvers as a courtroom adversary. He was ashamed to admit it now, but before, she was an object of alluring beauty, an intellectual challenge, a combination that he found strangely attractive.

Now, however, he had grown to care for her in a deeper, more substantial way. She was the brightest and most attractive woman he had ever met—her intellect and looks made him catch his breath—but it was the beauty of her character that had captured his heart.

And so, with this new challenge before him, with war and peace hanging in the balance, Zack decided that working long hours in his office might be too painful without Diane at his side.

He arrived home about 1700 hours, tossed the file on the ottoman in the small living room, stripped off his working khakis, and replaced the uniform with a black T-shirt and gray sweatpants.

When the first hunger pang struck his stomach, he thought about Red Lobster at Grossmont Mall. But then when he saw the mound of paperwork on his coffee table, he decided it would be quicker to walk to his favorite Mexican restaurant, Por Favor, only a couple of blocks from his house.

Captain Rudy's words from yesterday afternoon again echoed in his mind: *You're the only diplomatic solution to prevent an international standoff ... War could break out, depending on how this is handled ... I need to make sure your head's in the game.*

He scrapped Por Favor for a microwavable bag of popcorn and a caffeine-free Diet Coke.

With the steaming-hot bag in one hand and a cold Coke in the other, Zack settled into his large, comfortable club chair and kicked his bare feet up on the ottoman in the space between the stacks of reports about the attack.

He picked up the military service record for Lieutenant Commander Mohammed Quasay, USN.

Hmm. Excellent academic credentials. BS from Michigan. Honors graduate. NROTC. Dedicated Muslim.

What makes this guy tick? Why would a dedicated Muslim attack a Muslim holy site ... intentionally?

Whoever winds up defending these guys, these are exactly the questions they will raise. I can see it now. The "dedicated Muslim" defense. As in, "No dedicated Muslim would ever do such a thing."

He tossed the file back onto the ottoman and picked up the remote control. The opening of CNN's *Nightwatch* was almost like the view from the bridge of the *Starship Enterprise* at warp speed. The computer-animated introduction featured dozens of stars flying through the galaxy, accompanied by the music of trumpets and tympanis, as a deep, resonant voice announced from out of the blue, "This is *Nightside at 6* with Tom Miller."

In an instant, the image of Tom Miller, in a blue pinstripe suit and wire-rim glasses, the trusted dean of American newscasters, appeared. The sound of the trumpets and tympanis softened as Miller began his rundown of tonight's headlines:

"Good evening. I'm Tom Miller, reporting from Washington ..."

The sound of the tympanis and trumpets crescendoed, then gave way to a silent, black screen, the result of Zack hitting the off button on his remote control.

His eyes caught hers: the eight-by-ten color photograph of Diane Colcernian in her summer white uniform atop his small TV. He smiled at the picture, and it was almost as if he heard her say, "Stop worrying about me and get to work. You're a naval officer. You've got a job to do. Focus."

"Yes, ma'am," he said. He reached for a manila file with "LT Hosni Alhad, USN" written in black felt-tip on the front, and he was about to open the file when he heard the front doorbell ring.

Zack peered through the mini-blinds in the living room. A blue rental car was parked in the small driveway, behind his Mercedes.

CHAPTER 38

L'office de droit de Jean-Claude la Trec
56, rue Charles de Gaulle
Paris

The dark-suited lawyer rose from behind his ornate desk and walked across a luxurious Persian rug to bestow an affectionate greeting. And it should be affectionate, Abdur thought, especially after one hundred thousand nonrefundable U.S. dollars had been funneled through the Muslim Legal Foundation and transferred to la Trec's account just for the privilege of this meeting.

"*Bonsoir, Monsieur Rahman. Bienvenue á Paris.*" France's most famous lawyer, or avocat, extended his hand for a firm handshake with Abdur Rahman.

"It is good to be here again," Abdur replied in French.

"Please be seated," la Trec said, exuding charisma and pointing to one of two French provincial chairs side by side in front of the elaborate desk. "And to what do we owe this pleasure this evening?"

"Monsieur la Trec, I am here tonight on behalf of the Muslim Legal Foundation. We provide funding for—"

"Pardon, monsieur"—la Trec held up his hand—"but I am familiar with your outstanding organization. You provide funding worldwide for the legal defense of Muslims who may be the subject of political or religious persecution."

"You know of our organization?"

"But of course, monsieur. Your group underwrote Mr. Levinson's very handsome legal fee. Ten million dollars, was it? For the defense of the three Muslim chaplains last year as I understand it."

That comment took Abdur slightly aback. He knew la Trec's international underground contacts were good, but he didn't know they were that good.

"I am impressed, Monsieur la Trec."

"Don't be," la Trec said, smiling. "When your field is international criminal law, it is your job to stay abreast, shall we say, of the competition."

"By competition, I take it you mean Mr. Levinson?"

"A very fine attorney in his own right. And under those circumstances—a court-martial in San Diego—probably the right choice. The Yanks don't care too much for us Frenchmen these days. Would you care for some wine?"

"Yes, thank you." Abdur said. "Something red, please."

La Trec punched his intercom, and almost instantly an attractive secretary in a short, high-fashion dress brought in a silver tray with a bottle of pinot noir, flanked by two crystal wine glasses and a white plate with an assortment of cheeses. She poured the wine. La Trec sniffed it, sipped it, then nodded his head. The woman poured a glass for Abdur, who did the same.

"And so, Monsieur Rahman, to what do we owe the pleasure of your company here tonight?"

"First of all," Abdur said, "let me thank you for meeting me here with your staff at such a late hour."

"*C'est ne fait rien,*" la Trec replied. *It is nothing.* "One advantage of paying our retainer, monsieur, is that we are on call for our very elite clientele twenty-four hours a day. Even at a quarter past midnight, as you can see."

"Monsieur la Trec, let me get to the point. My organization wishes to retain your services."

"In what way?"

"First as a lobbyist, then as a litigator."

"Hmm." A curious look. A raised eyebrow. A sip of pinot noir. "And for whom and to whom do you wish to retain me to lobby?"

Abdur raised his glass, held it to the light, then took a sip. He nodded at the distinguished avocat. "The French government, monsieur. We wish for you to lobby your government for the introduction of certain measures before the Security Council of the United Nations."

The avocat smiled broadly. "And I suspect that in some way, this proposition might be connected to two American pilots, who happen to be Muslim, who also may happen to be in the hands of the government of our mutual thorn in the side, the State of Israel?"

"There is no such state," Abdur shot back. "But to answer your question, I suppose you suspect that, monsieur, because your natural instincts are impeccable. And because you are the greatest lawyer in the world."

"To my instincts." La Trec held his glass forward to clink it against Abdur's. "But I thought your friend Levinson was the best lawyer in the world." His voice held a hint of sarcasm. "After all, that's what his books say," la Trec added with a smirk.

"Levinson has now lost a case. You never have. Levinson tries his cases only in America. You are truly the world's greatest *international* barrister, having successfully defended such notorious characters as Igor the Barbarian and the Butcher of Bohemia. On the international stage, no lawyer in the world has a record that compares to yours, monsieur."

Jean-Claude la Trec smiled. "And when is it that you would like to have this resolution before the Security Council?"

"Sooner rather than later—*tomorrow*."

"You realize, do you not, that the tasks you are asking of me are far more formidable than what you asked, even, of Levinson?"

"And more expensive, I am sure. If that is your meaning, monsieur."

A pleased look crossed the avocat's face. He stood and gestured to Abdur to join him. "There is a view I want you to see from the far side of my office."

Abdur stood and followed la Trec to a floor-to-ceiling window behind the avocat's desk.

"Look to your right, Abdur."

Abdur complied. Not far off soared the majestic Eiffel Tower, and off to the left, *l'Arc de Triomphe*. Both were brightly lit and rose triumphantly over a million other lights.

"Your city is magnificent. Truly the most beautiful capital in the world," Abdur said.

"Paris." La Trec swirled his wine, then drank deeply. "*La Cité de Lumière*—the City of Light. Ours is a city that is growing friendly to Islam. And for the right price, it is a city than can be controlled by Islam."

Abdur let that comment sit for a moment, taking in the sight. Then, looking out over the moonlight-bathed Paris skyline, he asked, "And what price might that be, monsieur?"

Silence fell between them.

"If Levinson were worth ten million U.S. dollars in a losing effort," he said after a moment, "it seems that a price of fifteen million for the lobbying and fifteen for the litigation would be fair. Do you not agree? After all, you asked Levinson to affect the outcome of a court-martial. You are asking me to single-handedly achieve an international resolution *and*, I presume, defend these aviators?"

Abdur studied the avocat for a few seconds without speaking, then said, "We can have thirty million wired into your account by two in the morning, Paris time. But we need you to move out on the resolution immediately."

That brought a sly grin. "If, as you say, the funds have cleared by 2:00 a.m., I will arouse my contacts in the government at 2:01."

"Then we have a deal?" Abdur asked.

"We have a deal," la Trec said.

CHAPTER 39

LCDR Zack Brewer's residence
4935 Mills Street
La Mesa, California

Smiling and trim in well-tailored designer jeans, her hair almost glowing orange in the last rays of the setting sun, Lieutenant Commander Wendy Poole stood on his porch. She seemed ready to laugh at his surprise.

"Wendy, what are you doing here?"

Her smile softened, and she seemed almost apologetic. "Captain Rudy sent me."

"Captain Rudy?"

She laughed softly. "You *do* remember Captain Rudy—our commanding officer?"

"*Our* commanding officer? I thought Captain MacDonald at Appellate Government was your commanding officer."

"He still is. But I'm on TAD orders to San Diego as of this morning, Zack. I've been temporarily assigned to the Trial Service Office."

"What for?"

"The JAG has ordered me to serve as your assistant in the prosecution of the aviators," she said.

Zack could not speak.

"Captain Rudy made the request, Zack. He was worried"—she cut her eyes away from his for a second—"he was concerned that under the circumstances ..." She paused as if calculating how much to say. "He felt you could use some assistance."

"Some assistance?"

"This *wasn't* my idea, but they really liked the working model that you and Diane followed last year in the prosecution of the chaplains. So even though I'm technically senior to you, *Commander*, my orders are to support you in any way you see fit. Paperwork, tracking down witnesses, helping at trial. You name it. I'm officially at your disposal—*sir*."

Zack glanced at the mountain of paperwork on his ottoman.

I need to make sure your head's in the game ...

You're the only diplomatic solution to prevent an international standoff ...

War could break out, depending on how this is handled ...

I need to make sure your head's in the game ...

Then he looked back into Wendy's twinkling eyes.

"Know what?" he said. "I could use the help."

"Good," she said with a sigh of relief.

"See that paperwork over on my footstool?"

She stared at the pile of folders, then looked back to Zack with a confident smile. "So that's my homework?"

"*Our* homework ... after dinner. I was about to slap together a ham sandwich. How about if I make it two?"

"I'd love it."

CHAPTER 40

Secretary of State Robert Mauney, at the order of the president, had flown from Washington to New York. He sat with the United States ambassador and the rest of the U.S. delegation at the large conference table in the well of the Security Council chamber.

The specially called emergency session to deal with the "heinous American attacks on the Dome of the Rock" had been underway for two hours now. The secretary-general had announced that during the afternoon's session, two resolutions—the first, proposed by the Sudanese government, and the second, proposed by the French government— would be considered.

The first resolution, the Sudanese proposal, had been debated *ad nauseum* and was about to be voted on. The French resolution was yet to be introduced. Mauney remained uncertain about the French intentions. They had been typically tight-lipped.

This would be a high-stakes game of calculated mathematics. For the resolution to pass, nine of the fifteen members would have to vote for it. Each of the five members of the Security Council—consisting of China, Russia, France, Britain, and the United States—could exercise a veto and kill the resolution.

Mauney's instructions from the president had been clear: Use the veto only if it appears the enemy could muster the requisite nine votes to pass the condemnation resolution outright. Much would depend on the Brits and the French. If both stuck with the United States, either opposing the resolution or at least abstaining, the resolution could fall one vote short of passing. Both had remained lukewarm during the debates. Even still, Mauney doubted the Brits would actually vote to condemn. The French were another question altogether.

The resolution was called to order, and the secretary-general, Armani Ali of Egypt, took the floor to present the wording for an up-or-down vote by the fifteen members of the council.

"Resolved, on the motion of the Republic of Sudan, as follows:

"The Security Council of the United Nations does hereby condemn the United States of America for its unjustified and unprovoked military attack and destruction by United States Navy jets on the Dome of the Rock, a holy site sacred to the great and peaceful world religion of Islam.

"I will now begin the roll call on the resolution, proceeding in alphabetical order. Each nation will vote yea, nay, abstain, or veto as applicable."

One hour later, the balance on the condemnation measure hung with France. Seven members had voted to pass the condemnation resolution, and four had voted against it. Only two more votes were needed to pass it. The secretary came to France.

"The French Republic."

"Un moment, s'il vous plait, Monsieur Secretaire." This from Foreign Minister Louie Arant, who, like Secretary Mauney, had been dispatched by his president to personally oversee this international maneuvering.

Another minute passed. It seemed the French, in a typical grandstanding maneuver, planned to use the remaining two minutes to draw attention to themselves.

"Monsieur Secretaire," Foreign Minister Arant said. He hesitated a moment before continuing. "The French Republic votes—yea."

Applause erupted in the gallery and among the Arab delegations.

Secretary Mauney stared at his traitorous French counterpart, who did not return the look. The French, as they had done on so many other matters in the war on terrorism, had put the United States in a tough position.

"Order, please. Order," the secretary-general said, trying to calm the spontaneous anti-American celebration so he could proceed with the roll call. "The United Kingdom of Great Britain and Northern Ireland."

Lord, please don't let the Brits turn on us too.

"The United Kingdom of Great Britain and Northern Ireland," said Foreign Secretary Sir Victor McKibben, "Britain, in standing with her great ally in war, and her great friend in peace, the United States of America, votes—nay."

"Thank you," Secretary Mauney mouthed at Sir Victor, who smiled and nodded graciously.

"The United States of America."

"One moment, please, Mr. Secretary." Mauney turned to an aide and asked for the tally sheet of votes. So far, eight countries, including Albania, Angola, Bosnia, China, Egypt, France, Russia, and Sudan, had voted yes. One more vote would give the resolution the requisite nine votes needed to carry, thus delivering an embarrassing blow to the United States. After the U.S. vote, the Republic of Uzbekistan, a former Soviet republic with a predominant Islamic population, was up next, with a sure "yea" that would seal the deal.

Mauney looked to his immediate right to Caroline Ward, the forty-five-year-old U.S. ambassador to the United Nations. "What do you think, Madam Ambassador?"

"We've got to exercise the veto, sir," she said, telling him what he already knew.

"Vive la France," he said under his breath. "You're right, Caroline. It's the only way to block outright passage of a condemnation against the U.S."

"Let's ship the Statute of Liberty back with the foreign minister," Ward whispered in his ear.

Mauney rose, shooting another unreciprocated stare at the French ambassador before addressing the secretary. "Mr. Secretary, on the resolution by the government of the Sudan, now before the Security Council, and in exercising the authority granted to it by the Charter of the United Nations, as a permanent member of this Security Council, the United States of America does hereby exercise its right of veto over the resolution."

Hissing rose from the Arab section and from the gallery.

"Order. Order," the secretary-general said. "The United States of America having exercised its right as a permanent member of this Security Council to use its veto authority, and the chair having recognized the veto cast by the United States of America, the resolution is killed, and we will now move on to further business.

"Our next item on the agenda is a second resolution, and the chair recognizes the foreign minister of the French Republic."

"Merci, Monsieur Secretaire." French Foreign Minister Arant rose, nodding and smiling at everyone around the circular table except the American delegation.

"As you know, two days ago, the government of Israel announced that Israeli Special Forces had captured two United States Navy pilots, who are suspected to have launched missile attacks against the Dome of the Rock. While preliminary evidence suggests that Israeli forces may have crossed into Syrian airspace and actually captured these pilots on Syrian soil, a fact that, if true, could constitute an act of war against Syria, it is not our intention at this time to introduce any resolution on that matter. We do reserve the right, however, to hold that matter open as more evidence pours in on the method of capture of these pilots.

"Whatever the method, however, the fact remains that Israel has these pilots, and they are potentially not only war criminals, but criminals against humanity. To that extent, I yield the balance of my time to a very distinguished citizen of France, one of the world's foremost international criminal lawyers, Monsieur Jean-Claude la Trec, who has drafted a resolution, sponsored by the French government, that we feel would lead to the fairest and most just tribunal for dealing with these pilots under international law."

The foreign minister turned and nodded, and the tall, silver-haired avocat rose from amid the French delegation.

"*Merci, Monsieur Foreign Minister. Bon après-midi, Messieurs-dames.*

"As you know, ladies and gentlemen," the suave-talking gentleman began, "there is in the law, as we all know, the concept known as a *conflict of interest*. This concept is universally recognized not only in the body of law of every civilized nation on earth, but in the body of international law as well.

"The government of France would like to see this crucial international legal question involving disposition of these pilots in a way so as to avoid any charge of conflict of interest by any member state. Because these are American pilots, France feels it would be unfair to the United States government to be placed in a position of dealing with them."

La Trec, unlike his foreign minister, turned and gave a friendly nod at the American delegation. "Should the Americans prosecute these pilots, one of two things would happen. First, there would be so much international pressure to secure a conviction, the pilots might not receive a fair trial. On the other hand, if they were acquitted by an American tribunal, charges would arise, fairly or unfairly, that the system had been rigged."

La Trec again smiled and nodded to the Americans. Mauney glanced at Ambassador Ward, who rolled her eyes.

"This simply isn't fair to our American friends, and we wish to spare them such a potentially embarrassing situation.

"Likewise, should the State of Israel undertake such a prosecution, a similar conflict of interest would evolve. Although the attacks were against a Muslim holy site, that Muslim holy site was on soil controlled by the Israeli government. Like America, Israel would therefore be under enormous pressure from her own people to obtain a conviction, which may lead to an unfair trial for the pilots. An acquittal by an Israeli tribunal could lead to potential domestic chaos.

"Therefore, the government of France has authorized me to draft the following resolution for consideration by this honorable Security Council:

"Resolved: In the matter of seeking an appropriate international criminal forum for the potential prosecution of United States Navy pilots allegedly involved in the missile attack on the Dome of the Rock, and in order to prevent a potential conflict of interest by the United States of America or the State of Israel, both of whom may be faced with irreconcilable conflicts should either state seek to undertake such a prosecution, this Council calls upon the State of Israel to immediately hand over the pilots to military authorities of the United Nations for prosecution by the International Criminal Court, under the auspices of the Rome Treaty."

Rampant applause rose from the gallery.

"Of all the . . ." Secretary Mauney caught his tongue, then swallowed two large gulps of ice water.

Council of Ishmael headquarters
Rub al-Khali Desert

Excellent work, Abdur," Hussein al-Akhma said. "We've embarrassed the Americans twice in the same day. Already we've gotten more mileage out of this French fellow than we got out of Mr. Levinson."

"Yes." Abdur felt great satisfaction in the day's events. "No matter what the Americans do, we've succeeded in driving an even deeper wedge between them and the French."

"Although I am quite disappointed with the British. Just when I thought they might be coming around."

"They've been in bed with the Americans for a long time, Leader."

Hussein drained his glass. "Let's send a message to the Brits. Have our U.K. operatives arrange for five bombs to go off in various London-area elementary schools tomorrow. A bomb for every no vote cast today. They will pay with dead British schoolchildren."

"As you say, Leader."

CHAPTER 41

Prime Minister Rothstein took a sip of water, then met the gazes of the eighteen members of his cabinet. In a chamber normally filled with a barrage of verbal thunderbolts, rare silence reigned.

Rothstein set down the glass and commenced reading the final paragraphs of the communiqué from the president of the United States.

> And so, Mr. Prime Minister, we are pleased to accept your proposal, contingent, of course, upon the ability for the court-martial to function freely in Israel as it would anywhere else in the world. The defendants, of course, would have the right to counsel of their choice. If there is a conviction, the defendants would be released to American control. The same would be true if there is an acquittal.
>
> We are detailing Lieutenant Commander Zack Brewer as lead counsel to this case, as you suggested. Because of the complexity of the case and the importance of the outcome, the Judge Advocate General of the Navy is detailing an assistant prosecutor to serve with Lieutenant Commander Brewer. She is Lieutenant Commander Wendy Poole, a capable JAG officer who recently represented the Navy before the United States Supreme Court in the appeal of the convicted Navy chaplains shortly before their execution.
>
> In closing, Mr. Prime Minister, I realize that these are perilous times for Israel. To again underscore America's commitment to the security

of your country, I have ordered two additional carrier task forces to join the USS *Harry S. Truman* in the Eastern Mediterranean. Within a week, you can expect to see the *Truman* as well as the carriers USS *Ronald Reagan* and USS *Nimitz* off your shores.

Thank you for your friendship, Mr. Prime Minister. As always, we look forward to working with you as we strive toward our common goals of democracy, peace, and prosperity in the Middle East.

Very respectfully,
Mack Williams
President of the United States

The prime minister set down the letter, adjusted his glasses, and looked at his cabinet. "Comments?"

"The carrot and the stick," the minister of defense said. "Nobody does it better than the Americans."

"I would say that three carrier task forces is a pretty big stick," said Foreign Minister Alya Baruch. The defense minister looked at Alya, who had slipped on her glasses as she often did before making solemn observations.

"Three big sticks," she said, "that would be welcomed by every Israeli citizen right about now."

"I agree," the prime minister added. "Additionally, this cabinet needs to take decisive action to countermand the circus going on in the United Nations Security Council. I move that the cabinet accept the president's counterproposal."

A moment later, the cabinet approved a resolution by a vote of 19 to 0.

CHAPTER 42

Somewhere in Mexico

With the van obviously crossing some sort of bumpy, rocky terrain, Diane opened her eyes again, focusing on the dome light. It was still daylight, but she wasn't sure how long she had slept.

"Look who is awake." The man who called himself an Arab terrorist looked back as Diane did half a sit-up. She squinted in the bright sunlight. The terrain was remarkably similar to their last stop, except this time two large warehouses lay directly ahead of them.

"Where are we?"

"Somewhere southeast of where we were last time you were awake."

The van, crawling through dips and bumps, rounded the side of the outer warehouse ... which turned out not to be a warehouse at all.

A long, sleek Lear jet, its chrome twin engines brightly reflecting the hot Mexican sun, sat on a concrete pad just outside the left hangar. A concrete airstrip protruded out into the desert.

"You like flying, Lieutenant?"

"Not going to answer?" Mr. Terrorist stopped the van. "Not to worry. I will hold your hand if you become afraid." The man got out, slung an Uzi over his shoulder, and walked around to her door, sliding it open. "Out of the van, beautiful." He pointed the Uzi at her.

Oh dear God. I'm going to die.

"Walk to the plane. Move!"

She slid down, feet first, to the concrete. With the steel barrel of the Uzi pressed into the back of her neck, she slowly and painfully stepped across the hot concrete, her feet shackled, toward the aircraft. A retractable ladder was moved to the front section of the fuselage.

Our Father, who art in heaven, hallowed be thy name ...

"Faster, beautiful. We do not have all day!" Another shove of the barrel into her cranium.

Thy kingdom come, thy will be done ...

"Up the steps!"

... on earth as it is in heaven. Give us this day our daily bread. And forgive us our trespasses, as we forgive those who trespass against us.

"Faster," the terrorist demanded as she entered the door through the fuselage just behind the cockpit. Two Arab pilots in green army fatigues glanced up from their positions in the cockpit, while another Arab man, perhaps the flight steward, greeted her with a pistol to her nose. "Sit in the back," the pistol-bearing man said.

Lead us not into temptation ...

"Sit here!" said the man with the pistol as the driver followed her with his Uzi. She heard the cabin door close, then the whine of jet engines. Both terrorists sat in the seats behind her. Slowly the jet started rolling down the runway. Then faster, faster.

... but deliver us from evil ...

Liftoff. A steep ascent. Was this it? Why did she feel that this was the last time she would ever step foot, alive, in the Western hemisphere?

For thine is the kingdom ...

She felt the plane bank, level off, then bank again.

... and the power, and the glory ...

She flinched when she felt a hypodermic needle jab into her arm; she tensed as the terrorist pressed his thumb against the depressor, pushing whatever substance he desired into her body.

... forever and ever.

She looked out the window as deep wooziness began to overtake her. Eyes heavy, she watched the coastline transform into the rolling waters of the ocean. Which ocean? She wasn't sure. It didn't matter now ...

Amen.

Municipal Cemetery No. 8
The West Bank
Jerusalem

Alexander and Yael stood on the sidewalk near the cemetery gate. Fifteen acres of rolling green hills sprawled before them. Several dozen commemorative monuments were planted here, Stars of David rising from the ground to commemorate the lives of those whose families had somehow raised the money for a headstone.

Mostly just flat markers commemorated the graves. With numbers. Not even names.

Alexander Kweskin had no money to buy his precious daughter a headstone. So for now, in the eyes of the State of Israel, she was but a number. Grave marker number 318, Municipal Cemetery Number 8, in the Israeli-occupied West Bank of Jerusalem.

Three days had passed since her little body had gone back to the dust from which it came, and each day since then, he and Yael had come to visit her.

Alexander looked at his wife. "Ready?"

"Dah."

He took her hand, and they walked up the gravel path to where the ground was freshly broken at number 318. Alexander and Yael fell on their knees on each side of the grave. Their tears flowed as both of them laid a single rose on the ground.

"Oh God," Alexander prayed, "as the heavens are above the earth, so your ways are above our ways. We do not understand why we have come here to Israel, only to lose our precious daughter. May her death not have been in vain. May your vengeance be poured out on those responsible. May justice be yours. And may we now dwell in this land of yours in peace. Amen."

CHAPTER 43

Office of the Commanding Officer
Navy Trial Service Office
Building 73
32nd Street Naval Station
San Diego, California

vey, please send in the XO, and then I need to see Commanders Brewer and Poole."

"Yes, Captain." Ivey King, his civilian secretary, spoke in the sweet-sounding South African accent she still retained from her immigration thirty years before.

A moment later, a tall, lanky officer in his midforties, wearing the silver oak leaf of a full navy commander on his right khaki collar, appeared at Captain Glen Rudy's office door. The executive officer, known in navy lingo as the XO, was Rudy's second-in-command.

"We've gotten a call in from Washington. I've got to talk to Brewer and Poole. I need you to take over the uniform inspection this morning."

One of the more boring duties devolving on the commanding officer of a Navy Trial Service Office was that of uniform inspection. JAG officers, despite the fact that they were lawyers and had passed a bar exam in one of the fifty states or the District of Columbia, were part of the navy. And the navy was part of the military. And in order to maintain good order and discipline in the military, a proper, spiffy appearance was necessary. Today was the day.

"Aye, aye, sir. Consider it done."

"Thanks."

A few seconds later, Lieutenant Commander Brewer, in an inspection-ready working khaki shirt and pants, and Lieutenant Commander Poole, in an equally presentable working khaki shirt and skirt, appeared at the door.

"You wanted to see us, sir?" Zack asked.

"Zack, Wendy. Come in and be seated."

They complied.

"Admiral Stumbaugh just called. Official charges are being referred against our two pilots this morning in Norfolk. You need to be ready to fly to the Middle East in forty-eight hours. Are you ready for trial?"

Rudy saw Zack and Wendy lock eyes; then Zack's gaze met his. "Skipper, we think so. We've been working almost around the clock. Yes, I think we're ready."

"*Think?* Zack, I need more than that. I need—the president needs—to know we can win this thing."

"Captain, I always feel pretty confident about my chances at trial, as you know. But for a trial of this magnitude, this is coming down the pike awfully fast. We had at least ninety days of preparation time for the Olajuwon case. Enough time to work with the Naval Criminal Investigative Service to gather evidence. This attack occurred just *last week*, Skipper. I've never seen a court-martial convene so fast. We haven't even had the chance to go on board the *Truman* to interview witnesses."

Rudy ignored the comment, temporarily, and buzzed his telephone intercom. "Ivey, would you ask the master chief if he would mind bringing us a fresh pot of coffee?"

"Not at all, Captain," Ivey King said.

"I haven't either, Zack," Rudy said.

"Sir?"

"I've never seen a court-martial convene so rapidly. But this is being driven by international politics. The administration wants to seize the momentum away from this ludicrous French initiative. In other words, the JAG Corps has to respond, and respond effectively, even with a short prep time.

"Zack, the Israelis want you prosecuting this case as part of a very dicey diplomatic solution. Frankly, you'd probably have gotten the call to prosecute it even if we had brought these guys back to the States and had taken our sweet time to prepare.

"Wendy, I recommended that you come on board because I've seen your professionalism. You've impressed a lot of top brass with your

220 ★ DON BROWN

performance in front of the Supreme Court. I knew that Zack, despite his very healthy ego"—the comment brought sly grins from both Zack and Wendy—"would need a lot of help. Especially given the short time frame.

"Now, you two are going to be on the front lines in this thing, but just like last time, Zack, you'll have not only the full resources of the JAG Corps behind you, but also the full backing of the U.S. government."

"Thank you, sir," Zack said.

"Oh, and by the way," Rudy added, "just like you suspected, Zack, these guys have fired their navy defense counsel and retained Monsieur la Trec."

Zack again glanced at Wendy, raising his eyebrow.

"You were right," she said.

CHAPTER 44

Office of Lieutenant Commander Zack Brewer, JAGC, USN
Navy Trial Service Office
Building 73
32nd Street Naval Station
San Diego, California

1700 hours

Okay, Wendy, let's go over this checklist one more time and then take a break. You've been doing some digging on their educational and religious backgrounds?"

"Right," she said. "Both strict Muslims from strict Muslim families. Both went to college on scholarship with money from a charitable group called the Muslim Educational Foundation."

"Hmm." Zack frowned. "Let's pull the file from the Olajuwon case. I'm sure that's the same group that funded college and seminary for our three departed chaplains."

"Think there's a connection?" She shot him a curious look.

"Yes, I do, without a doubt." This time she noticed his voice held an air of confidence. More like the Zack Brewer she had seen on television dozens of times. The Zack who, with some help from Diane Colcernian, had whipped America's best trial lawyer. She also knew, as Captain Rudy had said, that to win this case, Zack would need to have his "head in the game."

"I'll pull their file and check."

L'office de droit de Jean-Claude la Trec
56, rue Charles De Gaulle
Paris

The man who was called "the greatest lawyer in France," "the most brilliant defense attorney in the world," and other sycophantic phrases by the international media looked up as the senior associate staff counsel, the lovely Jeanette L'Enfant, walked into his office.

"Ah, as always, you look more beautiful by the moment, *ma cher*," he said.

"And you, *mon beau* avocat, become more eloquent by the moment, which is why you are the world's greatest avocat." She sat down in the same French provincial chair occupied two days ago by Abdur Rahman and crossed her legs. "Even greater than the great Wells Levinson, *mon beau*."

"Oh, really?" He took a sip of mineral water from a crystal glass. "You're just saying that because you work for me, because I pay you more handsomely than any other law firm in France would, and because of certain other"—he cleared his throat and took another sip—"fringe benefits."

"You underestimate yourself." She shot him a knowing smile as she brushed a strand of blond hair over her shoulder. "Levinson is a self-promoter. How many resolutions could Levinson have gotten before the United Nations Security Council within a period of forty-eight hours? Or forty-eight years, for that matter?"

"Yes," he said, smiling into her eyes. He had met Jeanette L'Enfant at an international bar convention on the Riviera four years ago. He had not once regretted hiring her.

"Levinson is an American creation. A Jewish cowboy. Besides, the credible publications that really matter—the *Economist*, the *Telegraph*, *Le Monde*—all have said over the years that *you* are the world's greatest lawyer. But this you already know. But if it takes me stroking your massive ego to give you ... what is it the American's call it? The eye of the tiger? Then that I am happy to do."

He unbuttoned his gold cufflinks, dropped them into his desk drawer, then rolled up his sleeves. "As much as I do love your ego stroking, my intellectual kitten, you know as well as I do that the secret of my success is built not only upon, shall we say, healthy ego, but even more importantly upon preparation. Hmm?"

"Okay, okay," she said. "I can tell that you are in another one of those business-before-pleasure modes." She tossed the file across the desk.

"The dossier on Lieutenant Commander Brewer, I take it?"

"With every detail you asked for. His strengths, his weaknesses, his preference for women."

He opened the file and began perusing it. "Yes, well, one advantage we do have over Levinson. Brewer was an unknown when Levinson met him in court. Now he has a track record."

"Yes," she said. "A short but powerfully impressive track record."

He tossed the dossier back on the desk. "Why don't we start with an oral briefing?"

"His strongest attribute appears to be his media savvy and his ability to make powerful oral arguments. Not particularly the academic type. He finished in the middle of his class in law school and at the Naval Justice School—"

"Not exactly law review type, was he?"

"No, but where he may lack in classroom prowess, he more than makes up in rhetorical skills." She picked up the dossier and looked at it. "Law School Moot Court Champion, National Moot Court Team— runner-up regional semifinals, National Trial Team, Order of the Barristers, winner of the Naval Justice School Trial Advocacy Competition sponsored by the New York City Bar Association."

La Trec turned to look out the window at the Eiffel Tower in the distance. "Impressive, indeed. But with the exception of the navy award, all basically law school awards."

"It doesn't stop there. Brewer has been decorated by the secretary of the navy twice for his work in prosecuting highly publicized rape cases, and he first cut his teeth against Lieutenant Colcernian in a highly publicized rape case involving the niece of U.S. Senator Roberson Fowler."

"Yes, I remember reading about the case," la Trec said.

"Then, of course, *mon cher*, there was his most impressive victory against your friend Mr. Levinson."

"Yes, I must say I rooted for the young chap in that one." La Trec grinned. "Okay, so we know this naval officer has a flair for the courtroom. But there has to be a weak link in the chain. I want to know what he struggles with."

"As I said," she continued, recrossing her legs, "his strength is oral argument. He knows their rules of evidences and is extremely quick on his feet, both in meeting unexpected objections and in dealing with the media."

"Any video on him?"

She received a CD from the dossier. "There. Pop it in. Have a look."

La Trec placed the CD in his computer.

"This is from his closing in the Olajuwon court-martial."

The large, flat computer screen showed a frozen picture of a U.S. Naval JAG officer, standing in what looked like the well of a courtroom. After a click of the mouse, Brewer began to move and speak.

"If Harry Houdini were in this courtroom today, he'd be proud ... proud to see the world's greatest lawyer borrow the most fundamental technique of trickery from the world's greatest magician and bring it into the courtroom.

"Mr. Levinson seeks to hold out Harry Kilnap as the visual distraction while hiding behind his back the cold, stark truth of cold-blooded murder!"

The screen paused.

"So," la Trec said, "he is not afraid to go after a high-profile opponent in his closing argument."

"Not in the least bit intimidated," Jeanette replied with a sparkle in her eye.

"Run a little more," he ordered.

"Magic might be great for the stage, Mr. Levinson, but it won't work in a court of law. Not in this court anyway. Not when the cold, hard evidence against the defendants is so compelling, so condemning."

The screen paused again.

"Hard-hitting, isn't he?" la Trec said.

She smiled and raised a brow. "Check out the climax of his closing."

"And the religion we condemn is nothing more than a perverted philosophy that seeks to maim, kill, terrorize, and intimidate as a means of advancing its goals. A perverted philosophy—in the name of religion—the defendants have adopted and put into practice by taking the lives of American servicemen and innocent civilians.

"Send a strong message that murder, terrorism, and treason will not be tolerated. Not in my navy.

"Return with a verdict of guilty.

"Thank you."

"Enough!" la Trec snapped. "So obviously, he is a powerfully talented courtroom advocate. I'm not interested in his strengths. A chain is only as strong as its weakest link. I'm interested in his weaknesses. What do you have for me?"

"He doesn't show weaknesses, but they are there. Trust me." A comely wink.

"Show me."

She got up, walked around behind him, and started to lightly massage his shoulders. "His weakness is Delilah."

"What are you talking about, *ma belle?*"

"Commander Brewer is a Sampson in the courtroom, but like Sampson, his weakness is a woman. His Delilah is Lieutenant Diane Colcernian. Trust me on this. I know."

"How can you be so sure?"

"Call it womanly instinct." Her fingers dug deeply into his shoulders. "And you yourself have said that mine has never been wrong."

"Hmm," he mused as she nudged her nose along the right side of his neck. "So what are you saying, my dear?"

"You're the smartest lawyer in the world, Jean-Claude. I think you can figure this one out."

As she kissed him behind the ear, he picked up his cell phone and dialed the number for Abdur Rahman.

LCDR Zack Brewer's residence
4935 Mills Street
La Mesa, California

Zack was home alone, looking over his notes, when the doorbell rang. He checked his watch. Wendy was a few minutes early for their trial preparation session. He tossed the folder on the glass coffee table and opened the front door.

A delivery man stood in front of him holding a clipboard. "Lieutenant Commander Brewer?"

"That's me."

"I have a package for you, sir."

"Okay."

"Sign here, please."

The courier handed Zack a blue pen. He signed his name and took the manila envelope, which included his name and address but no return address.

"Thank you, sir."

As the courier puttered away in a Toyota Tercel, Zack reached into the envelope. He pulled out a photograph, facedown.

He turned it over.

Oh dear Jesus.

The eight-by-ten color photograph showed Diane, in civilian clothes, sitting on a stool in what appeared to be a cell block, with a black blindfold over her eyes. She was surrounded by two men wearing black ski masks and olive-drab fatigues, pointing Uzis at her head.

Zack felt as if he had been punched in the stomach. He heaved for breath. Cold sweat beaded on his forehead. He almost collapsed onto the sofa. For a moment he tried to breathe. Then he reached into the envelope and pulled out a single sheet of paper. It was a handwritten letter, printed in black ink.

Dear Lieutenant Commander Brewer,

Congratulations on your selection by the navy to prosecute yet another high-profile court-martial.

As you can see from the attached photograph, however, unfortunately, your favorite trial partner appears to be preoccupied at the moment and, consequently, will be unable to join you.

Not to fret, however, as I am sure that Lieutenant Colcernian will have her hands in this case and will be with you in heart.

Yes, and to ensure that this will happen, here is what we are prepared to offer for your peace of mind.

A motion to dismiss this case will most likely be made by your opponent, much in the way Mr. Levinson moved to dismiss the last court-martial you were involved in.

If the motion to dismiss is denied, that is when Lieutenant Colcernian will have a hand in helping you.

You see, as we understand American court-martial procedures, after the motion to dismiss is denied, you will get to make an opening statement to the members. Please be advised that at the moment you begin your opening statement, we will begin to, with the use of a sharp knife, amputate Lieutenant Colcernian's right hand. We will take our time, of course, ensuring the amputation process lasts precisely as long as your opening argument.

Then, when you deliver what will undoubtedly be a spellbinding closing argument, as you always do, we will repeat this procedure with her left hand. Won't that make for the most exciting argument you have ever delivered?

But wait.

There is more!

We understand that after closing argument, the jury will deliver a verdict. If the verdict is not guilty, we will release the handless Lieutenant Colcernian to return to freedom. But if the verdict is guilty, we will use our blood-stained knife to amputate her ears.

But even after that, there is still hope for the beautiful lieutenant. If the defendants are spared the death penalty, then we will return the handless, earless lovely into your arms.

But if either of these pilots is condemned to die, then we will proceed to slowly slit the good lieutenant's throat.

It all should be interesting, should it not?

Thank you, so much, for your consideration of this matter.

We look forward to working with you through the resolution of this case.

And may Allah the benevolent be glorified in all actions.

> Peace be unto you,
> A soldier of Allah

Eastbound California Highway 94
Approaching Lemon Grove Avenue exit
East San Diego County

Wendy tapped the brakes on the rental car, reacting to the slew of brake lights, an illuminated eastbound snake of traffic, now stalling in the late afternoon sun just west of the Lemon Grove exit.

She glanced down at her wristwatch: 5:45. She picked up her cell phone and hit speed dial. His answering machine came on. Then a *beep*.

"Hi, Zack, I'm stuck here on 94. I'm coming up on the Lemon Grove exit. I won't be there for probably another fifteen minutes. See you then. Bye."

Why was she disappointed he hadn't picked up? After all, she had worked with him at the NTSO all day today. And all day the day before. And three hours the night before that.

Today they had checked witness lists, traced documents on the educational funding of the pilots, and worked on potential cross-examination. When, earlier, Zack had to run to the military courthouse to deal with a guilty plea, they agreed to meet up again at his home in La Mesa, where they might grab a bite to eat, then work again until midnight.

In less than two days, she would be flying with him to Israel to take on a case that, no matter what the outcome, was bound to forge them together and perhaps change their lives forever. It was a pleasant thought.

She tried not to think about Diane. She had seen the pain in his eyes when discussing her disappearance. The great trial pit bull Zack Brewer had shown his emotional side over Diane's vanishing. His eyes had welled with tears several times at the mention of her name.

She prayed Diane Colcernian would survive. But for the good of the country, Wendy had to keep his mind off her. The nation could not afford to have Lieutenant Commander Zack Brewer distracted or slipping into depression on the eve of this court-martial.

Am I really trying to keep his mind off her in the name of the national interest? Or for my own interests?

She reached down and punched the radio on as, finally, her car reached the Spring Street exit.

The voice of a woman announcer: "More fallout today from the United States' controversial decision to prosecute the two pilots implicated in the missile attack on the Dome of the Rock. A number of the president's democratic opponents held press conferences criticizing the administration's refusal to adhere to the wishes of the UN Security Council. Among the most vocal of those critics, to no surprise, was the Reverend JamesOn Barbour of the Society Against Racial Discrimination. Here's what the Reverend Barbour had to say today from a press conference outside SARD headquarters in Chicago."

Barbour's voice came on the radio: "Why is it the United States has so cavalierly rejected this proposal from the great government of France? Is it because this administration has something to hide? Why is it this administration is so reluctant to submit to the sovereign authority of the United Nations?

"Other nations have done this already, but this administration wants to play cowboy on the stage of world politics. Is it because they have done something which they do not wish us to know? If the Williams administration truly has nothing to hide, then why not turn the matter over to the International Criminal Court to be judged by all nations!

"The Bible says the truth shall set you free. And I call upon this administration to submit to the UN, that great sovereign organization of nations, and to tell the truth!"

Enough of that buffoon. Wendy killed the radio as she pulled onto Mills Street. Zack's silver Mercedes was parked in the driveway, and even the sight of his car made her heart jump.

What's wrong with me?

She got out of the car, walked to the front door, and rang the doorbell.

No answer.

She rang again.

Same result.

She turned the doorknob. It was unlocked.

I wonder if I should just open it. Surely he won't mind. After all, he is expecting me.

She pushed open the door and saw him sitting across the room, on the sofa, his face buried in his hands.

"Zack?"

He didn't move.

"Zack!" She walked across the small room to him. He looked up at her. "What's the matter, Zack?"

"This came by courier just a few minutes ago." He handed her a large manila envelope.

Wendy stared at the photograph, feeling the blood drain from her face. *Lord, help me be strong.* "Zack ..."

His eyes, filled with raw pain, caught hers.

She wanted to take him in her arms. Instead, she said, "We've got to get this to Captain Rudy."

CHAPTER 45

8 East 4th Avenue
Coronado Island
Coronado, California

Fortunately, from Wendy's perspective, Zack had gotten his emotions sufficiently under control to take the wheel of his car and fight through the remnants of the San Diego evening rush-hour traffic. She did not judge him emotionally stable enough, however, to make the drive alone. So she insisted on riding with him to Captain Rudy's house.

He had offered no resistance.

A quarter moon hung over the white stucco cottage on posh Coronado Island as Zack pulled to the curb and parked the Mercedes.

"Want me to take the lead on this?" Wendy asked as they walked up the brick walkway.

"Technically, you *are* senior to me, ma'am."

"Okay. Say no more."

They stepped onto the front stoop and rang the doorbell. Captain Rudy, dressed in a golf shirt and blue jeans, opened the door.

"Zack. Wendy. Please come in." He motioned them into the living room.

"Sorry to bother you after office hours, Captain," Wendy said, "but shortly after Zack got home this evening, DHL delivered this package to him." She handed him the envelope.

He pulled out the photo. "Oh dear God, help us." He sat down.

"Captain, there's more in the envelope."

Rudy extracted the letter. His face, ordinarily ruddy, instantly paled.

"Okay. Okay." He ran his hand through his hair. "Listen, we've gotta stay cool here." He sighed heavily. "Zack, how are you feeling?"

"This has rocked me."

Rudy took a deep breath. "Okay, Washington needs to know about this immediately." He drew in another deep breath. "I'm going to the naval station." He ran his hand through his hair again. "And then I'll send a flash message to the National Command Authority. Okay?"

"Yes, sir," Wendy said.

"Depending on what Washington says, I may notify the FBI. Then I want you two to go back and keep preparing. I don't know how Washington will react to this, but we've got to be ready, as hard as this is, either way. Okay?"

They both nodded.

"Zack, are you going to be able to handle this?"

Zack looked at Wendy, then back to the captain. "Skipper, I don't know whether I can focus under these circumstances. It might be good if someone else prosecutes it." His voice wavered. He fell silent for a moment, then continued, his voice stronger. "But I'm a naval officer, sir. And you know that I will do my very best to carry out all the lawful orders of my superiors."

Captain Rudy stood, walked across the room, and gave Zack a reassuring pat on the shoulder. "I know you will, Zack. You're the finest officer who has ever served under my command."

"Yes, sir."

"Okay," Rudy said gruffly. "Let's get back to work."

"Aye, sir," Zack and Wendy said in unison.

White House Signals Office
Old executive office building

One hour later

It had been an unusually quiet night. Navy Captain Mike Stacks, duty officer in charge of the White House Signals Office, checked his watch: 11:45 p.m. He sipped his coffee as he walked between the rows of twenty-five military personnel from all five branches of the services, satisfied that all would remain quiet on his watch.

"Captain, we've got a Flash TS message from San Diego!" one of the air force duty sergeants called out. He referred to a top-secret message requiring the highest priority for action.

"Whatcha got, Sergeant?"

The sergeant ripped the top-secret message out of the printer and handed it to Captain Stacks.

Flash

Top Secret

From: Commanding Officer, NTSO San Diego

To: National Command Authority

Via: Navy Judge Advocate General

        Secretary of the Navy

        Secretary of Defense

        Chairman, Joint Chiefs of Staff

Re: Apparent Kidnap of Lieutenant Diane Colcernian, JAGC, USN

1. Please be advised that this command has been made aware of an anonymous letter threatening torture and execution of Lieutenant Colcernian in response to the prospective court-martial of navy aviators in Israel.

2. This command has also been made aware of a photograph of Lieutenant Colcernian, blindfolded, apparently in a hostage situation.

3. Threatening letter and photograph were initially delivered to the home of LCDR Zachary Brewer, JAGC, USN, who immediately made this command aware of same.

4. Copies of letter and photograph are being forwarded contemporaneously by scrambled facsimile.

5. Please advise ASAP.

> Very respectfully,
> A. G. Rudy
> CAPT, JAGC, USN

"Captain, the fax and photo just came across the fax scrambler."

Stacks looked at the photo, and his heart sank.

"Get the national security advisor on the hotline," he told the sergeant.

A moment later the sergeant handed the receiver to Stacks. "She's on the line."

"Miss Hewitt," Stacks said, his gaze still riveted to the picture of Diane Colcernian. "This is Captain Stacks, White House Signals Office Duty Officer. I apologize for the late hour, ma'am, but we've got a flash message and a photo from San Diego." He paused. "Lieutenant Colcernian has been kidnapped. They're threatening to kill her if the prosecution of the aviators proceeds."

He listened to her response before continuing. "Yes, ma'am," he said. "I understand. I'll notify the chief of staff and awaken the president. I'll get on it right away, ma'am."

CHAPTER 46

Despite Captain Rudy's order that they get back to work on the case, and despite their attempts to carry out the order, their efforts to comply had not been successful.

Maybe they should have gone somewhere other than back to his house, which was all too much a visual reminder of the photograph and letter he had received some six hours earlier.

Despite the strain, they had discussed the legal grounds on which la Trec might move to dismiss. Zack felt he would try to resurrect the International Criminal Court garbage he had smeared across the UN Security Council.

By midnight, Wendy was starting to nod, and Zack suggested they wrap it up. He helped her get her papers in her briefcase, then walked her to her car. She yawned as she stepped in and slid beneath the wheel.

"You okay to drive?"

"Sure," she said, smiling.

"I'm following you home."

"Zack, that's sweet, but you don't have to do that."

"You're sleepy; I'm not. I'm following you to make sure you're okay, and if necessary, I'll harass you on your cell phone to keep you awake all the way to the BOQ."

"You are persuasive. I see why they call you the navy's best litigator."

An hour and a half later, after having driven to the Bachelor Officers' Quarters at the North Island Naval Air Station, Zack pulled back into the driveway of his La Mesa home.

He got out of the car, closed the door, his heart pounding like a jackhammer. A Pavlovian reflex, no doubt. Just being here brought back the heart-wrenching moment when he received the envelope. Would it happen again? Would someone bring him a photograph of her dead body?

Get hold of yourself, Zack!

Stepping onto the front stoop, he pulled out his keys and jiggled the front door open. There were no more envelopes.

He dead-bolted the front door behind him, stepped into his bed-room, unbuttoned his khaki uniform shirt, and in his T-shirt and khaki uniform pants, lay down on the bed. The light from the living room lamp cast a pale light on the blades of the ceiling fan.

Lying on his back, he concentrated on the slow-moving fan, hoping the motion would tire his eyes and help him get to sleep.

What if they're outside? That thought jolted him. He reached into his bedside drawer and gripped his nine-millimeter Glock. Working the action, he laid the gun on his chest, then tried the eye-circling game again.

An hour later the digital clock showed 2:30 a.m.

The eye-circling game wasn't working.

He got up, laid the gun by his bed, then threw his uniform shirt back on. Thirty minutes later, the Mercedes rolled into the empty gravel parking lot at the summit of Mount Helix.

He cut the bright halogen headlights, and everything went dark. But in a moment, his pupils adjusted, and with the glow spilling over from the spotlighted thirty-six-foot cross, the images of the parking lot and the amphitheater came into focus.

Technically, the park closed at sundown, but Zack felt something tugging him beyond the low gate. He straddled it, hopped down, and walked across the amphitheater to the stone wall.

Looking west, the twinkling lights of San Diego spread across the vast vista below the mountain. Sweeping searchlights beamed into the sky from Lindberg Field, twelve miles or so straight ahead, from Brown Field, to his left just north of the Mexican border, and from MCAS Mira-mar, off to his right. Off in the distance, beyond Lindberg Field, the distinctive, silhouetted image of the Point Loma Peninsula jutted into the dark waters of the Pacific.

Zack lay down on his back on the stone wall at the edge of the park. A shooting star shot across the twinkling celestial canopy above the lit cross, visible in the right side of his peripheral vision.

"Father, at this very moment, more so than at any moment in my life, I feel a small semblance of what your Son felt that night in the garden of Gethsemane.

"Not that the terrible weight on my shoulders compares with the incomprehensibly heavy burden that caused him to sweat drops of blood that night, but for me, Father, your weak, earthly son, this burden is heavier than anything I have ever felt."

He sat up, turned away from the city lights, and faced the illuminated white cross.

"Father, out of sheer undeserved mercy, you gave me a remarkable talent for courtroom advocacy, for which I am grateful. And years ago, when I was accepted into law school, I told you that I would dedicate my profession to you and prayed that you would use my vocation for your glory.

"And since that day, Father, you have blessed me with success I never could have dreamed of and never could have achieved on my own. Indeed, Father, on my own, I would have failed miserably. Apart from you, I am nothing. And when I have strayed from you, I have fallen on my face, as I deserved to do.

"Father, for reasons I thought I may have understood, but now confess I don't understand, you brought Diane Colcernian into my life. At first we fought like cats and dogs. And then we became friends, Lord, and then we became more. Our feelings for each other grew. And although we never discussed it, I have wondered — and maybe Diane has too — if we were born for each other.

"But now, Father, after all that, if I obey the lawful orders of the officers above me, I could cause her to be slowly tortured and murdered. I don't believe I can do this. I feel that I just want to disobey this order and let them court-martial me. I know you would have me obey the orders of my superiors, but how can I, Father? How can I? How can I kill her, Lord? I want her back. Please, Father ..." His voice cracked and his tears streamed.

After a few minutes, he continued.

"Father, is there a way you can raise someone else up to prosecute this case? Will you please move on the Israeli government to consider another American they trust to handle this? Will you please change the president's mind about insisting on me?

"I didn't ask for any of this. I didn't ask to be the part of a diplomatic solution in a tense international standoff. Please, Father, if it be your will, take this cup from me. Please, please …" The tears were flowing again. He waited a few more minutes, wiped his eyes, and lay back down on the stone wall again.

He looked into the heavens. "But not my will, Father," he prayed slowly, "but your will be done. Give me the strength to follow your will, whatever that may be."

For the first time in days, a supernatural peace came over him.

"Thank you, Father. In the almighty name of Jesus of Nazareth, the Risen Savior and the Mighty Prophet of God, amen."

Zack closed his eyes and fell asleep.

CHAPTER 47

Office of Lieutenant Commander Zack Brewer, JAGC, USN
Navy Trial Service Office
Building 73
32nd Street Naval Station
San Diego, California

At the first signs of the gray, luminescent hue pushing back the stars, evidence that the sun was on its way somewhere over the eastern horizon, Zack's eyes opened. By the time the long orange rays of the morning sun had crested the mountain, he had driven home, showered, shaved, thrown on a set of fresh working khakis, and started to head down westbound California Highway 94 toward the naval station.

Zack checked his watch as he accepted and then returned the salute from the petty officer at the main gate of the 32nd Street Naval Station. Five minutes to eight. If he hurried, maybe he could get to the Navy Trial Service Office before colors.

Four minutes later he parked the 320 in his reserved spot. As he exited his car, he was stopped dead in his tracks—along with every other person and every car on base—by the sound of whistles blaring over the naval station loudspeakers.

Colors.

Zack came to attention, facing the nearest American flagpole, in this case, the flagpole in front of the NTSO. With the first note of "The Star-Spangled Banner," in accordance with naval customs and tradition, he snapped a sharp salute, holding the salute as the enlisted flag patrol hoisted Old Glory up the pole.

On board the USS *Ticonderoga*, moored at Pier 1 across the street, Zack saw dozens of sailors on deck, also frozen in salute; dozens of officers and enlisted men along the piers and sidewalks and decks held their salute. The scene was being repeated not only throughout 32nd Street, but at every U.S. Navy command and ship in the Pacific standard time zone at that very moment.

Zack held the salute until the last chords of "and the hooome of the braaave," then, with whistles blowing again, snapped down the salute just as crisply as he had rendered it. Cars started moving again, men and women resumed walking, and Zack headed into the NTSO, into his office, where he was met by his boss, a coffee-swilling Commander Bob Awe.

"Zack, the skipper wants you in his office right now."

"Aye, sir." Zack tossed his officer's cover on his desk and followed Commander Awe to Captain Rudy's office.

"He just came in, sir," Captain Rudy said, apparently into his speakerphone, then motioned for Zack and Commander Awe to come in and sit down.

"Zack, is that you?" A familiar male voice came over the speakerphone as Zack settled into the chair in front of Captain Rudy's desk. Zack couldn't quite place the voice, but if Captain Rudy referred to the speaker as "sir," then that was good enough for him.

"Yes, sir, this is Lieutenant Commander Brewer."

"Zack, this is Mack Williams."

And then, stunned recognition.

"Mr. President?"

"Yes, I think I'm still on the government payroll this morning."

Zack's eyes widened. He glanced at Captain Rudy, who smiled slightly and nodded his head.

"It's an honor to speak with you again, Mr. President."

"As one JAG officer to another, the honor is mine," the president said.

"Thank you, sir."

"Were you able to get any sleep last night?"

"Believe it or not, Mr. President, for the first time in my life, I slept outside on a park bench."

Zack saw Commander Awe raise an eyebrow at that remark.

"A park bench?" the president said. "Sounds like you couldn't have slept much."

"Maybe a couple of hours."

"I know it probably won't make you feel better, but just for the record, your commander in chief was up all night too. I've been on the phone with our intelligence people and with the prime minister of Israel working on the problem presented by the despicable letter and photograph that you received last night."

Zack took a deep breath. "Thank you, sir. I really appreciate that."

"Before I brief you on what I've been able to learn, is there anything I can do for you, Zack?"

Zack thought about that for a second, then realized that as a lowly lieutenant commander, he did not have the luxury of thinking too long, given the time schedule of the commander in chief. But for Diane's sake, it was now or never. *Do it, Zack.*

"There is one thing I'd like to ask you about, sir."

"Fire away, Commander."

"Sir, I would like to exchange myself for Diane. They would take me, and do whatever they want to me, but release her. Is there any way we could open up some sort of back-channel communication, maybe through one of our Arab allies, to make that happen?"

There was a moment of silence from the speakerphone.

"Zack, I'm not surprised at your request. I admire you for it, and I think if I were in your position, I'd feel the same way.

"You know as well as I do that every man and woman who puts on America's uniform does so knowing that he or she may have to pay for that privilege with his life. I wore the uniform with that knowledge, and I know you do, and I know Lieutenant Colcernian does.

"The hardest part about this job is making decisions about life and death. Personally, I'd rather give my own life than make a decision, knowing the consequences of that decision will mean the loss of life for someone's loved one. But like every president who has occupied this office before me, and especially in times of war—and make no mistake, we are at war here—my personal desires have to give way to what's best for America. Personally, I would truly rather sacrifice myself if it meant freedom for Diane. And I would in a heartbeat, if it were that simple.

"But for the good of the country, to try to ensure there won't be other kidnappings, to try to contain the power these evil monsters have, I can't do that. Do you understand, Zack?"

"Yes, sir."

"And while, as your president, I appreciate your willingness to make a personal sacrifice for Diane, even with your life, the problem is that we would have to negotiate with these terrorists to bring about that swap. And I don't know if they would accept the terms even if we tried.

"But we can't try, because the mere act of negotiating with them would be a reward to them for an unconscionable criminal act. That would set a precedent that anytime they wanted to bring us to the table, all they've gotta do is go kidnap a naval officer, or any other American, for that matter. Negotiating with them would lead to more deaths, to more torture. We can't do that. Do you understand my reasoning?"

"Yes, sir," Zack said. "Not only do I understand, but for what it's worth, I know it's the right policy."

"Zack, you should know two things. First, the CIA has been analyzing the letter and the photo, and Director Early informs me that this threat appears legitimate."

"I understand." Zack felt another lump in his throat.

"Having said that, we are devoting the full resources of the United States government to locating Diane, and if we can find her, we're going to do everything we can to go get her. But realistically, I can't promise we will be successful. Oftentimes, these animals act before we can do anything about it. But I can promise we will be diligent, relentless, and prayerful in our efforts to bring her home."

"Thank you, sir."

"Secondly, Zack, I spoke with Prime Minister Rothstein and shared with him copies of the letter and the photograph. He is as incensed about this despicable act as I am. I also discussed with him the possibility, given these circumstances, of having someone else prosecute these cases."

"Yes, sir?" *Please take this cup from me, Lord.*

"Zack, I'm sorry, but the answer is no."

A pause. A numbness.

"I understand, sir."

"Under the circumstances, I feel you're entitled to an explanation. First, the Israeli government is in a tough position politically. Their people think these pilots should be put on trial by an Israeli court. They say it's a question of Israeli sovereignty. And frankly, I can see their point. If somebody attacked a building in America, we would want to try them here in America, and indeed we have done that. If the Israeli government were to accede to our demands to turn over these pilots, that government could fall in a specially called election. Plus they're worried about an attack from Syria or maybe even Egypt if we brought the pilots back here to the States.

"For the most part, the Rothstein government has been very good in working with us. We can't afford to see that government fall, Zack. We need a government that is fully cooperative in Jerusalem.

"The only acceptable political solution to the majority of Israelis, short of putting these guys on trial themselves, is to have you go there and prosecute. The prime minister tells me that has not changed.

"Not only that, but the prime minister made another good point. If we back down and change prosecutors now, that would send a signal of weakness to these terrorists that their intimidation tactics can affect our policy. And frankly, we can't show one iota of weakness to them."

"Yes, sir."

"So, Zack, I need you to go back at this with a renewed determination. You've got another world-class defense attorney as your opponent. We know how good Mr. la Trec is. But I've seen you in action. I've got confidence in you.

"Your job is to go to Jerusalem and bring back a conviction. My job is to find Lieutenant Colcernian. You do your job, Commander, and I'll do my very best to do mine.

"Good luck, and Godspeed, Commander."

"Thank you, Mr. President."

CHAPTER 48

USAF C-17 Globemaster III
Special Mission 427218
Altitude 5,000 feet
Eastern Mediterranean

Their journey from San Diego began courtesy of the United States Air Force, which at the president's order had dispatched a sleek olive-drab C-17 to the North Island Naval Air Station to pick them up for the first leg of their twelve- to thirteen-hour flight.

In addition to Zack and Wendy, who would be sitting at counsel table and facing the cameras of the world, the official prosecution team included Zack's trusted military paralegal, Legalman First Class "Pete" Peterson, who had been with Zack through the Olajuwon court-martial; Legalman First Class Kim Benedict, who was Diane's military paralegal but was now temporarily reassigned to Wendy; and Captain Rudy and Commander Awe, who were along to provide whatever support Zack and Wendy might require.

Also aboard was a team from the Naval Criminal Investigative Service headed by Special Agent Shannon McGillvery, a petite strawberry blond and an eight-year veteran of the NCIS. Shannon was Zack's favorite NCIS agent. Her personality reminded him of a friendly stick of dynamite. He always preferred working with her on major general courts-martial because she was tough and smart. Plus they got along great. Shannon was one of Zack's jogging buddies, frequently joining him on 10K runs from the naval station down along Harbor Drive to the Broadway Pier and downtown San Diego and back.

A few times, Diane had joined them on the gorgeous waterfront run, but the threesome usually would become a twosome about three and a half miles into the run, as Diane, probably the strongest runner in the JAG Corps, would pick it up, leaving Zack and Shannon in the dust for the last leg of the run. That was okay with Zack, because he used the time with Shannon to talk about the cases he was prosecuting, many of which she was a witness in or had investigated.

Shannon held a PhD in criminal justice, spoke Italian and Spanish, and was literate in computer programming. Unlike Harry Kilnap, the venerable "old guard" NCIS agent from Norfolk who first cracked open and then almost lost the Olajuwon case, Shannon was a "new breed" professional agent who did things by the book, even if it meant losing a case for the prosecution.

As a result, she was popular with navy prosecutors as well as defense attorneys. Zack trusted her completely. If Shannon McGillvery spoke, you could trust her completely.

He had asked that she be assigned to the team, and that request was immediately granted.

After a one-hour layover at Dover Air Force Base in Delaware for refueling, the team flew to Sigonella, Sicily, where they picked up an NCIS advance team from the *Harry S. Truman* for the final leg of the C-17's flight to the Island of Cyprus. Zack was impressed with the advance team's in-flight briefings on the events leading up to the morning of the attack. Zack wrote furiously on his legal pad, while Wendy and Shannon took notes on their laptops.

Shannon at first seemed most intrigued by the strange radio communication from the Spanish boat. As the plane approached Cyprus, her Scotch-Irish temper erupted when the advance team admitted that no one had bothered to find the captain of the Spanish boat.

"There's a connection here. I can sense it," she snapped. "Nobody goes out in the middle of the ocean and starts transmitting 'Oscar India Golf,' for no reason. And the fact that no one has followed up on this is absolutely inexcusable!"

When the C-17 touched down at Cyprus, the prosecution team immediately transferred to two navy SR-60B Seahawk helicopters and, within ten minutes of landing, were airborne again, this time headed east at a low altitude over the blue waters of the Mediterranean toward the *Truman*.

Forty-eight hours later, the *Truman* had steamed to within four miles off the Israeli port of Haifa, and the prosecution team again boarded the Seahawks and took off toward the coastline. The choppers flew west over Haifa, then went into a steep bank before touching down in the Israeli desert, presumably the Negev. Blinding sunlight assaulted Zack's eyes as he stepped from the chopper and was directed to one of six Hummers waiting to transport them to Jerusalem.

Still in short-sleeve working khakis, Zack donned a pair of sunglasses to fight the glare. Under the brown-tinted shades, he saw that they had flown to a cryptic rendezvous point, out of public view. A squadron of well-armed United States Marines in battle fatigues stood by with several armored vehicles to accompany the convoy. A squadron of Israeli Army infantrymen, also heavily armed, was on hand too.

Zack stepped to the second Hummer in the convoy, accepted a salute from a marine sergeant, then slid into the back. Lieutenant Commander Poole, in her working khaki shirt and skirt, was escorted around to the other side; she also was saluted before slipping into the seat beside Zack.

The Hummer's engine was already running, the air conditioning working at full blast, much to Zack's relief. Commander Awe and Captain Rudy were led to the first vehicle in the convoy, and Shannon McGillvery and part of her NCIS team piled into the Hummer just behind Zack and Wendy. Zack figured that LN1s Peterson and Benedict were bringing up the rear.

Two hours later, the convoy approached Jerusalem's historic King David Hotel. Members of the international press were gathered around the roped-off perimeter of the magnificent old building. In addition to the prominent presence of the American networks, Zack saw the BBC, French and Russian television trucks, an Australian crew, and Al Jazeer, the prominent Arab television network known for its propensity to beam gruesome execution pictures directly into homes as a tactic for flaming angry Muslim furor against the West.

"It was supposed to be a secret that you were staying here, sir," the marine driver said. "Looks like somebody leaked to the press."

"Somebody *always* leaks. They're like bloodhounds, Sergeant; trust me," Zack said as the convoy pulled to a temporary stop just in front of the hotel. "Far more concerned with ratings than the truth or the good of the country."

"Yes, sir." The driver nodded. "Remember that time Dan Rather ran that story about President Bush's national guard service using fake documents?"

"You just proved my point," Zack said.

"You know, sir," the sergeant said, "we've heard rumors that the Reverend Barbour may be staying here for the court-martial."

"Oh, please." Zack rolled his eyes.

"Speaking of CBS, look." Wendy pointed across Zack's chest out the back right window.

A CBS television crew shone blinding spotlights through the back window. Zack and Wendy winced. At the same time, a blond with a CBS microphone banged on the same window, motioning for Zack to roll it down. A couple of U.S. Marines stepped in and gently backed her away.

The Hummer inched forward. Just ahead, the vehicle carrying Captain Rudy and Commander Awe stopped in front of the hotel entrance. Double columns of Israeli soldiers, armed and in riot gear, formed a human corridor that stretched from the vehicle to the lobby. Members of the press crowded in like maggots on a dead animal, rudely poking their microphones over the soldiers' shoulders, hoping for a comment, a word, anything from anybody.

A wave of flashbulbs moved slowly from left to right. Zack chuckled. "Captain Rudy and Commander Awe must be on the move."

"You'd think we were at the Academy Awards or something," Wendy said with a laugh.

"Most of them are a bunch of self-serving liberals who want to cede American sovereignty to the United Nations," Zack commented as the Hummer inched forward. "Supreme Court Justice Clarence Thomas once called them a 'high-tech lynch mob.' I think he was right." A pause. "Enough preaching," Zack said, catching himself. "Sorry about my attitude."

"Don't worry about it." Wendy patted his hand. "You've had practice dealing with them."

"Okay, Commander," the driver said as the Hummer stopped in front of the Israeli human shield, "in addition to these Israeli Defense Forces guys, each of you will be escorted by two U.S. Marines into the buildings. These marines will be assigned to you as part of your security detail during the course of the court-martial."

Two marine gunnery sergeants opened Wendy's door, and two others opened Zack's.

"Let's go," Zack said to the marines. Then he and Wendy hurried down the line of blinding flashbulbs, flanked by the four bulldog-looking marine gunnies.

"What do you think of Reverend Barbour's comments that this case should be tried by the International Criminal Court?" screamed a male reporter above the pack of yelping dogs.

"We've heard rumors that Lieutenant Colcernian will be executed if you prosecute this case, Commander Brewer. Is that true?"

That question stopped Zack flat in his tracks, just in front of the revolving door of the hotel. He turned, glaring into the sea of bright lights, searching for the idiot who had tossed that question for the world to hear. The blackmail note and the photograph had intentionally not been provided to the press for fear that going public would back the terrorists into a corner.

If the animals who had kidnapped Diane decided to go public with this, that was one thing. But so far, thank God, they had not. What was the press trying to do, get her killed for the sake of boosting television ratings? The question instantly microwaved his blood to the boiling point. He wanted to fly across the row of Israeli soldiers and strangle the irresponsible fool who had thrown out the question.

"Let's go, Zack."

Wendy's cool, velvet voice and her gentle hand, now in the middle of his back, nudged him through the front doors of the hotel.

There was work to be done.

CHAPTER 49

Room 204
King David Hotel
Jerusalem

Eight hours later

Sitting on the sofa beside his bed in a T-shirt and khaki pants, his black-socked feet kicked up on a coffee table, Zack checked his watch: 8:00 p.m.

Approximately twelve hours before showtime.

Tomorrow morning, the court-martial would convene under the watchful eye of Captain Thomas Norgaard, the senior military judge in the Navy-Marine Corps Trial Judiciary, Transatlantic Region, covering all courts-martial convening in Europe, Africa, and the Middle East.

Before Norgaard's transfer from San Diego to Naples, Zack had appeared in court before him about a dozen times. Zack had never lost a case under the snippety and snappy judge, but the mercurial Norgaard did have a reputation for ruling with the defense.

This fact had Zack slightly concerned, and when he thought about Diane, slightly hopeful.

Remember what the president said, Zack. You're a naval officer. We're in war.

The intense afternoon of preparation had gone well. Tomorrow most likely would involve defending against a motion to dismiss, and part of the problem here was shooting in the dark. No motions were filed, and as a consequence, neither he nor Wendy knew what they would be up against in the morning. But based on la Trec's show at the UN, Zack expected to hear more about the International Criminal Court.

Zack spent most of the afternoon beefing up an anticipated international jurisdictional challenge, while Wendy continued witness interviews. Assuming the motion to dismiss was denied, the rest of the day would be spent on jury selection.

Wendy had returned to her room to freshen up, and Zack decided to take a break before she got back.

Reaching for the remote control, he punched on the television and switched the channel to CNN.

A muted image of the Reverend JamesOn Barbour's saliva-spouting motor mouth was moving on the screen. He was standing at an unidentified podium fielding questions, or so it appeared. Zack was about to kill the power when a closed-caption message scrolled across the bottom of the screen: "Barbour offers to negotiate for Colcernian's release."

Zack pressed the audio button on the remote.

"As you know, since this administration has rejected the very reasonable proposal, I will be going to Israel to ensure that all the proper procedures are followed in this court-martial.

"I have also made myself available to travel, wherever I may need to travel, to negotiate the release of Lieutenant Colcernian. I made the offer to the administration this day."

A female reporter shouted to be heard. "Reverend Barbour, have you gotten any official reaction from the administration to your offer to negotiate Lieutenant Colcernian's release?"

"As I would have expected, this administration was uncooperative, but this will not stop me in my humanitarian efforts on behalf of this officer."

"Reverend," the familiar voice of Bernie Woodson boomed, "exactly where do you plan on going to negotiate for Lieutenant Colcernian, and just who do you plan to negotiate with?"

"Bernie, those whom I shall negotiate with know who they are, and those whom I shall negotiate with know where they are. Even though the administration will not cooperate, I hope this news conference will serve as an olive branch for peace.

"As far as the administration goes, as I have said, and as the late Mr. Johnny Cochrane has said, if the glove don't fit, you must acquit ..."

Click.

Take that, JamesOn.

The telephone rang.

"Lieutenant Commander Brewer speaking."

"Zack, it's Shannon."

"Hey, Shannon, what's up?"

"There's a witness here to see you."

"Yeah, who?"

"Belarusian Jew named Kweskin. He just immigrated to Israel with his family, Zack. His daughter was killed at the Dome. He's here with a translator. The translator's American."

"Where are they now?"

"In the lobby. Brought over here by Israeli police."

"Would you mind bringing them up so I can avoid dealing with the press camped out down there?"

"Be glad to."

"You're a sweetie, Shannon."

Five minutes later, Zack opened his door to Shannon, who stood by a brunette woman and a bearded man in a black shirt and black pants.

"I'm Kathryn Shadle." The brunette extended her hand and smiled. "I'm with the International Fellowship of Christians and Jews. I've heard a lot about you, Commander."

"Where are you from, Kathryn?" Zack released her hand.

"Covington, Louisiana. Not far from New Orleans."

Zack looked at the Orthodox Jew. *"Meen yah zah voot Zachary Brewer. Ochen Pree yet nah, Guspadyeen Kweskin."* My name is Zachary Brewer. Pleased to meet you, Mr. Kweskin.

That brought a smile from Alexander Kweskin's solemn face.

"You speak Russian, Commander?" Kathryn Shadle asked.

"Just a little. I've studied some on the side. Listened to tapes, that sort of thing. Not enough that I can afford to send you home," he said in English, giving her a wink. "Everyone please come in."

"We were just standing there, Commander, worshiping God at the temple wall. It was the fulfillment of our grandest dreams, the happiest day of our lives." Alexander's eyes moistened. "And then there was the roar of jets, and then a great explosion, and then"—tears dripped off his cheeks—"my Anna was lying in the courtyard bleeding. "She was my firstborn, Commander."

Alexander's eyes found Zack's, and Zack felt his heart swell with sorrow for the man's loss. "Now, in the eyes of the state, she is only a number in an Israeli cemetery. Grave marker number 318, Municipal Cemetery Number 8.

"But, Commander, I'm telling you," he said, now through sobs, "she was no number. Here. This is her picture. See? This picture is for you, Commander, to remind you that she was real and beautiful. If you have children one day, you will understand. Please don't let her death be in vain."

Zack choked back tears. He exchanged looks with Kathryn Shadle, who dabbed her eyes with a tissue. Shannon and Wendy, who had joined the group, looked down at the floor.

"Moi droog." My friend. Zack laid his hand on the man's back and looked into his black eyes. "I promise you. Your daughter will not have died in vain. Those responsible for this will be prosecuted and dealt with severely."

CHAPTER 50

Israeli District Court
Courtroom 3
West Bank Division

Courtroom 3, District Court of the West Bank, was packed to capacity with perhaps five hundred spectators when Zack led Wendy through the back double doors and up the center aisle. They laid their briefcases on the prosecution's table, which was on the right side of the courtroom.

Because Israeli courts typically do not have trials by jury, a makeshift jury box had been erected, obviously by a carpentry crew in a hurry. It did not match the otherwise ornate motif of the grand courtroom.

The high-rising judge's bench, still empty, sported a small nameplate front and center:

Captain T. D. Norgaard, JAGC, USN
Military Judge

Behind the empty bench, on the left and the right, the flags of the United States of America and the United States Navy stood guard like red, white, blue, and gold sentinels.

Other than the hastily constructed jury box, the room could have passed for an American military courtroom.

The two defendants were already at the defense table, also in service dress blues with gold aviator wings on their chests, having not yet been joined by their attorneys. A small army of armed shore patrolmen sat in the row behind them.

Zack looked around to the first row behind the prosecution table at the NCIS team. The one empty seat caught his eye.

"Where's Shannon?" he whispered to Wendy.

"Out in the field, working on some things. She promised to brief us tonight."

Zack heard a rumbling from the visitors' gallery behind him. He turned as a distinguished silver-haired gentleman in a blue suit entered, trailed by a younger, attractive blond woman. Behind them, three other well-dressed young men carried a variety of boxes and briefcases on portable rollers.

The silver-haired man strolled down the aisle with panache, exuding charisma without speaking a word. He stepped through the wooden swing gate, into the counsel area, and met Zack's eyes.

"A pleasure, Commander," Jean-Claude la Trec said, extending his hand. "I look forward to a hard-fought, honorable contest."

"*Enchantez de faire votre connasiance aussi, Monsieur la Trec.*" *Pleased to meet you also, Mr. la Trec.* Zack spoke in semifluent French, which brought a look of surprise to la Trec's face.

"*Est-ce que je peux vous prezentez Lieutenant Commander Wendy Poole?*" *May I introduce Lieutenant Commander Wendy Poole?* Zack gestured to Wendy, and la Trec bent to kiss her hand.

"And may I introduce my associate who will be assisting me at trial, Jeanette L'Enfant?"

"*Enchantez, mademoiselle.*" Zack took the hand of the elegant-looking blond.

"The pleasure is mine, Commander," she said, her eyes lingering on Zack's face before she exchanged pleasantries and a handshake with Wendy.

"I must say," la Trec whispered to Zack, "I am pleasantly surprised at your fluency in French, Commander."

Zack smiled. "As I am pleasantly surprised at yours in English, monsieur. But since American courts-martial are conducted in English, perhaps we should stick to that, at least until the guilty verdicts are announced."

Zack felt his adrenaline starting to flow. Litigation, even off-the-record verbal sparring with opposing counsel, especially against a courtroom giant with the reputation of a Jean-Claude la Trec, produced within him a sort of euphoria. For the moment, anyway, this "litigator's high" was taking his worry off Diane, the perfect antidote to depression.

"Guilty verdicts?" La Trec shot him a very French Cheshire grin. "That confident, are we?"

Zack folded his arms. *"Vous-avez les problemmes avec traduction?" You're having problems with translation?* He switched to English. "I can ask the court to provide a translator for you. I'm sure we can find someone who could drive down from our embassy in Beirut."

"All rise!"

Round one to the good guys.

With a commotion of clumping feet, the Honorable Captain Thomas Norgaard, Judge Advocate General's Corps, United States Navy, entered the side door.

The white-haired and stocky military judge, wearing a service dress blue uniform, stood for a moment in front of his chair and, with eyes that swept the room through wire-rim glasses, rapped his gavel once on the bench. "Be seated. This court is called to order."

CHAPTER 51

Restaurante Sol Elite Galivanes
Port Mahon, Minorca
Balearic Islands
Western Mediterranean

Shannon McGillvery wasted no time making friends. Sometimes she even befriended people before she met them. Such was the case with Dan and Ben, whom she had contacted before leaving San Diego and whose last names she neither knew nor cared to know.

The only thing she really cared to know about these black-mustached, rippling-muscled Israelis was who their employer was.

Dan and Ben were Mossad agents.

Mossad, as an agency of the Israeli government, had a vested interest in disproving that the attack on the Dome was a Yankee-Israeli conspiracy against Islam.

Her new, no-last-name friends worked for the Mossad's Special Operations Division, known as Metsada. The official mission of Metsada: highly sensitive assassination, sabotage, paramilitary, and psychological warfare projects.

In other words, these guys were some bad customers.

They had waited for her in the lobby of the King David, and two hours later, they were on an Israeli-government Lear jet headed to Minorca. Their mission: to find the captain of the *Bella Maria*.

Carlos Ortega had been sleeping, or so it appeared, when Shannon, who had left Dan and Ben lurking in the shadows but watching her from a distance, showed up at his apartment.

Flashing her credentials as a U.S. Naval Criminal Investigative Service investigator, lavishing him with fluent Spanish, and slipping him five hundred U.S. dollars as an incentive, she suggested that he meet her in an hour for lunch.

He met her at *Restaurante Sol Elite Galivanes*, a quaint café located on a vista overlooking historic Port Mahon bay.

"We believe that the transmissions from the *Bella Maria* are related to the attack on the Dome of the Rock. We don't suspect you, but we need to question the two Arabs." She looked at him with puppy dog eyes and touched his arm. "Your cooperation would be deeply appreciated by the United States government. And by me."

"One, I believe, has left the island." Ortega seemed mesmerized and at the same time a bit nervous. "The other one is still here."

"Can you take me to him?" Her fingernails, covered by cherry red nail polish, made light circles on the top of his hand.

"Of course." She saw him swallow hard. "I can take you there now."

He dropped her off in front of the small stucco house where the Arab named Falik was staying. She kissed him on the cheek and told him that she would meet him tonight at *Restaurante Sol Elite Galivanes*, that she could handle this conversation on her own. She lied about tonight.

When he drove off, Dan and Ben drove up. The threesome walked together to Falik's door.

"Hi, I'm Shannon, and these are my friends Ben and Dan." A furtive flip of her strawberry blond locks. "We'd like to come in and chat for a few minutes, if that's okay?"

"Anna nee barraf Pahangliski."

"Nice try," Shannon said. "But I think you do speak English when you want. At least you know three words. Do the words *Oscar*, *India*, and *Golf* ring a bell?"

"Anna nee barraf Pahangliski."

"Oh, really now?" She cocked her head and gave him a smile. "Not to worry. My friend Dan here is a translator." She looked at the big-muscled Israeli in the tight black T-shirt. "Dan, could you help Mr. Falik here understand what I'm trying to tell him?"

"Yes, ma'am."

The Israeli smashed his knee into the Arab's groin. The man reeled, then fell on his back, moaning, on the kitchen floor. Shannon and the boys came into the house, slamming the door behind them. She bent over as Dan and Ben whipped out razor-sharp daggers and held the tips to the Arab's throat.

"Now, I believe you were saying something like, 'Anna nee barraf Pahangliski'?"

"Ooh." Falik grabbed his groin area. "What do you want?" His English was suddenly fluent.

"Oscar, India, Golf. What is it?"

"I don't know what you're talking about."

"You know," she said, smiling, running her hand though his hair as though she cared about him, "my friend Ben here is an even better translator than Dan." She looked at Ben. "Ben?"

A smashing kick directly into the Arab's rib cage.

Falik grimaced and squirmed on the floor.

"Oscar India Golf, Mr. Falik?"

"I've never heard ..."

A furious punch in the mouth drew blood, which streamed from the corner of his lips.

"You know, Mr. Falik, unfortunately, we American spies cannot do certain things." She paused. "For example, by law, we cannot assassinate, maim, or torture a terrorist dirtbag like you. We are *so* humane, we Americans."

She looked up at Dan. "You know, Dan, I think I might like a cup of hot tea? It *is* about that time, isn't it?"

"Yes, ma'am."

"Would you do the honors?"

"A pleasure, ma'am."

Dan found a steel teapot, poured water into it, and struck a match, lighting the blue flame on top of Falik's stove.

"Anyway, where was I, Mr. Falik?" She pulled up a deck chair beside his supine position on the floor, crossed her legs, and rocked her pointed high heel in front of his face. "Oh yes. Now I remember. We American spies, because of our bleeding-heart, liberal Congress, can't have the type of fun that some of our counterparts have."

His eyes rolled toward her.

"For example, did you know that an American spy cannot legally assassinate an enemy operative? We can't maim or torture anyone like you Islamic fundamentalists can."

A faint whistle from the tea kettle grew shriller and shriller.

"Of course, nothing prevents us from watching our friends in the Mossad do their thing. Dan, how is our tea coming?"

Falik's eyes twitched at the mention of the word *Mossad*. Elevated fear seemed to crawl across his face.

"Oh, did I mention that my friends Ben and Dan are members of the Mossad?"

"Ready, ma'am."

Dan walked over to Falik and poured a stream of boiling water onto his arm.

"AAGGGHH!"

Shannon winced. "Now that's hard to watch."

Falik got up, trying to crawl like a wounded rat. That brought an immediate karate chop to the back of his neck and another knee to the groin, this time courtesy of Ben.

"OOHH!"

"Oscar India Golf, Mr. Falik?"

"Never!"

"Tsk-tsk." Shannon crossed her legs again. "Boys, would you see if there's something to drink in the fridge?"

"Bottled water okay?"

"Perfect." She accepted the bottled water from Dan, twisted off the cap, and turned the bottle bottoms up.

"Now, you know, Mr. Falik, it doesn't seem to me that our humane American techniques are working, now, does it? Let me try once more." A swig of bottled water. "Oscar India Golf?"

Nothing.

"Pity. Okay, let's see if the Mossad can come up with anything, shall we say, more persuasive." Another sip of water and a flutter of her hand. "Boys?"

Dan grabbed Falik by the hair, jerking him up from the floor as Ben twisted his arms tightly behind his back. Overpowering the smaller Arab, they pushed him into the kitchen, toward the blue butane flame leaping from the oven.

"No!" he screamed as the Israelis pushed his face down, closer to the leaping fire. "NOOO!"

"Oscar India Golf?" Shannon said calmly.

"Please! No!"

"Oscar India Golf?"

"Okay! Okay! I'll talk!"

"Now that's more like it."

CHAPTER 52

The Oval Office
The White House
Washington, D.C.

"Flip it on, Wally," the president ordered.

"Yes, Mr. President." The chief of staff hit the remote control, which brought to life the familiar face of CNN's Tom Miller.

"This is Tom Miller in Jerusalem, where in just a few minutes, the court-martial of two navy pilots, accused of launching missile attacks on the Dome of the Rock, are about to begin. And as we wait for the opening session of this, the second nationally televised court-martial in navy history, we are joined by our expert legal tandem of Jeanie Van Horton, a former federal prosecutor"—a smiling middle-aged blond appeared on the screen—"and of course, our own Bernie Woodson." A tough-looking African-American glared at the cameras.

"And we'll start with you, Bernie. What can we expect from this morning's session?"

Woodson frowned. "We don't actually know what Mr. la Trec will do, but we expect a defense motion to have the case dismissed. We believe that he will follow up on his argument that he made before the UN Security Council, that these pilots are accused of attacking an international holy shrine, are accused of killing foreign civilians, and therefore, the International Criminal Court in the Hague should be hearing this case, not a U.S. Navy court-martial."

"Jeanie Van Horton, what difference does it make which court hears the case?"

"Two things, Tom. First, la Trec is posturing politically. As you know, the international sentiment is boiling over against the United States and also Israel, and especially in the Arab world, where there is this notion that these attacks were some sort of American-Israeli plot to retaliate for 9/11. The U.S. reluctance to turn over the pilots to an international tribunal tends to fan those flames. So even if Jean-Claude la Trec loses this motion, he feels that he will have won in the court of international public opinion.

"Secondly, la Trec feels like he has a better chance for an acquittal of these pilots in an international forum. Assuming he makes the argument that the attacks were part of an American-Israeli plot and that his clients were just carrying out the orders of their superiors, the argument has a better chance of flying in the international court, where the U.S. is not so popular."

"Any chance Norgaard might grant this, Jeanie?"

"Obviously, Tom, we don't know. No such motion has ever been tried in a U.S. court-martial before. But here's what we do know about Captain Norgaard. He holds a master's degree in international law from Harvard, so he certainly will be attuned to such an argument, and more than any other navy judge he has a reputation for throwing out big cases on procedural or jurisdictional irregularities. And, Tom, he has a track record to back that reputation. So if there's any one judge in the navy who might actually toss the case on these grounds, it appears that Mr. la Trec may have found his judge."

"Thank you, Bernie Woodson and Jeanie Van Horton. Right now we've got to take a break, but we'll be back for continued coverage of the court-martial of the aviators right after this."

CHAPTER 53

Courtroom 3
Israeli District Court
West Bank Division

A re there any pretrial motions?" Judge Norgaard looked down from the bench over the top of his half-moon, wire-rim reading glasses.

Zack stood. "Nothing from the government."

"Your Honor"—la Trec stood and swept his hand forward, palm up, toward the judge, as if prepared to receive manna from heaven—"the defense will move to dismiss all charges and specifications for lack of subject matter jurisdiction."

A motion to dismiss this case will most likely be made by your opponent, much in the way Mr. Levinson moved to dismiss the last court-martial you were involved in.

"Very well," Norgaard said. "Let the record reflect that the defense has moved to dismiss for lack of subject matter jurisdiction."

If the motion to dismiss is denied, that is when Lieutenant Colcernian will have a hand in helping you.

"I will hear argument on your motion at this time, Mr. la Trec."

"Thank you, Your Honor." La Trec glanced at Zack. "Let me begin by saying that we respect the grand tradition of the United States military. Indeed, the U.S. military has had an indispensable hand in securing and maintaining freedom as we know it in the Western world, both in the twentieth and twenty-first centuries. And a great part of your awesome military has been the fair tradition of your military justice system." La Trec nodded humbly at Norgaard.

"While in most cases it would be most appropriate to bring a case involving U.S. Navy pilots before a U.S. Navy court-martial, I would argue, most respectfully, Your Honor, this is not such a case.

"This is a *unique* case involving well-established principles of international law recognized by all civilized nations, including the United States of America." He gestured grandly. "International law to which we contend the United States is bound."

"As you know, Your Honor, there are but two sources of international law recognized by the family of civilized nations. These are, one"—la Trec held up his index finger—"*custom*, and two"—his fingers now made a V sign—"*treaty*. The United States is bound to dismiss this court-martial and turn these defendants over to an international tribunal because of both custom and treaty.

"First, custom. Let me point out, Your Honor, that the United States government, to its credit, has a long and distinguished *custom* of endorsing international tribunals where war crimes are concerned.

"From the presence of American prosecutors for war crimes against Nazi officers at Nuremburg, to the prosecution of Yugoslavia's Slobodan Milosevic, America has supported, endorsed, and even participated in international tribunals for the alleged commission of international crimes." La Trec glanced at Zack.

"By its assent to international custom recognizing the use of such tribunals, America is now bound by international law. The only differences in the cases I have mentioned and in this case is that *these* defendants are Americans. But if America is going to support international criminal tribunals for the prosecution of defendants who are not Americans, she cannot credibly refuse to support such tribunals in cases, such as this one, where the defendants happen to be American."

La Trec stuck his left hand in his pocket, gesturing with his right.

"The second source of international law, in addition to custom, is the use of international treaties. In this case, the United States is also bound." La Trec raked his fingers through his hair.

"I speak, of course, to the treaty establishing the International Criminal Court, sometimes referred to as the Treaty of Rome, adopted by the United Nations Diplomatic Conference of Plenipotentiaries on July 17, 1998, in the city of Rome." La Trec paused, took a sip of water, and continued.

"Under this treaty, when there are crimes against humanity, when innocent civilians are attacked by military forces, as is the case here"—la Trec's voice rose—"the proper jurisdiction is the International Criminal Court, sitting in the Hague.

"Here is what the United Nations secretary-general, Mr. Kofi Annan, said about the International Criminal Court at its inception in 1998." La Trec extracted from his shirt pocket a sheet of folded paper, unfolded it, and laid it on the wooden podium. He slipped on his glasses and looked down, then read reverently, as if from a holy document.

"'In the prospect of an international criminal court lies the promise of universal justice. That is the simple and soaring hope of this vision. We are close to its realization. Let no State, no junta, and no army anywhere abuse human rights with impunity.'"

La Trec removed the glasses, folded them, and stuck them back inside his jacket. "Two years after Mr. Annan made those very eloquent comments, Your Honor, your great country, on New Year's Eve 2000, became the 139th and the last country to sign this treaty.

"The treaty was signed for your country by President William Jefferson Clinton, Commander in Chief of all United States armed forces. By taking this courageous step, President Clinton brought America more fully into the international family of nations, showing your country's willingness to relinquish just a small part of its national sovereignty for the better good of mankind.

"This court-martial is bound by both international law and the Constitution of the United States. Here, innocent civilians are said to have died as a result of the acts of military men. In such cases, America recognizes the use of international tribunals and has specifically assented to the establishment of the International Criminal Court in cases such as this. For these reasons, this case should be dismissed.

"I thank you, Your Honor."

La Trec nodded to the court, then turned and gave a slight, gracious bow toward the prosecution table before sitting down.

A motion to dismiss this case will most likely be made by your opponent, much in the way Mr. Levinson moved to dismiss the last court-martial you were involved in.

"Very well," Norgaard said. "Lieutenant Commander Brewer, what is the government's position?"

If the motion to dismiss is denied, that is when Lieutenant Colcernian will have a hand in helping you.

Zack pulled the small photo of a smiling, sparkly-eyed, curly-haired Anna Kweskin from his pocket. "This is for you, sweetie," he whispered to himself.

"Commander, did you say something?" Judge Norgaard snapped.

"My apologies, Your Honor." Zack rose, stepping confidently to the center podium the eloquent Frenchman had just abandoned. "Yes, we would like to respond." Zack glanced at the smiling la Trec, then back to Norgaard.

"First, Mr. la Trec's contention that the United States has assented to the use of a so-called international criminal court"—Zack made quotation marks with his fingers—"is inaccurate.

"While it is true that an American prosecutor was one of several lead prosecutors at the Nuremburg tribunals, it should also be remembered that Nuremburg was not just a single trial, as this court-martial will be, but was in fact *twelve* trials involving over one hundred defendants, taking place over a period of four years. That's hardly comparable, Your Honor, to the single, simple court-martial in this case.

"Plus, the host country at those trials, in that case Germany, was in shambles after World War II and had no legal infrastructure to support the prosecution of those defendants. Therefore, the International Military Tribunal convened at Nuremburg was the only practical way to get the job done.

"Here, we already have a practical way to get the job done. It's called this court-martial." Zack glanced at Wendy, then gestured to the water pitcher on the prosecution table.

"The Bosnian war crimes trials, which by the way have been the *only* example of any such other international war crimes tribunal convened since Nuremburg, are also a poor example. Mr. Milosevic and the others prosecuted were, like many prosecuted at Nuremburg, political or high-ranking military leaders.

"That simply is not the case here, Your Honor. There are no international or high-ranking military leaders involved. Just two renegade, traitorous"—Zack stopped and glared at the defendants—"Islamic terrorists masquerading as naval aviators.

"Mr. la Trec claims that the United States has assented to these types of tribunals since Nuremburg. He is wrong. As I just said, the only such tribunal convened since Nuremburg has involved the Bosnian war crimes trials." He took a Styrofoam cup of ice water from Wendy, nodding a thank-you.

"But even still, the United States military has retained jurisdiction over such cases, even where U.S. servicemen have been accused of crimes against humanity. The most prominent example of this, of course, is the well-known court-martial of Lieutenant William Calley, who was prosecuted, by a military court-martial I might add, for the execution of over one hundred civilians in what has become known by historians as the My Lai massacre, one of the most tragic events in the Vietnam War." He took a sip of water.

"The Calley court-martial was post-Nuremburg, and if the United States was going to hand over an American defendant to one of these so-called *international tribunals*" — Zack's voice took on a hint of contempt — "My Lai would have been the time to do it. But instead, the U.S. military properly retained jurisdiction and took care of its own business.

"A more recent example is the tragedy involving the nuclear sub the USS *Greenville*. In that case, the skipper of the *Greenville*, Commander Scott Waddle, was not turned over to some so-called international tribunal, despite the fact that his submarine was responsible for the death of dozens of Japanese civilians off Hawaii. That matter was handled by a *navy* court of inquiry, not by some bureaucratic arm of the United Nations.

"There are many other examples, and I won't belabor the point, except to say that my opponent's argument that the U.S. consents to such tribunals is flat-out wrong."

Zack took another sip of water and glanced at Anna Kweskin's picture, which he had laid on the podium.

"Permit me now to address Mr. la Trec's claim that the United States is bound by the so-called Treaty of Rome," he said with contempt, "which established what he calls the International Criminal Court." Zack again made air quotation marks.

"While it is true that former President Clinton signed this treaty, less than one month before he left office, let me also point out that Clinton was the *only* American president to date to ever consider the very radical notion that the United States should surrender or even partially abdicate its judicial sovereignty to the United Nations. All other American presidents have rejected this notion.

"Mr. la Trec's theory ignores Article 1, Section 2, of the United States Constitution, which allows the president to bind the United States by way of international treaties *only with the advice and consent of the Senate*."

"In this case, not only has the Senate *not* ratified this so-called treaty, but the administration of President George W. Bush specifically renounced the treaty and notified the United Nations that the United States will *not* be bound by its terms."

Judge Norgaard raised an eyebrow.

"So what does that leave us with, Your Honor?" Zack paused for a sip of water. "It leaves us with murder charges brought against two members of the United States Navy, convened in accordance with the Manual for Courts-Martial, under the legal auspices of the Uniform Code of Military Justice.

"The United States does not subscribe to the one-world government mentality underpinning this whole international tribunal thing." Zack chopped his fist in the air. "The jurisdictional requirements for proceeding with this court-martial have been met, and the defense motion should be denied.

"Thank you, Your Honor," Zack said, then sat down and glanced at la Trec, who still wore an arrogant grin.

"All right," Judge Norgaard said. "I commend both attorneys on some very excellent points in argument. Because of the complexity of this issue, I will defer my ruling until after selection of members, which I anticipate will last the rest of the afternoon. If I dismiss the case, the members will be released. If I deny the motion, both sides should be prepared to proceed. Any questions?"

"No, sir, Your Honor," Zack said.

"No, sir," said la Trec.

"Very well. The court will take a brief recess at this time."

"All rise!"

CHAPTER 54

Horse caravan
Mountainous terrain
Location unknown

The bumping against her spine brought her back to life as the effect of the powerful injections began to wear off again.

This time, the dome light from the Aerostar had been replaced by a deep-azure sky, flanked on the left and the right by high, rugged, sun-soaked mountain peaks. Gone was the hum of the Aerostar's engine, replaced by the *clop-clop* of horse hooves. Also gone—the chains around her hands and ankles.

Diane felt a cool breeze against her face, then pushed herself up and realized she was in a mule-drawn wooden wagon, being pulled along-side a river in a deep ravine. Four Arab men, all dressed like pictures she had seen of the Mujahideen freedom fighters of Afghanistan, all with AK-47s strapped over their shoulders, flanked each corner of the wagon on horses. The horses carried sacks strapped around them, behind the riders' saddles.

The sun glancing off the mountaintops was far from this chilly ravine. The chill hit her arms, creating goose bumps. She sat up and wrapped herself in the blanket that had been laid in the wagon for her.

One of the horsemen, the one just ahead of her and to the right, turned around and caught her eyes.

"Look who is awake." It was the man who had captured her. He gave her a sinister smile.

"Thank you," she said.

"Why are you thanking me?"

"For taking the chains off."

He shrugged. "What would be the point? Here, there is no place to run." He turned from her to face forward again.

She waited a few seconds, letting the mule and horses clop a few more yards along the river.

"So where is here?"

A few more clops. More cool breezes whipping down the ravine.

"Let me tell you where here is not," he said. "Here is not America. Here is not Mexico."

A few more clops. A whinny.

"Here is nowhere."

She sat up in the wooden wagon, Indian style, pulling the blanket around her arms.

"So where are you taking me?"

Another delayed response. "Only Allah knows from where we have come and to where we go."

"That's all you're going to say?" She waited for him to turn around. He did not. "It's not like I can do anything about it anyway."

"All I can say is this, Lieutenant." The *clop-clop* of horse hooves echoed through the ravine. "It would be wise to prepare your heart to meet Allah."

Mossad training facility
Central Negev Desert

Happy with what they had accomplished but still not satisfied, Shannon sat in the kitchen area of the Mossad training base and sipped on a bottle of water. "So how is our guest of honor?" She smiled as Dan, whom she had started thinking of as the Human Bicep, walked in.

"I think the interrogators are making him feel a bit more comfortable than we did."

"Still talking, is he?"

"Singing like a canary."

That thought brought a smile to her face. She cocked back her head and sipped more water. "Good." Another sip. "You know, I really should be getting back to Jerusalem. Poor Lieutenant Commander Brewer is going to think I've stood him up."

"From what I've seen of the commander, he can take care of him-self," the Bicep said, then opened the refrigerator, took out a bottle of orange juice, and tipped it up.

"Yes, I'm sure he can." She sighed.

"Miss McGillvery." Ben walked into the room. "Our intelligence people think they have spotted the wreckage of one of the F-14s."

She set the water bottle on the table. "Where?"

"Syrian Desert. Northeast of the town of Shabba."

"Where's that?"

"Had a feeling you would ask," he said, then rolled out a map on the table where they had been drinking coffee. "It's right about ... here." He pointed to a spot east of Damascus. "About 33 north, 37 east."

"How do we get out there?"

"Chopper low, due east, across the Jordanian border in the Negev. That's the trickiest part, not getting spotted crossing the border. If we cross undetected, we fly out to the Jordanian desert and turn north, going up the back side of the populated area of Jordan. We fly fifty feet off the deck to avoid radar.

"When do we go?"

"Tonight, under cover of darkness."

"I guess Commander Brewer will have to wait another day."

"You sure you want to go on this mission?" Dan frowned. "It's dangerous. A chopper is no match for an enemy fighter or any sort of ground-based antiaircraft fire."

"Look, Biceps," she said, giving him a friendly punch on his right rippling bicep, "I need the danger to get my adrenaline flowing."

CHAPTER 55

Courtroom 3
Israeli District Court
West Bank Division

His heart hammering, Zack watched as Captain Norgaard peered over his glasses at the packed courtroom.

"This court is back in session. Let the record reflect that all counsel and the accused are present."

Norgaard began to read his order: "The court has considered the defense motion to dismiss for lack of subject matter jurisdiction on the principle that international law, in this limited circumstance, would require referral of this case to an international tribunal. The defense has argued that the United States is bound to such a tribunal on the two internationally recognized bases of international law, namely, custom and treaty.

"The defense argues that by explicitly supporting international criminal tribunals at Nuremburg, and by implicitly supporting such tribunals more recently in connection with Bosnian atrocities, the United States has now recognized an international custom and is therefore bound to continue in that custom."

Norgaard paused to adjust his glasses and to take a sip of water.

"The defense further argues that the United States is also bound to turn these defendants over to the International Criminal Court by virtue of the fact that the Clinton administration signed the so-called Rome Treaty, establishing the existence of that court. On either of these grounds, either by custom or by treaty, this court, should it be persuaded of either argument, could dismiss and recommend to the navy that the case be tried by the international court."

"The prosecution has argued that the United States has not acceded to such forums by custom, and cites the Calley court-martial and the Waddle court-of-inquiry as examples."

Norgaard briefly looked down at the prosecution table.

"The prosecution, through trial counsel, has also argued that the United States is not bound by the Rome Treaty because it was not ratified by the Senate, and also because the George W. Bush Administration has specifically stated that the United States will not be bound by it."

"As a follow-up to the trial counsel's argument, claiming that the George W. Bush administration stated that the United States will not be bound by the Treaty of Rome, the court has conducted research on this issue and has discovered the following: On May 6, 2002, the government of the United States of America wrote to the secretary-general of the United Nations. That letter contained the following words concerning the Rome Treaty."

Norgaard laid down the paper from which he was reading and picked up a second piece of paper.

"'This is to inform you, in connection with the Rome Statute of the International Criminal Court adopted on July 17, 1998, that the United States does not intend to become a party to the treaty. Accordingly, the United States has no legal obligations arising from its signature on December 31, 2000.'"

Norgaard laid down the letter, removed his glasses, and peered out at the audience.

"After having considered the arguments of counsel, and after having reviewed the various principles of international and domestic law cited by both counsel, the court agrees with the prosecution that the United States is not bound to turn these defendants over to the International Criminal Court, and the motion is denied."

"Because of the lateness of the hour, this court will reconvene tomorrow morning for opening arguments. This court is in recess."

"All rise."

A blinding flash of light, followed by a ferocious blast, knocked Wendy into Zack's lap. Her weight carried them crashing to the floor. Zack's head slammed onto the deck.

When he opened his eyes, burning smoke nearly choked him. He squinted. Wendy was on top of him, screaming, trying to push herself up. The room, what he could see of it from under the table, whirled clockwise.

Shrieks and wails and shattered glass cut through the choking smoke. From flat on his back, the smoke cleared just enough to reveal the gold chandelier swinging overhead. A bitter, burning smell, the smell of gunpowder, filled the air.

"Everybody down!" someone screamed. "Everybody down!"

The Oval Office
The White House
Washington, D.C.

Mr. President." The voice of the president's personal secretary, Gail Staff, came over the speakerphone.

"Yes, Gail?"

"The national security advisor is here. She says it's urgent, sir."

"Send her in."

Mack stood as Cynthia Hewitt raced into the office, out of breath.

"What is it, Cyndi?"

"Sir, there's been a bombing at the court-martial in Jerusalem."

"What?"

"You should turn on your television, sir."

"This is Tom Miller in Jerusalem," an ashen-faced Miller said. "A bomb has exploded inside the courtroom in Jerusalem, where two American pilots are on trial in connection with the missile attack on the Dome of the Rock. There are reports of injuries, perhaps even deaths, inside the courtroom. It apparently exploded within seconds after the military judge, Captain Thomas Norgaard, denied a defense motion to dismiss and transfer this case to the International Criminal Court in the Hague. Details are still sketchy ..."

The screen went black as the president stood, fuming. "Cyndi, I want a National Security Council meeting in one hour."

"Yes, Mr. President."

Mossad training facility
Central Negev Desert

It was dusk in the Negev, the daylight now fading quickly, yielding to the canopy of stars starting to roll in from the east. The heavens' purplish hue brought a serene beauty of biblical proportions, Shannon thought momentarily. But this was no time for stargazing.

Shannon, Dan, and Ben, along with aviation reconstruction experts from the Israeli Air Force and the U.S. Navy, jogged to the first black, unmarked helicopter gunship. Its engines were already running and blowing a warm, windy draft. Shannon, dressed in black from head to toe, tried to hold her strawberry blond hair, which was blowing everywhere, into place. Her efforts were futile.

The second unmarked gunship, also black, was manned by a platoon of Israeli Special Forces commandos who were armed to the teeth, a fact that gave Shannon a degree of comfort, even though the commandos could do nothing to stop a Stinger missile that might be fired at either helo.

The choppers lifted off in unison, dipped their noses, and flew east, away from the vanishing dusk, perhaps no more than fifty feet off the ground. Within a few minutes, they had crossed the Jordanian border, apparently without being spotted. Shannon slipped on her night-vision goggles and gazed out at the landscape, looking almost like the surface of the moon as the choppers raced into the night.

Within fifteen minutes or so, the choppers made a great loop to the left, now on a northerly course that would take them into northern Jordan and then into Syria. Shannon reached into her pocket for her nine-millimeter. Feeling it gave her an additional sense of security. She disengaged the safety, then worked the firing pin.

Situation Room
The White House
Washington, D.C.

The vice president stood, signaling the other members of the National Security Council to stand as the president of the United States walked into the room.

"Sit," Mack ordered, almost curtly. The command was obeyed. "What have we got, Cyndi?"

"Mr. President," she began, "here's what we know. Two shoe bombs were worn by members of the Arab press. Their heels contained plastic explosives. These two were Al Jazeer reporters. Somehow they slipped in through Israeli security."

"Injuries and deaths?"

"Brewer and Poole were shaken up but are fine."

"Thank God."

"Judge Norgaard got hit in the hand with flying glass but has undergone stitches and will be okay."

"Good."

"But one of the defendants is dead, Mr. President."

Mack slapped his hand on the table and nearly uttered a curse word, then caught himself. "Which one?"

"Lieutenant Hosni Alhad."

"What about Commander Quasay and the defense team?"

"Just a few scratches. Alhad was killed when a flying shard of glass severed both his jugulars."

"What about members?"

"The members had been selected but were dismissed from the courthouse when the bomb went off."

"Thank God for that too."

"Yes, sir."

"Other deaths and injuries?"

"In addition to the two Al Jazeer suicide bombers, four other members of the press. Two British and two French."

"Make sure we send official condolences to the British and French governments."

"Yes, Mr. President."

"Mr. Secretary"—Mack looked at his secretary of state—"what's the official word from the Israelis?"

"Mr. President, I just got off the phone with Foreign Minister Baruch," Robert Mauney said. "They're embarrassed, of course, about the security lapse, but they've secured another courtroom in the same building. A carpentry crew has already started refurbishing the new jury box and can be ready as early as tomorrow morning. She also said, however, that if we wish to delay the proceedings a few days, the Israeli government will understand and cooperate."

"Mr. Secretary, cable the Israeli foreign minister. Court-martial proceedings will resume tomorrow morning.

"Secretary Lopez?"

"Yes, sir?" the secretary of defense said.

"Pass the word down the navy chain of command. I expect Brewer and Poole to be ready to go full steam ahead at sunrise."

"Yes, Mr. President," Lopez said.

"The United States of America will not allow Arab terrorists to inter-fere with or derail the manner in which we conduct our business."

"Yes, Mr. President."

"That is all." He hesitated. "For now."

Syrian Desert
33 degrees 15 minutes north latitude
37 degrees 8 minutes east longitude

It's an F-14, all right." Shannon trained the night-vision goggles on the aircraft's nose cone. "Or at least what's left of one."

In the moonlight, Shannon, flanked by Ben and Dan, stood about twenty feet from the wrecked nose cone, while Israeli and American military crash investigators combed the site. Several were already dig-ging into the remnants of the cockpit.

"We've got a body!" one of the investigators shouted.

"Somebody get a body bag!" a second investigator said.

"He's charred like burned toast!" came another voice from the cockpit.

Shannon cupped her hands to her mouth and called out, "Can you ID him?"

"Stand by."

A flashlight was pointed into the cockpit.

"Dog tag says Lieutenant Price."

"Get him bagged and let's get out of here!"

CHAPTER 56

Courtroom 4
Israeli District Court
West Bank Division

"All rise!"

"Be seated," Judge Norgaard said and then turned to the bailiff. "Please bring in the members."

A moment later, twelve U.S. Naval officers—a captain, eight commanders, and three lieutenant commanders—marched into the jury box.

Without a word about yesterday's bombing, Judge Norgaard, said, "We are now ready for opening statements. Is the government ready?"

"We are, Your Honor."

"Is the defense ready?"

"The defense is ready," la Trec oozed.

"Very well. The members are with the government."

Please be advised that at the moment you begin your opening statement, we will begin to, with the use of a sharp knife, amputate Lieutenant Colcernian's right hand. We will take our time, of course, ensuring the amputation process lasts precisely as long as your opening argument.

"Lieutenant Commander Poole will make the government's opening statement, Your Honor," Zack said.

"Very well."

Wendy stood, then walked across the well to the banister, in front of the senior member of the military jury.

"Mr. President, distinguished members, this is a very simple case.

"Unfortunately, it is a very simple case about murder, dereliction of duty, and treason.

"Lieutenant Commander Mohammed Quasay"—she pointed to the defendant—"is a United States Naval aviator." She lowered her arm and returned her gaze to the members. "At least, that was his cover."

"The United States government has spent hundreds of thousands of dollars on this officer. Investing in him from his early days at the University of Michigan. Putting him on an NROTC scholarship. Providing him with the best flight training in the world.

"Quasay worked his way up the ranks as a naval aviator. He was awarded a squadron command on board USS *Harry S. Truman*. He was a leader of men.

"But despite all that, despite everything the navy had done for him, as it turned out, Lieutenant Commander Quasay proved to be a traitor.

"On May 8 of this year, Quasay's air wing commander asked for volunteers to fly a very dangerous, low-level mission over Israel. The mission was dangerous, the air boss explained, because Quasay's jet would be flying within point-blank range of Stinger missiles. Quasay, along with the late Lieutenant Hosni Alhad, volunteered for this mission.

"As it turned out, unbeknownst to anyone, Quasay and Alhad had a mission of their own. It was a strange mission. It was a perplexing mission. It was a deadly mission.

"Next day, both jets took off from the *Truman*. Coming down low over Israel, they set a course over Jerusalem. Their official mission was to fly low, to show the flag of the United States, to bring a sense of comfort to the citizens of Israel.

"Their personal mission, however, was to unleash their missiles on Israel, to kill Israelis. Ironically, these two Muslim-Americans not only killed Jews, but killed Arabs as well. Their missiles struck the Dome of the Rock, destroying one of the holiest sites in Islam.

"These pilots were in command of their aircraft, ladies and gentlemen. They used their aircraft for great destruction, to kill innocent civilians.

"This we will prove, beyond a reasonable doubt.

"Thank you."

Wendy turned and walked away from the members. Zack prayed for Diane.

"Mr. la Trec," Judge Norgaard said. "Would the defense care to make an opening?"

"Indeed, Your Honor."

La Trec stood, nodding, then stepped into the well.

"Mr. President, members, as a citizen of France, it is indeed a humbling experience to stand before this tribunal, a military jury of the United States armed forces. We citizens of France have never forgotten, nor will we ever forget, the great sacrifice of blood and life spilled by Americans on the beaches in Normandy. And so as a result of your sacrifice, our friendship is forever cemented, and our respect for your constitution is deep and great.

"Mr. President"—la Trec gracefully swept his hand across the courtroom—"your constitution, and your fine legal system, which is as grand as any in the world, holds fast to the principle that unless the state can prove guilt in a trial, whether a civilian criminal trial or a military court-marital, an accused must be acquitted.

"In this case, the government's case will be fraught with reasonable doubt. You see, my friends, my clients"—he pointed to Quasay—"my client, is a Muslim-American. He is accused of deliberately, of his own accord, attacking one of the holiest sites in all of Islam.

"Would a Catholic attack the Vatican?

"Would a Jew attack the Wailing Wall?

"And likewise, why, ladies and gentlemen, would a Muslim-American deliberately attack one of the holiest sites in his own religion?

"Is reasonable doubt not already cropping into your minds by the very question, ladies and gentlemen? Is it possible that Lieutenant Commander Quasay or that his naval flight officer was ordered to launch this attack?

"What other reason would a naval officer, who happens to be Muslim, have for doing this unless he was ordered to? Is it possible the missile was actually fired by the naval flight officer, Lieutenant Mark Price, who is nowhere to be found? Does this raise questions in your mind? We fully expect the evidence will suggest this attack was ordered by those above Lieutenant Commander Quasay.

"And at the end of the prosecution's case, I promise you, ladies and gentlemen, that reasonable doubt will flood your minds, will dominate your thoughts, and at the end of the day, this case will scream for a verdict of not guilty.

"Thank you."

La Trec strode confidently back to the defense table and sat down.

"This court is in recess."

"All rise."

CHAPTER 57

United States Naval Hospital
Naples, Italy

Shannon McGillvery was sleeping on the utilitarian red leather sofa in the waiting area when a hand shook her shoulder.

"Special Agent McGillvery?"

"Zack?"

"No, it's Doctor DeSoto."

She rubbed her eyes and looked up, her eyes falling on the handsome young navy surgeon, a lieutenant commander, standing over her.

"What time is it?"

"Three in the morning."

"Are you finished?"

"Yes. It was messy."

"Aren't all autopsies messy?"

"The ones where the skin has turned to charcoal are especially messy."

"Thanks for ruining my breakfast."

"It's four hours to breakfast." He sat on the sofa beside her.

"Well?" She pushed herself upright on the sofa, her bare feet touching the cold floor as she felt for her loafers. "What's the verdict, Doctor?"

"Gunshot wound to the chest."

"What do you mean?"

"That's what killed this officer. A gunshot wound. That's what I mean."

Shannon felt her eyes grow wide. "Not the crash?"

"Not the crash."

"Do you know what kind of bullet?"

"I don't know anything about ballistics, Miss McGillvery, but I did dig this little puppy out of the lieutenant's chest." He reached into his pocket and pulled out a warped bullet in a small plastic bag. "By the way, there were two other bullet holes in his chest. But there were exit wounds in both cases. The other two are either still at the crash site or maybe in the Syrian Desert somewhere."

"Stay right here, Doc. I need to get my evidence bag. That's gotta go into chain of custody, and I've got to get it over to our ballistics lab right now."

Horse caravan
Mountainous terrain
Location unknown

Early-morning light filled the ravine, and Diane sensed the caravan was moving to higher ground. She raised herself up and looked out, then down. The river was now about one hundred feet or so below. The horses and mule were headed up a path with about a 20-degree incline.

The equestrian caravan clung to the mountain, steadily climbing upward in a series of hairpin turns, all the while making the river look more like a creek, then like a snake, then like a small string, maybe a couple of thousand feet below the road.

When they had climbed for several hours, they reached a level area in the side of the mountain. The spot was bathed in sunlight.

"Welcome home," Mr. Terrorist said.

"Home?"

"Get out. I will show you."

She stepped off the wagon, following him around a big boulder and into a narrow and deep cave. Inside were boxes of small rocket munitions and what appeared to be rocket launchers. There was also a cache of small weapons, mostly AK-47s, their triggers dead-bolted.

"There are some pillows and blankets and some foldaway cots a little ways back. Here is a flashlight." He handed it to her.

The small cot was spartan, but the pillows were inviting. If this was the place she was going to die, maybe she could die in her sleep.

She spread a blanket on her cot, lay down, and buried her head in the pillow.

And closed her eyes.

And prayed.

And fell asleep to the image of Zack Brewer.

CHAPTER 58

Courtroom 4
Israeli District Court
West Bank Division

Zack felt that the prosecution's case had gone well so far, and he had called a litany of witnesses to prove that missiles from Quasay's plane destroyed the Dome.

From the USS *Harry S. Truman*, the air wing commander, Captain J. Scott Hampton, testified that Quasay and Alhad had volunteered to fly the mission, low over Israel, and had been made fully aware of the dangerous consequences before volunteering. Under no circumstances, Captain Hampton testified, had either pilot been given authorization to fire on the Dome of the Rock. In fact, they were under strict orders not to fire unless in self-defense.

"Firing the missiles," Hampton said, "was a violation of a lawful standing order."

Israeli radar operators testified about the planes' flight paths over the Dome of the Rock, and forensic ballistic experts were called to testify that the missile fragments that destroyed the Dome were in fact fired from missiles traced to both planes.

Alexander Kweskin testified about the death of his daughter, breaking down on the stand several times. La Trec cross-examined him gently.

"Mr. Kweskin, I am so sorry for your loss. But the truth is, you don't know who fired those missiles or why they were fired, do you?"

"*Nyet*," he responded, after Kathryn Shadle translated.

The government had rested its case, clearly proving that Quasay's plane fired the missile. But the big, gaping question left in the government's case was, why?

Why would a Muslim intentionally attack his own holy site?

And unless Zack could pin down the answer, there was the legitimate chance that Quasay could walk.

And Diane might live. *Please be with her, Jesus.*

Would la Trec put on evidence? He would have to, in Zack's opinion, if he planned to build his defense on the theory that these attacks were ordered.

"Mr. la Trec." Judge Norgaard peered down from the bench. "Will the defense be putting on evidence?"

"We will, Your Honor."

"Very well. You may call your first witness."

La Trec rose. "Your Honor, this is somewhat problematic at the moment."

"Oh?" Norgaard adjusted his glasses. "And why is that, Mr. la Trec?"

"Because at this moment, our first witness is still aboard his ship."

"Who is your witness, and what ship is he on?"

"He is on the USS *Harry S. Truman*, Your Honor. Our witness is the *Truman's* commanding officer. He is Captain William Constangy."

A rumbling of whispers and murmurs arose from the gallery.

"Your Honor, I'm going to object." Zack rose to his feet.

"Your grounds, Commander?"

"Unfair surprise, Captain Norgaard. The Manual for Courts-Martial requires that the defense submit a witness list. Captain Constangy is not on that list. Besides, the *Truman* is on heightened alert right now, patrolling the eastern Med to try to deter any type of attack against Israel.

"We would argue that Captain Constangy would be disqualified because of operational requirements."

Norgaard peered under his half-frames at the Frenchman. "Mr. la Trec, two questions. First, is there a reason you did not put the captain on your witness list? And second, what relevance is he?"

"As to the first part of the question about a witness list, forgive me, Your Honor. As a Frenchman, not totally familiar with your Manual for

Courts-Martial, I must plead ignorance about the witness list requirement. But please, I beg of you, do not punish my client for his avocat's
mistakes. Certainly my clumsiness would constitute an ineffective assistance of counsel which would be reversible on appeal."

Norgaard frowned at la Trec.

Wendy leaned over and whispered in Zack's ear, "The ole ineffective assistance card. He knows exactly what he's doing. Using ineffective
assistance to get away with springing a surprise witness."

"Tell me about it," Zack whispered back.

"Now as to the second part of your question," la Trec continued,
"I can represent that the captain would be relevant to our defense that
this missile attack may have been ordered. Please, Your Honor, allow
this witness. My client faces the death penalty. Do not hold my incom-
petence against him."

Norgaard looked at Zack. "Lieutenant Commander Brewer?"

"Your Honor, Mr. la Trec has a reputation as being one of the world's
greatest avocats. He has a professional staff, many of whom are here
with him today. Therefore, it is unfathomable that he was not aware of
the witness disclosure rule.

"Mr. la Trec has undertaken the defense of Lieutenant Commander
Quasay, he has brought himself before this forum, and he is charged
with learning the rules and applying them just like any other defense
counsel. You can't just spring a witness on opposing counsel without
prior notice, even if you are one of the world's greatest ... what is it the
French call them? Avocats?

"The court must draw the line in the sand, Your Honor. I mean,
what's he going to want to do next, call President Williams to the stand
to support this ludicrous theory that this brutal attack was ordered by
those above him in the chain of command?"

Norgaard held up his hand, and Zack paused.

"Any more surprise witnesses, Mr. la Trec?"

"No, Your Honor. I assure you."

"Because if I do allow this witness to testify, I promise you that I
won't allow any more surprises."

"Of course, Your Honor."

Norgaard looked at Zack. "You were saying, Commander?"

"I was saying, Your Honor, that to allow Mr. la Trec to spring this
surprise would deprive the government of its right to a fair trial. And
our Supreme Court has held that the government has just as much
right to a fair trial as the defense.

"Surprise witnesses violate not only the rules of court, but traditional notions of fair play and fundamental justice." Zack glanced at la Trec, who was still smiling arrogantly. "The government asks that the motion be denied."

Judge Norgaard looked at la Trec. "Mr. la Trec, I'm going to give you one free pass. The court will order Captain Constangy be brought here to testify. I don't know how long that will take. Perhaps not too long, because the *Truman* just happens to be off the Israeli coast right now.

"But make no mistake. This is your only free pass. During the recess, I suggest you and your assistant over there go find a copy of the Manual for Courts-Martial and read it. Is that clear?"

"Yes, Your Honor. Thank you, Your Honor," la Trec gushed.

"Very well. This court is in recess."

"All rise."

Mountainous terrain
Location unknown

Zack held her in his arms, gently caressing her hair. And then he softly kissed her. *Thank you, Lord.* And then he released her from his embrace and reached into his pocket.

It sparkled in the orange light of the setting sun, a gem from the jewelers of heaven — the most perfect diamond she had ever seen.

"Diane, there's something I want to ask you."

Deep affection — love! — danced in his hazel eyes. His hands trembled. His voice shook as he descended to one knee. She had never before witnessed anything other than boldness from this most beautiful of men. He was the answer to her prayers. And his sudden vulnerability melted the very core of her soul.

"Yes?" A thousand thoughts whirled through her mind about the military wedding they would plan. Standing under an arch of glistening swords, to a round of applause, a couple in white, he in his choker uniform, she in her mother's wedding gown. *Ladies and Gentlemen: presenting Lieutenant and Mrs. Zachary Lawrence Brewer.* They would step forward, hand in hand, shielding their eyes from the bright flashbulbs and flying rice ...

"Would you consider ..."

The violent shaking in the cave brought her eyes open. Shrill whistling sounds filled the air. Rocking that grew into violent shaking threw her from her sleeping pallet. The sharp sound of rifle fire echoed, with a magnifying effect, through the cave.

She got up and ran around the corner, just behind the entrance. Her four captors yelled frantically in Arabic and fired their weapons. Another explosion almost knocked her to her feet.

"Get back!" someone screamed in English, then turned back to the fight coming from outside.

More yelling in Arabic. More confusion.

One of them scrambled for the rocket cache and fumbled around, obviously trying to set up the mortars.

More gunfire. One of the terrorists fell back, his skull transformed into a bloody orb.

There was a thump as one of the mortar rockets fired at the unseen enemy outside the cave.

Then another rocking explosion.

NCIS Ballistics Laboratory
U.S. Naval Station
Naples, Italy

Shannon McGillvery felt like she hadn't showered for days. So the hot water and warm steam from the shower in the women's locker room at the NCIS ballistics lab was heavenly. She closed her eyes, inhaled, and turned up the pressure, allowing the water to massage her shoulders for a few minutes.

She followed the trial on television when she could, and she was glad Judge Norgaard had put the court in recess so the defense could bring in Captain Constangy.

Shannon needed more time.

Zack was probably furious she had disappeared for three days.

But she would have done him absolutely no good sitting in Jerusalem. He needed more evidence, and she was determined to get it for him.

She stepped out of the shower and dried herself with a large, soft towel.

She took a few seconds to apply mascara and lipstick. She slipped her arms into a long-sleeved black blouse and then pulled on her designer jeans. Within minutes she was ready to head back to the ballistics lab.

"Is Agent Purcell finished yet?" she asked the receptionist, an Italian national.

"He said to please go back. He is waiting for you."

When Shannon walked into the room, Special Agent Joe Purcell was holding the bullet under a bright light with a pair of tweezers.

"Shannon, this is definitely a nine-millimeter. And we've got a match on the gun. You were right."

Shannon felt a smile crawl across her lips. "Go pack your bags, Joe. You and I have a plane to catch."

"Yes, ma'am," he said.

CHAPTER 59

Courtroom 4
Israeli District Court
West Bank Division

Only the sight of Diane Colcernian walking into the courtroom could have made Zack's heart leap more than seeing a smiling Shannon McGillvery striding confidently up the center aisle toward counsel table.

"Where have you been?" he whispered as she knelt down at counsel table between him and Wendy.

"Good news," she whispered back, smiling.

"All rise!"

"Here's my report." She slid a yellow manila envelope onto the table.

"This honorable court-martial is now back in session."

"You're not leaving again, are you?"

"Not on your life." She sat in a folding chair right behind counsel table.

"The record should reflect that all counsel and the defendant are present. And, Mr. la Trec, I understand that Captain Constangy has just been brought in by helicopter from the *Truman*." Norgaard's gaze locked on the skipper of the *Harry S. Truman*, who sat in the first row behind the prosecution table. Constangy was accompanied by the *Truman*'s senior JAG officer, LCDR Dewey Rouse. "Is the defense ready to proceed?"

"We are, Your Honor," la Trec said with a satisfying look. "At this time, we call Captain William Constangy to the stand."

"Captain Constangy, please take the stand to be sworn," Norgaard said.

In service dress blues with the four stripes of a navy captain on his sleeve and a colorful array of ribbons on his chest, Constangy walked to the witness stand and was sworn.

"Captain, did your ship recently detain a Spanish fishing vessel in the Mediterranean Sea?"

"We did, temporarily. Yes."

"Where in the Med, sir?"

"About fifty miles or so southeast of Minorca, as I recall."

"And why did you detain that vessel, sir?"

Constangy squirmed a little, looked up at Norgaard, then back at la Trec. "It was determined that the boat was emitting strange radio signals. They were irregular. They made no sense."

"What sort of radio signals?"

"They kept repeating the words *Oscar India Golf*."

"So you sent a SEAL team out in a helicopter to detain the boat?"

"That is correct."

"And when the SEAL team arrived on the vessel, what did they find?"

"It was manned by a crew of three. There were some small weapons on board. Nothing of real consequence."

"What was the nationality of the crew, Captain?"

"Two Saudis, one Spanish. What does that have to do with anything?" Constangy snapped.

Zack cringed.

"Please just answer his questions, Captain," Captain Norgaard ordered.

"You weren't pleased that there were two Arabs on board, were you?"

Constangy glowered. "I could care less about their nationality, monsieur."

"Well, isn't it true that you wanted to capture these Arab men and take them on board the *Truman*?"

"They were emitting strange signals. They might have been terrorists, monsieur."

"Terrorists." La Trec slipped on his glasses. "Just because they are Arab."

"I didn't say that!"

"You just said, and I quote, 'They might have been terrorists,' did you not, monsieur?"

"Yeah, but I didn't say they were terrorists because they were Arab." Constangy stared at Zack as if he was expecting Zack to object.

"You don't like Arabs, do you, Captain?"

"Objection. Relevance." Zack stood.

"We will establish relevance, Your Honor," la Trec countered.

"Overruled."

"That's ridiculous."

"You don't like Islamic people, do you?"

"Objection."

"Overruled. The witness will answer the question."

"I don't have anything against 'em."

"You don't have anything against 'em," la Trec repeated mockingly. "But isn't it true, Captain, that you said that Islamic fundamentalists are a bunch of animals?"

"I don't remember saying that."

"You didn't say that in the radio room of your ship, in front of your JAG officer, when you were debating whether to detain these Saudi citizens?"

Constangy, his face red, stared out to a spot just behind the prosecution's table. Zack turned around and figured he was making eye contact with his JAG officer, LCDR Rouse, who put his palm on his forehead and shook his head.

Great. He said it.

"Captain, I'm waiting for your answer."

"Okay, maybe I said something like that. But there was a lot of pressure. It's a dangerous world, monsieur. Something your country obviously doesn't care about. Well, the United States of America *does* care about it."

"Didn't you refer to a key ally of the United States of America, Saudi Arabia, as being like, and I quote, 'a horses rear'?"

Zack glanced at Rouse, who held his head down, grimacing.

"I don't know what I said. Maybe something like that. Look, we didn't know what was going on. It's a dangerous world. They were acting suspiciously."

"But you did refer to the Saudis as a horse's rear, didn't you?"

"Okay, okay. Maybe I did."

"Your JAG officer is right here in the courtroom. Do we need to call him to find out if you said these things, Captain?"

"Okay, I said 'em. Okay? There was a lot of pressure. I could've ordered that boat sunk. But I didn't. Okay?"

"Yes, you could've ordered that boat sunk, just like you could've ordered the attack on the Dome of the Rock."

"Objection!"

"Now see here, mister!" Constangy stood, his veins bulging.

"Sit down, please, Captain," Judge Norgaard ordered.

"I resent that, Your Honor."

"The objection is overruled. The witness will answer the question."

"I did not order the attack on the Dome," Constangy said through gritted teeth.

"But that wasn't my question," la Trec persisted calmly. "I asked if you *could* have ordered it."

Constangy sat, crossed his arms, and fumed. "Yes, I *could* have, but I did not."

"Do you know Lieutenant Mark Price?"

"Yes."

"He was Commander Quasay's navigator and weapons officer, right?"

"Right."

"Price led a Christian Bible study on board your ship, isn't that right?"

"Yes."

"In fact, he invited you, and you actually attended a few times, right?"

"Yes. Mark was a good teacher. And a good man."

"And wasn't Lieutenant Price teaching a course on biblical prophecy and the end times?"

"Yes. We had a number of men who'd read the Left Behind series. The Bible study grew out of that."

"And didn't Lieutenant Price teach that the temple would have to be rebuilt here in Jerusalem before Jesus returned?"

"Yes, I heard him say that a few times."

"And did he not also say that the Dome of the Rock was sitting on the site of Solomon's temple, and that it would have to be removed before the temple was rebuilt?"

"Yes. Mark felt, according to his teachings, that God, in his sovereignty, would somehow remove the Dome of the Rock."

"Did you ever have any discussions with him about how that would happen?"

"Maybe we had some discussions. Not many. Look, mister, I'm the captain of a United States aircraft carrier, something that the French don't have many of. It's not like I've got a whole lot of time to sit around and twiddle my thumbs or talk about Bible prophecy."

"Did you not suggest to him, when he and Commander Quasay volunteered to fly over Israel, that maybe God had called him to that mission?"

"I don't remember."

"Did you not suggest that perhaps a missile malfunction might destroy the Dome?"

"No!"

"Didn't you, in fact, order Lieutenant Price to launch that Sparrow missile from Commander Quasay's aircraft to destroy the Dome?"

"No!"

"Well, you didn't order my client to do it, did you?"

"I didn't order your client, and I didn't order Price either!"

"Sure you didn't, Captain."

"Objection!"

"Sustained!"

"I have no further questions for the Captain."

"Very well." Norgaard looked at Zack. "Cross-exam, Commander Brewer?"

Zack stood and rose to the podium.

"How long have you been in the navy, Skipper?"

"Graduated from the Academy twenty-five years ago, been on active duty ever since."

"How long have you been skipper of the *Truman*?"

"Going on two years now."

"I see your salad row is quite colorful, sir. What are some of the awards and decorations that have been bestowed on you?"

"Objection to relevance, Your Honor," la Trec said.

"Overruled. The witness will answer."

"Four Navy Achievement Medals, five Navy Commendation Medals, three Meritorious Service Medals, two Joint Meritorious Service Medals. I've had a stint with the Joint Chiefs. Five Sea Service Ribbons, four Overseas Service Ribbons, three Legions of Merit. Do you want me to continue?"

"No, sir. I think we have a feel for your background, Captain. But tell me this: What were the rules of engagement for U.S. fighters flying off your ship and over Israel on May 9?"

"Twofold. To take defensive measures if fired upon, and to seek out and destroy anything that looked like an enemy Scud missile launcher."

"Did the rules of engagement include the right to fire at any civilian targets on the ground?"

"No, they did not, Commander, and the rules of engagement have never included the right to attack civilian targets. We're Americans. We're better than that."

"Agreed, Commander. We are. But if Commander Quasay's plane fired a missile into the Dome of the Rock, was that a violation of the rules of engagement?"

"Of course it was." Constangy fumed. "And I never have and never will order anyone under my command to fire at a civilian target. The monsieur's question was the most insulting thing anybody ever said to me during my twenty-five years as a naval officer."

"Thank you, Captain. No further questions."

"Any redirect?"

"No, Your Honor."

"Very well. You may step down, Captain," Norgaard said. "Mr. la Trec, any more evidence for the defense?"

"One moment, Your Honor." La Trec and Quasay quietly conferred.

"Think he's going to rest?" Wendy whispered to Zack.

"Not in a million years," Zack whispered back. "He's putting his man on the stand. He's got to. Watch."

Zack looked again at the wallet-sized photograph of Anna Kweskin. The cross-examination of a defendant, next to closing argument, was the most important stage of any criminal trial for a prosecutor.

Lord, give me the strength to do your will.

"Your Honor, the defense calls Lieutenant Commander Mohammed Quasay to the stand."

A roar from the gallery.

"Commander Quasay, come forward please. Place your left hand on the Bible and raise your right hand, please."

"Your Honor, I would prefer to place my hand on the Holy Koran."

Norgaard looked around with a confused expression. "Have we got a Koran?" he asked the bailiff.

"No, sir," the bailiff answered. "Nobody ever asked for one before."

"Commander Quasay," Norgaard said, looking at the defendant, who was standing in the witness stand, "unfortunately, we do not have a Koran in the courtroom at the moment. The court will be happy to accommodate you in one of two ways. First, we can recess to find one. Or you can take the oath by simply raising your right hand."

"That is what I will do, Your Honor."

"The bailiff will administer the oath."

Quasay raised his hand and took the oath, then sat down as the French avocat took the podium.

"Commander, tell us in your own words what happened on the morning of May 9."

Quasay adjusted the tie on his service dress blue uniform. "It all started the day before. They called a special meeting of my squadron, Viper Squadron, and asked for volunteers for a dangerous mission over Israel."

"Who is 'they'?"

"The captain and the air boss."

"When you say the captain, are you referring to Captain Constangy, the skipper of the *Truman*?"

"Yes, sir."

"And what was the nature of this mission?"

"The Israeli government wanted low-level flights of U.S. jets as an assurance to the population that the navy would help deter any attacks by Syria. It was sort of a PR mission, I suppose, but it was dangerous because of the large number of Stinger missiles that have been brought into the country."

"And you volunteered?"

"I did."

"Why?"

"I was the squadron commander. It's my job to lead."

"And Commander Hosni Alhad volunteered also."

"He did."

"Why?"

"You'd have to ask him."

"All right. Tell us about the mission. What happened?"

"Mouse and I took off first; then we circled the boat and waited for Hosni and Pip.

"Who are Mouse, Hosni, and Pip?"

"Mouse is Lieutenant Mark Price, my naval flight officer. Hosni is Lieutenant Hosni Alhad, the other pilot. And Pip is Lieutenant Ricky Davis, his naval flight officer."

"Okay." La Trec nodded. "And after Hosni and Pip took off, what happened?"

"We dropped down low, maybe two hundred feet off the deck, and shot in toward the Israeli coastline. The plan was to fly in over the Negev, turn north, and then do a flyover of Jerusalem."

"Where over Jerusalem?"

"The first run would take us directly over the Old City. Sort of for symbolic purposes. Then we planned to do a loop north of the city and come back over the western suburbs. After that, we were going to fly over Tel Aviv."

"And what happened as you flew into Jerusalem from the south?"

"As I said, we were on a course straight in for the Old City. We were about five miles out, when next thing I know, Mouse had armed one of the Sparrows."

"And by 'Sparrows,' you're referring to one of the plane's missiles?"

"Right."

"And then what?"

"And as I was turning around to ask him what was going on, next thing I know, the plane jumped."

"Meaning?"

"He'd fired the missile."

"And then what?"

"Then I screamed at him. And I said, 'Mouse, are you crazy? What in the heck are you doing?'"

"And what did he say?"

"Objection." Zack stormed to his feet. "What a dead man said is hearsay."

"Mr. la Trec? Your response?"

"First, Your Honor, there's no evidence that Lieutenant Price is dead. He may be hidden in seclusion by the Israelis, for all we know. But at any rate, we would submit that his out-of-court statement is not hearsay because it goes to Lieutenant Price's state of mind. Also, under the circumstances, we believe it would fall within the excited utterance exception to the hearsay rule."

Norgaard scratched his chin. "The objection is overruled. You may answer the question."

"I forgot the question."

"What did Mouse say when you screamed at him and told him he was crazy?"

"He said that Captain Constangy had ordered him to fire the missile."

A roar of mumbling voices broke out in the back of the courtroom.

"Order! Order in the court!" Two whaps from Judge Norgaard's gavel. "Order!"

"Captain Constangy ordered Mouse to do it? Is that your testimony?"

"Yes, and Mouse said that the captain had ordered Lieutenant Price to fire a missile too."

More commotion. More rumbling.

"Order! Order!"

"What happened next?"

"I looked down from the cockpit, and we were passing over the Old City. The Dome was smoldering."

"And then what?"

"I kept yelling, 'Why did you do that, Mouse?' And he kept saying something about top-secret orders from the skipper."

"Top-secret orders from the skipper?"

"Right."

"And then what?"

"There was chaos in the cockpit. I kept thinking, *We're gonna get shot down, we're gonna get shot down!* I knew the Israelis would be scrambling their F-15s, and the only thing I could think of was that we were no match for the whole Israeli Air Force. I couldn't risk cutting west back across Israel to make a run for the Med. So I set a course for Syria."

"And you bailed out over Syria?"

"Yes, we both bailed out. Hosni and I were rescued. Unfortunately, Mouse and Pip are still out there." Quasay's voice trembled as if he were about to cry. He held his head low and wiped his eyes. "I pray to Allah every day they are still alive."

"I know, Commander," la Trec said in a consoling tone. "It is hard to lose those we care for."

"I am sorry," Quasay said, his eyes glistening as he looked at the members and then back to la Trec. "Could I have some water?"

"May I approach the witness, Your Honor?" la Trec pleaded.

"You may."

La Trec poured a cup of water from a pitcher on the defense table and brought it to the witness stand. Quasay drank as if he were suffering from dehydration in a desert. "Thank you."

"Commander, you're Muslim, correct?"

"Yes, sir. Devout."

"And you received a Muslim education growing up?"

"Yes, I attended The School of the Holy Prophet, located on the outskirts of Dearborn, Michigan."

"And you attended college, partially at least, on a Muslim scholarship?"

"Yes, with the help of the Muslim Educational Foundation."

"As a Muslim, what does the Dome of the Rock mean to you?"

Quasay took a deep breath, as if the very question was causing him anguish. Then he took another drink of water. "It is holy ground to the Muslim, sir. It is where the prophet—peace be upon him—ascended to Allah at the end of his night journey. Its destruction pains me personally. I would give my life to bring it back. How I wish I could give my life to bring it back."

"Thank you, Commander. No further questions."

"This court will be in recess."

"All rise."

CHAPTER 60

Courtroom 4
Israeli District Court
West Bank Division

Court had been in recess for about fifteen minutes, with Judge Norgaard off the bench for a prolonged break. Several members of the international press had tried approaching the counsel table for interviews with Zack.

But thanks to beefed-up security in the aftermath of the shoe bombing, Israeli police and U.S. Marines now formed a human barricade across the courtroom, just behind counsel table, denying even the press direct access to the JAG officers.

Zack could hear their shouts of "Lieutenant Commander Brewer!" over the tops of the marines' heads. But in the precious few minutes he had before commencement of cross-examination, Zack tried, albeit with some difficulty, to tune out their yapping. Instead, he studied Shannon McGillvery's report, cross-referencing pages and making notes on his legal pad.

"Anything I can do to help?" Wendy looked over his shoulder at the report.

She looked worried, undoubtedly thinking—as he did—that the defense had scored points with Quasay's performance. At this point, there was probably reasonable doubt. Zack would have to dent the defendant's credibility on cross-examination, or these terrorists might walk.

"As a matter of fact, yes. Why don't you throw these dogs a few innocuous bones"—he nodded to the press corps—"just to shut them up for a few minutes."

"What should I tell them?"

"Tell them the trial is going well, and we don't believe the defendant is telling the truth. Then smile and tell them the same thing again three or four times. By then Judge Norgaard should be back, and I can get through this report."

"Got it."

That quieted the vultures for a few minutes, allowing Zack to push through the fifteen-page, single-spaced NCIS report.

"All rise."

Zack turned around and gave Shannon McGillvery a wink and a thumbs-up.

"This court is back in session."

Shannon reciprocated.

"Please be seated. Lieutenant Commander Brewer, does the government have questions on cross-examination?"

"We do, Your Honor."

"Very well. You may proceed."

"Good afternoon, Commander Quasay."

"Good afternoon, Commander."

"Isn't it true, based upon the weapons configuration in the F-14, that either the pilot or the flight officer has the capability to launch a Sparrow missile?"

"That's true, but it wasn't me that launched that missile."

"But that wasn't my question, Commander." Zack wagged his index finger. "My question was that *you* as the commander of that aircraft *could have* launched that missile attack, with or without the consent or assistance of Lieutenant Price. Correct?"

After a moment of disgruntled silence, he said, "Correct."

"And as the commander of that aircraft, you could have set it down anywhere you wished, correct?"

"Yes, that was my prerogative."

"And you chose, voluntarily, to cross into Syrian airspace rather than trying to set her down in Israel."

"As I said, I was afraid we would get shot down in Israel."

"You didn't detect the presence of any Israeli fighters in the immediate vicinity, did you?"

"No, but an F-15 has supersonic capabilities."

"But you *could* have gone on the radio and declared an emergency, correct?"

"Of course. Any pilot can do that."

"And under the international rules of aviation, a pilot declaring an emergency has priority rights for landing at any airstrip, correct?"

"Correct."

"And you could have put your plane down, in *Israel*, within five minutes, if you had declared an emergency."

"Maybe, if we didn't get shot down first."

"You mean shot down by fighters that were not in the area?"

"Objection. Argumentative."

"Sustained."

"The navy has spent hundreds of thousands of dollars on your flight training, correct?"

"Correct."

"You've logged hundreds of hours in the cockpit of a jet fighter, correct?"

"Correct."

"You're required to be fully familiar with the international rules of aviation, correct?"

"Correct."

"Tell me, Commander, in all your hundreds of hours of training, and with hundreds of hours of cockpit experience, how many instances are you aware of in which an aircraft declaring an emergency has been shot out of the sky?"

Quasay looked at la Trec as if he was looking for an answer. Getting none, he glanced back at Zack. "I'm not familiar with one, but that doesn't mean it hasn't happened before."

"But isn't it true, under the international rules of aviation, that declaration of an emergency guarantees an aircraft *safe passage* to the nearest runway?"

"Yes, that's true."

"And there were airstrips in Jerusalem and the Negev where you could have landed, right?"

"Right."

"But you flew off to Syria instead?"

"Yes, and I told you why."

"And did it not occur to you, Commander, that an aircraft flying from Israeli airspace into Syrian airspace might get shot down, especially in this period of heightened international tensions between the two countries?"

Quasay looked at la Trec again. "Yes, I was concerned about that, and that's why we bailed out."

"Who bailed out?"

"Me and Mouse."

"Both of you bailed out?"

"Yes, that's right."

"Because you were concerned about getting shot down?"

"Right."

"So you were concerned about getting shot down over both Israel *and* Syria."

Another glance at la Trec. "Yes."

"Well then, why not just bail out over Israel?"

Shifting eyes. A hesitation. "Look, there was chaos in the cockpit, okay? I did not think about that at first. I'd like to see how you would handle the situation if your flight officer just shot a missile into the third holiest site in all of Islam!"

Zack smirked. He'd seen witnesses start to crack like this dozens of times. "Move to strike that last comment, Your Honor, and move for an admonition that the witness refrain from self-serving comments and just answer the question."

"Motion to strike is granted." Norgaard looked at the defendant. "Commander, you are warned against making such comments and are instructed only to answer Commander Brewer's questions. Understand?"

"Yes, sir."

"All right, Commander Quasay, after you bailed out, what happened?"

"I'm not sure what happened to Pip and Mouse, but Hosni's chute came down not far from mine. We got together and prayed that we would be rescued. Thank Allah that we were."

"Commander, you had a nine-millimeter Beretta issued to you as a sidearm, did you not?"

"Yes. Many pilots do."

"And you had that gun on you when you were picked up, right?"

"Yes."

"Now if NCIS ballistics reports were to show that your pistol was fired once, would you have any reason do dispute that?"

Another quick glance at la Trec.

"Actually, I did fire one shot at a jackal. I didn't know how long we were going to be stranded, and I knew we would need food. Unfortunately, I missed. I decided to save the other rounds for self-defense if we needed them."

"I see. And Did Lieutenant Alhad fire his weapon?" Zack could see Quasay's wheels spinning.

"Uh. Yes. Once, I think. He shot at the jackal too and missed."

"You know, we know all about Operation Islamic Glory, Commander. We know about al-Akhma, and we know you're a part of it."

"Objection, Your Honor. That's not even a question."

"Sustained."

Zack knew it wasn't a proper question under the rules of evidence. He hadn't intended it to be. He'd made the statement for shock effect.

"What does the phrase *Operation Islamic Glory* mean to you, Commander?"

Quasay's gaze shifted back and forth, between la Trec, Zack, and Judge Norgaard.

"You're wondering how we know about it, aren't you?"

"Objection."

"Sustained."

Zack looked over his shoulder at a grinning Shannon McGillvery.

"Islamic Glory," Zack persisted. "You are part of it, aren't you?"

"I ... I don't know what you're talking about."

Quasay's face looked drained of blood. His gaze darted from Zack to la Trec, then back again.

"Islamic Glory was a Muslim plan to have an American jet attack the Dome of the Rock to drive an irreparable political wedge between the United States and Israel, isn't that right?"

"Who told you that?"

Out of the corner of his eye, Zack saw la Trec shaking his head no.

"*Who* told me doesn't matter. *What* matters is that it's true, isn't it?"

"I wouldn't know anything about it."

"We also know that you shot Lieutenant Price three times in the chest."

Quasay's face flushed.

"Objection to form."

"Sustained. Please ask questions, Commander."

"Gladly, Your Honor. Commander Quasay, if a U.S. Navy coroner's report were to show that three gunshot wounds to the chest killed Lieutenant Price, and that those shots were fired by your gun, would you have reason to dispute that?"

A low rumble grew into a roar from the spectators in the back.

"Objection, Your Honor!"

"Order in the court!"

The roar continued.

"Order! Order!" Three whaps from Judge Norgaard's gavel restored quiet.

"What's the basis for your objection, Mr. la Trec?"

"Unfair surprise, Your Honor. We've not seen a copy of such a report, and if such a report existed, the government was required to disclose it before trial. Therefore, the defense moves to dismiss, or in the alternative, moves for a mistrial."

Norgaard eyed the members of the military jury. "Ladies and gentlemen, I'm going to excuse you while I take up a matter with counsel. Bailiff?"

The bailiff took the members out; then Norgaard looked at Zack. "Commander, I share Mr. la Trec's concerns about springing a question like that in the middle of a trial, especially if evidence wasn't turned over ahead of time. You know the requirements of *Brady versus Maryland* as well as I do. The disclosure requirement in the military is even more demanding than in the civilian courts. The defense gets everything. Your explanation had better be good, or I'm inclined to grant the defense's motion."

"Your Honor," Zack began, "I am, as you know from the previous times I've had the pleasure of appearing before you, very much aware of the military requirement of full disclosure prior to trial. However, in this case, the report was only made available to me just before the last break. I spent the time during the recess reading it, and therefore I haven't had the report long enough to disclose it."

"So there *is* such a report?" Norgaard asked.

"Yes, there is, Your Honor. I have it right here." Zack waved the NCIS report in the air.

"Why are you just now getting it, Commander?"

"Because, Your Honor, NCIS just found Lieutenant Price's body in the wreckage of the F-14 in the Syrian Desert. He had not ejected, by the way, contrary to the defendant's sworn testimony."

"You say NCIS found him?"

"Your Honor, NCIS Special Agent Shannon McGillvery was heading a team which included Israeli special forces and U.S. Navy crash experts. She's here in the courtroom today." Zack gestured to

Shannon, who nodded at Judge Norgaard. "The body was bagged, flown out of Syria—on a very dangerous mission, by the way—and then taken to Naval Hospital Naples for an autopsy. The navy medical examiner found three bullet holes in Lieutenant Price's chest, Your Honor, and one bullet, which ballistics traced to the defendant's gun."

"May I see the report?"

"Of course, Your Honor." Zack approached the bench and handed it to the judge, who studied it for a few moments. "Bailiff, please hand this to Mr. la Trec." The bailiff did. "Please take a few moments to read this, Mr. la Trec." He did, then looked up at the judge.

"Mr. la Trec, I've read many NCIS reports during my career in the JAG Corps. I have not yet admitted this into evidence, but at first blush, it *does* appear to be authentic, and the representations contained in it support Lieutenant Commander Brewer's assertion that Lieutenant Price's body was just found. Of course, you would have the opportunity to attack that premise by calling and cross-examining Special Agent McGillvery if you would like.

"I will tell you, however, that if I am convinced that the body was just found within the last two or three days, I will deny your motion to dismiss and also deny your motion for a mistrial. In fairness to your client, however, I will grant you a recess, for as long as you reasonably need, to build any defense."

La Trec leered at Zack. The arrogant facade was gone from his face. "Your Honor, I desire a short recess to discuss this with my client."

"Very well. This court is in recess."

"All rise."

CHAPTER 61

They've gotten to somebody!" Mohammed Quasay pounded his fist on the table. He stared at Jean-Claude la Trec, then at Jeanette L'Enfant. "My stomach is in knots." He dropped his head into his hands.

"It is going to be all right." Jeanette L'Enfant laid her hand on the back of his shoulder.

Was Allah really in all this? Why had he let Hosni Alhad influence him? Mouse Price was an infidel, but a friend. Maybe Allah wasn't in this after all. Maybe al-Akhma was a madman. Maybe Allah was now punishing him for destroying the Dome. If this were really Allah's will, why would he have been discovered?

This wasn't what al-Akhma had promised. He and Hosni were supposed to become heroes of the new United Islamic Republic. Now Hosni was dead, and Brewer was closing in like an American bloodhound tracking a wounded animal.

He looked up. "No. It's *not* going to be all right. I want to cut a deal. I want you to approach Brewer and offer my services as a material witness in return for them not to seek the death penalty. Otherwise, they'll fry me. Just like they did the chaplains. Tell them I'll sing about Islamic Glory. Anything they want to know."

La Trec and L'Enfant exchanged glances. "Are you out of your mind, Commander? What makes you think Brewer will deal even if we offer it? And if he takes it, do you really think the Council of Ishmael will let you live?"

"The Americans would protect me. Maybe put me in one of those witness protection programs."

"Commander, the Americans could not protect the World Trade Center. They could not protect the Pentagon. They could not even protect Hosni Alhad in this very courthouse. What makes you think they can protect you?"

He's right ... or is he?

"Look," la Trec continued, "the Council of Ishmael has paid *thirty million dollars* to hire you the best legal team in the world. They didn't hire me to plead you guilty. If I let you plead guilty, not only will they come after you, but they will come after me too. And that just is not going to happen. Do you understand?"

Why don't I trust him?

"Jeanette, I'm going to leave the two of you alone for a moment. Help him come up with an explanation before we have to go into court."

"Yes, Jean-Claude."

Courtroom 4
Israeli District Court
West Bank Division

Have you had sufficient time to confer with your client, Mr. la Trec?"

"I have, Your Honor."

"Very well. The bailiff will bring back the members."

With the members seated and Quasay back on the stand, Norgaard looked at Zack. "You may now resume your cross-examination, Commander."

"Thank you, sir," Zack said, then turned his gaze to Quasay. "Commander, let me repeat my question to you before the break.

"If a U.S. Navy coroner's report were to show that three gunshot wounds to the chest had killed Lieutenant Price, and that those shots were fired by your gun, would you have reason to dispute that?"

"Commander," Quasay said calmly, "no, I would not dispute that."

"Why not?"

"Because it is true." His tone sounded rehearsed. "I shot Lieutenant Price. I shot him in the cockpit."

Dramatic rumbles rose from the gallery.

"Order in the court!" *Rap! Rap! Rap!*

"I shot him to prevent him from launching more missiles. Innocent civilians had already died. I thought about Islamic pilgrims who had already perished at the smoking Dome below." He wiped his eyes. "I felt compelled to shoot him. It is the hardest thing I've ever had to do."

More rumbling from the gallery brought three more raps from the judge.

"So all this talk about shooting at a jackal was a bold-faced lie, wasn't it, Commander?"

"Yes, Commander, I regret to say that it was." Quasay looked down at his feet with a shameful head droop. "But what I am telling you now is the truth."

"Right. And your sworn testimony that Lieutenant Price bailed out was a lie, correct?"

"Again, I regret to say that it was. But I swear to you now, before Allah, that I am telling you the truth. And I say before Allah, Lieutenant Price destroyed the Dome, not me. As a good Muslim, I would never destroy it."

"Right. The truth is that you have lied here under oath, haven't you, Commander?"

"Yes, I am ashamed to say, but only about the death of Lieutenant Price."

"That makes you a liar and a perjurer, doesn't it, Commander?"

"Objection!"

"Order in the court! Objection is overruled."

"That makes you a liar and a perjurer *and* a murderer, doesn't it, Commander?"

"I will leave that for the members to decide, Commander."

"No further questions, Your Honor."

CHAPTER 62

Even though she was not an attorney, Shannon had been invited into the attorneys' lounge by Zack and Wendy. She was sitting on one of the comfortable sofas drinking a bottled water when they walked in.

"You did great." Zack gave her a high five, headed to a table, and sat down.

"I'm glad my part's over, at least." Shannon got up, crossed the room, dropped a few shekels in the snack machine, and reached for a bag of cashew nuts. "I've never been cross-examined like that. That French guy was good."

"You held your ground great." Wendy dropped shekels in the drink machine for a Diet Coke.

"Zack, do you think we're in good shape?" Shannon dropped a couple of cashews in her mouth.

Zack looked up from his legal pad. "Thanks to all your hard work, I think we're ahead on points. But we're not out of the woods yet. It could break either way. It all comes down to closing argument."

Shannon's cell phone chirped.

"Special Agent McGillvery." She felt the smile instantly evaporate from her face. "Okay ... Are you sure? Are they credible? ... How long ago? ... I understand. Yes, sir. I'll be right there."

"Is everything okay?"

Shannon looked up and saw that Wendy was frowning. Zack had glanced up from his legal pad again. She was not about to reveal that Diane Colcernian had possibly been spotted.

Not now.

Not when he was about to make perhaps the most significant closing argument in his career.

The distraction, she knew, would be overwhelming.

"Yes, everything's fine. Just some peripheral business I need to go check on. Look, I'm not going to be able to stay for closing arguments. You guys take care, and good luck this afternoon."

Zack stood, and so did Wendy.

Shannon gave Wendy a hug and Zack a friendly peck on the cheek.

Then she was out the door.

Courtroom 4
Israeli District Court
West Bank Division

The atmosphere was tense as Zack sat at counsel table with Wendy. Across the aisle, la Trec and L'Enfant furiously scribbled notes. Quasay looked on stoically.

La Trec was a formidable opponent, but not as ruthless as Wells Levinson. Perhaps the fact that Zack had already beaten Levinson made la Trec seem less of a giant.

The prosecution was ahead on points, he felt, and with a hard-hitting closing argument, the case could be put away.

And so could Diane.

Please be advised that at the moment you begin your opening statement, we will begin to, with the use of a sharp knife, amputate Lieutenant Colcernian's right hand. We will take our time, of course, ensuring the amputation process lasts precisely as long as your opening argument. Then, when you deliver what will undoubtedly be a spellbinding closing argument, as you always do, we will repeat this procedure with her left hand.

Zack prayed silently again for strength, for wisdom, and for Diane.

"All rise."

"Are the parties ready for closing argument?"

"We are," la Trec said.

"The government is ready," Zack said with his index finger on the picture of Anna Kweskin's angelic face.

"Very well. The government has waived the opening section of closing argument. Therefore, the members are with the defense. Mr. la Trec?"

"Thank you, Your Honor," la Trec said. He seemed to have regained the panache he had before his client was caught in a lie. He strode confidently to the middle of the chancel area.

"Mr. President, distinguished members of this court-martial, I promised you that at the end of this case, there would be more questions about what really happened than answers. That there would be questions as to why a good Muslim would deliberately assault and destroy one of the holiest sites in all of Islam."

A few of the members nodded as la Trec paused, stepped back, surveyed each member, and then continued.

"I believe that the evidence before this jury, unfortunately, is one of the most puzzling, unintelligible morasses of disjointed information that I have ever seen in a criminal trial, and I've been involved in hundreds of trials all over the world.

"But before I discuss the poor state of the prosecution's evidence in this case, I want to make a comment about the great American system of government that has been the beacon to oppressed nations since the early 1900s.

"One of the greatest historians my nation has ever produced is the late Alexis de Tocqueville. Ironically, it is not a study of France, or of the French Revolution, or of the kings and queens of Europe that de Tocqueville is known for. Rather, it is his influence on your country that has made him famous. I speak, of course, of the immortal work of literature *Democracy in America*.

"Ladies and gentlemen, I became a student of de Tocqueville and of America as a boy. And I often wondered, as a boy, what is it that makes America great? What is it that causes thousands of your men and boys to spill their blood and their lives for those whose language they don't even speak and for strangers they don't even know?

"And in my studies, I came to the conclusion that the answer is in one word.

"*Freedom.* The one great principle that separates America from all others is her dedication to freedom for the individual.

"Totalitarian governments like the Nazis that would murder a man without a hearing and without a fair trial are an anathema to freedom.

And that's why you came to our beaches. Because you could not stand by and let such regimes oppress and murder and maim. Because at your very core, you are good. Because you believe in the teachings of the great philosopher, who said, 'Greater love has no man than he who would lay down his life for a friend.'

"There are principles that make America the undisputed leader of the free world, I have learned. And one of the greatest principles that separates you from all others is the great principle of *reasonable doubt*.

"You Americans are so committed to freedom that you have declared that government cannot convict a man unless the government proves each and every element of its case *beyond all reasonable doubt*.

"Your system says that even if you believe a man is guilty, that alone is not enough to convict him. If there is any *reasonable doubt* whatsoever about any element of the crime, then that man must go free.

"Your founding fathers, those men like Franklin and Jefferson, those men who were dear friends of Lafayette and of other great Frenchman in the infancy of your republic, believed that if nine men were guilty and one was innocent, better to let all ten go free than to punish the one who is innocent.

"These lofty ideals, these sublime commitments to freedom, are hard for the world to understand. But these are the ideals that make America, in the words of your great former president Ronald Reagan, 'a shining city on a hill.'

"Just as your men poured over the cliffs at Pointe du Hoc and shed their blood for France, as an indebted Frenchman, I feel privileged to give something back in their memory by standing here and by embracing and defending the principle that Jefferson and Franklin and thousands of your countrymen fought and died for—the principle of reasonable doubt.

"Just as you, distinguished officers of the United States Navy, are part of the military wall against totalitarianism, likewise the principle of guilt beyond a reasonable doubt is the legal wall against the despot.

"And having said that, we ask the question, has the government really proven beyond a reasonable doubt that Lieutenant Commander Mohammed Quasay, a devout Muslim and an American naval officer, *intentionally* launched a missile attack against one of his religion's holiest sites? Does the very question itself leave you scratching your head and asking why?

"Let us take a look at what the evidence shows in this case.

"First, we know that my client's flight officer, Lieutenant Mark Price, was by all accounts a religious fanatic. He actually led a *Bible* study on board a U.S. Naval warship. And what was it that caused him to start this Bible study? Some fanatical sailors were reading a fantastical, apocalyptic account of the end of the world, the Left Behind series, and actually *believed* the books.

"According to Price's own commanding officer, Captain William Constangy, Price started the Bible study to explain the events of the so-called end times." La Trec made air quotation marks.

"We know that Price actually believed the Dome of the Rock must be destroyed so that Solomon's temple can be rebuilt before Jesus comes back.

"We know Price even had these conversations with Captain Constangy himself.

"We know, from the captain's own admission, that he despises Islam. Consider his reaction in the *Truman*'s radio room when he detained a boat with two Saudi citizens. He referred to Islamic fundamentalists as 'a bunch of animals.'

"A bunch of animals? What kind of talk is that coming from the captain of a U.S. Navy supercarrier?

"And what's significant about Constangy's testimony is not just what he said, but also *what he did not say*."

La Trec stopped, walked over to counsel table, took a sip of water, then turned to the members and resumed.

"Constangy testified for the better part of an hour the other day. And not once did he disassociate himself with Price.

"Oh sure, he denied ordering the missile attacks. What do we expect him to say about that? But not once did he deny being a fundamentalist Christian." His voice was heavy with contempt. "Not once did he say he did not believe Price's fantasy about the Dome needing to be destroyed before Jesus returns.

"What kind of a man is this commanding one of the world's most powerful warships?" La Trec turned his hands palms up, as if in supplication.

"Is Constangy a religious fanatic who would order his warplanes to destroy buildings for the advancement of what he considers to be his God's purposes? Isn't that exactly the kind of fanatic who destroyed American buildings and took American life on 9/11?

"The testimony we heard from Constangy was bone-chilling. Constangy ordered this attack, ladies and gentlemen, and Mouse Price carried out that order.

"Now in a few minutes, Lieutenant Commander Brewer will appear before you for the government's closing argument. And what is it you will hear? He will argue that my client lied about shooting Price.

"Okay. But there is a reason that Commander Quasay had to shoot Price. And the reason was to protect innocent life. Price was a man gone mad. He had to be killed.

"Should Commander Quasay have come clean with this at first? Of course he should have. But it was Price who started this whole thing. Quasay panicked. Who wouldn't?

"And please don't let yourselves become distracted by this red herring about who shot Price. My client is not charged with shooting Price. He is charged with launching a missile attack against the Dome of the Rock. And the question is, can the government prove *beyond a reasonable doubt* that he *intentionally* carried out that attack?

Put another way: Which is a more reasonable explanation of what happened here? Explanation one—that a couple of fundamentalist Christians, Price and Constangy, believing that the Dome must be destroyed for Jesus to return, took it upon themselves to take matters into their own hands; or two—that a Muslim pilot intentionally destroyed one of the holiest sites in his own religion?

"It raises questions in your mind, doesn't it? Of course it does. And if there is a question in your mind, then this case screams of reasonable doubt.

"Do your duty, ladies and gentlemen. Return with a verdict of not guilty."

An eerie silence fell over the courtroom. For the first time in the trial, la Trec had worked the spellbinding magic for which he was internationally famous. Wendy looked worried. Zack gave her a wink.

"Is the government ready for closing, Commander Brewer?"

"Absolutely, Your Honor."

Zack stood, glanced at Anna Kweskin's smiling picture on his table, inconspicuously blew her a kiss, and stepped into the well and eyed every one of the members.

"Mr. President, distinguished members, it is a sick and twisted irony that my distinguished opponent, in all his swooning eloquence, would invoke the name and the blood of thousands of fallen Americans at Normandy for the sake of somehow pleading for the exoneration of an admitted liar, an admitted perjurer, and an admitted murderer.

"Mr. la Trec"—Zack stared at his famous opponent—"make no mistake about it. The Boys of Pointe du Hoc, the Rangers of Omaha Beach, the Screaming Eagles of the 101st Airborne Division, and every other man and woman who spilled precious American blood on your beaches, did not do so for those who would shoot an American officer point blank in the chest, lie about having done so, and then blame his own crimes and offenses against a defenseless dead man."

Zack's voice echoed across the courtroom and through television sets around the world, as an army of reporters scribbled furiously.

"Yes, it is true, Mr. la Trec, that guilt beyond a reasonable doubt is the bedrock of the American system." Zack turned from la Trec and back to the members. "But even before that, sir, and even above that, the American system was built on truth.

"Our Declaration of Independence declares that 'we hold these *truths* to be self-evident ...'

"The Holy Bible on which our jurisprudence was built, the book on which your client refused to place his hand, declares, 'You shall know the *truth*, and the *truth* shall set you free.'

"Perjury, Mr. la Trec, strikes at the very heart of the American system that your fellow Frenchman, Mr. de Tocqueville, studied so assiduously. And to come into this court and suggest that Commander Quasay can lie, commit perjury, and then ask these members to believe that a good man like Captain William Constangy ordered an attack on civilians, is insulting to every American and every Frenchman who died liberating your country from the subjugation of the Nazi jackboot."

Pacing down the banister rail, Zack eyed the members, now speaking softly. "Ladies and gentlemen, this notion of proof beyond a reasonable doubt doesn't require that we throw common sense out the window. Let's take a commonsense look at how the evidence plays out in this case.

"The first commonsense principle is that a liar and a perjurer cannot be believed and cannot be trusted. Quasay first said that he shot a jackal and claimed that Mouse Price bailed out of the F-14. And then, when he realized we had a ballistics report showing that his gun was used to murder Price, and that Price's body was found inside the wreckage of the cockpit, he changed his story.

"Caught red-handed in his lie, he said, 'Well, okay, I lied about that little minor detail'—as if murder is a minor detail—'but everything else is true.' After that pathetic performance of perjury, is there anyone here who would trust Mohammed Quasay with the truth?"

Three members shook their heads.

"The second commonsense principle is a time-honored navy tradition that the commander of a ship or the commander of an aircraft is responsible for the actions of that aircraft. How many navy captains have lost their command when their ships ran ashore or collided with other vessels? Commander Scott Waddle of the USS *Greenville*, for example, was taken to a court of inquiry when his submarine surfaced and collided with a boat carrying Japanese tourists. What's the bottom line here? Quasay was commander of that plane and is strictly liable for its actions.

"Third commonsense principle. How can a dead man fire a missile? Quasay already admitted that he murdered Lieutenant Price. If Lieutenant Price had three bullets in his chest, who else could have fired the missile? Now, Lieutenant Perjurer Quasay claims that he shot Price *after* the attack on the Dome. But does that make sense? First of all, he is an admitted liar. So you can't believe anything he says anyway.

"But he also said that there was chaos in the cockpit. His own lawyer just said he panicked. In fact, I wrote down exactly what Quasay said."

Zack held up a legal pad. "He said, 'I knew the Israelis would be scrambling their F-15s, and the only thing I could think of was that *we were no match for the whole Israeli Air Force*.'

"Now, distinguished members, murder is a premeditated act. How can he be"—Zack made mock quotation marks—"thinking about getting away from the Israeli Air Force and then have the presence of mind to turn around and pump Lieutenant Price's chest with lead?

"Is that even logical?

"Or is it more logical that he murdered Lieutenant Price in the cockpit during the flight from the aircraft carrier, which gave him plenty of unencumbered room to maneuver?

"Of course that's more logical. Especially if, in his own words, 'there was chaos in the cockpit' after the missile attack and his only concern was escaping from the Israeli Air Force.

"Keep in mind, also, that a missile was fired not only from Commander Quasay's aircraft, but also from Lieutenant Alhad's. He, of course, died when an Islamic suicide bomber attacked this courtroom. Like Commander Quasay, and like the suicide bomber who killed him, Lieutenant Alhad was also Islamic.

"Now this punches a huge hole in the defense's despicable character assassination of Captain Constangy and Lieutenant Price.

"Mr. la Trec jeers and sneers over the fact that Lieutenant Price was a Christian and perhaps Captain Constangy is too. If they are believers in Jesus Christ, he insinuates that they are fanatical zealots capable of the type of mass murder that radical Islam is responsible for.

"Well, I've got some news for you, Mr. la Trec"—Zack looked over at the Frenchman—"you say you're a student of America. Then you should know that many of America's great military leaders, from George Washington to Stonewall Jackson to Robert E. Lee to Omar Bradley, to thousands of American boys who hallowed your beaches at Normandy with their precious blood, were Christian.

"And by the way, monsieur"—Zack wasn't finished lecturing—"the *great philosopher* you quoted in your closing argument, the guy who said, 'Greater love hath no man than he who would lay down his life for a friend'—that philosopher, as you call him, was Jesus Christ." Zack turned his focus back to the members, now lowering his voice.

"Do we really believe, ladies and gentlemen, even if we were to consider the ludicrous notion that Bill Constangy ordered Mouse Price to launch his missile against the Dome, that he also would have taken a chance by ordering Lieutenant Pip Davis, the other naval flight officer, to do the same?

"Distinguished members, just like the two planes that smashed into the World Trade Center, these two planes acted in concert. There was a meeting of the minds between these two planes.

"Now that meeting of the minds was either between the two pilots, or between the two flight officers." Zack paused, stepped back into the center of the well, and eyed the six members sitting in the first row.

"Is it coincidental that both pilots were rescued but both flight officers are missing?

"Is it coincidental that the sidearms of both pilots were fired?

"Thankfully, Mouse Price's body was discovered." Zack stopped, turned, and gazed at the defendant, then back at the members.

"And somewhere on the wide expanse of the Syrian Desert, the decaying body of Lieutenant Pip Davis is pinned in the crumpled wreckage of a cockpit. And in that poor man's body, you would find a bullet. A bullet fired from the sidearm of Lieutenant Hosni Alhad.

"So why would a couple of Islamic pilots want to destroy one of the holiest spots in Islam?

"A fair question … And here's why.

"If an Islamic fundamentalist will sacrifice his own life to advance the cause of this so-called Allah, then why not sacrifice a building if doing so would advance their political agenda? If life means nothing to them, and poor Anna Kweskin's life meant nothing to them, then why should a building mean anything?

"Remember when I asked Quasay about Operation Islamic Glory? Remember the look on his face when I asked him if Islamic Glory was a secret Muslim plan to destroy the Dome and blame it on America to drive a wedge between the U.S. and moderate Muslim governments?"

There were a few head nods.

"Ask yourselves this: Did it work? Is the gap wider now between the U.S. and the Arab-Islamic world?

"Yes, it worked. Every Islamic-Arab government — in fact, almost every government in the world — has condemned America in the United Nations, and hundreds of thousands still pour into the streets even today as a result of this conspiracy."

Nods came from three of the members in the front row.

"There has never been a more barbaric, more savage, and more evil force to tramp across the earth than militant Islam. Hitler, Kahn, Stalin, Nero, all the nefarious faces to flash across and then fade from the stage of world history — all these look bland in comparison to militant Islam. For the scoundrels whose names I have mentioned, as horrible and ruthless and heartless as they were, for all their atrocities and crimes against humanity, at least their inexcusable brand of evil was isolated, more or less, to one geographic region. And they were all defeated, all subdued, sooner or later gone from the face of the earth.

"But with militant Islam, there is no geographic border, no socio-economic limit, no border of morality or decency at which this unprecedented cancer of evil will stop.

"They kidnap people, hold them hostage" — Zack's voice cracked as the picture of Diane bound and gagged flooded his mind — "spread their pictures to willing media outlets around the world, make their families suffer a public agony, and then these militant animals decapitate their victims' heads on television with dull axes and celebrate in the streets at the pain and spilled blood of the innocent. Age and gender provide no safe haven from their barbarism. Anna Kweskin was but a child … a girl …" Struggling to keep his voice from cracking, Zack solemnly held up the girl's picture and walked up and down the jury box. "A girl who was fulfilling her family's dream of returning to Israel." He turned and pointed at the defendant. "But militant Islam ripped her from her family, forever." He dropped his finger and turned back to the members.

"When they murdered thousands of innocent American citizens on September 11, despite the very muted and restrained obligatory condemnation from moderate Arab governments, hundreds of thousands of Islamic militants poured into Arab streets expressing wild-eyed celebration at American death and destruction.

"Remember that, ladies and gentlemen? How can we ever forget?

"And so, it is from this savage and uncivilized belief system that the defendant, Lieutenant Commander Mohammed Quasay, and his late colleague, Lieutenant Hosni Alhad, emerged." Zack paused, took a sip of water, and brought his voice to a lower pitch, slowing his cadence.

"The 'politically correct' way of thinking we have adopted over the last few decades told us that despite their religious beliefs, despite the fact that others who embraced their philosophy had already murdered thousands of innocent Americans, we told ourselves that despite all that, Islamic pilots could be trusted to fly their missions as Americans first, sworn to uphold the Constitution of the United States and obey the lawful orders of their superior officers."

He turned and looked at Quasay, then back at the members. "In this case, we were wrong.

"Your verdict today will not win this ongoing war against terrorism. But a verdict of guilty will be a victory in a major battle. A verdict of not guilty would be a major defeat for the cause of righteousness.

"Did their plan work?

"Yes, it worked. Now the question is, will they get away with it?

"Do your duty, ladies and gentlemen. Return with a verdict of guilty."

Zack turned and walked across the hardwood floor, his black leather shoes clicking and echoing into the far corners of the eerily silent courtroom.

"This court will be in recess."

"All rise."

CHAPTER 63

Courtroom 4
Israeli District Court
West Bank Division

The members had been out for two hours. Zack and Wendy were waiting in the attorneys' lounge, trying to relax and avoid the press, when the knock came on the door from the bailiff. For the first time in his career as a prosecutor, Zack was afraid of a guilty verdict.

But if the verdict is guilty, we will use our blood-stained knife to amputate her ears.

Ignoring more press questions, Zack and Wendy entered the packed courtroom. The defense team was already in place. A tense excitement permeated the jam-packed gallery, as evidenced by the whispers and murmurs as they walked up the corridor splitting the gallery.

"All rise!"

Judge Norgaard entered before Zack and Wendy could get to their seats.

If the members convicted Quasay, the next stage of the trial was the sentencing stage.

Zack's orders if they got to sentencing: Obtain the death penalty.

"Please be seated," Norgaard said, then turned to the bailiff. "The bailiff will bring in the members, please."

They filed in with stoic looks on their faces. No smiling, no eye contact with anyone except Captain Norgaard.

"Mr. President," Norgaard said to the senior member, "I understand the members have reached a verdict."

"We have, Your Honor."

"May I see it, please?" The bailiff took the verdict sheet from the senior member to the military judge.

"The verdict appears to be in order. Bailiff, please hand this back to the president."

But if the verdict is guilty, we will use our blood-stained knife to amputate her ears.

"The accused and counsel will rise and face the members."

Lord, please be with Diane.

"Mr. President, you may read the verdict."

"Lieutenant Commander Mohammed Quasay, United States Navy, this court finds you, on the charge of disobeying a lawful order ...

"Guilty.

"On the charge of conduct unbecoming of an officer and a gentleman ...

"Guilty.

"On the charge of intentionally firing into a civilian population area ...

"Guilty.

"On the charge of first-degree murder ..."

Zack winced. *Please be with Diane.*

"Guilty."

The courtroom was filled with oohs and aahs and rumbling chatter.

"Order in the court." *Whap! Whap!* "The court will come to order." The crowd quieted.

"The members having spoken, we will now move into the sentencing phase of the trial. Lieutenant Commander Brewer, is the government prepared for sentencing?"

But even after that, there is still hope for the beautiful lieutenant. If the defendants are spared the death penalty, then we will return the handless, earless lovely into your arms.

But if either of these pilots is condemned to die, then we will proceed to slowly slit the good lieutenant's throat.

It all should be interesting, should it not?

"We are, Your Honor." Zack prayed silently for her safety. It was time to build the case that Quasay should be executed.

"Mr. la Trec, is the defense ready for sentencing?"

"Your Honor." La Trec stood slowly. "My client and I have had a philosophical disagreement on how to proceed at this point. He has requested to address the court at this time."

Norgaard raised his eyebrow. Zack exchanged a look with Wendy.

"That's a bit out of order, Mr. la Trec. Normally at this phase of the proceeding, the government gets to go first." Norgaard looked at Zack. "Commander Brewer, do you have any objections to this request?"

Zack looked at Wendy again, who unobtrusively shrugged her shoulders.

"Your Honor, it is a bit out of order, but the defendant has already been convicted at this point. If that's what he wants to do, that's fine."

Norgaard looked at Quasay. "Lieutenant Commander Quasay, you wish to speak?"

Quasay rose slowly and looked over at Zack, then at the judge. "Your Honor, I wish to relieve my attorney at this time."

"Say it again?"

"I wish to fire my lawyer and represent myself."

This guy is out of his mind.

"And why is that?"

"Because he went against my specific instructions on how to defend my case."

"Commander, do you understand that we are beginning the portion of the proceeding where the government will seek the death penalty against you?"

"Yes, sir. I realize that. I wish to speak with Lieutenant Commander Brewer in private first, please, sir. Then, afterwards, I wish to represent myself."

Norgaard scratched his head and raised his eyebrows. He looked at Zack.

"Commander Brewer, what's the government's take on all this?"

"My concern, Your Honor, is that this may be a ploy to raise ineffective assistance of counsel as grounds for an appeal."

"Please, Commander." Quasay looked over at Zack. "I will waive my rights to an appeal if only I can speak to you privately. Please, I appeal to you as a naval officer."

Zack turned to Wendy. "You're the appellate expert," he whispered. "See any problems with talking to this guy?"

"I'd insist on having a court reporter present, and a lawyer there to represent him if he needs it."

"Okay," Zack whispered. "Your Honor, I will agree to speak with Commander Quasay on the following conditions. First, that a court reporter be present to record for the record everything that is said. And second, that an attorney, either Mr. la Trec or someone else, be present for him to consult with if needed."

"Commander Quasay, I'm inclined to agree with Lieutenant Commander Brewer. The conditions he has requested are the only circumstances under which I am inclined to grant your request. My problem is, if you're planning to fire Mr. la Trec, another attorney would have to get familiar with your case, and I'm frankly not inclined to delay your sentencing for that."

"I want her!" Quasay pointed at Jeanette L'Enfant. "She knows my case. She can go into the conference with me."

Jeanette L'Enfant's eyes widened. She pushed a strand of blond hair from her face.

"You want Miss L'Enfant with you?"

"Yes."

"Miss L'Enfant, are you willing to sit in on this conference with the defendant and Lieutenant Commander Brewer and provide any assistance the defendant needs?"

Jeanette L'Enfant glanced at la Trec, and when he gave a single nod of the head, she turned back to Norgaard. "Yes, Your Honor. I am willing. But for the record, Lieutenant Commander Quasay is proceeding against our advice."

"Very well," Norgaard said. "Commander Brewer, where would you like to set up this meeting?"

"The attorneys' lounge, Your Honor, provided we can arrange for adequate security."

"That can be arranged," Norgaard said, then turned to the bailiff. "Ensure that U.S. marines provide security for the movement of the prisoner and for the meeting itself."

"Aye, aye, Your Honor."

"Until then, this court is in recess."

"All rise."

CHAPTER 64

Attorneys' lounge
Israeli District Court
West Bank Division

Zack, Wendy, and the court reporter sat on one side of the table when the shore patrol and the marine security unit arrived with Quasay, who was in handcuffs and leg chains.

Zack stood as Quasay approached the table.

"So what did you want to talk to me about, Commander?"

"I wish to plead guilty."

"Plead guilty?" Zack looked at Wendy, then at Quasay. "You've already been *convicted*. We don't need your guilty plea."

"Please, Commander." Quasay's voice trembled, and his eyes were moist. "I do not wish to die."

"You don't wish to die."

"Please." A tear rolled down his cheek. "I wanted to plead guilty earlier. My lawyer would not let me."

"Is this true?" Zack asked L'Enfant.

"Yes, there was a fundamental philosophical disagreement between the commander and Mr. la Trec on how to proceed with his defense."

"So you just took the stand and lied and trashed the reputations of good naval officers who couldn't defend themselves to protect your hide."

More tears from Quasay. "Yes. I did not want to."

"Look at her." Zack slid the photo across the table. "She was nine years old, Commander. She was the apple of her father's eye. Now she's just a number without a tombstone in a nondescript Israeli cemetery. Thanks to you."

Quasay's eyes lingered on Anna Kweskin's picture. He put his hands over his face and wept.

"Commander Brewer, I almost did not do what I did. I was terribly misguided. I regret the killing and the lies. If you let me live, I will provide all the information I know about Operation Islamic Glory. That much I can do for Mouse Price and the little girl, Anna." He looked Zack in the eye. "I can be far more valuable to you alive than dead."

The proposal made sense. Maybe this was an honorable way to avoid the death penalty. And by avoiding the death penalty, maybe Diane would live! And maybe he *would* be more valuable alive than dead. Perhaps even a material witness in future trials against the ringleaders of the Council of Ishmael.

Of course, for this to work, news of the deal could not be leaked. If the terrorists knew that Quasay was spared the death penalty to testify against them, then Diane might be doomed. Still, Zack felt a strange sense of relief.

Thank you for possibly opening this door, Lord.

"I can make a recommendation on your request, Commander Quasay, but the decision on whether to cut such a deal is not mine. That decision would most likely be made in Washington. But I suspect that for such a proposal to fly, two things would be necessary. First, we would need to hear everything you know about Islamic Glory, and second, you would have to agree to life in prison."

"Agreed on both counts." Quasay did not bat an eye.

"Very well. I'll message Washington, inform Judge Norgaard of what's going on, and get back to you with an answer."

"Thank you, Commander."

"Bailiff, please remove this man from my sight."

"Aye, aye, sir."

Courtroom 4
Israeli District Court
West Bank Division

Four hours later

Commander Brewer." Judge Norgaard looked out over the packed courtroom. "I understand the parties have reached a sentencing agreement?"

"That is correct. We have, Your Honor."

"May I see it?"

"Permission to approach the bench?"

"Yes."

Zack handed Judge Brewer the terms of the agreement. The judge examined them, then looked at Quasay.

"Commander Quasay, as I understand this agreement that trial counsel just handed me, the government is not going forward with the death penalty and is instead recommending that you serve a sentence of life in prison, in return for you voluntarily agreeing to waive any and all rights to a possible appeal. I understand that this arrangement is your proposal and that you have been advised by counsel against accepting this agreement. Is that right?"

"That's correct, Your Honor," Quasay said.

"Miss L'Enfant, is it correct that you have advised your client against this arrangement?"

"Yes, Your Honor. This is his proposal and is against our advice to him."

"Commander, do you realize that by waiving any and all appeal rights, you would never be able to challenge any ruling of this court, and as a consequence, a sentence of life in prison would remain the permanent sentence which you must serve?"

"Yes, I do, Your Honor. This is my idea and my wishes."

"Has anyone said anything to coerce or induce you into entering this agreement?"

"No, sir."

"Has anyone made any promises to you to cause you to accept this agreement?"

"No, sir."

"Lieutenant Commander Brewer, are these terms and conditions acceptable to the government?"

"Yes, Your Honor. The government recommends that the court accept the terms of the agreement."

"Very well. I find the terms of the agreement are freely and voluntarily entered into between the defendant and the government, that no hidden threats, inducements, or promises have been made to the defendant that would make this agreement involuntary, and that the agreement is in the best interests of both parties, and so the terms contained herein are approved.

"Will the defendant and counsel please rise and face the court?"

Quasay rose with Jeanette L'Enfant. La Trec did not rise.

"Lieutenant Commander Mohammed Quasay, United States Navy, this court sentences you as follows: to be reduced to pay grade E-1, to forfeit all pay and allowances, to be dishonorably discharged from the naval service, and to be confined in a military prison for the remainder of your natural life.

"Is there anything else from the defense?"

"No, Your Honor," Jeanette L'Enfant said.

"Is there anything else from the government?"

"No, Your Honor," Zack said.

"Very well. This court is adjourned."

"All rise."

CHAPTER 65

King David Hotel
Jerusalem

Zack was almost buoyant in the back of the Hummer during the ride from the courthouse back to the King David Hotel. Not because he had again beaten one of the world's greatest lawyers, but because he hoped that a life sentence might spare Diane.

He had been sure, barring a miracle, that the death penalty for Quasay would have meant the end for Diane. He had asked to be spared the task of essentially driving the nail in Diane's coffin.

And just when it looked as if he would have to argue for Quasay's execution, this!

He thought of Abraham, raising the sword to slay Isaac, and then, when the Lord saw that he would be obedient, mercy.

The Lord had provided a solution that was in everyone's best interest. Already, Quasay had given enough information to allow NCIS to root out other terrorist cells that had been implanted in the navy. Details of Operation Islamic Glory had been spelled out. The last five hours, since Quasay's declaration that he was firing Monsieur la Trec, had been a bonanza for navy Intelligence.

How the Lord's ways are so far above the thoughts of man. How he remains in control!

The Humvee stopped in front of the King David. Zack and Wendy stepped out, again under heavy guard, and again under a barrage of flashbulbs and reporters' questions.

"Commander, was any deal cut with Quasay for information?" someone from the press corps shouted.

Zack saw a podium of microphones set up in the lobby to satisfy the press corps. A navy public affairs officer, a full commander, intercepted Zack and Wendy.

"Public affairs wants a brief statement, Commander Brewer. Nothing fancy or elaborate is necessary. This request comes from Washington."

"Yes, sir," Zack said. With Wendy at his side, he followed the commander to the makeshift podium. He squinted in the bright glare of television lights.

"Ladies and gentlemen, on behalf of the United States Navy, let me say we are very pleased with the result of this court-martial. You heard the plea agreement read in open court earlier today. This arrangement will save the government the time and expense of a lengthy appeal, while at the same time ensuring the terrorist who co-opted U.S. Navy missiles will never again see the light of day. The man directly responsible for the missile attack on the Dome was convicted. The other man responsible for the attack is dead. Justice was served. That is all."

"But, Commander. Commander!..."

Zack stepped away from the microphone bank, waved, smiled, and with Wendy at his side, walked away.

The elevator reached the second floor, and Wendy gave him a congratulatory hug.

"I'm going to my room to freshen up and change into civvies," she said. "Want to grab a bite a little later?"

"Sure. Maybe we should track down Shannon, Captain Rudy, and Commander Awe and see if they want to go too."

He turned, walked down the hall, then inserted his room key into the electronic receptacle. The two marines guarding the door came to attention.

"At ease, gentlemen," he said as the security light on the door flashed green and he pushed it open.

"Shannon. Captain Rudy."

They were sitting on the sofa waiting for him. Their faces were uniformly solemn. Something was wrong. He could sense it.

"Sit down, Zack," Captain Rudy ordered.

"Is everything okay?"

"I think you should sit, Zack," Rudy repeated. Zack complied. "Shannon, tell Zack what we know."

"It's about Diane, Zack."

Oh dear Jesus.

"What about her?"

"We believe she's dead."

No. Please.

"What do you mean you *believe* she's dead? Either she is or she isn't! What are you saying, Shannon?"

"Calm down, Zack," Rudy ordered in a calm voice.

"U.S. intelligence operatives in the Tora Bora Mountains in Afghanistan caught wind of a small caravan of armed Arab men moving through the mountains with a redheaded woman fitting Diane's description. They followed the group high into a mountain range. Apparently the group spotted the operatives."

"Wait a minute, Shannon. What do you mean when you say 'U.S. intelligence operatives'? Are these Americans you're referring to?"

"Unfortunately not. And that's part of the problem. They were Afghani nationals working for the CIA. Anyway, the group that had the woman fitting Diane's description spotted the operatives and started firing. The operatives fired back. The firing escalated to mortar and rocket attacks. When it was over, the cave from which the rebel group was firing had collapsed.

"Several bodies were found of Islamic fundamentalists linked to terror groups. A CIA forensics team was choppered in. Diane's body was not found, but hair samples were. A DNA match showed the hair to be hers. We believe she's buried in the rubble deep in that collapsed cave, Zack."

Zack felt numb. His worst nightmare was unfolding. "Why can't somebody dig through the rubble and see if she's there? I mean, if we haven't found a body, she could still be alive, right?"

"Zack, there are tons of heavy rocks collapsed in that cave. They cannot be removed by hand, and the altitude and the steep incline are such that we can't get the heavy equipment up there."

"I don't buy that!" Zack fumed. "If we can put a man on the moon, we can get a bulldozer up the side of a mountain."

"Zack, it's too late. Even if we *could* get a bulldozer up there, which we can't, no one inside that cave could have possibly survived. Anyone inside would have been buried under tons of boulders, and even if they hadn't been crushed by the rocks, they would have suffocated by now."

"How do you know that, Shannon? Have you been out to the site?"

"No, I haven't."

"Then what kind of an intelligence agent are you, anyway?"

"Zack, that's enough," Captain Rudy said. "Shannon, show him the pictures."

She handed him a manila envelope with twelve eight-by-ten color photos taken from the site.

"Oh dear Lord," Zack said, studying the photos one by one. Lifeless legs and arms were protruding from the rocks. Tears flooded his eyes.

"I'm sorry, Zack," Shannon said. "We've lost her."

CHAPTER 66

The Lawn
University of Virginia
Charlottesville, Virginia

From his wooden chair behind the podium on the steps of Charlottesville's famed Rotunda Building, a building that had been designed by Thomas Jefferson himself, Zack listened as the president of the University of Virginia eulogized Diane Colcernian.

"She was a woman of great intellect, of great character ..."

Zack swallowed hard, combating the tears with all his might. He was up next, and it wouldn't look right for a United States Naval officer in full service dress blues to take the podium as an emotional mess.

"She bore the name of her great-great-great-grandfather, Diane *Jefferson* Colcernian, and she bore his wit, and forethought, and ...

Refocus, Zack.

He gazed at the sea of students gathered on the Lawn, the long, rectangular grassy area at the heart of the university's academic center. Their eyes were locked attentively on their president, whose words he was tuning out for the sake of emotional self-preservation.

His imagination rewound to her college days, when she was an undergraduate here. And when in the distance, behind the crowd of two thousand or so students, he saw a redheaded coed strolling across the Lawn at the opposite end, her books in hand and an orange sweater tied around her neck, he felt himself smile. And felt himself wishing he could have known her during her college days and law school days. That would have given them another seven years.

He flicked a tear from his right eye. It splatted on the brick just to the right of his shoe. Blinking rapidly, he looked up at the deep blue Shenandoah sky just above Cabbel Hall at the opposite end of the Lawn.

The cool crispness of the mountain air and the blazing colors of autumn leaves reminded him that life is cyclical, and somehow, somewhere, someday, he would see her again.

"And now, please welcome, from the U.S. Navy JAG Corps, an outstanding officer, and a close personal friend of Diane's, Lieutenant Commander Zack Brewer."

A light round of applause turned to a standing ovation.

Keep it together, Zack, he thought as he stood and shook hands with the university president, then stepped to the podium. *Keep it together.*

"Thank you," he said, politely waving them to be seated. "Thank you."

They sat, their silence giving way to the rustling of trees in the breeze and a few honking horns from McCormick Road along the perimeter of the Lawn.

"My friends, we are at war. In the ninety days that have passed since the court-martial of Lieutenant Commander Mohammed Quasay, the international situation for the United States has deteriorated.

"Quasay's conviction and life sentence have not satisfied the howling throngs of angry Islamic-Arab protestors, thousands who pour into the streets of Arab capitals on a daily basis, chanting 'Death to America,' burning both the American flag and President Williams in effigy, and calling for retaliation against American targets worldwide.

"As you know, in San Francisco, a huge cache of dynamite was discovered underneath the Golden Gate Bridge. Fortunately, it was extracted by demolition experts only hours before an automatic detonator would have sent the bridge into the bay.

"The cities of Washington and New York have not been so fortunate. Islamic suicide bombers have attacked the metro systems in both cities, resulting in dozens of men, women, and children dead and others permanently maimed.

"Islamic terrorist groups proudly take credit not only for the murder of innocent Americans in New York and Washington, but also for the Stinger missile attack of British Airways 747, bound for New York, which was blown out of the sky seconds after liftoff from London's Heathrow International Airport. This attack was to 'teach Britain a lesson' for siding with America before the UN Security Council, according to an Islamic group taking credit for the mass murder.

"In Moscow, the Russian government, obviously hoping to regain grandeur as a world superpower, has courted the Arab States with military and financial aid, obviously hoping to establish a beachhead in the ruins of America's misfortune.

"This is the state of the war we find ourselves in." He paused to soak in the moment. The next part of the speech would be the hardest.

"My dear friend, Lieutenant Diane Colcernian, a beloved daughter of this great university"—he paused, inhaling deeply—"is both a heroine and a victim in this war." He exhaled, paused, slowing his words.

"Personally, I've had a hard time over the last ninety days. The truth about Diane's disappearance has been tough. I have hoped against hope that the absence of her body would mean that she would one day walk through the doors of my office, flash her sparkling green eyes and magnetic smile, and suggest that we go for a run along San Diego's waterfront.

"But as spring turned to summer and summer to fall, I have come to realize that this season of my life, which included the first woman I have ever loved, may be fading into winter."

The wind blew hard across the lawn, sweeping a few sheets of notebook paper out of book sacks. No one moved.

"Even so, closure has not yet come. Perhaps soon, but not yet. I am not ready to let go. I cannot let go. Not yet.

"But before I leave to do what I must do, I want to share a story about Diane." He reached into his U.S. Navy uniform jacket and extracted a sheet of folded paper, unfolded it, and laid it on the podium. "I'm a Carolina grad, and as you know, Diane is from here, UVA." A mild round of applause. "She used to tease me about spending all my undergrad days at the Dean Dome watching basketball games. So I teased her about spending her time in the library."

That brought a few chuckles.

"Of course, she really didn't mind me teasing her about that, because it was true. I admired her for her intellect. And one of the reasons she loved the library so much here at UVA is because there is a fabulous collection of original works here by her favorite poet, Alfred, Lord Tennyson.

"This morning when I arrived on campus, I visited the Tennyson collection, looking, searching for a few lines of the poet that might stir her heart if she were here.

"This is what I found, from the poem 'Marriage Morning.'"

He glanced at his audience. Their eyes were transfixed upon him. Many wiped away tears. He prayed silently for the strength to get through this. Then slowly, deliberately, the words of Tennyson echoed across the lawn.

"Light, so low upon earth,
You send a flash to the sun
Here is the golden close of love,
All my wooing is done.
Light, so low in the vale,
You flash and lighten afar,
For this is the golden morning of love,
And you are his morning star."

Zack folded the poem, tenderly placed it back in his pocket.

"Good-bye, Diane. You are the light of my life."

A standing ovation greeted his last words. He waved, shook hands one last time with the university president, then accepted a police escort to the car that was waiting for him nearby.

Western Union office
Charlottesville, Virginia

Two hours later

With Shannon McGillvery at his side, Zack stepped into the Western Union office and nodded at the white-haired clerk.

"How much money did you say you wanted to wire, Commander?" She gave him a kind smile.

"Five thousand dollars, please, ma'am." Zack handed her an envelope stuffed with cash.

She licked her fingers, then counted each hundred dollar bill with her thumb. "And where did you say you wanted to send it?" She adjusted her hearing aid.

Zack leaned over, smiled, and deliberately spoke a little louder. "Jerusalem, ma'am." Shannon smiled as Zack slid a piece of paper toward her. "Here's the address."

"Oh, Jerusalem! Okay, Commander. Just let me get you a receipt."

A moment later, she handed him a receipt and a copy of the wiring form. The destination address was right. Apparently nothing was wrong with the lady's reading and writing.

"The money will be there in less than twenty-four hours, Commander."

"That's perfect, ma'am. Thanks."

"Come on, Zack," Shannon said. "I'll drive you to Dulles Airport."

"Let's go."

David Ben Gurion International Airport
Tel Aviv, Israel
Three days later

4:00 a.m. Jerusalem time

Traveling in civilian clothes, he arrived at Ben Gurion Airport at four in the morning, still under the cover of darkness. He hailed a taxi for Jerusalem and gave the driver the address.

The sun was coming up when the driver dropped him off on the side of the street. The vista from here was gorgeous, the gold synagogues and mosques of the Holy City glistening in the glow of the orange sun rising over the Mediterranean in the distance.

Jerusalem's streets were coming alive with the sounds of sirens and honking horns as Zack sat on the sidewalk and waited. A half hour later, he saw three figures walking up the hill toward him: a young woman with long brown hair and a middle-aged Jewish couple holding hands.

"Welcome back, Commander," the young woman called in an accent that revealed her to be American.

"Thank you for meeting me here, Miss Shadle," Zack said as a smiling Alexander Kweskin extended his hand and said, "Welcome, my friend."

"You've been working on your English, I see." Zack patted the man's shoulder.

"Dah," Alexander said, smiling.

"He's doing great, Commander," Kathryn said.

"Obviously he has a good tutor."

"Thank you, Commander." She blushed. "And, of course, you've met Mrs. Kweskin."

"Yes, I have." Zack smiled at Yael, and she gave him a brief hug. "Thank you all for meeting me," he said.

"You're welcome," Alexander said in a Slavic accent.

"There's something I'd like to ask of you, Alexander," Zack said, gently resting his hand on Alexander's shoulders.

"Anything," Alexander said through Kathryn's translation.

"I still have this picture of your daughter." He held it out. Alexander's eyes moistened almost instantly. "Although I never knew her, she helped me get through the trial. Her life meant something to the cause of justice, Mr. Kweskin, even after her death."

He caught Kathryn's brown eyes.

"I was wondering if you and your wife could take me up there"—he pointed to the rolling cemetery—"to the place where she's buried. I'd like to pay my respects."

Kweskin smiled. "We haven't been there in a month. We need to visit our daughter too. Yes, it would be an honor to lead you up."

"Thank you, sir. If this is a good time, I will follow you."

Alexander turned, and with Zack and Yael on one side and Kathryn on the other, he led them through the gate into Municipal Cemetery Number 8 and along the central walkway for about a hundred yards. Zack could see that Alexander was counting the rows of graves. And then, when he had counted fifteen or sixteen, Alexander turned left at marker number 311. Marker 312 had the name Cantor. Numbers 313 through 317 remained anonymous.

"Slava Bogu!" Praise be to God!

Alexander sprinted the short distance to what had formerly been an anonymous grave marker and fell on his knees crying. Yael followed him, sinking to her knees beside him.

Zack looked down and saw it for the first time. The monument company had done a tasteful job.

> *Anna Kweskin*
> *Who gave love and strength*
> *in life and death.*
> *Never, ever forgotten*
> *Isaiah 53:5–6*

"She is no longer a number, Guspadyeen Kweskin. She never was."

From his knees, his eyes glistening, Alexander looked up at Zack, then stood and lunged at him, giving him the biggest bear hug Zack had ever received.

Motioning with his left arm, he brought Yael and Kathryn into the midst of the embrace. And then, his tearful eyes looking into Zack's face, he mumbled something in Russian that Zack didn't understand.

"What did he say?"

"He said, 'Lieutenant Colcernian will never be forgotten.'"

EPILOGUE

Eternal Father, strong to save,
Whose arm hath bound the restless wave,
Who bidd'st the mighty ocean deep
Its own appointed limits keep;
Oh, hear us when we cry to Thee
For those in peril on the sea!

William Whiting
"Eternal Father, Strong to Save"
Hymn of the United States Navy

DON BROWN

THE NAVY
JUSTICE SERIES

TREASON

IN THE COURT-MARTIAL OF THE CENTURY, JAG OFFICER
ZACH BREWER FACES AMERICA'S TOUGHEST ENEMY YET.

ZONDERVAN

Read an excerpt from Don Brown's *Treason*,
Book 1 in the Navy Justice Series.

PROLOGUE

Black Forest Café
Near the Limmat River
Zurich, Switzerland

Abdur Rahman Ibn Auf checked his watch as the meeting adjourned. Quarter to twelve. Good.

Enough time for a little walk, maybe some sightseeing, and perhaps even lunch and a couple of drinks before summoning his pilot for the return flight to Riyadh.

He donned the jacket of his Armani business suit and stepped from the front door of Barclays onto the sidewalk beside Zurich's world-famous, charming Bahnhofstrasse. Squinting into the bright sunlight, he slipped on a pair of designer sunglasses. Around him bustled serious-looking businessmen speaking into cellular phones, young mothers—or perhaps au pairs; he could not tell the difference—pushing prams, laughing young lovers, and groups of beautiful women carrying smart bags from expensive clothing boutiques. On either side of the street, flower vendors displayed profusions of colorful bouquets, and halfway to the corner, a group of students crowded around a bakery window.

A cool breeze hit his face, and he closed his eyes, drawing the pristine Swiss air into his lungs. He breathed in, almost smiling at the invigorating result.

Why did Allah place the great cities of the faith in the middle of a scorching, God-forsaken desert rather than in a place like Zurich? At home, survival was impossible without air-conditioning. Here, nature provided it. But the Great Faith had spawned where it had, and Allah had his purposes. Perhaps to avoid distractions, which abounded here.

Abdur headed south down the Bahnhofstrasse by foot in the direction of the Arboretum and Bürlki Plaza on Lake Zurich. A traffic light stopped him just before he reached the Swiss National Bank Building, and he turned left toward Stathausquai, on the east bank of the Limmat River.

The deep blue waters of the river, fed by the melting snow from the Alps, flowed into Lake Zurich a few blocks to his right. Abdur never grew tired of this view. If paradise was like any city in the world, surely Zurich would be at the top of the list. He watched two tour boats churning south toward the lake.

The sounds of laughter—young and feminine—broke into his thoughts. He turned toward a sidewalk café across the street, on the bank of the river.

There were four in the quartet—or perhaps he might say the bouquet—of exquisite Swiss fräuleins. They sat giggling under an umbrella at a white wrought-iron table. He did not need to blink even twice to see they were blond, well figured, and perhaps in their midtwenties. They were all blue-eyed. They were Swiss; how could they not have eyes the color of a summer alpine sky?

One of the fräuleins, the prettiest, with shoulder-length hair and wearing a navy business suit, seemed to sense his gaze. She shot him a coquettish smile, tilting her head slightly toward an empty table next to hers.

The outdoor café on the riverbank would make a perfect spot for lunch and a cocktail. And who knew? Perhaps this was his lucky day. A successful business session in the morning. An unanticipated rendezvous in the afternoon before leaving the country?

Blond European women seemed to be inordinately attracted to clean-shaven Arab men in expensive business suits. This trend had been established, luckily for him, by the late Princess Diana of Great Britain and Dodi al-Fayed. Or so he had been told when he studied at Oxford.

Abdur sat at the table next to the foursome. They spoke German, which was no impediment to his eavesdropping. He was fluent in the three official languages of Switzerland—German, French, and Italian—in addition to having mastered English and, of course, his native Arabic.

Such were the privileges of an educational pedigree for which money had been no object.

He inched his chair closer to the pretty one, and now she was only a stone's throw from him. When the wind shifted, he caught a whiff of exquisite perfume. Is it hers? He couldn't tell.

As he listened, he heard her speak in a low, velvety tone as she announced she had ended her relationship with her boyfriend. She sighed deeply—for his sake, perhaps?—then went on to tell her friends she would have to take holiday this year in Monaco without him. "He deserved it. Such an unfaithful dog."

An unfaithful dog.

Was that a calculated message, intended not only for her attractive fräulein companions, but also for his ears? Or merely coincidence?

Nothing is coincidental. Everything is calculated.

Abdur ordered a cocktail and contemplated his next move. Perhaps a round of complimentary cocktails for the fräuleins would attract their attention. Or maybe he would trail her home when she left.

"Ahff wun, yah eff." The sudden deep sound of a man's voice over his shoulder distracted Abdur. "Excuse me, mister," the man repeated in Arabic. "Her name is Marta."

Abdur turned, frowning. The man was handsome, Middle Eastern, and perhaps in his early thirties. He wore an expensive suit, tie, and shoes, all of which were white.

"You contemplate luring her to your hotel." The man's Arabic was flawless. "Except you did not reserve a room, because you had planned on flying back in your Cessna Citation this afternoon to report to Riyadh. But now, with the bat of her eyes, the scent of her perfume, the crossing of her legs, you are contemplating, shall we say, a slight change of plan?"

Abdur rose to his feet and met the man's black eyes. The penetrating quality of the man's gaze was instantly gripping, as if he had the power to hypnotize. Abdur felt a chill shoot down his spine.

"Do not fear, my brother," the man continued. "And I assure you, my sudden intrusion has not compromised your opportunity with this Swiss maiden. You will have your opportunity, if it is what you want. She will cooperate. Trust me."

"Do I know you?"

"I have been searching for you, my brother."

"You look familiar." Abdur frowned again, trying to read the other man's expression. He was unsuccessful.

"I am Hussein al-Akhma of Kuwait."

"Un hum del Allah. Praise be to God." Abdur had seen Hussein's picture in Arab newspapers. But this was the first time he had seen the man in person. "Of you I have heard much, Brother Hussein."

"And I, of you." Hussein inclined his head. "But then, we are a small brotherhood, are we not?" Hussein gave Abdur a friendly pat on the shoulder, and Abdur relaxed. But not much.

"When I was at Oxford, you were at the London School of Economics. But we never met." Abdur was getting his voice back.

"An unfortunate crossing in the night. But Allah has his purposes and his timing. And this moment has to do with the latter."

Abdur pointed to the chair across the table. "Please, be seated."

He studied the mysterious man, rumored to be both a billionaire playboy and a stalwart man of the faith. Was this an oxymoronic combination? Perhaps not. Abdur felt the same tug-of-war within. The prophet Muhammad himself—Peace be upon him—certainly had felt the same struggles.

"Brother Abdur, though we have never met personally until now, I have known you for some time." Again, a fiery, magnetic flash lit Hussein's eyes.

"What do you mean?"

"You are searching for the purpose of life. I believe Allah has called you. Like me, you have been entrusted with much at a young age. But it is all meaningless unless we are called to a higher purpose." Hussein's voice was smooth, hypnotic . . . as if he saw through the windows of Abdur's soul.

How can he see my struggles? My demons?

"Next to the prophet Muhammad—Peace be upon him—there had been no greater Muslim to walk the earth than the servant of Allah, Osama bin Laden," said al-Akhma. "Not since the British burned the White House in the War of 1812 has a foreign enemy struck the heart of America. But one man on September 11, 2001, carried out what the Japanese, the Germans, and the mighty Soviets did not.

"Drew American blood.

"On American soil."

"He was so bold. So daring, was he not?"

"Yes, he was, my brother." Hussein smiled. "But even Osama was not perfect. The brilliant hero of 9/11 failed to realize that to defeat our great enemy, one must become invisible, blend in with their forces."

Abdur studied his companion. "I do not follow you."

"That was Osama's Achilles' heel. He and his cronies all looked and spoke Arabic. Of course, our Arabic heritage is glorious and to be embraced. But Al Qaida cast the perfect stereotype for the Zionist media to beam over the airwaves into American homes and plaster on the front pages of the New York Times and the Washington Post.

"Al Qaida," he continued, "gave the world the image of bearded-looking, turban-wearing 'terrorists' firing AK-47s into the air in frenzied jubilation whenever a bomb went off in Israel. Meaningless. What did we ever accomplish by blowing up a civilian bus on the streets of Tel Aviv? Nothing. Yet all this fueled the Zionist propaganda machine around which Christians and Jews wrapped their anger. It caused them to turn their political and military power against Islam."

"It does make sense," Abdur said.

"I am recruiting a new, more sophisticated breed of Islamic fighter. A fighter who can blend into the Western landscape with fluency in English, with the ability to instantly ditch his turban for a business suit . . ." Hussein's black eyes glinted, drawing Abdur in. "A fighter with the willingness to don a U.S. military uniform for the cause of Allah. These characteristics will epitomize Council of Ishmael operatives.

" 'Know thine enemy,' " Hussein quoted in Arabic. "Allah has laid it upon my heart, Brother Abdur, to assemble a council of twenty rulers to govern this new breed of fighter and to advance this unprecedented worldwide organization."

Goose bumps crept up Abdur's neck, and he sat forward.

"All who have been called to this council are wealthy beyond earthly measure—among the wealthiest men in the various Islamic nations they represent. All are British- or American-educated. All are fluent in English and fervent in their devotion to Islam. All loathe the three great enemies of Allah—Israel, America, and Christianity."

Hussein put his hand on Abdur's shoulder, paused, then met Abdur's eyes. Something supernatural seemed to hold Abdur in his chair.

"Allah has told me, Brother Abdur, that you are one of the chosen twenty."

Chills shot down Abdur's spine.

"One of his coveted Council of Ishmael." Hussein seemed to caress each word as it passed from his lips. And then he stared at Abdur, silent.

The sounds of summer in a busy European city returned to Abdur's ears: car horns honking, birds chirping, trolley bells ringing, the wind blowing off Lake Zurich. All provided a surreal backdrop that Abdur felt was somehow divine.

His gaze wandered to the table next to them that was now empty. Sometime within the last few minutes, Marta had left, and he had not even noticed. He turned again to his companion. "I feel, Brother Hussein, that this is a divine moment. An appointment with destiny preordained by Allah himself. Beyond that, my words have left me."

Hussein's smile was gentle. Abdur noticed his teeth were nearly as white as his suit.

"Abdur, you need not give up your lifestyle. You are not called to poverty. Only to glory. To use all you have been blessed with—your language abilities, your educational background, your resources—for the glory of Allah. You were born for this day. You were blessed for this reason. Very few Muslims the world over possess your combination of talent, skill, and resources.

"Say only this: that you will come, that you will follow me. That you will say yes to Allah's call. That you will become an adopted son of the Council of Ishmael."

Femme du Monde School of Modeling
International Headquarters
North American Division
Madison Avenue, New York City

Diane Colcernian ran her hand through her hair and took a swig of bottled water. She was standing near the elevated runway down the center of a mirrored room that served as a combination lecture hall and practice studio. Four other models lolled against the runway, listening to Monica, the agency's artistic coach, deliver another of her dull lectures on the importance of runway posture.

Angelica, a long-legged blond, rolled her eyes toward Diane, and dark-haired, gamine Corrine snickered. This brought a glare from Monica, who then continued her delivery in her pseudo French accent.

"Next she'll show us an example of her runway work in Paris," whispered Sybil. A moment later, Monica, dressed in designer warm-ups, did exactly that. She floated up the runway stairs and signaled the technician to start the strobe lights and music. Then, head back, body thrust forward, she moved along the runway, her long legs in a fashionable strut. She snapped into a turn and returned to where her young students waited by the runway.

"Now, your turn," Monica said above the music. The women lined up at the stairs, and Diane, who was first in line, climbed up, ignoring the snickers of "Teacher's pet."

Monica made no secret that she was grooming Diane to step onto the runway as a world-class supermodel, just as Monica herself had done twenty years earlier. Diane suspected it was her wavy, flame-colored hair—which, according to photos she'd seen, was much like Monica's in her youth—that endeared her to the artistic coach. Their physiques were similar: tall, lithe, long-limbed, with an almost liquid manner of movement. Because Monica had chosen Diane as heir apparent, she was often harder on her than on all the others; her expectations were greater.

Modeling had been Diane's dream since she was a teenager. She'd thought it would be glamorous—bright lights, public adulation, photographs on the cover of Glamour and Vogue. But in reality, it was excruciatingly hard work. Monica monitored every bite she and the other girls ate. If she gained even a half pound, lunches and dinners consisted of iceberg lettuce and low-fat yogurt. She spent hours with studio makeup artists, still more hours with the studio hairdresser as he twisted her tresses into extreme—and sometimes painful—designs. Then there was her personal trainer who put her through a tortuous daily workout to keep her body toned. And the hours spent under bright, hot lights often left her with a migraine. When she and the others went out on the town, it was only to be seen. Not to be real. Not to enjoy real conversation with real people. Not to laugh and talk about books and world affairs.

She missed that. Her father had brought her up to think for herself, to enjoy stretching her mind with the classics, with art and music, to debate politics and world affairs. His dream, especially after her mother died, was for Diane to go to college, to continue to stretch her mind. To practice law.

But in a fit of rebellion, she'd announced that she planned to follow her dream—no matter what he said. She was going to New York. Her words had broken his heart. She hadn't cared.

Now Diane looked up at Monica, who frowned as she gestured for Diane to join her on the runway. With a sigh, she took her place beside the artistic coach and struck a ten-point model's pose, pasting on the traditional hollow-cheeked, bored expression. Oh yes, she was almost there. She had almost reached her dream.

Why did she feel so empty?

The music throbbed as she slithered down the runway. Seven liquid steps, then snap to a turn. Seven more, turn again . . .

The studio door burst open, and the office manager, Janice Jeffers, a plain but pleasant woman, stepped into the studio. Her heels clicked and echoed like tap-dancing shoes against the polished hardwood floors as she crossed the room.

"Diane, telephone call!" Janice almost shouted to be heard above the runway music.

Diane halted midstep; Monica signaled the engineer to turn off the strobes and music. "Can't it wait?" She shot Diane a glare, then looked back to Janice. "As you can see, we're just beginning the exercise."

"Sorry, Monica," Janice said. "It's an emergency."

"It better be," Monica snapped, then frowned at Diane. "Make it quick, honey."

Diane hurried down the runway steps and jogged to the door, where Janice put her arm around her. "You can take the call in my office." She led Diane down the long hall.

"Who is it?"

"Your father's aide. He said it was urgent." Janice opened the glass door to her office and gestured toward the telephone on her desk.

Diane lifted the receiver to her ear. "Hello?"

"Diane, this is Lieutenant Commander Wilson."

"What's going on, Mitch?"

He hesitated a moment—though it seemed like an eternity—before answering. "Your father's in the hospital. I think you should catch the next flight down here."

Her heart pounded. "What happened?"

"Maybe you should wait until you can talk to his doctor."

"I'm not waiting. Tell me now, Mitch!"

Another hesitation. "Diane . . . the admiral has had a stroke. It's serious . . . I'm sorry."

This isn't happening. This is a bad dream.

"Diane?"

"Is he going to make it?" She blinked back the sting of tears.

"The doctor thinks so, but it'll be touch and go for the next few days."

"Where is he?" She sank into the swivel chair by the desk.

"Portsmouth Naval Hospital. He's getting the very best treatment the Navy can provide. Listen, I've arranged for your plane to fly into Oceana Naval Air Station. I'll meet you there in two hours."

They said their good-byes, then Diane dropped her head into her hands.

"Diane?"

She felt Janice's arm ease across her shoulder.

"I'm sorry . . . Your father's aide didn't want me to tell you. He called us thirty minutes ago to discuss transportation arrangements so you didn't have to worry with them yourself. Mr. Rochembeau is in Paris, but I called him on his cell phone. The company jet will fly you to Virginia Beach."

Two hours later, the Femme du Monde Lear jet touched down at the Oceana Naval Air Station in Virginia Beach. Diane put on dark sunglasses to conceal her red-rimmed eyes, long since washed free of makeup by her tears. She stepped from the jet into a sunny Tidewater afternoon.

Her father's aide waited, his expression lined with concern. When she reached him, he took her by the arm and guided her to the admiral's staff car. He returned to the plane for her luggage, placed it in the trunk, and slid into the driver's seat.

Before he turned the key in the ignition, she touched his arm. "How bad is it, Mitch?"

The aide hesitated and then let his hand drop to his lap. "He's paralyzed on the left side of his body. He drifts in and out of consciousness. Both times he regained consciousness, he whispered your mother's name." He met her gaze. "And yours."

"My mother was a wonderful woman. I wish you had known her."

"The admiral has often said you're just like her. Strong, smart, resolute."

"I don't feel so strong and resolute right now." She pulled out a tissue and dabbed her eyes, praying for a dose of the same strength she remembered in her mother. Most of all, she prayed for her father. And tried not to think of her regrets.

U.S. Naval Medical Center
620 John Paul Jones Circle
Portsmouth, Virginia

As the car approached the main gate outside the huge Portsmouth Naval Hospital, Diane still fought to control her tears. A few minutes later, her father's aide steered the car into the flag officers' parking spaces near the front entrance of the hospital.

He came around to the passenger side and opened the door. "Your father is the strongest man I know," he said as Diane swung her legs out of the car. "The sound of your voice will give him strength."

Diane and Mitch got off the elevator at the sixth deck. A slim officer in a khaki uniform, wearing the silver eagle of a Navy captain pinned to one collar and the gold oak leaf and silver acorn of the Navy Medical Corps on the other, stepped forward and greeted them. "I'm Captain Ornsbee. Lead physician in charge of your father's treatment."

"Is he going to be okay, Doctor?"

"It's still early. These next few hours will be crucial. We're worried about the possibility of an aneurysm. We're giving him blood thinners and watching him constantly."

"May I see him?"

"Yes. I'll take you. But be prepared. He's had a massive stroke. The left part of his body is paralyzed. He may not recognize you."

"I want to see him."

He gave her a solemn nod and then led her down the corridor, past the nurses' station, to a hospital room on the other side.

She halted midstep, stunned. The proud body that was once Vice Admiral Stephen Colcernian lay in a helpless form attached to wires and tubes. "Oh, Daddy." She swallowed the tears at the back of her throat, willing herself not to cry.

The doctor's voice was low. "Your father may be able to hear you. I know it's hard, but try to stay strong."

"Okay." She wiped her eyes, took a deep breath, and moved closer to take her father's hand. "I love you, Daddy. You'd better not leave me. Not now. Please. You're so strong. You're going to be fine." Please, God. Let him hear me. "I came as soon as I found out. Bob has been great. You'd be so proud of him. He arranged to have a plane take me from New York to Oceana. He's a great admiral's aide, Daddy."

Nothing.

Please, God . . .

"Squeeze my hand if you can hear me, Daddy."

Was it her imagination?

"Daddy, can you squeeze it again?"

It was faint, but this time, definite.

Thank you, Lord.

"Daddy, I'm leaving New York, coming home to be close to you. And when we get you up and on your feet, I'll go to UVA so I can come see you on the weekends."

Another squeeze.

She drew in a shaky breath and cleared her throat. "I know how much it means to you to have someone in the family uphold our Navy legacy. I want it too, Daddy, not just for you, but for me. And I was thinking on the plane coming down here. I'm going to go to UVA, and then I'm going to apply for law school. And then I'll apply for a direct commission in the Navy JAG Corps. And I'm going to be the best JAG officer the Navy's ever seen."

This time, it was different. The squeeze was still faint, but twice as strong as the others.

"I won't let you down, Daddy. I promise."

Treason
The Navy Justice Series
Don Brown

In the Court-Martial of the Century, JAG Officer Zack Brewer Faces America's Toughest Enemy Yet.

The Navy has uncovered a group of radical Islamic clerics who have infiltrated the Navy Chaplain Corps, inciting sailors and marines to acts of terrorism. And Lieutenant Zack Brewer has been chosen to prosecute them for treason and murder.

Only three years out of law school, Zack has already made a name for himself, winning the coveted Navy Commendation medal. Just coming off a high-profile win, this case will challenge the very core of Zack's skills and his Christian beliefs—beliefs that could cost him the case and his career.

With Diane Colcernian, his staunchest rival, as assistant prosecutor, Zack takes on internationally acclaimed criminal defense lawyer Wells Levinson. And when Zack and Diane finally agree to put aside their animosity, it causes more problems than they realize.

Softcover: 0-310-25933-9

Pick up a copy today at your favorite bookstore!

ZONDERVAN™

GRAND RAPIDS, MICHIGAN 49530 USA

WWW.ZONDERVAN.COM